Ask No Questions

A DETECTIVE
CAELAN SMALL NOVEL

ASK NO
QUESTIONS

LISA HARTLEY

CANELO

First published in the United Kingdom in 2017 by Canelo

This edition published in 2019 by

Canelo Digital Publishing Limited
57 Shepherds Lane
Beaconsfield, Bucks HP9 2DU
United Kingdom

A CIP catalogue record for this book is available from the British Library.

Print ISBN 978 1 78863 386 4
Ebook ISBN 978 1 911420 66 8

Look for more great books at www.canelo.co

Printed and bound in Great Britain by Clays Ltd, Elcograf S.p.A.

For my family, and in memory of Wack Woollas (1927 - 2009)

The blood haunted her.

She saw it pool beneath her feet when she walked down the street, felt it spatter her skin as she showered.

The images she could pretend she had forgotten: Nicky on the floor, the blood leaking from her throat, arcing across the room close to where the body lay.

The body.

The small, thin, curled-up ruin of a child.

No, the images were there too, stuck in her head, replaying on a never-ending loop of horror.

At the hospital, when they undressed her, dried blood cracking and flaking from her clothes as they were removed, she had remained silent. When she saw her stained knees and hands, Nicky's blood branding her, she had said nothing.

She knew she had failed.

Two bodies. Two lives snuffed out.

A team of police officers who should have known better, who could have done more.

And Caelan herself, who had fought to save her colleague's life, and failed, watching Nicky's gasping, choking dying moments every time she closed her eyes.

And the blood. The blood would never leave her.

As she opened the door, the heat flew at her, wrapping itself around her like warmth from an oven. Yesterday, the temperature had reached twenty-six degrees and today promised to be hotter. October was proving the perfect time to escape the grey misery of Britain for Egypt's winter warmth.

She slipped on her sunglasses, the white tiles on the stairs outside her door appearing to glow in the glare of the sun. People were already in and around the kidney-shaped swimming pool, children shrieking as they leapt into the water. Caelan kept walking towards the double doors of the restaurant. Several people smiled as she passed, and she nodded at them, her eyes busy behind the dark lenses, ever alert. She had pulled her hair back into a ponytail and wore a baseball cap. In this heat, a hat was wise, but in Caelan Small's life, blending in had always been advisable.

In the restaurant, she removed the sunglasses and hat, collected a plate of scrambled eggs and toast and set it on a table. As she sat down, a smiling young waiter approached, dressed in white trousers and a shirt printed with palm leaves. He had a silver jug in each hand, and he held them both aloft as he said, 'Good morning. Tea, coffee?'

Caelan turned a teacup the right way up on its saucer. 'Coffee, please. Thank you.'

The waiter bent to pour the thick brown liquid into the cup.

'From England?' he asked. Caelan nodded. 'Cold there? Rain?'

She smiled. 'Yes. We do have sunshine, but it's never as hot as it is here, even in summer.'

'I would like to see snow. One time.'

Pouring milk into the cup, she nodded. 'I hope you do. Snow's pretty, but I prefer your sun. Thank you.'

He moved away, still smiling.

She ate quickly, then sat for a while, taking her time over the coffee, the only person who was breakfasting on her own. As usual, the observation didn't bother her. Being alone meant fewer complications.

After collecting her snorkelling equipment from her room, Caelan strolled through the lush green gardens, threading her way between the terracotta-painted blocks of bedrooms and down towards the beach. She stopped to take a bottle of water from the fridge that stood next to the beach bar, found a sunbed and stripped down to her bikini. She had a paperback with her, but for now, she was content just to lie there, watching and listening.

–

Richard Adamson reversed into a parking space, tension beginning to knot his stomach. The summons to an anonymous hotel could have only one meaning.

They were worried.

A threat, a person of interest. A risk. Discreet phone calls here, clandestine meetings there. Consequently he had been asked to leave his cosy office and drive down here, taking the usual precautions.

He reached up to twist the rear-view mirror towards him, checking his appearance. He had no idea who he would be meeting, but it paid to look the part. The right facade was key in this game, and it *was* a game, to him at least. Cat-and-mouse, hide-and-seek. He strode across the car park, buttoning his jacket.

The receptionist was a young man, fiddling with a smartphone that he hurriedly shoved into his pocket as he saw Adamson approaching.

'I have a room booked in the name of Lysander,' Adamson said. The receptionist's hands moved over the keyboard of the computer that sat on the desk in front of him. He nodded, turned to lift a sheet of paper from the printer behind him and pushed it across the desk.

'Room 205. If you could fill in your car registration and sign here, please.'

Adamson scribbled a jumble of letters, including an approximation of the name that was not his own. Once he had his key, he turned away and made for the stairs. He never used lifts if he could help it, a trick he'd been taught early in his career. A closed box that could be halted at any point, made unreachable and inescapable? No thank you.

He reached the top of the stairs and pushed through a fire door. As he passed Room 201, the door opened. He hesitated. They had been watching, then. He turned his head, sensing movement inside the room, then moved closer to the door. A man stood inside it. Richard smiled to himself. Cloak-and-dagger. He stepped inside.

The room was the usual budget-hotel mix of clean white bedlinen and muted paintwork. At the desk in the far corner a woman sat, her gaze fixed on a laptop computer. He waited, studying her profile. This was a surprise. He had met her before, but not for a while, and never like this. Whatever the reason for his presence here, it was obviously serious. Elizabeth

Beckett had any number of assistants and lower-ranking officers she could have sent in her place. She was an assistant commissioner, responsible for Specialist Crime & Operations, and part of the Metropolitan Police's senior management team. In Richard's small and discreet corner of the Met, Beckett was God.

Interesting.

He stood perfectly still, hands by his sides. After a minute or so, the woman turned in her chair. She smiled, got to her feet. She was in her early fifties, her silvery hair loose around her shoulders, a pair of glasses lying on the desktop. Rubbing her eyes, she stepped forward.

'Richard. It's good to see you. Thanks for coming.'

Not that he'd had a choice. He shook her hand, her grip firm, her skin cold.

'You're welcome,' he told her.

'Coffee?'

'Please.'

She glanced over to the man who still stood by the door. 'Will you organise some, Davy? Thank you.'

Davy's lips tightened, but he nodded and left the room. A spark of amusement flared in her pale-green eyes as she watched him go. He clearly resented being used as a waiter.

'Shall we sit down?' She waved Richard towards the navy-blue sofa that stood under the window, then dragged the chair from the desk and settled into it. 'You're no doubt wondering why you're here.'

He smiled. 'And why *you* are, ma'am. With respect, I wasn't expecting you.'

'The Home Secretary insisted I talk to you myself.' She watched his face, but he was ready for her.

'The Home Secretary? I see.'

4

She laughed. 'As inscrutable as ever, Richard.'

'I knew it must be important.'

'We're being discreet. Though,' her gaze roamed the room, 'hiding out in a hotel does seem rather ridiculous. I arrived here in the early hours, scurrying up the stairs like a teenager late home from a night out.' She sighed, and Richard wondered if she was thinking of her own children, away at university as far as he knew. Leaning forward in her chair, she set her hands on her knees. 'We have an issue, and we would appreciate your help.'

'I'll do all I can, as you know.'

'I do. It's part of the reason I wanted to speak to you myself, regardless of the Home Secretary's wishes.'

He raised his eyebrows, happy to let his guard down slightly, though he knew flattery when he heard it. There was silence until the man she had called Davy knocked on the door and came back in bearing a wooden tray. He set it on the desk, and Beckett leant over to pour three cups of coffee from the insulated jug, a delicious aroma drifting through the room as she did so.

Silently she handed Richard a cup and saucer. Davy went to the door, locked it and engaged the security chain. When Beckett glanced at him, he nodded, moving back to pick up his own drink. Beckett sipped, gazing over towards the window. Richard waited, knowing she would not be rushed. Eventually she raised her eyes to his.

'This is difficult.'

'What's the problem?' Richard concealed his impatience.

She cleared her throat. 'We believe a person has entered the country whom it's necessary to find and then keep within sight. Discreet but nevertheless careful surveillance.'

Another surprise. This was not what he had been expecting her to say. In fact, he was disappointed. But then she had to be referring to someone notorious, or it would be being dealt with further down the ladder. Much, much further.

'Okay. And how do I fit in?'

Elizabeth Beckett took another mouthful of coffee, then set the cup on the saucer and replaced it on the tray. She held his gaze, and when she spoke, her voice was little more than a whisper. 'Caelan Small.'

Richard's throat tightened, though his expression didn't change. 'What about her?'

'We want her to do this for us.'

'But—'

Beckett held up a hand. 'We need her, Richard.'

He was already shaking his head. 'There's no way.'

'We think there's a good chance she'll agree.'

'Caelan made it clear she would never work for us again. I'm sorry, ma'am, but it's impossible.' And why would they want her to? It was a puzzle.

Beckett was quiet, her eyes studying his face. He stared back, knowing that what he had said was true.

'We'd like you to talk to her,' she said eventually.

'Me?' Richard suppressed a snort of amusement. 'Caelan wouldn't listen.'

'She has in the past.'

'No. She may have ignored me slightly less often than she did most people...'

'You had a relationship with her.'

Now he did laugh. It was no surprise that they knew. 'That's not how I'd describe it.'

'Nevertheless, we'd like you to try.' Her tone made it clear there was no room for argument.

Davy had resumed his position by the door. He shuffled his feet and touched a hand to his jacket, by his hip. Richard swallowed.

'I don't even know where Caelan is.'

Beckett smiled. Safe ground again. 'We do. Egypt.'

'Egypt? Why?'

'Even Caelan Small goes on holiday.'

'Under which name?'

'Her own, for a change. Perhaps her guard is down.'

Richard doubted that. He sighed as Beckett slid a bulky white envelope from the inside pocket of her jacket.

'Stay in the room that was booked here for the rest of the day,' she continued. 'A car will pick you up at seven, and your flight leaves at nine. I presume you have a bag packed?'

He dipped his head. 'Yes, ma'am.' It was part of the job to be ready to leave at a minute's notice.

'Excellent. You'll be met once you land at Sharm El Sheikh.'

'And what shall I tell Caelan?'

Beckett held out the envelope. 'That we'd like to talk to her, in the first instance. She's due to fly home in three days anyway. Someone will be waiting for her at the airport then too.'

'And if she refuses?' He took the envelope, turning it over in his hands. It would contain his tickets, a passport and driving licence, credit cards, and cash; both Egyptian and sterling. The name on the passport and other items would not be his own.

'If she refuses, we'll keep trying to persuade her.' Beckett's back was straight, her shoulders back, confident that Caelan would listen to them and be ushered back into the fold. Richard wasn't so sure.

'How?' He hoped he didn't sound as sceptical as he felt. Why would they even consider asking Caelan? There were other officers who would be eager to step in, himself included. He gazed at Beckett, considering the possibilities. What was she up to?

She stared back at him, her eyes narrowing. 'Let us worry about the detail. Talk to her, get her to see sense.'

'I have to be honest, ma'am, I'm not sure that anything I say will make a difference. Caelan walked away from the job with no intention of coming back.'

'I'm aware she resigned. We're still paying her, though.'

'That was part of the agreement.'

Beckett lifted her chin, her eyes cold. 'Well, then the deal has changed, or it could easily do so. We want her to do this, and we think she'll agree.'

The skin on his arms was prickling, part of him understanding already.

'Who will she be finding?'

Elizabeth Beckett turned away, her hands clenching into fists in her lap. With a sharp, quick movement, she turned back, meeting his gaze and holding it. She said the name softly, as if it were a curse. It was what Richard had expected to hear, but still he wanted to cover his ears, to leave the room, climb into his car and drive away.

Instead, he closed his eyes, remembering.

2

How the hell was he supposed to find her? The receptionist had insisted he could not give out Caelan's room number, and the hotel grounds were extensive – he could wander around all day and still not see her. Richard swore under his breath, wiping his hand across his face, sweat already soaking his back. In his cotton chinos and polo shirt, he felt ridiculous. As he crossed a sun-drenched courtyard, he saw a few shops and hurried across to them.

Back in his room, he pulled on the swimming shorts and flip-flops he'd purchased, applied plenty of suncream and went outside again. In this heat, she would surely be by the pool, or on the beach.

He tried the pool area first, examining the women who were possibilities without appearing to stare. It was tricky searching the crowd with bikini-clad bodies in all directions. His sunglasses would help disguise what he was doing, but he didn't want to give the wrong impression and risk drawing attention to himself.

There was no sign of her.

He strolled around the edge of the pool, then sat on the side with his legs dangling in the water. A rest wouldn't hurt. He was considering grabbing a beer before heading down to the beach when a touch on the back of his neck caused him to freeze.

'What are you doing here?' The voice was quiet but unmistakable.

Caelan.

He kept his eyes on the water in front of him. Wearing only shorts he felt strangely exposed, as if he were naked and utterly defenceless. As usual, Caelan was in control of the situation. He could feel her fingernail on his skin, not painful, not yet, but there all the same. He had been stupid to sit down here, leaving himself vulnerable. Mistakes like that could be costly.

'Looking for you,' he said.

Caelan snorted. 'Well here I am. What do you want?'

Richard hunched his shoulders, willing her to remove her hand. 'Could we find somewhere quiet to have a drink? I want to talk to you.'

'Want to, or have to? I'm sure I can guess.'

She moved away, and he clambered to his feet, turning to look at her. Her hair was dark, her eyes hidden behind her sunglasses. He had no idea what Caelan's natural hair or eye colour were because both had changed so often in the time he had known her. Sometimes he thought she did it for her own amusement, keeping the mystery, the illusion, of Caelan Small alive.

She stalked away. He hurried after her, aware that she could disappear into the sprawl of the hotel again if she chose to.

'Where are you going?' he asked.

'You didn't answer me, not that you needed to. I doubt you turning up here is a coincidence. I'm going back to my room.'

More apprehensive than ever now that he had found her, he followed, surprised when she made no attempt to stop him. When they reached her door, she removed her sunglasses and glared at him. He forced himself to meet her gaze. Brown eyes. Hazel? Probably her natural colour; he was close enough to guess she wore no contact lens. She truly was on holiday. High cheekbones, small nose. Neat eyebrows, drawn together in a frown.

'Can I come in?' he asked. She shrugged as she removed the card that served as a room key from her shorts pocket and unlocked the door.

Inside, the air was cool, the air conditioning whirring away high in the corner. Richard took off his sunglasses and glanced around. It was a mirror image of his own room. Bathroom to the left of the door, then a square area beyond, the floor tiled in terracotta, the walls painted white. Two queen-size beds. A chair, upholstered in a burgundy and gold fabric that matched the bedspreads. Dark-wood furniture – a square table, a wardrobe and a desk with a cupboard built in, a chest of drawers. Her suitcase stood in the corner, padlocked. She threw her snorkelling gear and hat onto one of the beds and rounded on him.

'Drink?'

Thrown, he nodded, and she bent to open the cupboard. Inside was a fridge. She removed a can of beer and handed it to him, then took out a bottle of water for herself.

'Thank you,' he said, then, after some hesitation: 'Look, Caelan, I'm sorry. I know it's a shock to see me...'

She gulped some water and gave a bark of scornful laughter.

'It's a surprise, not a shock. Who sent you? Nasenby?'

Nasenby had been Caelan's boss, the head of the Metropolitan Police's Intelligence & Covert Policing section. He had accepted her resignation with reluctance, though he had understood. She remembered the day she had told him – his sadness, and her resolve. Her time lurking in the shadows was over.

But Richard was shaking his head. 'Higher than Nasenby.' There was no reaction. 'They want me to offer you an opportunity.'

'I don't work for them any more. I told them I never would again.' She screwed the lid back onto the bottle and turned away, pulling back the curtain from the window to stare out at the gardens beyond.

Richard glanced around. 'Are we okay to talk in here?'

'I thought that's what we were doing.'

'You know what I mean.'

Caelan kept her back turned. 'Where else do you suggest?'

'The beach? A walk?'

'The beach is busy, and there's nowhere to walk.'

'Do you mind if I check around?'

'Fuck's sake,' she muttered, opening the door to the balcony. 'I've done it, but please yourself. I'll wait out here.'

Richard watched her march onto the balcony and throw herself into a chair. Reluctantly he turned back to search the room, scouring every inch of it. The drawers and wardrobe were empty. Her clothes must still be in her suitcase, as his own were. Force of habit. He wondered if she had brought a weapon. It seemed unlikely, airport security being what it was, but you could never be sure with Caelan. He saw no sign of one in the room. Her shorts and vest top wouldn't provide any hiding places, and the safe in the wardrobe wasn't big enough to conceal a gun.

When he was satisfied, he stuck his head outside and spoke quietly. 'Will you come back in, please?'

She turned, her expression mutinous. At first he thought she would refuse, but eventually she stood and moved across the balcony. His eyes scanned the gardens outside, and he took in the sounds of children playing and splashing drifting from the pool area. An elderly couple sauntered along the nearest path, arm in arm, both streaked with sunburn. Further away, a man hauled a squeaking trolley of clean bedlinen along. Caelan pushed past Richard, and he closed the door, drew the curtains.

'Are we going to sleep?' She stood by the wall, her arms folded.

'Wouldn't be the first time we've shared a room,' he grinned. Her face was stony. 'Come on, Caelan, I'm joking.'

'Tell me what you want, Richard.'

'All right. I was called to a meeting yesterday, told to come out here to see you.'

'By?'

'Does it matter?'

'Does to me.'

Richard moved closer, lowered his voice even further. 'Elizabeth Beckett, on instructions from the Home Secretary.'

There was a pause. Caelan gave another snort.

'Aren't we honoured?'

'They have a proposal for you.'

'Not a chance. Goodbye, Richard.' She jerked a thumb towards the door.

He reached out a hand to touch her arm, then thought better of it. 'Caelan, listen. I was given a name.'

'Who?'

'Seb Lambourne.'

Her jaw clenched, but when she spoke, her voice was even. 'He escaped. Left the country.'

'They think he's back.'

She considered this, her head tipped to the left, fiddling with her bottle of water. Richard waited.

'What are they going to do?' Caelan asked eventually.

He held up his hands. 'I agreed to come and talk to you, that's all. They want you to find him. I don't know what they're planning.'

'That's reassuring.'

'Don't shoot the messenger.'

She made a gun from her fingers and aimed it at him, one eye closed.

'Who's involved? How do they know he's returned to the UK?'

Richard moved over to the nearest bed and sat down. 'Like I said, I don't know. All I've been told is that it's about Lambourne.'

'And they think that'll tempt me out of retirement?'

'Has it?'

'No.'

3

In a bland conference room, three men sat around an oval table, a laptop idling in front of them. Deputy Assistant Commissioner Michael Nasenby was in his mid fifties: grey-haired, slim and elegant in a dark suit, white shirt and plain charcoal tie. The second man was younger, but not by much. Commander Ian Penrith was overweight, balding. His face had a world-weary, battered appearance, as if his every experience was displayed there for all to see. A scar sliced through his left eyebrow; his nose had been broken more than once. He was sweating through a too-tight shirt, his dark blue tie covered in a busy pattern of tiny white rugby balls. The third man was the youngest: mid thirties. He wore a well-cut suit and expensive shoes. Tim Achebe was one of the few black police officers in the country to hold a rank above that of inspector, and those in the know were tipping him as a future assistant commissioner, possibly commissioner, of the Metropolitan Police. Achebe himself quietly hoped their predictions were true.

Caelan Small stared out from the laptop's screen as they studied her photograph. Tim Achebe stared at the image, trying to reconcile her face with the stories he had been hearing.

'That's her?' He was sceptical. Caelan Small looked… ordinary. He knew better than to judge by appearances, but he would need convincing. It was vital that the assignment they had been discussing was a success. Anything less would be disastrous.

Nasenby spread his hands. 'She's the best we have. Had, I should say.'

It might have sounded like a boast, but it was a simple statement of fact. To illustrate his point, Nasenby clicked the mouse and a second face was displayed. Achebe squinted.

'And who's that?'

With a smile, Nasenby said, 'Caelan Small again.'

Achebe let out a whistle. 'Bloody hell.'

The faces appeared to belong to two different women. The colour of her hair and eyes was different in the second photograph; even the shape of her eyebrows and the set of her shoulders. Achebe had to admit, he was already impressed. Beside him, Penrith screwed up his face.

'Some facial padding and a hell of a lot of make-up,' he scoffed. 'Caelan Small is a liability.'

Nasenby coughed. 'That rather depends on who you ask, Ian.'

'Since I was invited here, I'd presumed my view would be valid,' Penrith snapped. He lifted the water jug that sat in the middle of the table, slopping the liquid as he filled a glass. Nasenby frowned at the mess.

'How old is she?' Achebe ignored the interruption, still marvelling over the photographs.

Nasenby leant back, crossed his legs. 'Twenty-eight.'

'We thought perhaps she could pose as a student. A mature student, admittedly...' Achebe said.

'It won't be an issue. Caelan's been anyone we've asked her to be in the past.'

Achebe ran a hand along his jawline.

'You're certainly confident about her abilities.'

Nasenby leant forward to pick up the jug of water. He poured himself a glass but didn't drink. 'As I've already mentioned, Caelan has proved herself time and time again.'

'But Lambourne has seen her before. He'll know who she is.'

'He doesn't know Caelan Small. She was Kay Summers for that assignment. There's no way he will recognise her, I'd bet my pension on it.'

Achebe nodded, satisfied. He had to trust them, after all. This wasn't his show. 'Is she back in the country?'

Flicking up his shirt sleeve, Nasenby glanced at his watch. 'She should have landed by now. We've time to have some lunch.' He sipped his water, brightening at the prospect of food, then set the glass down.

'And is she alone?' Achebe asked.

'Yes. One of our people went to speak to her, but he flew back the next day.'

'Has she said she'll do it? I understand there have been some issues.'

'Yes, Caelan did tender her resignation.' Nasenby held out a hand to examine his fingernails.

'Why?'

'She didn't agree with a decision that was made.'

Achebe frowned. 'And that prompted her to resign? That concerns me.'

'It needn't,' Nasenby told him. 'Several of us saw the decision as poor judgement, justifiably as it turned out.'

'But you didn't all throw the towel in?'

Nasenby laughed. 'No. Probably because we didn't have the guts.'

'But Caelan Small did?'

'It was more personal for her. Someone was sacked, made an example of. Another officer.'

'A friend of hers?'

'Well, someone she had grown to trust. I'm not sure she has friends.'

'She works well alone?'

'I'd say that Caelan does everything alone.' There was a trace of sadness in Nasenby's voice, and he cleared his throat. 'She seems to prefer it that way.'

—

At East Midlands Airport, Caelan walked past the only man in arrivals wearing a suit without looking at him. In the toilets, she splashed water over her face and stared into the mirror. She didn't want to be dragged back into their world, but since Richard Adamson had mentioned that name, she had known that she had no choice.

Seb Lambourne.

'You fucker.'

She hadn't realised that she'd said the words out loud until a middle-aged woman who was drying her hands turned to look warily at her. Another woman, late twenties, glanced her way and smiled. Caelan gazed back, eyes appraising, and watched her blush. Washing her hands, she wondered what the woman would do if she stepped closer, slid her arms around her waist and backed her into one of the cubicles.

Not today. Today she would go out and be driven back to her old life. She was reluctant, but Seb Lambourne had evaded her once. She wasn't going to let it happen again.

The young woman let the door swing closed behind her. Setting her jaw, Caelan followed her out. She disappeared into the crowd without a backward glance as Caelan smiled to herself.

He was still standing there, his gaze fixed on the passengers flooding through passport control. Caelan stepped up close behind him and tapped him on the shoulder. He jumped, then whirled around to face her. Late twenties, broad shoulders, military bearing. She had never seen him before. Smiling, she flung her arms around him, kissed his cheek.

'Lovely to see you.' Then, with her mouth close to his ear as she hugged him: 'Play along, all right, and keep your voice down.'

She linked her arm through his as he recovered himself.

'You're Caelan Small?' He murmured the name uncertainly: *Carlin*.

'It's pronounced *Kaylen*,' she told him. 'And yes, I am.'

'I was expecting a man.'

Caelan rolled her eyes, pulling her arm away from him.

'I can see you've been well briefed. Sorry to disappoint you.'

'No, I mean… I thought Caelan was a man's name.'

She waved a hand. 'Call me Colin if it makes you feel better.'

He flashed an uncertain smile. 'I assume you're here to take me to a meeting?'

He hurried after her as she started walking. 'Yeah, I—'

'I'm also presuming you don't want to broadcast the fact to the world?'

Blushing, he tried to take the handle of the suitcase that she was wheeling along, but she pushed his hand away. 'What's your name?' she asked.

'Davies. Ewan Davies.'

'And where's your car, Ewan?'

They left the airport building, emerging into a grey, damp and cloudy afternoon. He nodded towards a queue of shivering people, most still wearing shorts and T-shirts. 'We have to get a bus to the car park.'

They joined the end of the line, Caelan grateful that she had worn jeans to travel in. Ewan straightened his tie and brushed his jacket sleeves with his hands. Caelan watched, amused.

'What's wrong?'

Again, colour flooded into his cheeks. 'Feel a bit of an idiot wearing a suit when everyone else is in holiday gear,' he mumbled.

'They probably think you're arresting me.'

'Don't they come onto the plane to get you if they're doing that?'

'Do they?' She craned her neck. 'Here's the bus.'

—

In the car, Caelan leant back in the passenger seat and closed her eyes.

'So where are we going?'

Ewan hesitated. 'I was told not to say.'

She opened her eyes again, fixing him with a hard stare. 'You're not allowed to tell me?'

'I'm sorry.'

'Ridiculous. Well, I'll assume London.'

He started the engine. There was a silence, and then Caelan yawned.

'Wake me when we get there.'

After a minute or so, Ewan risked a glance. She seemed to be asleep already. He realised his hands had the steering wheel in a stranglehold, and made a conscious effort to relax them. Why hadn't he been told she was a woman? Someone's idea of a joke, no doubt, allowing him to blunder in unprepared. His lips tightened as he accelerated past a truck that was lumbering its

20

way down the dual carriageway. Hilarious, and so professional. As he knew only too well, being unprepared could cost you your life.

Caelan shuffled in her seat, her head tilting slightly as a small sigh escaped her lips. Ewan kept his eyes fixed on the windscreen for a few seconds, but she soon settled again. It felt strangely intimate to have her asleep in the next seat. Most of his passengers sat in the back and barely acknowledged his presence. Not her. She had hoisted her suitcase into the boot, then started to walk around to the driver's side before remembering and turning back. No doubt she would have driven herself if she'd had the chance.

Ewan's orders were clear, even if the details of the passenger he had to collect hadn't been. He was to park the car, escort his charge into the building and up to the second floor, then wait outside the room for further instruction. Under no circumstances was she to be allowed to wander off on her own. He wondered what he should do if she wanted to use the toilet – wait outside, he supposed. If she was determined to get away from him, he wasn't confident he would be able to stop her. She radiated capability. He glanced at her again, trying to determine exactly what it was about her that intimidated him so much.

–

'Ms Small?'

Caelan felt a tentative hand on her shoulder and brushed it away impatiently. There was a pause, then the voice tried again.

'We're here, Ms Small.'

Instantly she was awake, her eyes focusing on Ewan's face.

'Where?' she demanded, passing a hand over her dry mouth.

Ewan reached for his door handle. 'We need to go inside.'

She sat up straight, narrowing her eyes at the anonymous office building that filled the windscreen. She didn't recognise it.

'Who do you work for, Ewan?' she asked softly. He half turned towards her, his hand straying up to the knot of his tie, resting there for a second and then fluttering back down to the steering wheel.

'I'm not sure I should—'

'Who?'

He lifted his chin.

'They'll be waiting.'

She smiled, clearly surprising him, then leant forward and touched his knee with her fingertip.

'Come on then.'

—

Ewan tapped a number into the keypad that was fixed to the right-hand side of the blue-framed glass door. Caelan grinned as the locks clicked and he stood back, waiting for her to enter the building first.

'Two six nine four,' she teased, as they crossed towards the empty reception desk, their footsteps muffled by the expanse of thick grey carpet.

'Wrong.'

Caelan laughed. 'No I'm not.'

He ignored her, knowing he was blushing again. It happened to him too often. Not ideal, especially in this line of work. They approached the lift, and he pressed the button to open the doors. Caelan shuffled her feet.

'Can't we use the stairs?'

He frowned. 'Why?'

She didn't reply, but stepped inside the lift and stood with her back to the mirrored wall, clearly reluctant. Ewan selected the next floor up and waited as the doors closed, conscious of her watching him.

'Who are we going to see?'

He cleared his throat. 'I don't know. I was told to bring you here, but no more.'

'And will you be driving me home afterwards?'

'I'm not sure.'

The lift arrived with a clunk and the doors opened. Ewan stepped aside to allow Caelan to exit. She didn't, hanging back instead.

'What is it?' He felt a stab of panic. Was she trying to trick him, planning to send the lift back downstairs?

'I'm deciding whether I want to hear what they have to say.'

'You've changed your mind?'

Caelan considered it, then stepped forward, out of the lift and onto more luxurious carpeting, navy blue this time.

'No, I'll hear them out. Why not? We're here now.'

–

Nasenby slid his mobile phone back into his jacket pocket.

'They've arrived.'

Ian Penrith rolled his eyes and fidgeted in his chair as Achebe straightened his tie. Achebe was nervous, which surprised him. Caelan Small was one of them, on their side, despite the stories he had heard about her. They knew how she worked – her motivations, and her weaknesses, such as they were. Still, he was apprehensive. Penrith had made his opinions clear, and he was a man whose views Achebe had listened to before. He lifted his chin, not acknowledging Penrith now, closing out the older man with his grubby suit and gloomy features. This time Achebe would make up his own mind.

There was a tap on the door and Nasenby strode over to fling it open.

'Caelan. Lovely to see you.' His tone was that of an indulgent father welcoming a much-loved child back into the fold. Achebe glanced at Penrith, glimpsing the sneer as the other man made a show of studying the tabletop. Penrith had protested against the idea of Caelan Small's involvement from the beginning, and he wasn't a man to take being ignored lightly.

Caelan paused in the doorway, smiling at Nasenby.

'Hello, Michael. Would you mind telling me where we are? I had a nap in the car.'

Nasenby's eyebrows lifted. 'London, of course.' As if there was nowhere else. 'The outskirts.'

'That narrows it down. Is Ewan coming in?' She glanced behind her.

'Ewan?' Nasenby peered around Caelan, clearly confused. 'The driver? No, we don't need him.' He raised his voice. 'Go and get yourself a drink, but hang around. Good man.'

Achebe winced at Nasenby's tone. Public school, with a hint of bluff country gentleman. Patronising, thoughtless and offensive. He'd heard it often enough, especially recently. Working with this lot was proving to be an education in itself. He watched Caelan Small's eyes narrow, obviously unimpressed herself by Nasenby's attitude.

'If I agree to do this, I want Ewan with me,' she told them. Nasenby looked aghast for a second before collecting himself.

'With you? What do you mean?'

'I want him to work with me. You've spoken before about me having a partner, Michael.'

'Yes, but not…' Nasenby paused. 'I meant one of our own officers. Richard Adamson would—'

'I'm not working with Richard again.' Caelan was definite.

'Mr Davies hasn't been through our training programmes, he doesn't have your experience.'

'You wouldn't have sent him to collect me if you didn't trust him,' Caelan pointed out. 'I'm serious, Michael. If I'm going after Lambourne again, I don't want to do it alone.'

Behind her, the man in the corridor blushed. Caelan turned to him with a smile, and he returned it, shuffling his feet.

'What do you think, Ewan? Is that okay with you?'

He nodded. 'If my bosses agree. If I'm suitable.'

Half in love with her already, Achebe decided.

'You'll do,' Caelan grinned.

'But we have plenty of people who could partner you, if that's what you want,' said Nasenby. 'I'm sure Mr Davies is effective in his field, but that doesn't mean he's suited for this particular assignment.'

'I think he is.'

'It's not your decision.' Nasenby's hands were on his hips.

'Really?'

'I'm not going to argue with you, Caelan. The answer's no.'

'Then I'll leave now. You forget, Michael, that *you* came to me. I'll listen to what you have to say, and then I'll make a decision about my future, but if you want me, you'll have to have Ewan too.'

Nasenby held up his hands. 'Fine. But if he catches a bullet in the head, don't blame me.' He threw open the door. 'Come in then, Mr Davies. That was the shortest selection process I've ever seen. Welcome aboard.'

Caelan stood aside and, clearly bemused at this extension to his assignment, Ewan Davies stepped forward.

'Have a seat,' Nasenby told him, as he marched back to his own chair. 'Why not?'

Caelen stepped further into the room, her eyes missing nothing. Eventually they rested on her own face, still displayed on the laptop screen. Achebe got to his feet and approached her, his hand outstretched.

'Detective Chief Inspector Tim Achebe. Pleased to meet you.'

She looked up at him with a smile as she shook his hand. 'Hi, Tim. Have you been looking at my mugshots?'

He laughed. 'You could say that. We've been hearing all about you too.'

Caelan turned away, flashing another smile, to focus on Penrith, who hadn't moved from his seat. He lifted his head as she neared him, his face blank.

'Oh, Ian,' Caelan said. 'Still hate me?'

His lips parted, grey teeth flashing as he gave a mirthless smile. 'Good afternoon, Caelan. You resigned. As far as I'm concerned, you've been put out to pasture, so I'm not sure why the possibility of you being involved should even be discussed. We have plenty of people who do still want to work for us.'

Caelan pulled out the chair between Nasenby and Davies and sat down. 'I haven't said I'll do it yet.'

'You should never have been given the option, and now you're being allowed to recruit your own assistant? Even for you, it defies belief.' Penrith folded his arms.

Nasenby closed his eyes for a second. 'Thank you, Ian. Your objections have been noted, as they were well before this meeting. Now, we all know why Caelan's here.'

Penrith snorted. 'Because she's bloody lucky.'

'*Thank* you, Ian. Enough. Caelan is one of our most experienced officers, and, of course, she knows Lambourne. Knows what he's capable of.'

'She was there in that fucking bloodbath, you mean,' Penrith spat. 'Watching while the whole situation went to shit.'

Caelan was silent, but Nasenby frowned. 'No one was "watching", Ian, you know that. What happened was… unfortunate, but in the end, unavoidable.'

Penrith's cheeks were stained deep red. His fists clenched on the tabletop. 'Unfortunate? Fucking unfortunate? A ten-year-old kid dies, his murderer escapes, and it's unfortunate?' Nasenby didn't respond, and eventually Penrith gave a deep sigh. He turned to Achebe, who was beginning to wish he had never agreed to be at the meeting. Regretting, in fact, agreeing to be involved at all. He had enough crap to wade through at his own station without becoming caught up in all this cloak-and-dagger bollocks. He was ambitious, yes, but fighting amongst colleagues, senior colleagues, he could do without.

Penrith hadn't finished. 'The official line was that yes, the child was dead before our people showed up.' He announced this as if it was news. Achebe opened his mouth, despite having no idea how to respond, but Caelan Small got there first.

'The official line? Come on, Ian, they killed him as soon as they realised we were on our way. He was dead when we entered the building, you know that.' Her voice was weary. 'It's the truth.'

Penrith gazed at her, his pale-blue eyes desolate. 'Is it? There were only four other people in that room besides you – I'm not counting the dead child.'

Caelan took a deep breath. Achebe saw the flicker of emotion, watched as she brought her face under control. He wondered where Penrith was going with this. He'd heard about

Lambourne and the boy, of course – the whole country had been outraged – but this? What was Penrith suggesting?

'The dead child? His name was Charlie.' Now Caelan's voice was taut.

'I know what his name was, Caelan. I can hear his voice, see his face. I saw every photograph his parents had ever taken of him, watched every scrap of video, spoke to everyone who knew him. Three weeks: searching, hoping, waiting. Eighteen-hour days, the press baying for blood, everyone up to the Prime Minister involved. And then we track his kidnappers down, move in – and suddenly he's dead. Ten years old, face down on the floor, hands and feet still tied, a bullet hole in the back of his head.' Penrith lifted a hand to his face, drew it over his lips. Achebe's palms were damp, his shirt sticking to the small of his back. He wondered what Davies was thinking. Caelan Small might not be such a paragon after all, whatever they had all been told.

Silence. Caelan's face was blank, her right foot soundlessly tapping the carpet, over and over again.

'Ian…' Nasenby tried again. Penrith glared at him, holding up a hand, his fingers extended.

'Lambourne was in that shitty house with Charlie Flynn. So was Lambourne's right-hand man, Glen Walker.' He folded his thumb and index finger down, his eyes fixed on Caelan's face. 'Then, our brave officers of the law: Clifton, Sturgess and Small.' He made a sound that could have been a laugh but was closer to a snarl. 'Nicky Sturgess: well, she's dead. Poor Nicky, but it was an honourable death in the line of duty. More importantly, she can't tell any tales.' He folded down his middle finger. 'Next: Sam Clifton. He was in charge, he shouldered the blame. He was dismissed, disgraced, lambasted by the media,

28

shunned by his friends. Now he spends his days drinking away the memories.'

'Sam was scapegoated,' Caelan said.

'I agree, he was. And so you resigned. A protest against Clifton's treatment. A gesture, in any case. Designed to protect yourself, of course. Anything Sam said afterwards would be disregarded as the ramblings of a drunk, a broken man. And if he stumbles in front of a lorry or a train one day, well, wouldn't that be tragic?' Penrith shook his head, snatched his glass of water up, gulped some down. The others sat as if mesmerised.

'So, back to that day, that almighty fuck-up.' Penrith held up his little finger. 'The fifth and final adult in that house: Caelan Small. Afterwards, when the bodies had been tidied away, you disappeared. Still on full pay, of course – can't be bad. And here you are: alive, on the payroll, still respected and recommended. Undercover officer extraordinaire. Professional. Capable.' He sneered. 'But you fucked up, didn't you? You underestimated Lambourne.' His voice was soft now, hypnotic. 'He killed Sturgess, slit her throat and stepped over the body. But he didn't kill you, and he didn't kill Sam Clifton. Why? Lambourne had a knife, so did Walker. They killed Sturgess without a second thought, but you and Clifton – not a scratch. Strange, that. You were all armed, weren't you?'

'You know we were.'

'And yet no shots were fired. Not one. Not by Sturgess, not by Clifton, and not by you. Not when Sturgess was attacked and killed, not even when Walker and Lambourne were making their escape. That strikes me as odd. It's as if they had a hostage. A young, *vulnerable* hostage.' He glanced at Achebe, who was now extremely uncomfortable. 'Wouldn't you say, Tim?'

Achebe cleared his throat, totally thrown. 'Well, I... I wouldn't like to speculate.'

Penrith nodded, a savage jerk of his head. 'Sensible. Well, I wonder – I'll speculate, if you like. Because not only did you have a gun, Caelan, you had an armed response unit as backup. There were vanloads of officers waiting outside, panting to get to Lambourne and Walker. Myself included. We could hear what was going on, see some of it. But not what happened to Charlie. We never heard his voice, never saw his face. Not until it was over.'

'Nicky was wearing the camera. When she was killed...'

'Yes, the only thing we saw after that was the ceiling and her blood flowing over the lens.' Penrith bit back. For a second, Caelan closed her eyes.

'Ian, enough.' Nasenby was shaken, the first time Achebe had seen him remotely off balance. 'This is ridiculous. What's your point? What are you trying to say? Mistakes were made in the Charlie Flynn case, we all know that, none more so than Caelan. Regrettable as the boy's death was—'

Now Caelan leant forward, interrupting her boss. 'What is it you're accusing me of, Ian? What do you think I've done?'

Achebe's mouth was dry. Penrith took a breath, visibly steadying himself.

'Done? At best, believed your own press, thought you were untouchable. Gross incompetence. Disregarding orders. Endangering life. At worst...' He paused. Achebe suppressed a groan, fearing Pandora's box was about to be opened. 'At worst, you were working for Lambourne. Corrupt. In his pocket. Whatever you want to call it. And you probably still are. How else did he escape, surrounded as he was by armed officers? Roadblocks, dogs, a helicopter, his name and face on every news channel and all over the internet? Someone had to have helped him. You. Or Clifton. Or was it both of you?'

Nasenby shoved back his chair and lurched to his feet, his hand shaking as he thrust a finger towards Penrith. 'Get out.'

'I'm—'

'Go, Ian. Before I call someone to remove you.'

Penrith smirked, but got to his feet. 'You'd do that, would you? You're still protecting her? She's making a fool of you, Michael.'

Nasenby's lips were pressed together, his hands gripping the edge of the table. Penrith picked up his briefcase and marched towards the door. He turned as he reached it. 'I'll be taking this higher.'

'Do that,' Nasenby told him.

Penrith lingered. 'The truth will come out eventually.'

Caelan gazed at him. 'It already has.'

'The inquiry? A joke,' Penrith spat.

'There's no conspiracy here, Ian, I swear.'

Penrith laughed. 'You swear? *You* do? Someone who lies for a living? Forgive me if I'm sceptical.'

Then he was gone. Caelan exhaled, while Nasenby picked up his water and drained the glass. Unsure of what to say, how to react, Achebe kept his mouth shut.

'Well, that was fun,' said Caelan. She was totally calm now, Achebe realised. Amazing, and not a little frightening.

'He won't let this lie, you're aware of that, aren't you?' Nasenby asked her.

'It's bollocks, Michael, you know it is. How long has he been cooking up that little theory?'

'It's been mentioned before. He came to me a few days ago wanting to discuss it. I told him to bugger off.'

Achebe cleared his throat. 'I hope this... difference of opinion won't affect the operation?'

31

Nasenby guffawed. 'Because Ian's had a hissy fit? Of course not. He might think he's important, but I can assure you he doesn't have too much sway. Now, let's talk about how we're going to approach this.'

'Tell me how you know Lambourne is back in the country,' Caelan demanded.

Nasenby flicked a glance at Davies. 'That's not important,' he said.

'I disagree.' Caelan looked at Achebe. 'Tim?'

An easy question to answer truthfully. 'I don't know,' he said. 'I'm only involved because the Charlie Flynn kidnapping and murder was on my patch.'

Caelan studied him, and Achebe had the sudden, unnerving impression that she could read his mind.

'If Lambourne's in London, we'll struggle to find him,' he told them.

Caelan was losing patience. 'Right. So what exactly do you want me to do?'

'He's here in the UK.' Nasenby held up a hand, silently asking Caelan not to interrupt. 'How we know that isn't important? A trusted source is all I'll say.'

'A snitch. We could have done with one when we were first trying to find him, when he kidnapped Charlie Flynn,' Caelan put in. Nasenby ignored her.

'The problem is, we don't know where he's hiding. London is the obvious place, hence Tim being on board, but he could be anywhere. He has the money and the contacts to stay well out of sight for as long as he needs to. However, someone like Lambourne won't keep quiet for long. He'll get itchy feet, and that means only one thing: problems for us.'

'He has a son who's at university in Lincoln,' said Achebe. 'We thought perhaps you could go up there, pose as a student for a while. It makes sense that Lambourne would try to contact him – Ronnie's his name.'

'A student?' Caelan wrinkled her nose. 'What's he studying?'

'Accountancy. You wouldn't need to enrol, though,' Nasenby told her. 'We have places in mind where you could work, as an alternative. Bars, a café, a bookshop. Anywhere you'd have the chance to chat to Ronnie Morgan. Of course, you could simply follow him around for a while, until he meets his dear old dad.'

'That might be the best approach,' Caelan said. 'I'm not sure I want to be tied to a job, working set hours, because Ronnie won't be, not as a student. He calls himself Ronnie Morgan?'

'He took his mother's name after the Flynn case.' Nasenby nodded. 'Wouldn't you? It would ruin a legitimate career, being known as the son of Seb Lambourne. I'd imagine he keeps it quiet.'

'Though if you were going to be a criminal, it would be top of your CV,' Achebe grinned, grateful of an opportunity to attempt to lighten the mood.

'Okay, I go to Lincoln, find Ronnie Morgan, hope he leads me to his dad. And then what?' Caelan asked.

Nasenby said, 'We go after Lambourne. Discreetly, of course. As we know, he's wanted for blackmail, kidnap, at least two charges of murder, and God knows how many other offences. We capture him quietly, if we can. If he starts his old tricks again, though, especially if he takes another child, we'll need a different approach.'

'Sounds straightforward,' said Achebe. Nasenby gave him a sharp look, as if suspecting him of mockery. Achebe kept his face straight. He wasn't taking this lightly, far from it, but Nasenby's pomposity was beginning to grate. Caelan raised her hands, as if she too had heard enough.

'All right,' she said. 'I'll go to Lincoln. Never been there, so why not? No promises though, Michael.'

Nasenby exhaled, a release of tension he immediately concealed in a cough. Caelan heard it, though; Achebe saw her hide a smile. He checked his watch.

'Can I leave you to confirm the details? I've another meeting shortly.'

After another round of handshakes and assurances of continued contact and information-sharing, Achebe left the room and found himself hurrying out of the building. He had wanted to be involved in this, had argued and blagged his way in, but now... now he was feeling the beginnings of regret. In the past, he had kept his head down, played safe. His career had been built on solid foundations. Attempting to capture a criminal such as Seb Lambourne could make a reputation, or it could destroy it. As he unlocked his car and slid behind the wheel, he shuddered. Sam Clifton, someone Achebe knew, had met in his early days on the force, was testament to that.

–

'So what did you think?' Nasenby asked. Caelan sipped from a glass of water before replying.

'About Achebe? He's nervous.'

'Of course he is. He's ambitious. He couldn't resist muscling his way onto this case, and now he's wondering if he's done the right thing.'

'Aren't we all?'

Nasenby ignored that. 'Which legend do you want to use? We'll need one for Mr Davies here too, if you're determined to insist he tags along.'

'Which I am.'

Sighing, Nasenby got to his feet. He went over to the window, pulled the vertical blinds to one side so he could peer out. 'I'll have to speak to his superiors. They won't like it, I can tell you. You don't make my life easy, Caelan.'

Caelan continued as though Nasenby hadn't spoken. 'None of the identities I've used before are suitable. We'll need new ones.'

'If you like. We can sort out a flat for you in Lincoln. I was going to suggest a room in a shared house, but now there are two of you to consider... Listen, Caelan, are you sure about this? No offence to Mr Davies, but he's an army man, not used to libraries and lecture theatres.'

Ewan raised his eyebrows, hearing his intelligence and capability being dismissed in one plummy sentence. Caelan lifted her chin.

'He can be my partner, fresh out of the army, looking for work. Though I'm sure he could pass as a student if he needed to.'

Nasenby eyed Ewan doubtfully. 'Oh, I'm sure.' He leant forward, shutting down the laptop. 'Why don't you spend a few days at home, give us time to put everything in place? You still have your apartment in town?'

'Yes.'

'Good. I'll be in touch, one way or another.'

Caelan stood, eager to leave. 'We'll see ourselves out.'

Ewan followed as she crossed the room.

'And Caelan?' Nasenby called. She turned back. Nasenby was leaning against the wall, his hands in his trousers pockets. He smiled.

'Don't get yourself killed.'

4

Back in the car, Caelan pulled her seat belt across her chest. 'Did you mind me recruiting you, Ewan?'

He cleared his throat. 'What if I'd said no?'

'I had a feeling you wouldn't.'

Switching on the engine, he checked his mirrors. 'I might have done. Where are we going?'

'You heard Nasenby. To my flat. We've been ordered to have a couple of days off.'

'We?'

'You're stuck with me now, Ewan. Rotherhithe. Near the tunnel. You know London?'

'Like a cabbie.'

She laughed as he reversed out of the space and headed for the car park's exit. 'That's a bonus. So, I'll ask again. Who do you work for?'

'Your boss told you. I'm an army man.'

'At one time, maybe.' He was silent. 'Come on, Ewan. You know all about me.' Though he didn't, not at all.

Caelan turned to gaze out of the window as an RAF base came into view. She recognised RAF Northolt, to the west of the city. She settled back in her seat, knowing it would be at least an hour before they reached her flat. Meanwhile, she wanted to find out all she could about the man at her side, the man she had, rather impulsively, recruited as her partner. She had accepted the job, as she had known she would from the moment Adamson had appeared at her hotel. Lambourne had to be captured, and made to pay.

'You must be more than an ex-soldier boy, otherwise you would never have been allowed to pick me up and take me to see Nasenby. To have access to the building, much less know the entry code.' She hoped she was right. Otherwise she had misjudged him, and he would have to go.

'They'll have changed the numbers by now.'

She waved a hand. 'No doubt. The point is, you were trusted with it at all. Not many people would have been.'

'I joined the army at sixteen. I served for thirteen years, then I was discharged. Now I work for the Metropolitan Police.'

'There, didn't hurt, did it?' Caelan grinned. 'And? What do you do?'

'Protection.' He said it quickly, as if doing so would mean he hadn't revealed anything.

'I knew it. SO1?'

He grinned, raised an admonishing finger. 'That's not what it's called now.'

'Same thing. Protecting the royal family, the Prime Minister and various minions, plus anyone else who needs it. Royal properties and visitors, high-risk prisoners.'

'High-risk undercover police officers.'

'I'm honoured.'

He accelerated past a lumbering lorry. 'Don't be. I'm obviously not so good at it.'

Caelan laughed. 'Really? Reassuring. You mean because you weren't briefed properly for the airport? Maybe it was deliberate. Perhaps they'd like you to lose me.'

-

The pale-yellow-brick building was six storeys high, built on the banks of the Thames not far from Canary Wharf. Its numerous windows were painted royal blue, as were the doors. CCTV cameras kept a watchful eye from each corner of the building, and Ewan knew there would be secure parking, as well as a concierge team.

Caelan said, 'Before you say anything, I inherited the flat.'

'None of my business. It's impressive.'

'Wait until you see inside.' It wasn't a boast. Caelan sounded embarrassed, and Ewan wondered why. What concern was it of his if she owned an apartment in a place like this? Her job was difficult and dangerous, no doubt commanding a decent salary. Someone in her position would need a home they could feel secure in, even more so than the average person.

'I'll have to return the car,' Ewan told her. 'I'll see you tomorrow.'

She smiled. 'You're not coming in?'

Ewan knew he was blushing again. 'Well, I…'

'Because if we're going to make this work, we need to be seen together. Do you live in London?'

'My sister does. I've been staying with her.'

'Okay. Get some clothes, toiletries, whatever you need, then come back here. Don't worry, I've got two bedrooms.' She climbed out of the car, went around to the boot to retrieve her suitcase, then ducked her head back inside. 'I know Nasenby said a few days, but it won't be. He'll move quickly, it's his way. We'll probably be in Lincoln tomorrow.'

Ewan tried to protest, but Caelan slammed the door and trotted around the corner of the building, out of sight. Slowly he eased the car into gear and drove away.

5

The restaurant was one of the most expensive in the city, and Richard Adamson was glad that he would not be paying the bill. The Mayfair location, the à la carte menu – Adamson felt out of place and underdressed. In his career he had mingled with people from every conceivable background, from royalty to the most impoverished. Yet there was something about places like this that reduced him to the snivelling lad who'd wet his pants on the first day of primary school.

In the chair opposite Adamson's, Ian Penrith sipped at a glass of red wine. With one hand resting on his belly, his eyes creased in pleasure, he resembled a well-fed pig. Is there any other kind? Adamson asked himself, taking a swallow of his own exorbitantly priced mineral water.

'Well, what do you think?' Penrith asked. Adamson wiped his lips on his napkin, purely to give himself a few seconds to formulate his reply.

'You're asking me to keep an eye on Caelan. In effect, to spy on her.' His voice was flatter, his tone blunter than he had intended. Penrith tipped back his head and laughed.

'Nonsense, not at all. I'm concerned about her suitability for the assignment. I wanted you to be the one to track down Lambourne, as I told Nasenby. He's desperately clinging onto Caelan's past successes, and it's pathetic. She's not up to the job.'

'I'm not sure I agree.' Adamson scooped a morsel of the fancy dish he had ordered onto his fork and nibbled at it. He still wasn't sure what it was – meat of some kind? He had chosen to point at it on the menu rather than attempt to pronounce its name and risk looking ridiculous. Penrith would have loved to see him trip himself up. 'You know I've worked with Caelan several times before. Do you seriously believe I could follow her around without her realising? She'd be onto me in a heartbeat. I think, as Nasenby does, as Elizabeth Beckett and the Home Secretary do, that Caelan is the best undercover officer we have.'

Penrith set his glass on the table with rather more force than he needed to.

'She's not, but that's irrelevant – we can't use her to find Lambourne. The whole scheme's doomed to fail. He's seen her, spoken to her. I don't care if she was in one of her clever disguises, he'll know he's seen her before. He's not stupid.'

'I'm aware of that, but I've walked past Caelan on the street myself when she's been undercover and not recognised her. She has a gift for it, a talent. She doesn't just put on the outfit; she becomes the person. Lambourne will never know.'

Ian Penrith shook his head. 'Another one who fancies her rotten.' Adamson began to protest, but Penrith held up a meaty hand. 'Mind you, you got further with her than most men have.' He leant forward, leering. 'You shared a bed with her for a while.'

'During an operation, because we had to. The trouble with Caelan is, it's hard to know where the legend ends and the real person begins. Or if there's even a difference any more.'

'Spare me.' Penrith pushed a forkful of steak into his mouth. 'Look, Richard. Bottom line. Are you going to do this or not?'

Adamson swallowed. 'Not.'

Penrith tipped his head to the side. 'Where's your ambition gone? A few years ago, you'd have jumped at the chance.'

'To undermine one of my colleagues? I think you're confusing me with someone else.'

Penrith started a slow handclap, causing every other diner to turn and look at him, and Adamson to blush a furious shade of red. He contemplated walking out of the restaurant, but then Penrith would have won.

'How about if you work alongside her, then? Go to Lincoln, shadow Seb Lambourne's son yourself.' Penrith chewed, swallowed. 'Two heads are better than one and all that crap.'

Richard frowned. 'Would Caelan know about it?'

'I'd have to tell Nasenby, get him to sign it off, and that's tantamount to telling Caelan anyway. You know she's his pet.'

'Which is hardly Caelan's fault.'

'No, to be fair, she doesn't encourage the old goat. Now, do we have an agreement?'

Pouring himself another glass of water, Richard nodded. It was no doubt a mistake, but what choice did he have? Penrith smirked, took his time picking a piece of meat out of his back teeth with his index finger. 'Good man, Richard. And now you can order dessert.'

—

Ewan stood next to the intercom, feeling ridiculous having to squat to speak into a metal box. He didn't even know which flat number to ask for. The intercom buzzed and a voice said, 'Can I help you, sir?'

He'd been spotted. It was no surprise. The place had more security than Downing Street. 'I'm here to see Caelan Small.' Shit. Would she be using her own name? Too late now. 'I'm afraid I don't know which flat she lives in.'

There was a pause. 'I'll call Ms Small now, sir. Your name?'

Ewan gave it, then stood back, smoothing his hair. Was the concierge still watching? No doubt. He half hoped Caelan would deny all knowledge and he could go home. Then the door beside him opened silently. Picking up his canvas bag, Ewan stepped through it.

The area inside had a white tiled floor, gleaming under chrome spotlights. Ewan realised, far too late, that he had traipsed mud all the way across it. Behind the reception desk, the concierge thinned his lips as he took in the perfect imprints of Ewan's size twelves.

'Ms Small is on her way down to meet you, sir,' he said, his tone implying that he had no idea why Caelan would be bothering with such an oaf.

'Thank you.' Ewan stepped back, bumping into a low trough filled with an array of exotic plants. The concierge's eyebrows lifted a fraction. Ewan moved away with an apologetic smile, only to fall over his own bag, which he'd set at his feet. 'It's a lovely place,' he said, to cover his embarrassment. The concierge nodded, though his expression didn't change.

'Yes, indeed.' He turned back to his computer. Ewan took the hint and shut up.

On the cream walls, black-and-white photographs of various London landmarks were framed in dark wood. In case the residents forgot where they lived, Ewan thought with a smile. Their rent or mortgage payments would soon remind them of that. He had no idea what it would cost to live here, but it had to be astronomical, especially by his own modest standards. He had bought a semi-detached house in a village near the Welsh border, not far from where he had grown up, and the mortgage payments on it still pained him. One of these apartments would no doubt set him back four or five times what he had paid for his house. Not that he would want to live here. Caelan had said she'd inherited the place. Ewan sniffed. Couldn't be bad. He wondered who had bequeathed the apartment to her. It wasn't the sort of place an elderly person would choose to live in.

The lift doors slid open and he picked up his bag again. Caelan appeared, obviously happier using the lift on her own territory. She raised a hand to Ewan before going over to the reception desk, smiling at the man behind it. His face lit up.

'Good evening, Peter. How's your wife?' she asked.

'Not so bad, thank you. She loved those flowers you sent, wanted me to thank you for thinking of her.'

'You're welcome. Is she out of hospital yet?'

Peter shook his head. 'Another few days, they say. They're looking after her, though the nurses are run off their feet. Never enough of them after all these cuts they've made. It's criminal, though they still manage to do an amazing job. Anyway, I won't keep you when you've a guest.'

'Thank you, Peter. I see he's made a mess.' Caelan grinned. Ewan blushed, but said nothing.

'Not to worry. I'll get the mop out, soon have that sorted. Have a good evening.'

'You too, Peter. Say hello to your wife for me. Come on, Ewan.'

Ewan followed her into the lift. 'You don't mind using it then?'

She pressed the button for the top floor. 'What do you mean?'

'The lift.'

'There's six flights of stairs if you'd rather.' She shrugged. 'The lift's fine here. There's no danger.'

She said it as though trying to convince herself. Ewan wondered how many places she hadn't felt safe in. More than him, no doubt, and he'd been deployed to Iraq and Afghanistan.

'You know the receptionist well?'

'Porter. He doesn't like being called a receptionist. He's ex-army too; you should have a chat with him.'

'I think I pissed him off.'

'Wipe your shoes next time. This is a posh gaff.' She grinned at him.

–

Her apartment was number 135. He committed the number to memory as Caelan unlocked the door.

'I thought you'd have a fingerprint entry system at least.'

'It's not the Batcave.' She smiled. 'Come in.'

He followed her inside, where he slipped off his trainers.

Caelan watched him. 'Good thinking. I'd hate to have to throw you straight back out.'

The living room was larger than he had anticipated, about twenty-five feet by twenty. One wall was brick, and because it was a corner apartment, there were two huge windows, one overlooking the Thames, one the street below where Ewan had entered the building. She would be able to see anyone who approached, he realised. The walls were painted white, bare of pictures or any other decoration. Beneath his feet were wooden boards. Two charcoal sofas were separated by a bookcase, with a TV and games console on a low table in one corner. There was a dining table with six chairs under one of the windows, though Ewan doubted Caelan did much entertaining. The place had the feel of a show house. He had the impression she didn't spend a lot of time at home. It made sense.

'Fancy a takeaway?' Caelan wiped her hands down the sides of her jeans, and Ewan noted the gesture with interest. Why would someone so self-assured be nervous in her own home?

–

Later, after a curry and three beers each, Ewan felt brave enough to ask the question he'd been holding back since their meeting with Achebe and Nasenby.

'Why me?'

Caelan was sprawled on one of the sofas while Ewan sat at the dining table. She looked at him, narrowing her eyes, then made the decision.

'I need someone I can trust, rely on,' she said.

'But you don't know me.'

'And you don't know me. That's part of your appeal.'

'Can't you trust your colleagues?'

She shrugged. 'Not any more.'

'Nasenby?'

'Yes. I trust Nasenby, unless he gives me a reason not to.' She folded her arms. Ewan saw the gesture, decided not to pry any further. 'What did you tell your sister?' she asked.

'The truth, to a point. That I was going away for work, I didn't know how long for and I'd be in touch when I could. She's used to it.'

'No partner?'

'Not now. I was married briefly, but she… Well, she didn't cope well once I'd left the army and was around all the time.'

'Really?'

'Neither did her boyfriend.'

'Ah.'

He shrugged. 'Better to find out now than in twenty years' time. At least we hadn't got around to having kids.'

Caelan had drawn up her knees, wrapping her arms around them. Ewan took this as a sign that her personal relationships were not up for discussion. Her phone, which she'd thrown carelessly onto the sofa beside her, began to ring. She picked it up, checked the screen.

'That was quick.'

From her side of the conversation, it was clear she was being given instructions. Ewan got up and wandered over to the window, gazing down at the Thames far below. He didn't want her to think he was listening, though she could have left the room if she had wanted privacy. He leant closer to the window, rested his forehead on the cool, damp glass. If he was honest, the task before them excited him. Caelan was in charge, of course, the star of the show, but to have even a bit part was more than he could have hoped for. After spending so many years being shot at in every war-torn hellhole on earth, the move into protection had been a real comedown. It might sound exciting, but Ewan knew the truth. He was a tiny cog in a huge machine, and it didn't matter whether he was there or not. The thought of being out in the field again had lit a fire in his belly, one he'd believed long extinguished. People had trusted him once, relied on him. He'd let them down. Here was a chance to put his experience and training back into action. He wasn't an investigator, far from it, but he knew how to keep someone alive. If he could do that for Caelan Small, it might help him sleep at night.

Might help him forget their faces.

'Ewan?' Caelan was standing beside him. 'That was Nasenby. We're leaving in six hours. We need to get some rest.'

6

He couldn't remember her name. Strands of her blonde hair fell across her face as she grumbled in her sleep. As she turned over, Ronnie Morgan took the opportunity to slide his arm from beneath her, then slowly, carefully pivoted on the bed so he could set his feet on the ground. Reaching forward, he picked up his clothes, wallet and phone and crept into the tiny en suite bathroom. He didn't dare shower in case the sound of the water woke her, so he put his hands under the tap and splashed his face instead. Then he picked up her toothpaste, squirted some onto his finger and rubbed it on his teeth. Considering how much he'd had to drink the night before, he didn't feel bad. A slight headache, a dry mouth, that was all.

Once dressed, he went quickly, quietly to the door and let himself out. No point disturbing her to say goodbye.

That was what he told himself as he opened the door onto the street and slipped through it. He felt guilty now, though she had wanted it as much as he had. She had invited him back to her room, so it wasn't as if she was expecting a game of Scrabble when they got there.

Walking quickly to put as much distance between her and himself as possible, Ronnie headed for a café where he knew he could get a decent breakfast. At a cash machine he was relieved to see that another five hundred quid had been credited to his account. The money came from his dad, of course, though that was a secret. His mother didn't know about it, and

Ronnie certainly wasn't going to tell her. She hated his dad and wouldn't have let Ronnie touch his money. The way he saw it, though, why shouldn't he? It wasn't as though the old man had contributed much when he was growing up. He'd been in prison when Ronnie was born, stayed there until a few days before his son's seventh birthday, arriving at the party bearing a carload of gifts. At that age, the presents mattered. No matter that his mum had raised him alone, worked every hour she could to make sure he had everything he needed. Seb Lambourne had strolled back into their lives as if he had never been away, and Ronnie had loved him for it.

He hadn't known where his dad had been all those years. Then, during his teenage years, the truth had slowly dawned. His dad was a criminal, a crook. It had seemed glamorous at first, and Ronnie had been impressed, despite himself. The cash, the cars, the house and the holidays... His mum had warned him, told him repeatedly what Seb Lambourne was like. But he was Ronnie's father, and that counted for something. At least it had back then.

Then Charlie Flynn had disappeared, and Ronnie's world imploded. His dad was the most wanted man in Britain, hated and despised. He and his mum had to go into hiding, leave their home and their lives. At first his mum had refused to go, but when someone poured petrol through their letter box, followed by a lit match, even she had to admit they weren't safe. The man she had married twenty years previously was a monster, worse than even she had suspected. And now Seb Lambourne was paying for his son's nights on the piss.

Ronnie wiped the last traces of egg yolk from his plate with a piece of toast and pushed it into his mouth. He had a lecture at ten and he'd have to hurry. Hopefully the blonde girl from the night before would have forgotten his name and what he looked like. He would probably bump into her again, but he would ignore her. A relationship was not part of his plan – not yet. He had his life mapped out, and though he was happy to accept his father's money, he would never follow in his footsteps.

There was a homeless man sitting on the pavement with a paper cup in front of him. Ronnie dropped a folded ten-pound note into it, and the man looked up in surprise.

'Cheers, pal.'

Ronnie grinned, nodded. 'You're welcome, mate.' No skin off his nose. *Thanks, Dad – you've bought some poor sod his dinner, maybe contributed to his next fix or bottle of spirits.* The thought amused him. Ronnie had direct debits set up all over the place too – children's charities, refuges, animal sanctuaries. A generous donation to each one every month, paid for by Seb Lambourne's fatherly guilt. Served him fucking right. About time he helped other people for a change.

Ducking into a newsagent's, Ronnie bought a notepad and pen. He might enjoy himself, but he was serious about his studies too. Get his degree, pass his professional exams and leave Seb Lambourne far behind. He'd shed the old man's name, but there was no fighting genetics. Still, Ronnie did his best.

He made the lecture theatre in plenty of time, had a chat with a few mates from his course as he went inside, and didn't give his dad another thought.

7

Caelan cooked breakfast: bacon, fried eggs, sausages and toma-
toes. Ewan had been surprised when she had offered, expecting
her to start her day with muesli or fruit. Then again, the curry
the night before should have given him a clue. As he was
buttering a second slice of toast, the apartment's entry phone
buzzed. Caelan looked up from loading the dishwasher.

'Here we go.' She set the plate she was holding on the
worktop and went over to pick up the receiver. After a quick
conversation, she replaced the handset and raised her eyebrows
at Ewan. 'There's a parcel downstairs. Ready to meet your new
identity?'

He frowned. 'Meet him?'

'It can feel like that,' Caelan told him. 'This isn't quite the
same, because you're not assuming a concrete role, but you'll
need to be convincing.'

'That's what worries me,' Ewan admitted.

Caelan ignored that. 'I'll go down and fetch the parcel.' She
bent to slip her shoes on.

'Let me.' Ewan chewed his last mouthful of toast. 'You
cooked.'

Caelan smiled. 'Don't get used to it; that was a one-off.'

–

In the lift, Ewan stared at his reflection, wondering how he could disguise himself if he needed to. All he could think of was fake glasses and facial hair. Not exactly in Caelan's league.

On the third floor, a woman got into the lift. She smiled at Ewan, then turned away, obviously not wanting to talk. That suited him. Perhaps he shouldn't have volunteered to come down here after all. People would expect to see Caelan, but not him. Then again, Caelan had wanted him to stay. Although they had only met the day before, Ewan already felt comfortable in her presence. She was easy to talk to, and though he had felt intimidated on meeting her, it had quickly given way to respect, especially after seeing the way she had dealt with Ian Penrith at the meeting.

What Penrith had said troubled Ewan. He couldn't believe Caelan was guilty of any wrongdoing, though how could he know for sure so soon after meeting her? He had lain awake the night before in Caelan's guest room, thinking about the accusations Penrith had made. He knew he would be reliant on Caelan for however long it took to flush Lambourne out. This was her field of expertise, not his, and that alone caused him to feel vulnerable. But he had no choice but to trust her after she had dragged him along for the ride.

After the beer, the amazing curry and a warm shower, he had expected to fall asleep immediately. That hadn't been the case, and he was feeling the effects of too little sleep already. Life in the army had never been nine to five, but his work for the Met had been a little more routine. Now he was going to be on duty twenty-four hours a day until Lambourne was caught. The thought was not comforting. Working so closely with Caelan was going to be difficult too. He thought he could trust her, but how could he be sure? Time alone would tell.

Caelan went quickly into the bedroom Ewan had slept in and picked up the khaki canvas bag he had brought with him. She shook her head with a smile. Lucky his story was going to include an army background. Knowing that she had at least five minutes before he returned from reception, she had planned to search through the bag, more out of habit than any sense of mistrust. Now, though, seeing his phone on the bedside table, his wallet, she hesitated. He would probably realise what she had done, and any camaraderie that was beginning to grow between them would be destroyed. No. It was better to wait. If he gave her any reason to doubt him, then she would act, and swiftly. She'd done it before.

–

As Ewan stared down at his own face on the passport Caelan had handed him, he wondered how they had found a photo of him. It was obvious when he thought about it. From his real passport. They'd even put a few stamps inside the new one, made it look battered. He had credit and debit cards too, and a driving licence.

He read the name from the document. 'Edward Devlin.'

'Same initials as your own. The date of birth will be your real one too. If you hesitate when someone asks you, it's a dead giveaway,' said Caelan.

'What do I call you?' he asked. She held out her own new passport for him to inspect. 'Karen Devlin,' he read aloud.

'We're married, by the way,' Caelan told him, unfolding a certificate and waving it at him. Ewan gaped, and she laughed. 'Congratulations. Do you want to phone your mum?'

'We're… Is that real?'

'Absolutely. At least, if anyone cares to check, all the official records will show Edward Devlin marrying Karen Shaw in a lovely country hotel two years ago. They might have problems finding someone who attended the ceremony, though. We have joint bank accounts, insurance, all the usual stuff. There'll be social media accounts, even photos. Places mainly, not people, as you'd expect. Enough of a presence to be convincing. Someone will update all that for us periodically. There's a car waiting for us too, one that Edward and Karen have been making loan payments on for the past eighteen months.' She brandished a car key, jangling on a fob with a couple of others. 'The rest are the keys for our house in Lincoln.'

Ewan shook his head, overwhelmed. 'And Nasenby set all this up overnight?'

'Not personally. A lot of it was probably already in place, waiting for people to fit the roles. They want us in Lincoln quickly.'

'Okay. I'm worried I'll call you by the wrong name,' he admitted.

'Don't call me anything if you can avoid it. People don't use each other's names that much in conversation. If you use it too much it sounds weird, and weird means noticeable, which we don't want.'

'Right. Maybe I should be taking notes.'

-

Three and a half hours later, after an uneventful journey once they had escaped the London traffic, they arrived in Lincoln. The address they'd been given proved to be in an area called Birchwood, to the south of the city. The house was semi-detached, on a wide main road and next to a T-junction.

'Nowhere for us to be boxed in.' Caelan nodded approvingly as she reversed the car onto the brick driveway. 'And no nosy neighbours.' The adjoining property was empty, a faded 'For Sale' sign lolling in the overgrown front garden.

'When do we start being Edward and Karen?' Ewan asked.

'Now,' she told him. He nodded, the enormity of what he had agreed to hitting him again.

Inside, the house was clean, though with a musty smell suggesting that the windows hadn't been opened for a while. The furnishings were comfortable but functional, nothing too lavish. Pale wood veneer tables, a brown leather settee, a few bland paintings. The windows had blinds as well as curtains, meaning the occupants of the house could be totally invisible to anyone outside if they closed both.

'Is this a safe house?' Ewan asked, noting the bolts on the front door. Caelan shrugged as they went upstairs.

There were two bedrooms, one with a neatly made double bed, wardrobe, drawers and en suite, the second smaller, with a single bed but no other furniture.

'Sparse,' Caelan said.

Ewan smiled. 'I've slept in worse places.'

'All those years in the army.' Caelan dumped her bag on the floor. 'Do you want the right-hand drawers, or the left?'

Ewan stared at her for a second. She gazed back, widening her eyes, sending him a non-verbal message.

'Don't mind,' he stammered. 'The left?'

'Goes with your side of the bed.' Caelan nodded, beginning to scoop clothes out of her bag and into the drawers.

Ewan swallowed. They were going to share the bed. Why had he not thought of that? True, they were posing as a married couple. But who would know? There was a single bed in the second bedroom. If he slept there, what difference would it make? Sharing a bed with Caelan would be excruciating, especially as the nearest thing he had to pyjamas were his boxers and an old T-shirt. Caelan turned, her eyes bright, clearly finding his discomfort amusing. She quirked an eyebrow, and he managed a smile. This was going to be even more difficult than he had imagined.

In the kitchen, they discovered that the fridge was full of food, as were the freezer and cupboards. Caelan didn't comment, filling the kettle and flicking it on to boil. Ewan eventually found tea bags and a jar of coffee, as well as chocolate digestives. Leaning back against the worktop, Caelan tore the packet open and took a couple.

'I'm going to look at the rest of the house,' she said through a mouthful of crumbs. 'Will you make the tea?'

Ewan nodded, knowing an offer of help would be refused. He would be useless anyway. This was Caelan's territory.

There was a dining table against the wall that separated the kitchen from the living room. Ewan carried the two mugs over to it and pulled out a chair. As he dunked a biscuit into his tea, he could hear Caelan moving around in the next room. What she was doing, he had no idea. He took out his phone, scrolled through the news, the latest football results. Sipped his tea, ate another biscuit. Wished himself miles away.

Ten minutes later, Caelan reappeared. Her hands were empty and she didn't tell him what she'd been doing. Ewan decided he didn't want to know.

'Your tea will be cold,' he said. With a smile, she picked up her cup and drank.

'What do you want to do tonight?' she asked. Ewan stared, wondering what he was supposed to say. Was she asking him as Ewan, or as Edward? She raised her eyebrows. 'Ewan?'

'I didn't know who you were talking to.'

She laughed. 'In the house, we're Caelan and Ewan. We're safe here, free to talk. The second we step out the front door, we're Edward and Karen.'

'Okay. Won't it look strange to the people who live around here, us arriving with hardly any luggage? Moving into a house so well furnished that even the beds are already made?'

Caelan dropped into the chair beside his. 'Don't worry. Hopefully we won't be here long, and most people are far more worried about their own lives than their neighbours'.'

'Lambourne's a threat, though, isn't he? He killed one of your colleagues, not to mention a ten-year-old child.'

Pushing back the chair, Caelan stood and turned away, massaging her temples with her fingertips.

'He doesn't know we're here, and he's not likely to find out,' she said.

'But if we're following his son...'

'*We're* not. Karen Devlin is.'

'He's seen your face.'

She rounded on him. 'If you don't want to be involved, there are plenty of trains out of here. You could have said before we left London.'

'I've never done this before. I don't know about surveillance, counter-surveillance, any of it.' Ewan spoke quietly, and Caelan's face softened.

'I wouldn't have brought you if I'd had any doubts. You don't have to do anything but stay close to me. I don't see this as a difficult assignment. We're not going to confront Lambourne, or even interact with him. That's not our job.'

He smiled. 'All right.'

She moved over to the kettle again.

'My turn to make the tea.'

They watched TV for a while – mindless quiz shows and then the soaps. As the evening drew in, Ewan offered to cook, and Caelan was happy to have some time to read the information they had on Ronnie Morgan. She didn't want to hide it from Ewan, but there was no need for him to see it. He knew what the young man they were here to follow looked like, and that was enough.

She curled on the sofa, flicking through the information she had been provided with. Ronnie Morgan was young, and innocent. He couldn't be blamed for the sins of his father, but Caelan felt fury build in her stomach as she read about him. Lambourne's criminal activities had no doubt paid for his son's toys and clothes, his school shoes. Ronnie Morgan had the chance to succeed, to thrive – and Charlie Flynn was dead.

Caelan didn't believe Seb Lambourne would arrive in person to see his son – he wasn't that stupid. He must realise he was a wanted man. He would also guess that Ronnie might be watched. He would either contact the young man secretly to arrange a meeting, or have him collected and brought to him. Either way, Caelan intended to find Lambourne. He had killed one of her colleagues, wrecked the life of another and brought her own professional reputation into doubt. Thinking about his son merrily living his life infuriated her. Lambourne had destroyed every life he had touched, and then escaped without a scratch.

When she found him, when they were face to face again, Caelan had plans of her own to deal with him.

He would be made to pay.

This time, he wouldn't walk away.

8

The hotel room was too warm. Richard Adamson felt perspiration prickling his back as he swung his bag onto the bed and kicked off his shoes. He removed his coat and picked up the tiny white kettle that stood on the desk. As he left the bathroom after filling it, he saw there was a thermostat on the wall near the door. There was no way he would sleep if the temperature remained as it was. Knowing from long experience that the window would be impossible to open, he stepped back across the room, his phone beginning to ring as he fumbled with the thermostat.

'Not interrupting anything, am I?'

Richard frowned. 'What do you mean?'

'You sound out of breath,' Ian Penrith chuckled.

'My room's on the fifth floor and the lift isn't working.'

'Been missing your gym sessions, have you? Tut tut.'

Richard visualised Penrith – the beer belly, the too-tight suits. 'What do you want, Ian?'

Penrith heard the bite in his tone, and matched it. 'How long have you been at the hotel?'

'Five minutes.

'And what are you planning to do now? Few pints, a meal and a long hot bath?'

'I hadn't—'

'I want you out on the street, Adamson. You need to find the son before Caelan does, then track down Lambourne himself.'

Richard went over to the window and pulled back the curtain. He could see the cathedral, dwarfing the buildings around it, glowing golden against the night sky, illuminated by spotlights he couldn't see. The effect was impressive.

'Adamson?' Penrith barked.

'Have you spoken to Nasenby?' Richard asked, his eyes still on the cathedral.

There was a pause, then Penrith said, 'I told you I would.'

'Doesn't mean you have.'

'Are you calling me a liar?'

Richard sighed. 'Never.'

'Caelan's already in Lincoln, with her new assistant.' Penrith snorted. 'What a bloody joke. The man has no experience, no clue about what we do. It's Nasenby indulging Caelan's whims again. She'll lose him his job one day.'

'Employing her hasn't done his career any harm so far.'

'Because her mistakes are covered up, her failures ignored. She should have been sacked over the Charlie Flynn case, maybe even faced criminal charges. And what happened? Nothing.'

'Listen, Ian…'

'You're going to stick up for her. There's a shock. When you find Lambourne and you're the hero of the hour, when Caelan admits defeat, remember who sent you up to Lincoln. Who believed in you? It wasn't Michael Nasenby.'

Richard had heard enough. 'I'm going to speak to Nasenby myself.'

'Do that. Ruin your career, your prospects. Nasenby's floundering, Richard. He's desperate for a result on Lambourne, because it's the only way to save his job. His and Caelan's.'

'Rubbish.'

Penrith laughed, a wet, mocking chuckle. He spluttered, cleared his throat. Richard held the phone away from his ear for a second.

'Not sure, though, are you? Take it from me, Nasenby's old news. You'd do well to decide where your loyalties lie before it's too late.'

'Goodbye, Ian.'

'Remember what I've said.'

'Oh, I will.'

'And do your job. Find Seb Lambourne.'

As Penrith ended the call, Richard turned from the window, threw his phone onto the bed. Why was he here? Penrith obviously hadn't spoken to Nasenby about him being in Lincoln. Nasenby would soon realise he wasn't around, and then what? Richard liked Michael Nasenby, and respected him. What would he think when he discovered Richard was treading on Caelan's toes?

Pacing the room, he made his decision and picked up his phone again. It rang twice before Nasenby answered.

'What can I do for you, Richard?'

Richard swallowed. 'Michael, I…'

'Let me put you out of your misery. You're in Lincoln?'

Surprised, Richard sank onto the bed. 'I didn't think you knew.'

'Ian may think his actions go unnoticed, but I can assure you they don't. He is supposed to report to me, after all. I'm pleased you phoned.'

Richard licked his lips, wondering what to say. 'You are?'

'It proves you're not completely under Ian's control.'

There was a silence. Richard closed his eyes, opened them slowly. 'He said he'd tell you.'

'And you believed him?'

'We're supposed to be on the same side.'

'You'd think. The Charlie Flynn investigation left its mark on Ian.'

'On all of us.'

'Quite,' Nasenby said. 'But Ian more than most.'

'He blames Caelan for the boy's death.'

'Easier to blame someone else than yourself. Ian worked eighteen-hour days throughout the Flynn investigation, was one of the first officers through the door after Lambourne made his escape. He feels he let everyone down.'

'I know.'

'He's a good officer, a decent man. His judgement is perhaps... clouded when it comes to Caelan. He thought Charlie would be brought home safely.'

Richard began to speak, then hesitated. He wanted to ask what happened the day Charlie Flynn died. How Caelan and Clifton had escaped unscathed, how Lambourne and Walker had managed to get away unseen.

'Richard?'

'I'm here.'

'Did Ian tell you his theory about Caelan and Seb Lambourne?' Nasenby asked. Richard marvelled, not for the first time, at Nasenby's ability to seemingly read his mind. They weren't in the same room, not even the same city, but Nasenby knew what he was thinking.

'He did say he has questions about our officers' confrontation with Lambourne and Walker.'

'I'm sure. Anything else?'

'He... suggested Caelan might be working with Lambourne. Working for him, I should say.'

'And what do you think?'

Richard passed a hand over his eyes. 'I've heard Caelan's account. I've read the reports.'

'And there are holes in her story. We all know that,' Nasenby said. 'You're wondering if Ian's right? If Caelan can be trusted?'

Richard shook his head, unwilling to voice the thoughts that had tormented him. 'No. I know her.'

Nasenby sighed. 'Do you, Richard? I thought I did too.'

'You can't believe Ian's nonsense? Caelan's our best officer, you told me so yourself. Why did I go to Egypt to bring her home if we don't trust her? Why is she here, looking for Lambourne's son?'

Nasenby was silent, ignoring the questions. Richard realised he was supposed to join the dots himself. He wasn't sure he wanted to.

'I didn't say I don't trust her.' Nasenby's voice was quiet.

'You want to keep her close, and have her find Lambourne at the same time? Two birds with one stone?'

'Partly. I also want to keep her safe. Save her from herself, if you like. Why do you think she was in Egypt?'

Richard frowned. 'She was on holiday.'

'And?'

'What are you saying, Michael?' Blinking, Richard tried to clear his head. 'I don't understand.'

'Have you ever known Caelan go on holiday before? She barely even takes her leave.'

'But she'd handed in her notice, finished work. I thought she wanted a break. She travelled under her own name...'

'Which makes sense if she wanted it to be clear where she was. She resigned, went away. Disassociated herself from the Met, and from the aftermath of Charlie Flynn's death. Absolved herself from blame.'

'But…' Richard floundered as he tried to make sense of what the other man was saying. Eventually Nasenby took pity on him.

'It doesn't matter, Richard. Stay in Lincoln, keep an eye on Caelan. If you can, find Lambourne.'

'And if Caelan sees me, recognises me?'

'Don't let her. She mustn't know, Richard. If she thinks we're watching her, she'll run. The only reason she agreed to this at all is because Lambourne's involved.'

'And she has a partner now, one of her own choosing,' Richard couldn't help but point out. Nasenby laughed.

'Ewan Davies? Do you know his history?'

'How could I? I'd never heard of him until Ian told me he was working with Caelan.'

'Jealous, Richard?' Nasenby chuckled.

Richard attempted to conceal his irritation. 'Not at all. It's none of my business if Davies is considered an asset.'

'Caelan thinks so, and for now, it's in all our interests to keep her happy. If or *when* Davies ceases to be useful, he'll be removed.'

Richard swallowed. 'Removed?'

'Well, sent back to guard duty. He's ex-army, left after some nasty business in Afghanistan.'

'Oh?' Richard didn't much care.

'Limped home, tail between his legs. Fared better than several of his men, though, who came home in coffins – those they were able to collect the pieces of, I mean.'

There was a silence, Richard still trying to gather his thoughts.

'And now he works for us?'

'For the Met, yes.' Nasenby paused. 'You probably believe I'm indulging Caelan, don't you, Richard?'

'I...'

'No doubt Ian thinks so, but I think we need Caelan if we're to find Lambourne.'

'I agree,' Richard said quickly.

'Excellent. I'll expect daily updates.'

'What about Ian?'

'Let's keep this conversation between ourselves, shall we?'

Richard grunted. 'You don't want me to tell Ian I've spoken to you? Then I'm left in a rather awkward position.'

'That can happen when you try to please everyone. Good-night, Richard.'

Richard paced over to the window again, furious. Though neither would admit it, Nasenby and Penrith had similar personalities. Both ambitious and confident, skilled at manipulating the will of others. And now Richard was stuck here, trapped between the pair of them.

'Fucking great,' he muttered to himself. He could go to Elizabeth Beckett, explain what the two men were up to, but Beckett was unpredictable, as likely to tell him to get on with it as she was to side with him. Worse, she might ask him to give her daily reports too, provide another tune for him to dance to. No, better to stay here and follow orders.

Someone's orders, anyway.

Caelan was out there in the city somewhere, making her preparations. Richard had been provided with the same information Caelan had about Ronnie Morgan – it was sparse, and Caelan would know she was at risk. Surveillance was usually carried out by a team. If Morgan saw Caelan too often, if he realised she was following him, all would be lost. Richard didn't envy Caelan her task, but then his was no easier. Morgan was unsuspecting; Caelan might not be. Watching her without alerting her to his presence would be close to impossible.

Ducking back into the bathroom, Richard glanced at the kettle he'd filled earlier, then turned away, deciding to head down to the hotel's bar instead. Once he was trailing Caelan, he would have no time to relax.

9

After a shower, Caelan put on the jogging bottoms and T-shirt she would sleep in. On the floor beside the bed she placed a rucksack containing a change of clothes, some cash and her Karen Devlin identification. She set her phone on the bedside cabinet, adjusted the position of the pillow and climbed into bed. Ewan was showering in the bathroom across the landing, and Caelan knew she had five minutes to read the information collated on Ronnie Morgan a final time before she destroyed it. Perhaps she was being overly cautious, but having the few sheets of paper in her possession made her uncomfortable. Having a hard copy delivered into her hand by a trusted courier was secure enough, more so than receiving it by email would be. Still, she didn't want to keep the information any longer than necessary.

On the first page was a colour photograph of Ronnie Morgan, as well as details of his height, weight and distinguishing features. Caelan studied the photograph, noting Morgan's resemblance to his father, particularly the dark eyes and the shape of his mouth. She had seen enough images of Seb Lambourne to discern the echoes of him in the face of his son, and wondered if Ronnie and his mother saw them too.

Having memorised Ronnie's address, a flat in a block of student accommodation, Caelan tore the thin sheets of paper into narrow strips. Then, glancing at the open bedroom door, she shredded the strips to tiny pieces, which she deposited on the bedside table. In the morning, she would burn them. She picked up her phone, scrolling through her emails. Nothing of note. No missed calls, no texts. As usual, she was entirely alone.

She heard the toilet flush and smiled to herself. Not alone at all, not this time.

Ewan stood in the bedroom doorway, dressed in a T-shirt and jeans, but barefoot.

'Okay?' Caelan said, understanding his hesitation. Being thrown together with someone who was in effect a stranger was never easy. During one of her first undercover operations, she had posed as the partner of Richard Adamson, who at the time she'd barely known. Sharing a house and a bed with him for six months had been difficult, at least at first. Eventually, as with genuine relationships, the awkwardness dissipated. At least Adamson had kept his hands to himself.

With a hesitant smile, Ewan said, 'Do we have to share the bed?'

'We need this to look real. I know it's weird, I understand.'

'Who's going to know if I sleep in the other room?'

Caelan leant back against the headboard. 'Honestly? Probably no one. I'm being overcautious.'

'You mean I can take the single bed?'

She laughed at the relief on his face.

'Go for it,' she told him. Ewan flushed, clearly wondering whether she was insulted because he didn't want to leap into bed with her. Caelan held his gaze with a smile. She wasn't, not at all. 'Goodnight, Ewan.'

'What time...?'

'I'll knock.'

'Okay.' Ewan saw the rucksack Caelan had set at the side of the bed and frowned. 'What's in the bag?'

Caelan explain what she'd packed. 'If we're called away quickly, or if something happens and we have to get out, everything I need is in there. Stuff I've unpacked I'd leave behind.'

'Should I do the same?'

'Might be a good idea.'

Ewan nodded. 'See you in the morning.'

He closed the door and Caelan heard him go into the other room. She gave him a few minutes to undress, then climbed out of bed and went downstairs.

The kitchen was dark, silent except for the fridge grumbling away to itself. Caelan took a glass from a cupboard, filling it with cold water from the tap. She gulped down a few mouthfuls, knowing she should rest but also recognising that her mind was too busy for sleep to come easily. She could go for a run, but it was late and she might draw attention to herself. People rarely took to the street for a jog close to midnight. Where might Ronnie Morgan be tonight? Tucked up in his bed already, or in a bar? From the scant intelligence provided on the young man, Caelan guessed the latter. She would never find him tonight. Lincoln wasn't a large city, but without a clue, without following Morgan from the second he left his flat, it would be pointless.

She drained the glass and set it in the sink. Leaning against the worktop, her arms folded, she stood listening to the unfamiliar noises of the house settling for the night. Pipes clicked as the central-heating system cooled, floorboards creaked. She went into the darkened living room and stood to the side of the window, where the blind met the frame. She would have a better view of the street from her bedroom upstairs, but there was no harm in having a glance through the window here too.

The houses across the road, exact replicas of the one they were staying in and its neighbour, were in darkness. As Caelan watched, a shadow passed the first-floor window of the house directly opposite. The curtains were open, the room beyond dark. Caelan tensed, certain she couldn't be seen but wary all the same. She didn't move, her eyes fixed on the window. Counting off the seconds, she waited. Someone readying themselves for bed, no doubt. But why not close the curtains, switch on the light? She frowned, annoyed at her own nervousness. The night before an operation began was usually tense, but she had never doubted herself like this before. She was paranoid – seeing phantoms, creating monsters. Remembering ten-year-old Charlie Flynn lying dead on the cold concrete floor of the damp, dark cellar he'd been held prisoner in, she swallowed. Charlie should be alive – going to school, laughing, playing. Growing, living his life. Instead, he was dead, killed after being caught up in a mess he had not created. The monsters were out there, Caelan knew. Her job was to find them.

She counted to three hundred, but the shadow did not return. Slowly she withdrew from the window and hurried back to the kitchen. After scanning the back garden and seeing nothing untoward, she picked up one of the dining chairs and took it up to her bedroom. Leaving the vertical blinds closed, she drew back the curtains, knowing that she would be able to watch the house through the slats of the blind without being observed. Pulling the duvet from the bed and wrapping it around her, she settled into the chair. Across the street, the house was still dark. Caelan huddled deeper into the duvet, her gazed fixed on the window. It would be a long, cold night, and she would be tired in the morning.

This time, though, she was leaving nothing to chance.

10

The coffee shop was already open as they approached the door a few minutes after seven thirty the next morning. The place was handily situated opposite the building where Ronnie Morgan lived, and Caelan knew that lingering over an early breakfast would give them plenty of time to wait for him to appear. The timetable she had been provided with informed her that Ronnie's classes started at nine, but since his flat was only a few minutes' walk from the university buildings, she wasn't expecting him to emerge for some time. As there was no guarantee he had slept at home, she had wanted to be outside his address as early as possible. Even so, they'd been in the area for only half an hour. Wandering around empty streets well before anyone else was up and about might have drawn attention to them. The coffee shop was a bonus, one they hadn't been informed of. Caelan had been fully prepared to wait on the street.

Caelan led Ewan to a table towards the back of the shop that afforded a clear view of the door to Ronnie Morgan's building without them being too visible to passers-by. The place was small, pine tables and chairs jostling for space on wooden floor-boards. For now, they were the only customers. Behind the counter, a middle-aged woman and a younger man yawned their way through preparing for the day. Caelan picked up the menu from the table, and studied it. She wasn't hungry, but she knew she should eat while there was an opportunity. After a long, cold night on the dining chair watching the window of the house opposite, coffee was required. Her caution had likely been unnecessary, but she knew she wouldn't have slept if she had gone to bed.

'Full English for me,' Ewan smiled.

'Have a bacon baguette,' Caelan told him. 'If we need to leave, you can take it with you. I'll have one too.'

Ewan nodded his understanding. 'I'll go and order.'

As he stood, Caelan allowed her gaze to drift back to the double glass doors of Ronnie Morgan's building. There were shops on the ground floor, then four floors of university-owned apartments above. Ronnie's studio was at the top. He rented a room with a private kitchen area, as well as a bedroom and shower room. Extra facilities would mean extra costs, and Caelan wondered how he afforded them. They knew he didn't have a part-time job like many of his fellow students to make ends meet. She made a mental note to ask Nasenby if Ronnie's finances had been examined. Probably not at this stage. He wasn't suspected of any crime, and there would be no grounds for it.

Ewan returned to the table, bearing two white mugs. Caelan thanked him as the welcome aroma of strong coffee reached her.

'Bacon butties on their way,' Ewan said. He drank from his cup and set it on the table. Caelan nodded, her eyes still on the doors of the building opposite. There was movement behind the smeared glass and she reached for her coffee as she waited to see who would emerge. As she watched, the door opened and a blonde-haired girl emerged, rubbing bleary eyes. Her padded jacket hung open, revealing a McDonald's uniform. She checked her watch, then allowed the door to swing closed behind her as she strode away.

'There's an intercom entry system for visitors, but I'm sure if you pressed enough buttons, someone would buzz you in without asking too many questions,' Caelan said, her voice quiet enough that Ewan had to lean closer to hear.

'You think we might need to get into Morgan's room?' Ewan didn't look thrilled at the prospect. Caelan shrugged.

'Hopefully not. Being arrested for burglary wouldn't be a great idea.'

'True. Might blow our cover.' Ewan nodded. Caelan smiled, amused by his choice of words.

'There shouldn't be any need. If we do our jobs properly, he won't even know we've been here.'

The bell above the café door jangled as a group of workmen clumped inside. Wearing fluorescent clothes and muddy boots, they looked like builders or road workers. As they gathered around the counter, laughing and jostling, Caelan caught Ewan's eye. He needed to remember who they were supposed to be. When the café had been empty of customers, Caelan hadn't minded relaxing their guard a little, but now, with others around, it was imperative to be on their guard. Ewan grinned, and Caelan knew he had realised what she was trying to communicate. Time to put on the mask.

Recruiting Ewan had been impulsive, many would say foolish. Nasenby certainly would, and no doubt Ian Penrith was broadcasting his complaints about Caelan's involvement to anyone who would listen. Caelan knew Nasenby would continue to defend her, but for how long? What Penrith had said about Lambourne's escape and her own possible involvement in it was nonsense, but there were plenty of people looking for someone to blame. Charlie Flynn's family, the press, the public. There were blogs and comments on social media questioning what had happened, how Lambourne had been allowed to escape. Theories had been publicised, discussed. Caelan and her colleagues had never been mentioned by name, because no one outside of their own unit had known they were involved. Caelan didn't understand how, but Sam had been identified at once, and thrown to the wolves. That didn't mean people hadn't tried to find out who else was to blame. The operation had been secret, the culmination of months of surveillance on Lambourne. He had been suspected of various serious crimes, but never kidnapping. Not until Charlie Flynn went missing and the police came to believe Lambourne was involved. Then all bets were off. The softly-softly approach was useless with a child's life at stake.

But it had been futile.

Lambourne must have heard their approach, their footsteps. They had been expecting an empty house, not a bloodbath. Caelan remembered the smell of it, the smears of blood on her face, her clothes. Nicky's blood. She hadn't seen Charlie, not clearly. Sam had thrown himself down beside the boy, but it was too late. The hope they had felt, the anticipation that they were here to save him, to rescue his young life, died in their chests as they saw his body. Then Lambourne lurched out of the darkness, knife held high, and in a second Nicky was down. Caelan watched the scene again, as she had thousands of times since it had happened. Every movement a blur, events unfolding so quickly it was impossible to remember the facts. All she knew was that Nicky had died, slumped face down, her eyes instantly losing their light. Caelan had fallen to her knees, bellowing desperately into her radio, knowing it was already too late. Nicky's life had puddled on the floor before the first back-up arrived. Caelan was still kneeling there as they thundered into the room, and persuaded her gently away from the body.

Sam was beside her, his face white, the horror Caelan would carry every day reflected in his eyes.

They were to blame, and they knew it. They were following orders, had done as they were told, but two deaths was a burden impossible to carry. Sam had struggled, floundered, and Caelan knew she was doing the same. Now she had to stand up, to square her shoulders and fight. Lambourne was out there, and she would find him.

She should have shot him while she had the chance, and fuck the consequences.

Caelan blinked, her gaze still fixed on the entrance to Ronnie Morgan's building. She would find Lambourne, and he would pay.

'Karen?' Ewan was speaking to her, his face concerned. Caelan looked at him, smiled.

'Sorry, love. Miles away.'

Ewan raised his eyebrows a fraction as their food arrived. Setting the plates down on the table, the waiter blocked Caelan's view of the door for a second. They thanked him, the smell of the bacon and freshly baked baguettes igniting Caelan's appetite. She picked up the tomato ketchup from the table and squeezed a generous amount over the bacon. As she did so, the door opened again and another customer entered the café. Caelan watched, still chewing.

It was Ronnie Morgan. He stood behind the gaggle of workmen, who were still placing their orders. Caelan watched as he pulled his phone out of his pocket, wondering again about his income. How many students could afford breakfast in a café? It wasn't an expensive place, granted, but it wasn't the cheapest either. Morgan had probably chosen it for convenience, since it was on his doorstep. Caelan swallowed her mouthful of food, glancing at Ewan. Had he realised that Morgan was here?

Under the table, she moved her foot to nudge his. He kept chewing, but his eyes met hers, letting her know he had seen their quarry too.

Caelan took another bite as Morgan shuffled closer to the front of the queue. She didn't want to rush her food. If Morgan was going to sit down to eat, they'd need to make their own breakfasts last so they could follow when he left. If he was going to place a takeaway order, however, they'd need to be quick.

Morgan spoke to the woman behind the counter and handed over his money. She was laughing as she turned to the till, Morgan grinning. He stepped away from the counter and made his way to a table, choosing one close to Caelan and Ewan. He didn't look at them as he sat, concentrating on his phone again. Caelan continued to eat, wishing she could see what he was studying so intently. When she spoke to Nasenby again, she would ask about access to Morgan's mobile phone records. It seemed unlikely that Lambourne would contact his son through his regular number, but if he were desperate, he might take the chance. Nasenby and his colleagues believed Lambourne and Ronnie to be estranged, but Caelan knew better than to make assumptions, however reliable the intelligence purported to be. She didn't trust the information she had been given.

Not any more.

Ronnie drained his coffee, set the cup on the table. Time to go. Having checked the opening hours of the ticket office on his phone, he knew he would have time to spare before his seminar began. As he got to his feet, he saw the queue, now six people deep, and picked up his mug and plate. He returned them to the counter, earning a quick smile of gratitude from Sue who owned the place.

Threading his way through the crowd, he pushed open the door. Outside, the first drops of rain falling from the bulk of a black cloud overhead, he glanced at his building. It was only one night. He already had his rucksack on his shoulder, filled with textbooks, notepads and his laptop. He could shove boxers, socks and a T-shirt in the front pocket, save himself the hassle of coming back here, catch an earlier train. Why not?

Decision made, he hurried across and let himself into the building, unaware of the eyes monitoring his every move.

–

'Why would he go back inside?' Ewan spoke softly, though there was no one nearby.

'Forgotten something? I don't know.' Caelan had turned away, knowing Ewan was watching the door. Her eyes scanned the street. It was still too early for shoppers, and the few people wandering by wouldn't provide much cover. Every second they stood here made them more conspicuous. They were outside a department store, its windows illuminated, mannequins staring glumly at them. Ewan checked his watch.

'If Ronnie's class doesn't start until nine, he could be inside for close to an hour,' he pointed out. 'The university building's only a two-minute walk away.'

Caelan turned, her gaze fixed on a shadow, a man in a dark overcoat who was crossing the road thirty metres or so away. There was a pedestrian crossing, but he'd ignored it. He had a dark beard, his eyes lost behind his glasses, a smart leather briefcase in one hand, cup of takeaway coffee in the other. A gaggle of people thronged the pavement opposite, and he sidestepped them, disappearing into the supermarket that stood on the corner of the street. She frowned, then shook her head, dismissing him.

'What do we do?' Ewan asked.

Caelan raised a hand, gesturing towards the window display. 'Admire this for another couple of minutes.'

'And then?'

'We split up.'

She saw panic freeze his face. 'Split up? But…'

'You walk around the block, find a cashpoint, whatever. I'll go to the supermarket. I'll be able to watch from there.'

'I don't understand.'

'We'll have our phones if absolutely necessary, but we'll have to be discreet, stay in character.' A woman was approaching, and Caelan gripped Ewan's arm. As she passed, Caelan said, 'The door to his building's opening again. Don't look, don't turn around.'

Ewan bent closer to the window. 'I do like that jacket.'

'It's him. He's turned right, away from the university. Let's go. We'll stay on this side of the road for now.' She took Ewan's hand as they began to walk. Across the road, Ronnie Morgan sauntered along, not looking back.

'Wonder where he's going,' Ewan said.

'To meet a mate, a girlfriend? Not the library, that's the other direction too.'

'It'd be closed anyway.'

Caelan shook her head. 'It's open twenty-four hours.'

'Really? Why? Who's going to want to study at two o'clock in the morning?'

'Someone who's left their assignment until the last minute?'

Ewan laughed. 'I'm guessing you used to?'

'Every time.' Caelan smiled to herself, remembering. It was true.

77

As Ronnie disappeared around the corner, they crossed the road.

'He's heading towards the main shopping area,' Caelan said. 'Brayford Wharf's down there.' She pointed. 'There are bars, restaurants, even a cinema I think. Perfect location for a university, and for students to live.'

'If you have the money to go to those places.'

'And Ronnie certainly seems to have.'

They were on the high street now, lined with shops and businesses, a few cars meandering past. Ronnie wandered along, clearly not in a hurry. Soon they neared the railway line that sliced through Lincoln's city centre. It was still quiet, but soon the area would be busy with students, workers, shoppers. The city would wake. Ronnie hesitated, checking right and left, then jogged across the road, slipping through the traffic with ease. Caelan frowned, concerned.

'We'd better cross.'

They did so, Ronnie not far in front now. They stepped over the railway lines, hurrying past a church, incongruous here, situated beside a busy crossroads and the railway line. It was their first glimpse of historic Lincoln, but they had no time to appreciate it. Ronnie had disappeared in the shadow of the church, and around the corner. The shopping area of the city stretched in front of them, but he had ignored it.

'He definitely went round the corner, didn't he?' Caelan knew the answer but wanted confirmation. Ronnie heading for the shops would have made sense, even this early. His turning right didn't.

'What's round there?'

'As I remember, the railway station.'

Ewan tightened his grip on her hand for a second. 'You think he's going to catch a train? Where would that leave us?'

'A few seats behind him.' Caelan increased her pace.

'You mean we'd get on too?'

'Wouldn't be doing a good job of following him if we didn't, would we? He could be going to meet his dad.'

'You think?'

'I don't know.'

Ronnie was ambling across the station car park now, heading for the entrance.

'Maybe he's meeting someone off a train,' Ewan suggested.

'Could be. Let's hope it's Lambourne.'

When they entered the station, however, Ronnie was queuing for a ticket. Glancing up at the monitor displaying the trains soon departing, Caelan thought quickly. This was unprecedented. The first day of their surveillance and their subject was forcing them to change their plans. She hesitated. Was it a trap? It was a hell of a coincidence. She pushed the thought away, knowing she had no choice but to follow.

'We need to know where he's going.'

They joined the queue, a young woman and an elderly man between them and Ronnie. Caelan had plenty of cash as well as Karen Devlin's credit card in her bag, but this was unexpected. Again she wished she could have seen what Ronnie had been studying on his phone so intently earlier. He was now at the head of the queue, and, concerned that they wouldn't be able to hear what he was saying, Caelan slipped closer, taking a timetable from a plastic holder bolted to the wall to disguise her action. As she flicked through it, Ronnie asked for a return ticket to King's Cross. *Shit.* She hadn't imagined they would be back in the capital so soon. She beckoned to Ewan and they went outside.

'What is it?'

'He's going to London. So much for the committed student I was told about. He hasn't missed a class yet this year, but here he is jumping on a train even though he has a full day of lectures.'

'You think it's suggestive?'

She lifted her shoulders, let them fall.

'I doubt he'd miss his classes for something trivial.'

'What are we going to do?'

'The train's due to leave in seven minutes. I'm going to be on it.'

'You? What about me?'

'We don't know how long he's going to be in London. I need you to go back to the house. Collect our stuff, then drive down to meet me. I'll keep in touch.'

She could see he was disappointed, but there was no time to worry about it. She pulled the car keys out of her bag and handed them to him.

'I'll see you soon then.' Ewan blinked.

She stepped forward and kissed his cheek.

'Drive carefully,' she told him. Without looking back, she strode into the station.

The cost of the ticket seemed astronomical to Caelan, and she was grateful for the credit card.

'Change at Newark,' the man behind the counter told her. She thanked him and hurried to find her platform. She saw Ronnie Morgan waiting by a vending machine, and moved to stand behind a middle-aged couple, as close to him as she dared. Ronnie's hands were in his pockets, headphones on, gazing down the track as if urging the train to appear. He had no suitcase and Caelan would have been willing to bet his journey was unplanned and unexpected. She would have to let Nasenby know what was happening. Not yet, though. Not here.

When the train arrived, wheezing and rattling its way to a halt, Ronnie was one of the first to board. Caelan made sure she noted where he sat. There were only two carriages, the seats battered and frayed, and she knew it would be easy to watch him. He showed no sign of having noticed her, hadn't even glanced in her direction. So far, so good.

She sat towards the back of the carriage, in the left-hand row of seats. Ronnie was on the right, near the front. If she leant forward, Caelan could see the side of his face. She was confident he hadn't seen her, but she knew she couldn't be too careful. She took off her jacket and shoved it into her bag, then pulled out some black-framed glasses and slipped them on. It was an old trick, but a different-coloured top and pair of glasses was a subtle way to change her appearance quickly. She had straightened her hair that morning, and now pulled it back into a ponytail rather than leave it loose around her shoulders. Taking out her phone, she settled back in her seat. They would be in London in less than three hours, and then she would need to concentrate.

11

It was warmer in London, the sun trying to peer around the clouds.

'We've left the station,' Caelan said. 'We're in King's Boulevard.'

There was a pause. 'Which is?' said Nasenby.

'Between King's Cross and St Pancras.'

'Got it.' There was another silence. Caelan assumed Nasenby was pinpointing their location on Google Maps. Then again, it was possible he still used an A–Z. 'You're heading towards Camden Town?'

Caelan considered it. 'If we keep going in this direction, yeah, I'd say so.'

'Keep me informed.'

Nasenby ended the call and Caelan kept walking. They were passing between the two railway stations, in a pleasant pedestrianised area with a few trees and potted shrubs. There were coffee shops and restaurants, a vendor selling hot dogs from a barrow. Frying onions scented the air, an elderly man hobbling in front of Caelan pausing to take an appreciative sniff. To the left of the path was a circular concrete platform, and people sat on the steps leading to it, enjoying the sunshine. Though the sky was bright, there was a chill in the air here, and Caelan was tempted to put her jacket back on. Not yet. There was a group of people wearing business suits, chatting and laughing, between her and Ronnie, and she was confident he hadn't noticed her. He hadn't looked around, or checked over his shoulder. Caelan knew that being ultra-aware of her surroundings was part of her job, but she was always surprised how little notice others took of those around them. Vigilance could help you stay alive. Her eyes searched the crowds constantly, her mind recording details of those she saw. She smiled to herself. No one was invisible.

The day Charlie Flynn had died barged into her head again. The house had been nondescript from the outside, a tiny terrace at the end of a row of identical properties. The adjoining house had been a squat, the people sheltering there unable to answer any questions about the comings and goings next door. They'd seen nothing, heard nothing.

Smelt nothing.

When they'd entered the house, silently, covertly, the smell had confirmed they were in the right place. Urine, faeces and the underlying stench of fear and desperation. Next to Caelan, Nicky Sturgess had frozen. Caelan had guessed her imagination was conjuring terrible images, halting her, forcing her to take a breath and calm herself. There was no indication that Charlie was already dead, not then. They'd found the cellar door quickly, reinforced with metal bars and double-padlocked. Overkill when the prisoner was a skinny ten-year-old boy. Sturgess had laid a hand on Caelan's arm as Sam Clifton worked on the padlocks. 'Steady,' she had said. She hadn't taken her own advice, had rushed inside, her training, her caution evaporating when she had seen the huddled form of the boy lying against the wall. Lambourne had been waiting in the shadows. His knife had torn into Nicky's throat before Caelan had even realised he was there. As Nicky hit the ground, Lambourne strode forward, stepping over her body. In Caelan's mind, he was smiling.

She dragged herself back to the present as ahead of her, Ronnie Morgan stopped, gazing around. Rebuking herself, Caelan pulled her phone from her pocket and lifted it to her ear as if receiving a call. She stopped walking, waited to see what he was doing. He had paused outside a restaurant, steps leading up to an outside seating area, white-shirted serving staff visible flitting between the tables inside. She watched as he bounded up the stairs. A young woman approached with a smile, handing him a menu. Ronnie spoke to her and she nodded, waving him inside. Caelan called her boss again.

'You think he's meeting someone?' Nasenby wanted to know.

'It seems likely. A place close to the station, easy to find...'

'Can you get inside?'

Caelan shifted her feet, peering at the restaurant.

'There are plenty of free tables, but it's open-plan. There's no cover.'

'If he's there for a meeting, I want to know who he's with and what's said. This could be vital.'

'You want me to go in there.' It wasn't a question. 'What if he's meeting his father?'

Nasenby snorted. 'In the middle of London? Lambourne wouldn't take the risk.'

'He doesn't know we're watching him.'

'Of course he does. He'll guess. He might even be expecting us to follow Ronnie.'

'No doubt, but expecting and knowing are two different things.'

Nasenby sucked in a breath through his teeth. When he spoke again, his tone was decisive. 'Go inside. You know how to play it, Caelan.'

Pushing the phone back into her pocket, Caelan strode towards the entrance, knowing Nasenby was right. She could do this. Her stomach jolted, anxiety she hadn't experienced since her first days of training coursing through her as she asked for a table for one.

–

As each minute passed with no sign of the person who was supposed to meet him here, Ronnie Morgan grew more self-conscious. *What a twat.* He'd followed the instructions in the letter he'd received without question, and now he was sitting here alone. No one was coming. He'd been set up. His cheeks were red as he bent his head to study the menu again.

'I think I'll go ahead and order now,' he told a passing waiter, who gave him a sympathetic smile.

When his food arrived, Ronnie dug into the burger and fries hungrily. As he chewed the last mouthful, the waiter approached again.

'There's a call for you,' he said. His expression remained neutral, but receiving telephone calls for customers was clearly a new experience for him. Hiding his own surprise, Ronnie wiped his mouth and pushed back his chair. His mobile was in his pocket: full battery, decent signal. He'd passed on his number, so why call the restaurant?

He followed the waiter over the scuffed floorboards to the bar. It was semicircular, built in the centre of the restaurant, allowing the staff to keep an eye on their patrons wherever they sat. Above it, rows of glasses loomed, hanging from wooden frames, reflecting the faces of those scurrying below on each gleaming surface. Ronnie gazed up at them as he reached the bar, wondering if they were ever used. The waiter beckoned to him.

'Here you go, mate.'

Ronnie took the handset with a nod of thanks, waiting for the waiter to move away before lifting it to his ear.

'Hello?'

'Ronnie. Enjoy your meal?'

A male voice, distorted and tinny, with no discernible accent. Not his father, at least he didn't think so. The caller sounded amused, and Ronnie glanced around, startled. How did they know he'd finished eating? Was he being watched? There were a few other people dining, but no one seemed to be paying him any attention. A middle-aged couple ignored each other at one table, while at another, a woman with glasses and a ponytail stirred a cup of coffee. There was a man eating alone in a booth close to the bar, but his eyes were fixed on his plate as he concentrated on shovelling pieces of gammon into his mouth.

Ronnie moistened his lips, wishing he had stayed in Lincoln. He was being dragged into his father's world, ignoring the promises he'd made to his mother and even to himself.

'I did, thanks,' he managed to say.

Another bark of laughter. 'Good. Now, leave the restaurant. Get the tube to Northolt. We'll be waiting.'

He was gone. Ronnie blinked, confused. Where the hell was Northolt? He'd never heard of it. Fear danced around his head. This wasn't what he had agreed to.

The waiter was back, his smile fixed in place.

'Your friend paid the bill,' he said. Ronnie stared at him.

'My friend?'

The waiter nodded to the phone Ronnie was still clutching. 'The one you were supposed to be meeting? He paid by credit card, over the phone. His treat, as an apology for not showing up, he said.'

'Okay...' The man eating the gammon had finished. He glanced at Ronnie before getting to his feet. As he headed for the bar, Ronnie thrust the phone back at the waiter and fled.

–

'She's ditched the boy wonder already,' Richard Adamson murmured.

'I can't hear you,' Nasenby complained. 'Either speak up, or ring back when you can talk freely.'

Richard swore to himself. Speaking to his boss while following Ronnie Morgan and Caelan Small was no easy task. Caelan had removed the glasses again, allowed her hair to fall around her face. Richard swerved around a group of giggling American tourists as he followed Caelan back towards King's Cross. He hadn't risked following her inside the restaurant, choosing to hide behind a newspaper outside, knowing she would recognise him instantly if she saw him. His grey woollen beanie and two-day growth of stubble wouldn't fool her.

'I said there's no sign of Davies.'

Nasenby chuckled. 'Already? Well, you know Caelan works best alone. It took a few years, but even I accepted it.'

Richard hesitated as Caelan was caught up in a crowd of people outside the familiar red and yellow brick arches of the King's Cross St Pancras Underground station. Within seconds, she had disentangled herself and disappeared inside. She didn't look back.

'I'll call you again when I know where we're going.' Adamson knew he'd have to hurry. Losing them now would end his assignment, leave him in disgrace.

'Be sure you do, Richard,' Nasenby said. 'Have a chat with our friend Ian too, won't you?'

Furious, Richard cut Nasenby off without replying or saying goodbye. More than ever, he felt like a puppet, one with two puppeteers.

–

The train was busy. Caelan pushed her way aboard, squeezing in behind a woman wearing a brightly patterned hijab. Ronnie Morgan stood to her left, further along the carriage, his back to her. If she stayed in position, she could watch him without turning her head. She rolled her shoulders, tensing then relaxing her neck. As she raised her head, a baby peeked at her over the shoulder of the woman in front of her, its face breaking into a smile as Caelan stuck out her tongue. Grinning back, Caelan flicked her eyes towards Morgan. The baby ducked its head for a second, then popped back up, giggling. The woman turned briefly. Caelan met her eyes, and she gave a shy smile. The baby reached a chubby hand towards Caelan, but its mother took a step away, lowering her eyes apologetically. Caelan understood. A parent providing an early lesson on not talking to strangers. She concentrated on Ronnie. As she watched, he shifted, lifting his head, studying the list of stations displayed near the roof of the carriage. She readied herself to follow if he left the train.

They arrived at the next station, Warren Street, but Ronnie didn't move to disembark. As passengers left the train and more boarded, Caelan studied their faces quickly, scanning their features, disregarding them. No threat. No danger.

Then, through the crowd, she saw him.

12

Caelan froze, the baby and their game forgotten. He hadn't looked at Ronnie Morgan yet, but this could be no coincidence. Glen Walker, Seb Lambourne's right-hand man, only one rung below his boss on the ladder of Britain's most wanted, was on the train. He hadn't been seen since Charlie Flynn's death, and it had been assumed he had left the country with Lambourne. Now here he was in London, a scruffy beard offering scant disguise. Caelan recognised his eyes, a cool grey, and his broad frame. He stood at the far end of the carriage, beyond Ronnie and thirty other innocent people. Caelan shifted her body. There was no way she could get between Ronnie and Walker, but she could observe.

What was Walker doing here? Was he the person who had asked Ronnie to travel to London, who had phoned him at the restaurant? Was he still working for Lambourne? Caelan knew that Nasenby, Penrith and their superiors had scoffed at Walker, labelling him the brawn behind Lambourne's intelligence and cunning. Caelan had never been convinced. Walker was no fool. She watched his eyes as the train began to move, the possibility that he would recognise her racing through her mind. Should she abandon Ronnie and attempt to apprehend Walker? Down here, beneath the city streets, there was no way of contacting Nasenby for instructions, no opportunity to call for backup.

As she watched, Walker allowed his gaze to settle on Ronnie. A curious expression crossed his face, gone before Caelan could fully process it. Fury? Anticipation? As if Walker were a starving man, and Ronnie a plate of his favourite food. Her heart rate increasing, thumping a warning, Caelan took a step to her left, jostling the man beside her, who frowned. Muttering an apology, she stood still, knowing that drawing attention to herself would be a mistake. She looked up at the list of stations again, confirming what she already knew. The next stop was Oxford Circus. It would be busy with shoppers, tourists and other travellers. It would be easy to lose sight of Ronnie, and Walker too if he intended to stick around. It was possible to board trains on the Bakerloo and Central lines at Oxford Circus, as well as remaining on the Victoria Line. The number of locations Ronnie could head to from here was frightening. If he went out onto Regent Street or Oxford Street, the crowds would make tailing him even more difficult. If she lost him now, there would be no chance of finding him, and their link to Lambourne would be gone. If he was going to exit the train at Oxford Circus, as she believed he would, she had less than a minute to decide on a course of action.

The train slowed again and Ronnie turned towards her. Walker watched, noting the movement from his end of the carriage, and Caelan knew she had no option. Ronnie was her priority. She had no way of knowing what Walker was planning to do, but she would have to alert Nasenby to his presence as soon as she could.

On the platform, Ronnie glanced left and right. Caelan pushed through the crowd and paused by the wall, pretending to tie her shoelace as Walker stepped onto the platform. He smirked as he saw Ronnie's confusion, and Caelan straightened as he approached the younger man, one hand in his jacket pocket. Her mouth was dry, adrenalin coursing through her as she took a step towards Ronnie. What was Walker planning? More importantly, what did he have concealed in his pocket?

'Are you lost?' Even in the hubbub of the station, Walker's voice was easy to hear. Ronnie frowned.

'No. No, I'm fine, thanks.'

Walker lifted his shoulders. 'Suit yourself. Thought you might need a map.'

Caelan tensed, raising herself onto the balls of her feet, ready to spring at Walker if necessary. Walker whipped his hand from his pocket and thrust it towards Ronnie, who flinched. Caelan took a breath, telling herself to calm down. Walker was holding out a Tube map, the pocket-sized version you could pick up in most Underground stations.

'Take it,' he urged. Obviously uncomfortable, Ronnie did as he was told, and Walker nodded, satisfied. He stepped back, was soon lost in the crowd.

Ronnie stared after him, bemused, then opened the map and studied it. Once again, Caelan wished she could see through his eyes, read what he had read. After a moment, he lifted his head, stuffing the map into his jeans pocket as he began to walk. They were heading for the Central Line, Caelan realised. Ronnie was planning to catch another train. No British Transport Police officers down here, no way of passing a message on to Nasenby. She would have to allow Walker to disappear again, for now.

–

Ronnie's stomach felt as though it had liquidised. He held onto a nearby yellow metal pole as the train hurtled through the darkness, keeping his eyes on the floor. This had been a mistake. Glen Walker was here. He hadn't recognised him at first, but when the man's face had twisted, somewhere between a smile and a grimace, he had remembered the face leering out from the news reports and photographs. His father: dark-haired, handsome. Beside him, Glen Walker: bald and built like the proverbial shithouse. And the map he'd forced Ronnie to take. What had that been about? Was he part of the scheme to lure Ronnie to London? There was nothing written on the folded paper, no directions or messages. It was just an Underground map, indistinguishable from thousands of others. Ronnie had to assume Walker was making a point, letting him know he was in London, and worryingly, terrifyingly, that he knew Ronnie was too.

Walker had been around occasionally when Ronnie had spent time with his father, back when he had thought his dad worth the effort. Before he'd fully realised what sort of man Seb Lambourne was. He hadn't wanted to see him again after the kid had died, but when the letter had arrived… Maybe it was a misunderstanding. Maybe his dad could explain why he'd killed a child and allowed his son's life to be destroyed.

Tightening his grip on the handrail, Ronnie made his decision. He would go to Northolt, but no further. If no one showed there, if he was sent to another far-flung part of London, he would be on the next train back to King's Cross. His gut was already telling him his trip down to the capital had been a mistake, but he needed to hear the truth. They'd banked on his curiosity being stronger than his fear, and it had been, until the phone call at the restaurant. Now, fear had the upper hand.

Thirteen stations before Northolt. Ronnie shook his head. He knew such superstition was nonsense, but a shiver passed through him all the same. Maybe he should get off at the next station, ignore their command and head home. He swallowed, longing for a drink of water. At least Walker had disappeared.

As the train halted at Bond Street, Ronnie hoped never to see his dad's old mate again.

-

They emerged into choking fumes and drizzle. Four lanes of traffic halted while people scurried over a pedestrian crossing. Directly outside the station, a metal railing prevented people from crossing the road wherever they felt the need. There were bicycles padlocked to metal stands along the length of it. Ronnie Morgan was still standing in the entrance to the station, so Caelan walked past him. On the pavement outside, she joined a few other people who were milling around, mobile phones held to their ears, deep in conversation. She sent Ewan a text, telling him where she was, then called Nasenby to update him.

'Wherever he goes, follow him,' Nasenby instructed. 'Northolt's the arse end of nowhere. Why the hell has he gone there?'

Caelan stuck her index finger in her ear, attempting to block out the traffic noise as vehicles thundered past her. 'I've no idea.' She turned, watching as Ronnie took out his own phone. 'Looks like he might be receiving a call.'

Nasenby grunted. 'All right. Stay in touch, Caelan. And be careful.'

-

'You're at Northolt?' The same voice, distorted and metallic, as at the restaurant. Ronnie took a step back, moving inside the station. There was a tiny kiosk selling newspapers, cigarettes and sweets in one corner. He sidled behind a gang of kids who were hanging around the counter, loudly attempting to persuade the proprietor to sell them some fags.

'Ronnie?' He was becoming impatient, Ronnie could hear it.

'Yeah, I'm here.'

There was a pause, then, 'Go out of the station, turn left. Keep walking.'

Ronnie exhaled, suddenly exhausted. 'No. I'm not moving until you tell me what's going on.'

'Then your father's dead.' He hadn't missed a beat.

'What... what did you say?'

'He's here with me. If you want to see him, start walking.'

Panic seared Ronnie's belly. This was the stuff of low-budget cop shows. 'You're lying.'

'Can't take the risk, though, can you?'

'All right, okay. I'm going.' He clenched his jaw, furious.

'You've made a sensible decision.'

Ronnie swallowed as his throat tightened. This was not going to plan. He was certain the man was bluffing, but...

He started walking.

–

Caelan began to move, having allowed Ronnie a thirty-second head start before following. There was only one man between herself and her quarry, and she couldn't risk him seeing her. The road was long and straight. Letting him get a little way ahead was fine; she would be able to watch him from a distance.

Except.

Except Ronnie had disappeared. Caelan hesitated, her eyes scanning the scene ahead of her. Across the road, a red double-decker was chugging at a bus stop. Adrenalin began to course through her as she searched the people crowding onto it.

No Ronnie.

He wouldn't have had time to cross the road, would he? Caelan took a few deep breaths, attempting to stem the wave of panic. Shit. She'd lost him.

Ronnie Morgan had vanished.

13

He couldn't be on the bus, there had been no time. He wasn't on the pavement in front of her. Maybe he'd climbed into a car... Caelan pushed the thought away. She would have seen it stop. Increasing her pace, she kept walking. She'd taken her eyes off him for a second, no more. She would not allow herself to give up.

And then she saw it. Invisible until you were beside it, a gap between the end of the brick railway bridge she had just crossed, and the start of a metal fence. A narrow set of stairs, leading down to an underpass. Thumbing a text to Nasenby, Caelan plunged down the steps. The underpass yawned in front of her, the entrance dark and forbidding. The other end was visible, but the interior was gloomy. She couldn't see Ronnie, couldn't hear anything but the roar of traffic on the road above. She took a breath, refusing to believe she had lost her quarry. She was better than this.

Wasn't she?

The underpass was chilly, dank and dark. There were lights set at regular intervals into the wall, but they had all been smashed. Caelan pulled out her phone, switched on its torch.

Saw the body.

He was lying at the far end of the underpass, blood leaking onto the damp tarmac. An involuntary noise escaped Caelan as she ran to throw herself down beside him. She attempted to find a pulse, gave up, pressed her cheek close to his lips. Tiny wisps of air against her skin – he was breathing, but only just.

'Ronnie? Ronnie, can you hear me?'

No response.

Footsteps behind her, quick and urgent. She lifted her head, knowing who was approaching.

'What the hell...?' Richard Adamson was beside her, his mouth working. Caelan pushed him away. Ronnie's eyes were open but unfocused, a soft keening sound escaping his lips. Caelan leaned closer, muttering words of comfort.

'Call an ambulance, Richard!' she ordered.

Adamson started, pulling his phone from his trouser pocket. 'Jesus, Caelan. What happened?'

'I don't know. I lost sight of him for a few seconds. I saw nothing, heard nothing. Did you?'

He shot a glance at her. 'How did you know I...?'

'I saw you, Richard. Several times.' She took Ronnie's hand, feeling for the pulse in his wrist, furious with Adamson, with Nasenby – with the whole fucking lot of them.

Adamson flushed, turning away. She heard him request an ambulance and police presence.

'They want to know about his injuries.'

'Tell them he's leaking blood like a fucking tap.' Caelan yanked Ronnie's jacket and T-shirt up, her own blood thundering in her ears when she saw it. 'Shit, it's a gunshot wound.'

She wrenched off her coat, folded it and laid it beneath Ronnie's head. She needed to stem the flow of blood, but with what? She could use her hands, but they would be filthy from the train and Tube. It didn't matter. If she didn't staunch it soon, Ronnie would never have to worry about picking up an infection again.

Adamson was relaying information about their exact location to the emergency services operator. Caelan looked up at him.

'Give me your shirt.'

'What?'

'Your shirt, Richard.' She glared at him. 'Now would be good.'

Adamson nodded his understanding and began to remove his coat one-handed, phone still at his ear. As he struggled with the tiny shirt buttons, Caelan lost patience and leapt to her feet. Frantically, she undid them herself and yanked the shirt away from Adamson's body, wadding it as neatly as she could and pressing it to Ronnie's stomach.

'We're applying pressure to the wound, but he's lost a lot of blood,' Adamson gabbled. Caelan stared at her hands, Adamson's white cotton shirt already stained red, her mind alive with questions.

'Ask them how long,' she demanded.

'She says a few minutes.'

Caelan clenched her teeth. 'Hang on, Ronnie.'

Adamson squatted, placed a hand on Caelan's shoulder.

'Do you think you're helping?' He didn't speak, but stood and took a pace away, turning towards the road. Caelan lifted her head. 'I can hear sirens.'

Her phone was ringing too. With both hands wet with blood, she had no way of answering. She could guess who it would be: Nasenby. Well, he could wait. The shitstorm was inevitable. This was a gift for Penrith, and anyone else who thought Caelan Small's career should have ended after the Charlie Flynn case. She closed her eyes, knowing that if she had done her job properly, she would have seen the gunman, at least. By allowing Ronnie to disappear from her line of sight, she had provided an opportunity for his attacker.

Ronnie shifted, his right hand flailing, trying to reach the wound in his abdomen. Caelan spoke gently to him again, knowing all too well the agony he would be in. She had the scar in her thigh to prove it.

Above them, the traffic noise lessened as blue lights strobed. The thump of feet on the concrete steps, two paramedics jogging towards them. Caelan scrambled to her feet, a sense of relief flooding her as they took over.

'Will he be okay?' It would be a natural question for anyone to ask, whether they knew the victim or not. Caelan knew Richard hadn't given his real name on the phone, and she would be using her Karen Devlin identity until told otherwise.

'We'll do our best,' one of the paramedics said, his face grim.

Caelan moved away, wiping her hands on her trousers, knowing it would take more than a few washes to rid herself of the sight and smell of Ronnie's blood. Adamson held out a bottle of water and she took it gratefully, managing to swallow a few mouthfuls.

'Okay?' he asked, his voice hardly more than a whisper. She met his eyes, shook her head.

'You?'

'We're in the shit. Nasenby's on his way.'

'He's coming here? It's a crime scene, needs securing as soon as possible.'

'It will be.'

Caelan turned her body away from the paramedics, though she doubted they were listening.

'And who are we?'

'As far as anyone else knows, two passers-by.'

'Who don't know each other?'

Adamson nodded. 'Fair point.'

They moved apart. Richard pushed his hands into his trouser pockets, his eyes on the ground. Caelan wanted to leave, to put some distance between herself and this place. She couldn't even move outside, take a few breaths of fresher air. The person who shot Ronnie must have made their escape through this end of the underpass, otherwise she would have seen them. It meant the whole area would be cordoned off and meticulously searched by scene-of-crime investigators.

The underpass was illuminated suddenly by the beam of a powerful torch. Caelan straightened as four uniformed police officers marched towards her, closely followed by someone she recognised.

DCI Tim Achebe.

14

'You're telling me they didn't find him?' Caelan asked. Across the table, Michael Nasenby shook his head. 'But he had nowhere to go.'

'Like Ronnie Morgan when you lost sight of him?' Ian Penrith sneered.

Caelan lifted her chin. 'Why don't you ask Richard? He lost Ronnie too.'

Penrith coloured slightly. 'Richard was acting as an observer only, Caelan. He was there for your safety.'

'Yeah, I'm sure.'

'You weren't supposed to be aware of him.'

Caelan gave a scornful laugh. 'I knew Richard was around before we left Lincoln. I saw him more than once.'

'As I was saying,' Nasenby cut in, 'they didn't find the gunman. Forensics are at the locus now. When you exit the underpass, you're back on the road where the station is, but obviously on the other side of the street. There's a lane by the exit leading to a water treatment facility. Disused.'

'Did they check—'

'There was no one hiding there,' Nasenby confirmed.

'On one side of the lane is overgrown waste ground – trees, bushes, junk. Then the railway line. On the other, houses. There's a bus stop across the road – he could have started down the lane, jumped a fence and strolled off leaving no trace.' Penrith pulled out a handkerchief and wiped his forehead. 'The helicopter went up, we had an armed response unit sitting on their arses. He, or she, vanished.'

'They're doing a fingertip search of the underpass now, and will broaden the area to include the waste ground and lane. It could take days.' Nasenby's voice was flat. 'Door-to-door enquiries have begun; appeals for witnesses will be included on the evening news.'

'Has Ronnie's mum been informed?' Caelan asked.

Nasenby sighed. 'She has, and she's understandably devastated. A family liaison officer is with her. There's no way of telling Lambourne, of course.'

'Oh, he'll know,' Penrith said. 'Then more shit will start flying.'

'Thank you, Ian.'

Penrith stuffed the handkerchief back into his pocket. 'Come on, Michael. You think Lambourne will take this lying down? His son's been murdered.'

Caelan's stomach somersaulted. 'What did you say?'

Nasenby shot Penrith a glare. 'I'm sorry, Caelan. Ronnie died on the operating table. They did all they could to—'

Caelan was on her feet before she knew what she was doing. Her voice shook. 'And you didn't think to tell me?'

'Please sit down, Caelan. We—'

'Neither of you had the decency to inform me that the boy whose blood I was covered in was dead? I sat there with him for fifteen minutes, trying to stop his blood leaking all over the pavement with my fucking hands...' She held them up, scrubbed clean now but feeling filthy.

'It was seven minutes, based on Richard's emergency call.' Penrith held her gaze. 'Blood on your hands, Caelan. Who'd have thought it?'

She lurched across the table towards him, Nasenby seizing her by the shoulders and pushing her back into her chair as Penrith began to laugh.

'Go home, Caelan,' Nasenby told her. 'Get some rest.'

She narrowed her eyes at him, hatred for Penrith coursing through her like poison. 'I want to find whoever did this.'

Penrith snorted. 'You're a witness. At least…'

'Could you leave, please, Ian?'

'Leave? We're supposed to be debriefing her together.'

'I can manage.' Nasenby's voice was as cold as Caelan had ever heard it. Penrith, breathing heavily, lumbered to his feet.

'I'll go and have a chat with Richard Adamson. See if he can enlighten me about what the *fuck* happened out there today.'

Ramming his chair hard beneath the table, he bent towards Caelan. 'Another boy's dead because of you. Remember that.'

As the door slammed behind him, Caelan muttered, 'As if I'm going to forget.'

Nasenby leant back in his chair, linking his fingers in his lap. 'This is a disaster, Caelan.' He was as calm as ever, not fazed in the slightest by another ugly scene with Penrith.

'I know.'

'With Lambourne involved, it's catastrophic.'

'I *know*.'

'Ian suspects you of the shooting.'

Caelan opened her mouth, blinking. 'What?'

Nasenby shrugged. 'It's ludicrous, of course, but there it is.'

'But…'

'I know. And Caelan, your clothes were covered in blood; no doubt gunshot residue will be found on them, and on your skin. Swabs were taken, weren't they?'

'I lifted Ronnie Morgan's top to find the source of the blood, I touched his clothes, his skin. I was in the place where the gun was fired immediately after it happened. Finding gunshot residue on me is guaranteed. No doubt Richard's covered in it too.'

'How do you know where the gun was fired?' Nasenby's eyes were cold. 'He could have been shot at the entrance to the underpass, staggered to the end and collapsed. It was too dark in there for you to see any traces of blood. We don't *know* yet where the shot was fired.'

'All right, I'm making assumptions. But I was there, Michael.'

'So was I, but we both know better than to speculate.'

'When…' Caelan swallowed, her mouth dry. 'When's the post-mortem?'

'Not until tomorrow. DCI Achebe is SIO.' Nasenby cleared his throat. 'Can't say I envy him. We'll be working closely with him, of course.'

'Good. I want to—'

He held up a finger. 'Not you. You return to being retired.' She knew that tone. He wouldn't be persuaded, not about this. Nevertheless, she had to try.

'Michael, please. Let me work with Achebe.'

His expression changed, became fatherly again. 'You made a mistake, Caelan. It happens to us all, but in our game, mistakes can cost lives.'

She tipped her head to one side, regarding him steadily. 'Why are you talking as though you're in a spy movie?'

'Let me speak plainly then.' His face hardened. 'I need to mop up your mess. I can't do that if you're still here. Penrith thinks you shot Ronnie Morgan. The evidence will no doubt suggest it as a possibility. I know you didn't, but if I'm to have a chance of saving you, you need to be nowhere near this investigation. Do I make myself clear?'

Caelan pushed back her chair. 'You do. I'll be at home when you all come to your senses.'

She walked away from her friend and mentor without looking back.

15

'Who's in Battersea?' Ewan asked, changing gear as they joined a queue of traffic at a red light. Caelan turned her head away from him, not wanting him to see how rattled she was. The events of the day were taking their toll, and she wanted to go home, take off the horrible sweatshirt and jogging bottoms she'd been given when her own clothes had been taken from her, and have a long shower. She should have trusted her instincts, resisted being persuaded to dance to their tune again.

'A friend,' she said, scrubbing at her eyes with her fingertips. 'Someone I need to talk to.' Whether he would be in any state to even answer his door this late in the day was another matter.

–

The area was grim, a block of flats amongst several others, huddling against the grey sky. Five floors, bright red doors looming out of the gloom on each level. Satellite dishes everywhere, the scent of onions frying. A group of children booting a football around a muddy patch of grass. 'No Ball Games' signs, litter. Teenagers grouping around a lad on a BMX. Money changing hands, packets concealed in pockets.

'Aren't they buying...?' Ewan whispered.

'Yeah.' None of their business. Caelan kept her head down, climbed the stairs. A balcony ran along the front of each floor, the doors of the flats on that level opening onto it. She picked her way through the rubbish and debris, rounded a fat, miserable-looking ginger cat, stopped outside flat 19.

She touched Ewan's arm. 'Let me do the talking, okay?' He nodded. 'Sam's a good bloke, but he's got himself into a state since he left the force. He might be pissed. No, he *will* be.'

'But you think he can tell you something?'

'Hopefully.'

She knocked on the door. Silence. Wondering if she was making a mistake, Caelan stepped back, close to the edge of the balcony. Below them, the BMX and its rider had vanished, though the kids were still there. One of the youths saw her looking down, said something to his mates. He blew her a kiss, grabbing his crotch. Caelan's expression didn't change. She stared back at him, his acne-scarred cheeks, his tight jeans and huge trainers. He laughed and turned away. Posturing, but she'd be wary when they went back to the car. She hated the tiny echo of fear, and stamped it down. He was not a threat; he was a kid showing off to his friends, no more. She knew she could render him helpless within seconds, but he had the power to unnerve her all the same, and she hated him for it.

Behind her, Ewan cleared his throat. Caelan was pleased he had remained silent, not interfering or offering to protect her. Not his job, not his place. She moved back to the door, hammered on the flaking paintwork again.

'Maybe he's out,' said Ewan.

'Maybe he's shit-faced.' Caelan bent towards the letter box and poked it open. A dim hallway, scuffed laminate flooring and woodchipped walls. 'Sam? Come on, Clifton, open the door.'

There was a thump, the rustle of movement. A burst of laboured coughing, then: 'Who is it?'

'Open the door and you'll find out,' Caelan called back.

A pause. 'Caelan?'

'Bingo. Come on, Sam.'

He shuffled into view, and took his time removing chains and undoing bolts. At last he appeared in the doorway, dark blond hair plastered to his head, unshaven, blue eyes shuttered. He wore an old England football shirt and scruffy jeans, his feet pushed into a pair of battered leather slippers. The waft of warm air, takeaway food. Male sweat. Caelan swallowed.

'Can we come in?'

Sam squinted at Ewan. 'Who's he?'

'A friend.'

A humourless laugh. 'You still have some then? Lucky you.'

He led them into a tiny living room, a huge TV muted, a video game paused on the screen. The coffee table swayed beneath the weight of hardback books, newspapers, beer cans and food wrappers.

'It's a bit of a mess,' Sam said unnecessarily. He waved them towards the sofa, then lowered himself unsteadily into a beanbag, pushing a three-quarters-empty vodka bottle beneath it with his foot. Caelan removed a plate containing the remains of a curry from the settee before sitting. She leaned forward, elbows on her thighs.

'How have you been, Sammy?'

He looked around pointedly. 'Top of the world, love, as you can see.' He didn't sound drunk, but he spoke carefully, enunciating each syllable slowly, as though locating the words in his brain was an effort.

'I need your help.'

'And here's me thinking this was a social call.' Sam stared at her, brow furrowed. 'What the hell are you wearing?'

'What does it look like?' Caelan glanced down at the thin grey sweatshirt and jogging bottoms.

'Stuff they give criminals to put on after they seize their clothes for evidence.'

Caelan said nothing, and Sam raised his eyebrows. 'Are we playing twenty questions?'

'Haven't you seen the news?'

He sniffed, raising a hand to rub at his nose. 'Not since I was the lead story. I tend to avoid it these days.' He pushed himself to his feet and left the room; returned carrying a cardboard box. 'Beer?'

Ewan refused, but Caelan accepted a warm bottle of lager, nodding her thanks. Sam slumped into the beanbag again, popped his own beer open and said, 'How have you fucked up this time?'

'This time?' Caelan cocked her head. Sam drank, tipping his head back as far as it would go, his eyes fixed on the grimy ceiling. He scrubbed a hand across his mouth.

'I've been told to keep my trap shut, stay away from you,' he said. 'To stay away from everyone.'

'Is that why you've got a thousand locks on your front door?'

'The only door. And yes.'

Caelan absorbed this. 'No one's been in touch?'

'Are you kidding? I'm a fucking pariah. Even my mum avoids my calls.'

'I'm sorry, Sam.'

He exhaled sharply through his nose. 'Are you?' He drained his beer. 'What's this news?'

Caelan took out her phone, scrolling through the news app until she found the headline. She handed the handset to Sam, who scanned the story.

'Yeah, and? Some bloke's been shot.' He looked up at Caelan, taking in the police-issue clothing again. Her expression. She saw a flicker of fear in his face, a shiver touch his spine. 'Who? Who was it?'

Caelan told him. Sam froze as the words penetrated his fogged brain. He drew his knees close to his chest and wrapped trembling arms around them. 'Oh fuck.'

'You see why I'm concerned.'

'Concerned? You should be shitting yourself.'

Caelan gestured at her clothing. 'I've a feeling I'm about to become the prime suspect.'

'You?'

She explained what had happened without telling him why she had been near Ronnie Morgan, or revealing that they believed Lambourne to be back in the country. Sam raised his eyebrows when he heard that she had found Ronnie in the underpass, but didn't push the issue.

'You're here to warn me, then?'

'I doubt anyone will do it officially.' Caelan shrugged.

'You said you needed my help.'

She nodded. 'You and I are the only ones left who were there.'

'Charlie Flynn?'

'Penrith is asking questions.'

'Are you surprised? It was a disaster.'

'He's suggesting...' Caelan set her jaw, made herself say the words. 'He's suggesting I was working for Lambourne. You too. He thinks Charlie was alive when we got to the house.'

Sam stared at her, his shoulders hunching. 'Then he's full of shit.'

She nodded. 'Charlie was already dead. I know it, so do you.'

'You don't sound convinced.'

Abruptly, Caelan stood. She paced to the door, her eyes burning with tears, the dread Ian Penrith had given voice to pushing its way to the front of her brain. 'He didn't move, he didn't speak. The post-mortem proved he'd been drugged for a period before he died. What if we were wrong, Sam? What if Charlie *was* still alive when we arrived at the house?'

Sam was on his feet, taking two wobbly steps towards her. 'He wasn't. Listen to me: you're going to drive yourself mad thinking like this. We checked for a pulse, he wasn't breathing. Lambourne and Walker ran while we were distracted because they'd killed him.'

Caelan grabbed his arm, held it, her fingers biting into his flesh. 'But there was no blood, Sam. I didn't see any damage to his head.'

He squirmed, trying to release himself. Caelan held on, not looking at Ewan. Every doubt, every worry she'd had about what had happened was rushing into her mind, falling out of her mouth. She hadn't planned to say any of this, but now she had started, she found she couldn't stop.

'It was dark,' Sam choked out. 'He was lying on his front, we wouldn't have seen any exit wound. We couldn't even see our own hands in front of our faces until I switched on my torch. Caelan, he was dead.'

Her breath shuddering in her chest, Caelan turned away, not wanting to look at him. Ewan jumped up to follow as she stormed towards the front door. Sam stumbled after them, still bleating, and as Caelan wrenched at the door, she rounded on him.

'Keep telling yourself he was dead, Sam. I've tried to, but it won't work. It makes no sense, doesn't add up.'

Sam gazed at her, his lips trembling. 'Caelan, someone killed him. You know they did.'

She nodded slowly, all at once perfectly calm. 'Yes, Sam. The question is, who? And when?'

16

In the car, Ewan was silent. Caelan let him drive for a few minutes before she said, 'I'm sorry you heard all that.'

She saw his hands tighten on the steering wheel. 'Is it true?'

She turned her head, unable to find the words. 'I don't know,' she said eventually.

'Clifton seemed sure.'

Caelan glanced at Ewan's profile, unable to read his expression as the street lights and headlights of other vehicles sent shadows flitting over his face.

'Lambourne escaped while you went to the victims?'

'Yeah. Sam ran to Charlie, I tried to help Nicky, but there was nothing I could do.' Caelan clamped down the memory as it threatened to ambush her. Nicky's face, Nicky's throat, Nicky's blood…

'So you only knew Charlie was dead because Clifton told you so,' Ewan pointed out gently.

'I had no reason to doubt it.' *Not then.* 'Penrith won't be the only one asking questions. Now Lambourne's back, Ronnie Morgan's dead and I'm being pushed away.'

'You told Clifton you thought you'd be the prime suspect in Ronnie Morgan's murder. Do you believe that?'

She watched the world outside blur past for a few seconds before replying.

'It makes sense, doesn't it?'

'But you didn't kill him.' It wasn't a question, and Caelan didn't bother to answer. She closed her eyes, wishing she was already home. The flat would be cold, dark and never hers. But there was security, a stout door.

'Drop me at the side of the road,' she heard herself say. Ewan glanced at her, eyebrows raised. 'I'll make my own way home. Go and see your sister. I'll be in touch.' She attempted a smile, but it was all wrong. Her face wouldn't co-operate, her shoulders heavy with the burden she was dragging back upon herself.

'Let me take you to your apartment first.'

'No need.'

'Where are you going?'

She gave him a hard stare. 'I told you. Home.'

He said nothing more, but she knew he didn't believe her, that he was concerned. *Get away from me while you can*, she wanted to tell him. She should never have involved him in this.

As Ewan guided the car towards the kerb, Caelan wondered how Sam Clifton, unemployed and supposedly penniless, was finding the money for takeaways and premium brands of vodka and lager.

–

Sam popped the cap on another beer, chasing the first mouthful down with a hefty swig of vodka. He curled into the corner of the sofa, allowed his head to fall onto a well-worn cushion. Caelan Small. He hadn't been expecting her to arrive at his home, but if Lambourne's son was dead, all bets were off. He had spent the final nine months of his career deep undercover, attempting to discover who Lambourne employed, who he trusted. Who could be used, possibly turned. The answer had been obvious from the beginning: no one. Lambourne was a shadow, a ghost. When he was spoken of, it was in hushed tones, with reverence. Sam had considered himself good at his job – a success. He had cosied up to more criminals than he cared to remember. Lambourne, though – Lambourne was different. No one dared even speak about him. The man and his inner circle remained a mystery.

Until Charlie Flynn.

Why Lambourne had decided to dabble in kidnapping, Sam had never figured out. It was difficult, and risky; there was a good chance anyone attempting it would be caught. Lambourne had made his money in drug dealing and extortion – much safer bets.

Sam poured more vodka into his mouth, relishing the cold, hard taste. Had Caelan thought about the reasons behind the kidnapping? No doubt. Charlie Flynn's family had been reasonably well off but not stupidly rich, not by London standards. In any case, Lambourne had not made a ransom demand. Cradling the vodka bottle in his lap, Sam took a mouthful of lager, swilling the lukewarm liquid around his mouth before swallowing it. There were so many unanswered questions. Until Caelan had stormed back into his life, though, whether Charlie Flynn had been alive or dead when he and Caelan left him had never been one of them. Never.

Until tonight.

When the knock came, Sam took his time, finishing both the vodka and the beer before dragging himself to his feet. He stood in the centre of the living room, the walls on a fast spin around him.

A second knock, louder than the first. No voice through the letter box this time. Sam shuffled closer, using the wall to keep himself upright. There was a peephole fitted in the door, and he closed one eye, tried to line up the other with the hole. Missed.

He stumbled, his forehead crashing off the frame of the door. He began to laugh, though when he touched his face, his hand was red. He was on the floor, he realised, the laminate cold on his back, his legs braced against the door.

Another knock. The letter box moving now, opening a fraction.

'I know you're there, Clifton.'

Sam's head jerked, realisation hitting him like a slap. Danger. He pushed himself onto his knees, his head lolling.

'Clifton?' A pause. 'I can see you, you fuckwit. Let me in.'

Sam scrabbled on the floor, trying to stand. 'No. No way.'

'Come on, Sam. I've brought a bottle.'

'Leave me alone.'

There was a chuckle, then the clink of glass against the letter box. 'Don't be like that. We'll have a drink, nice and friendly.' Another pause. The voice now more like a snarl. 'I'll count to three, then I'll force the door.' Sam gulped, aware now that he hadn't replaced the chains and bolts. Knowing the door without his extra security was about as strong as a cardboard box.

He staggered towards the living room, terror sharpening his senses. He stared around, his eyes searching for the escape he knew didn't exist. No hiding place, no camouflage. No hope.

He heard the door open easily, footsteps on the laminate.

'Wasn't even locked,' the voice called cheerily. Sam backed into a corner, his arms tight around his body. He wasn't a religious man, had never prayed in his life, but he was pleading now, asking God to help him.

'There you are, Sam.'

It seemed God was not in the mood to listen. Sam noticed the smile first, wide and mocking.

Then he saw the gun.

He managed to whisper, 'What do you want?'

A shrug. 'To talk. And then...'

Sam swallowed. 'Then?'

'Depends what you tell me, doesn't it?'

'What do you want to know?'

'I'm not your first visitor tonight, am I?'

Shaking his head, the motion prompting a wave of nausea, Sam answered quickly. 'No. Someone else was here.'

'I'm pleased you've decided to tell the truth.'

'You knew?'

'It was a test. I saw them leave. What did she want?'

Sam moved away from his corner, towards the sofa. The intruder's gun hand twitched. Sam froze, raising his own hands in submission.

'To check on me, see how I was.' He was aware of the tremor in his voice. He'd been trained to survive interrogations, to preserve his cover identity at all costs and give away nothing. Now look at him. Panicking at the first sight of a gun. Tears blurred his vision as he was reminded again how far he had fallen. The drink, this dump of a flat. His own face, haggard and unshaven.

'Is that right? Interesting. No one seems to have bothered before.'

His face flushing, Sam said, 'She was in the area.'

A mocking laugh. 'How convenient. Who is she?'

Sam lifted his chin. 'A friend.'

'Give me a name.'

Fear rushed through him again. 'No.'

The gun came up, aimed squarely at Sam's chest. He clenched his teeth together.

'No? Even though I'm the one with the gun?' A glance at Sam's lower body. 'Even though you've just pissed yourself?'

'If you kill me, you'll never find out.'

Laughter again. 'You think?' Two steps closer, the gun now trained on Sam's head. 'Tell me.'

Sam forced himself to keep talking. 'How did you know where to find me? How did you know who I am?'

The gun wavered for a second, then was lowered again, pointing at the floor. 'You need to ask? You were all over the news: Sam Clifton, king of the fuck-up. But your colleague was never named. It was her that came here tonight, wasn't it?'

'No.'

Two more steps, a fist bunching Sam's football shirt around his throat, the gun rammed against his temple. His vision spun and lurched, his knees sagging. A moan escaped his throat before he clamped his lips closed again.

'Liar. I'll give you one more chance to tell me.'

Sam stood perfectly still, refusing to speak. If this was his end, so be it. He'd let Charlie Flynn down, but he wouldn't do the same to Caelan. Knowing he had one chance, he allowed his body to go limp. The gunman hesitated, and in that second, Sam arced a hand towards his throat. The gun fell, the man's eyes wide as he choked and fought to reach the knife Sam had embedded in the side of his neck. Sam dropped to the floor, panting, grabbed the gun, straightened up. Stepped away from the blood. The other man was on his knees, then his back. Sam stood over him, the gun trained on his face. He wasn't going to get up again, Sam knew, but no harm in being careful. Careful could save your life.

The gunman was breathing raggedly now, blood pumping from the wound. Sam knelt beside him.

'Who sent you?'

A cough, a splutter of blood. 'Fuck you.'

'Come on, tell me. Was it Lambourne?' The man's eyes were rolling back in his skull. Sam knew he didn't have long. 'Tell me, and I'll make it quick.' His turn to brandish the gun.

'Fuck you.' It was a whisper, little more than a breath.

Sam turned away, slumping to sit with his legs outstretched. 'Your choice.'

When Nicky Sturgess had bled out on the floor of the cellar, her death had seemed instantaneous, though he knew his memories were unreliable. He had tried to forget it had happened at all.

He was shivering now, the adrenalin giving way to sickening realisation.

A dead body, and a lot of blood.

He dragged himself to his feet again. He needed help. His phone was on the sofa, pushed between the cushions. He retrieved it, scrolled through his list of contacts. Names and faces, people he had once trusted. Not any more.

He found the name he needed, and stared at the screen. Would the number still work? Would he even answer?

Four rings, then his voice, clipped, impatient.

'What do you want, Sam?'

'I need your help.'

17

Caelan hadn't gone home. After calling into a supermarket for a change of clothes, she was on a bus, heading back to Northolt. As she had expected, the Underground trains weren't stopping at Northolt station, indicating that the area was still being examined by scene-of-crime officers. She expected they would be busy there for hours yet.

She sat a few seats behind the bus driver with an elderly woman falling asleep by her side. Slowly, trying not to disturb the woman, who now was leaning against her, Caelan slid her phone out of her pocket. Having found her location, she decided to get off at the next stop and see how close she could get to the station. She still had her own identification and warrant card. Nasenby should have taken them from her, if she was being forced back into retirement. An oversight, perhaps. She shouldn't have had her warrant card at all, not since before she went to Egypt. Not since she had handed Nasenby her letter of resignation. Caelan smiled as she stepped onto the pavement on Mandeville Road, judging she was about half a mile from Northolt Underground station. Penrith would have taken her ID and no doubt had her slung in the cells too.

As she neared the station, she saw the cordon. Traffic was backing up along the road, people opening car doors to peer out, even abandoning their vehicles entirely to gawp. A shooting in the UK was a rare occurrence, and would surely be a major news story for some days to follow. Uniformed police officers were standing guard, not allowing people too close, fending off journalists and television cameramen. Undeterred, people held up mobile phones though what they were filming was unclear. Behind the cordon, around the station, the bridge and the entrance to the underpass, there was no visible activity. Caelan slowed her pace, considering her next move. She took out her phone again.

Voicemail. She ended the call without leaving a message, and waited. In less than a minute, her phone rang.

'Good evening, Tim.'

'Detective Small. I've been informed you were told to go home.'

'By Michael? He told me to leave the area, but he didn't specify where I should go.' She waited. Achebe was silent, and she could hear another voice in the background. Who?

'Where are you, Caelan?' Achebe said.

She moved her phone away from her ear, holding it out so the cacophony of noise in the street would be heard. Shouts, sirens, people chattering as they rushed past her.

She returned the phone to her ear. 'Are you here too?'

Another whispered discussion. 'I'm at South Harrow police station, where you were brought after... after the incident. We're basing the inquiry here.'

Drizzle was beginning to fall, and Caelan ducked into a doorway. The choke of the car engine fumes and the press of people hurrying towards the action made her wish she had stayed away.

'Have you found the gunman?'

A pause, then Achebe ignored her question. 'Come to South Harrow, Caelan. We can discuss what's happened here.'

'Nasenby won't be happy.'

She ended the call, checked the location of South Harrow police station on Google. Two and a half miles away. She buttoned her new jacket, deciding she would walk. Solitude and time to think would be welcome.

–

Tim Achebe looked exhausted. His pale-blue shirt was crumpled, his tie askew. He sat behind a scruffy wooden desk in a tiny office, frowning at the screen of a laptop. Caelan watched him for a second before rapping her knuckles on the glass in the door. Achebe started, closing the laptop as if he'd been caught looking at something he shouldn't have been. When he recognised Caelan, he waved her inside.

Caelan sat in the only other chair in the room, facing Achebe. There was no one else in the office, and she wondered again who Achebe had been talking to when he phoned her.

'Coffee?' Caelan accepted, and Achebe stood. 'Won't be a second.'

He left the room, closing the door behind him. Caelan looked at the laptop, tempted to nip around the desk and see what Achebe had been studying. But he could return quickly, and being caught snooping wouldn't be ideal.

He set a mug on the desk in front of her and sat back down, rubbing his forehead.

'Long day?' Caelan took a mouthful of coffee. Achebe gave a tired smile.

'Not as long as yours.'

She nodded, acknowledging the point. 'Tell me about the gunman.'

Achebe sat back in his chair, studying her face. 'Michael Nasenby has forbidden me to speak to you.'

Not unexpected when she was supposed to be kicking her heels at home. 'So why am I here?'

'Because he's not my boss.' Achebe smiled.

'Does he know you've called me in?'

'Yeah, but he thinks I'm going to tell you we've discovered nothing about what happened today and send you on your way.'

Caelan stared at him, trying to read his expression, guess his intention. Ignoring Nasenby's command was an interesting move, and not one she would have predicted him to make. She'd already decided he was a yes-man, committed to furthering his own career and no more.

'He won't like it.'

'Then he can talk to the person who made the decision – Detective Chief Superintendent Adele Brady.'

Caelan recognised the name. 'But Nasenby's my boss.'

Achebe smiled.

'Do you have your warrant card?'

She took it out, slid it across the desk. He picked it up, studied it.

'What about Ian?' Caelan said.

Achebe handed back the warrant card. 'Ian Penrith? Still spouting nonsense.'

'Nasenby said Penrith suspects me of the murder.'

'The murder of Ronnie Morgan, or of Charlie Flynn?'

His tone implied the idea was ridiculous. Caelan knew he was observing her closely. She was unperturbed. Let him look. She had nothing to hide.

'I meant Morgan, but probably both.'

'Have you heard about the third death?' Again Achebe's eyes were fixed on hers. Caelan's mind blanked. What was he talking about?

'The third?'

'Did you go to see an ex-colleague of yours this evening?'

Caelan stared at him, mouth open.

'Sam Clifton? You're not saying he's dead?'

He shook his head. 'I'm saying he was threatened in his home by a man with a gun. Fortunately, or perhaps not, Mr Clifton remembered his training. It's the intruder who's dead.'

'Sam killed him? The man who shot Ronnie Morgan?'

Achebe shrugged. 'We don't know if it was this man who killed Morgan.' He pushed back his chair, lifted a wool overcoat from the back of it. 'Want to go and see?'

'What about Nasenby?'

'Like I said, if he has a problem, he can to talk to the boss.'

–

The windows of Achebe's car were already covered with a thin sheen of shimmering ice, the first frost of the year making its presence known. Inside, Achebe sat blowing on his hands, waiting for the heated windscreen to do its work. In the passenger seat, Caelan huddled deeper into her coat, wishing she had taken the opportunity to go home for a proper change of clothes.

An intruder showing up at Sam's door with a gun raised questions. Though she welcomed being told to accompany Achebe, because it gave her a chance to be part of the investigation, she felt reluctant too. Her career had been built on her undercover work, her talent for disappearing in a crowd, her observation and acting skills. Achebe was clearly quietly ambitious; making certain he was part of the operation to locate Seb Lambourne proved as much. His superior officer, Adele Brady, was well known in the force. Caelan had never met her, but she would be more than a match for Nasenby, even at his most imperious.

Achebe sped as quickly as possible through the darkened streets. He was silent, songs Caelan didn't recognise playing softly on the car's music system – acoustic guitar, heartfelt lyrics. Crossing Battersea Bridge, his phone began to ring. A female voice with a pronounced northern accent filled the car.

'Tim? Is Detective Small with you?'

Achebe glanced at Caelan. 'She is.'

'Good. I want you to give her a full briefing. You understand me, Tim? A *full* briefing.'

Caelan saw Achebe's Adam's apple jerk as he swallowed. 'Ma'am…'

'As we discussed earlier. She needs to know everything.' The blast of a car horn echoed down the line, followed by a tirade of swearing. Achebe and Caelan exchanged a glance.

Caelan mouthed, *Brady?*

Achebe nodded.

'Bloody taxis,' Brady muttered. 'Tim, change of plan. Bring Detective Small to see me when you've finished at Battersea, please.'

Achebe drummed his fingers on the steering wheel. 'It's already late, ma'am.'

'You think any of us will be going to bed tonight?'

Achebe sighed. 'Where?'

'I'll go to South Harrow.'

The music resumed as Brady disconnected.

Caelan glanced at Achebe. 'A full briefing? What haven't you told me?'

'You heard her. She'll speak to you later.'

–

When they reached Battersea, Sam Clifton's building had no cordon, no visible police presence. As Achebe parked the car,

Caelan looked around for Nasenby's vehicle, expecting him to be waiting for them. She had no idea what he was driving these days, but it would be large, new and expensive. None of the cars nearby were likely candidates.

Between the blocks of flats the patch of tattered grass was deserted, though as they climbed out of the car, a black cat sauntered into view, pausing to sniff at a fast-food wrapper.

Achebe took in the scene. 'What a shithole.' He locked the car doors, his eyes searching the shadows.

'Worried it'll be nicked?'

'Wouldn't be surprised.' He glanced at Caelan, ran a hand across his mouth. 'I grew up a few miles away.'

Considering the neighbouring areas, she guessed, 'Camberwell?'

'Peckham.'

'Cushty.'

Achebe laughed. 'These days maybe.'

Sam's front door was closed, but as they approached, it swung open. Ian Penrith stood there, his face expressionless.

'Caelan.' He didn't look surprised to see her. 'It seems Nasenby's orders are meaningless, even though he outranks all of us.'

She lifted an eyebrow. 'I wasn't expecting you, Ian.'

Smirking, Penrith nodded. 'I bet. But you know how it is. Sam might be useless now, but he was one of us once. We'll help him clean up. You, though,' he stabbed a finger at her, 'should be at home.'

'Take it up with the Chief Super,' Achebe told him. 'Are you going to let us in?'

Penrith inclined his head. 'Tell me why you're here.'

'It's a crime scene. We're detectives.'

'A crime scene?'

'A man's dead.'

Penrith stepped aside, allowing them into the narrow hallway. Achebe hesitated.

'No protective clothing? No cordon, no scene-of-crime personnel?'

'No need.'

Achebe stared. 'But—'

'Door's wide open.'

A new voice, loud, coming from behind them. Caelan turned to see a woman enter the flat. Her dark hair was cut in a chin-length style, emphasising strong cheekbones and wide green eyes. She paused, staring at them.

'Where's the body?'

'Good evening, ma'am,' Achebe murmured. Penrith had paled, his fury clear.

'Caelan, this is Adele Brady. She seems to think she's your new commanding officer.'

Detective Chief Superintendent Brady laughed. 'Because I've asked Detective Small to come here? I want to know if she recognises this man.'

Penrith's voice was condescending. 'And a photograph wouldn't have done?'

'Not if we want an identity confirmed tonight.' Pointedly Brady turned away from Penrith, smiling at Caelan. 'Well? Do you recognise him?'

'I haven't seen him yet,' Caelan had to admit. Brady tutted, nodded towards the other end of the hall. 'In the living room. You know where it is, don't you? Hard to miss it in a place this size.'

Caelan moved forward. Brady was clearly aware that she and Ewan had been here earlier, and was letting her know as much. The feeling of unease, present since Ronnie Morgan had boarded the train bound for London, intensified as she approached the living room door. It was closed, but she could smell blood, sense the unnatural stillness of the room beyond.

She pulled back her shoulders, seized the door handle, conscious of Brady and Achebe close behind her.

Inside, Sam Clifton sat on his beanbag, as she had seen him earlier. His knees were drawn up to his chest, his arms wrapped around them. He stared at the floor, not seeming to register their presence. Tim Achebe glanced at him, but Sam didn't respond.

The dead man lay on his back, eyes open, lips drawn back over his teeth. A knife handle protruded from his neck, blood pooling beneath on the grubby carpet. Caelan stepped closer, studied his face.

'Well?' Brady demanded.

Caelan raised her head. 'I don't know him.' She stared at Sam. He hadn't moved. Brady's hands were on her hips.

'You don't know him? Or you've never seen him before? Two different things.' Her eyes searched Caelan's face. Caelan turned away, her stomach lurching.

It couldn't be.

Sam stirred, lifting his eyes to meet Brady's. 'He wouldn't tell me who'd sent him.'

Shut up, Sam, Caelan silently urged.

'Detective Small?' Brady was watching her with interest, and Caelan knew she had to be careful. She had no reason to trust the Chief Super.

'Like I said, I don't know who he is.'

Penrith sauntered into the room.

'She doesn't recognise him, Superintendent. Now, can we all go home?'

Brady shook her head. 'I'm not stupid.' No one replied, and eventually she gave a huff of disgust. 'You can go, Detective Small.'

Caelan stared at her. 'Sorry?'

'Have I been unclear? If you don't recognise him, you're no use to us. Forget what I said about us chatting.'

Tim Achebe cleared his throat. 'Ma'am—'

'Go back to South Harrow, Tim. I'll join you later.'

Achebe tightened his lips. 'Fine.'

'Don't slam the door on your way out,' Brady grinned. As he left the room, she jerked a thumb at Caelan. 'Off you go.'

Penrith was in the hallway, concentrating on his phone. Caelan turned her head as she passed him.

'I'm leaving too,' she said.

'So soon?' Penrith drawled.

Caelan marched out of the front door. How the hell was she going to get home? On the balcony, she took out her phone. Clapham South tube station was a couple of miles away, but the quickest route there would mean her going via Clapham Common. At this late hour, she opted for the longer way, which meant she would be on residential streets instead. It would take an extra ten minutes, but she hoped it would be safer.

She had been walking for less than five minutes when a car drew up beside her. She ignored it, gripping her phone, ready to run. It crept closer, the passenger window down.

'Get in,' Adele Brady called. Caelan stopped, surprised. 'Come on, I haven't got all night.'

—

Brady's car was small, its silver paintwork filthy. In the passenger footwell, a pair of muddy wellington boots took up most of the legroom.

'Where do you live?' Brady asked as Caelan fastened her seat belt.

'Globe Wharf.'

'Which is?'

'Rotherhithe.'

'Thought you were going to say Manchester or somewhere.'

'Would I still have had a lift?'

'Depends.'

'On what?'

Brady glanced across. 'On you. Why do you think I wanted you brought here tonight?'

'No idea.'

'After the incident earlier today? The death of the person you were tailing?'

Caelan tipped her head back against the headrest. 'You know.'

'Most of the bloody Met knows. Your name's being kept out of it for now, but there are those who think you should be spending tonight in a cell.'

'You mean Ian Penrith?'

'Amongst others.' Brady paused. 'Listen, Caelan, you're in the shit. Tonight, Sam Clifton killed a man. He's not said much yet, but we'll be interviewing him thoroughly.'

'I'm sure. And then?'

'His mess will be cleaned up.'

'Meaning?'

'You know how it goes. He won't face criminal charges.'

'Which indicates that you know the identity of the man he killed, regardless of what you said before.'

'Why does it?'

'Because if you didn't, you'd be handling his death differently. He could have a family waiting at home for him who wouldn't take kindly to his body being quietly cremated and no more being said, but you must know he hasn't.'

Brady said nothing, which Caelan took as acquiescence. When the other woman spoke again, her voice was quiet, contemplative.

'I think you can help me.'

'Why?'

'You have an excellent reputation. That doesn't disappear overnight.'

Caelan laughed. 'I think mine might have.'

'And tomorrow, you'll probably be arrested. Gunshot residue will be found on the clothes you wore earlier; forensics will prove it's on your hands too. You had the best opportunity to shoot Ronnie Morgan.'

'What's my motive?'

'That's easy.'

'Then tell me, because I don't have a clue.' Caelan knew her voice was shaking. Why had she got into this woman's car?

'You wanted to draw Seb Lambourne out of hiding. What better way to do it than murder his son?'

Caelan laughed at the absurdity of it. 'Seriously?'

'Why else would you travel to Egypt using your own passport, making no attempt to disguise your face or your identity? You'd heard Lambourne had been there. You wanted to sniff around.'

'Bollocks. I was on holiday. I never left the hotel grounds.'

'No. You didn't need to.'

'What?'

Brady turned, glaring. 'Don't take the piss, Caelan. We've spoken to your assistant.'

'My—'

'The poor sod you used as an amateur detective in Egypt – Atem? Name ring a bell?'

Fuck, Caelan thought. 'Listen—'

'No, you listen. There are people, influential people, who are trying to destroy what's left of your career. You seem to have been doing your best to help them. Ian Penrith wants you in prison. I think we both know how long you'd last if you were locked up.'

Caelan set her jaw. 'I'd be okay.'

Brady snorted. 'Like fuck you would. You'd be lucky to last the first night. I want to help you, but you need to be honest with me. People are out to get you, Caelan. I think you know that.'

'You're paranoid.'

'Why did you ask Ewan Davies to stay with you then? A man you didn't know?'

'Because I trust him.' Caelan's voice was little more than a whisper. She cleared her throat, tried again. 'He doesn't know me, hasn't heard—'

'He didn't know you were there when Charlie Flynn was found. He had no preconceptions about you.' Brady nodded. 'I can see how that would be appealing.'

Caelan turned to look at Brady, her mind hurtling through the possibilities. Someone had been talking, and it had to be Achebe. He'd been at the meeting where Ian Penrith had thrown his accusations out into the open. Brady was Achebe's boss – he would have briefed her. Then Ronnie Morgan's murder had blown the operation to use him to get to his father wide apart. She gave Brady a sidelong glance.

'What do you want?'

Brady sighed. 'To keep you out of prison. And the same as you – to put Seb Lambourne away for the rest of his life. But like I said, you need to be honest with me.'

Caelan knew she had no choice. Brady's record was exemplary. She was clearly intelligent, and she would take no shit. Someone Caelan could imagine working with. They were in Lambeth, Brady driving steadily through the quiet, darkened streets. As they passed Lambeth Bridge, turning eastwards, Caelan made her decision, blowing out her cheeks.

'Fine.'

Brady nodded. 'Good. Did you kill Ronnie Morgan?'

Caelan shook her head. 'No.'

'Do you know who did?'

'No idea. Whoever did must have been waiting in the underpass, or at the other end. Ronnie was directed to Northolt; he must have been told exactly where to go.' She told Brady about the phone call she'd seen Ronnie receive. Brady pursed her lips.

'We're accessing his mobile phone records, tracing his movements.'

'Glen Walker approached him on the Tube.'

Brady paused. 'What did you say?'

Caelan told her about Walker appearing on the train, the strange expression she'd seen on his face. She described watching him handing Ronnie the map, surprised that Richard Adamson hadn't already briefed his superiors. 'Was the map found on Ronnie's body?'

'I don't know. You're certain it was Walker?'

'Yeah. We've met before.'

'I know. Can't be coincidence.'

'No way. He knew Ronnie would be there.'

'We need to find him. Do you think he's behind Ronnie's decision to come to London?'

'If he's still working for Seb Lambourne, maybe, though I doubt even Lambourne would kill his own son. Walker might be working alone, I suppose. We've assumed he and Lambourne went their separate ways after Charlie Flynn.'

'When they evaded capture.'

'Yes.'

'Escaped from vanloads of armed police officers, dogs, helicopters?'

Caelan chewed the inside of her cheek. 'Yep.'

'How did they do it?'

'I've no idea. We've never managed to explain it.'

Brady nodded. 'I think we need to.'

'Okay, well good luck. We've been trying ever since it happened.'

'I've read the reports, your account of the incident.'

'I told the truth.' Caelan was aware of how defensive she sounded.

'Why did you want to see Sam Clifton today?' Brady's voice was soft, persuasive. Caelan looked at her, but the Chief Superintendent's eyes were fixed on the road.

Brady knew.

Somehow, she had begun to ask the same questions that were hurtling around Caelan's brain.

'You're asking me to trust you. How do I know I can?'

Brady lifted her shoulders, allowed them to fall. 'If you don't, expect to be arrested tomorrow.'

'Blackmail, Chief Superintendent?' Caelan lifted an eyebrow, her tone belying her panic.

'Friendly advice.'

Brady knew more, much more, than Caelan had anticipated. Being honest was her only option. 'I went to see Sam because I wanted to talk about Lambourne. About that day.' She relayed their conversation to Brady, holding nothing back.

'So you're concerned that Charlie Flynn was alive when you left the building?'

'Concerned? I'm fucking terrified. I couldn't live with it, not if we left him there when we could have saved him.'

'You trusted your colleague, you believed Sam when he said Charlie was dead.'

'I know.'

'What if Sam lied?'

'I—'

'You've already asked yourself the same question, haven't you, Caelan?'

She studied her lap. 'Yes. I didn't see Charlie, not clearly. I tried to help Nicky, but it was hopeless.'

'Nicky Sturgess.' Brady tapped the steering wheel a few times, an irritating rhythm.

'You're not going to suggest she was still alive too? I saw Lambourne slit her throat, had her blood all over me. They did a post-mortem! I went to her funeral, for fuck's sake.'

Brady laughed, a quiet, dry chuckle. 'You're not naïve. A funeral is easy to arrange. Doesn't mean the right person's in the coffin. Doesn't mean there's *anyone* in the coffin.'

Caelan rubbed her eyes, her mind freewheeling, wanting Brady to shut up. More guilt, more burdens to bear. The image of Nicky lying on the filthy floor, her throat a vivid mess of blood, the rattling, gasping breaths… Blinking, she forced the memory away. 'What are you suggesting?'

'My turn to be honest with you. I suspect there was more to the Charlie Flynn case than anyone realised. I think lies were told, assumptions made, mistakes ignored. Who was the man Sam killed?'

Caelan pressed her lips together. 'He's irrelevant.'

'Is he? He won't be when Sam Clifton is tried for his murder. I'll ask again. Who was he?'

'I thought I recognised him, but I can't be certain. Someone from my past.'

'Your past as a police officer? Someone you've arrested, questioned?'

She shook her head. 'I'm probably wrong.'

'Your career has depended on your ability to identify targets, integrate yourself with them. I doubt you're mistaken. Tell me.'

'Run his fingerprints. You never know your luck.'

'Caelan...'

'All right.' She closed her eyes briefly. 'I don't know his name, but he worked in a pub I used to meet Sam in when he was trying to get close to some of Lambourne's people. We knew he was dealing drugs from the premises. In fact, Sam was a regular customer. The merchandise was properly stored as evidence, of course.'

'Naturally.'

'One night, Sam and I were in the bar. Not together; we never spoke in there if we could help it. He saw a bloke leave – someone he needed to stay near. He followed him, and I got up too. I was Kay Summers then – blonde hair, Geordie accent. Short skirts, plenty of make-up. It wasn't subtle. As I was leaving, the man Sam killed tonight barred my way, tried to chat me up. Managed to back me into a storage cupboard. By that point, it was clear he wasn't going to take no for an answer.'

Caelan swallowed. Brady turned her head.

'What happened?'

'He grabbed me, pinned me against the wall. I knew I had to maintain my cover, no matter what. Couldn't scream for help, not in that place. Anyone who came running would probably have joined in. He had his knee between my legs, his hand around my throat...' Caelan paused again, licked her lips.

'Take your time,' Brady said softly.

'I knew I could fight him off, but if I did, I'd risk giving myself away. The woman I was supposed to be wouldn't have had much training in unarmed combat.'

'But in that situation—'

'I had to maintain my cover.'

Brady was silent, then said, 'What did you do?'

'Managed to stamp on his foot, knee him in the balls. Ran. Was lucky enough to find a taxi.'

'You didn't have a pen handy?'

'A what?'

'I was told you once killed a man with a pen.'

Caelan shook her head. 'Not true.'

'I didn't say I—'

'It was a pencil.'

Brady stared, forgetting the road. Caelan laughed at her expression.

'I'm joking.'

Brady smiled. 'Sam would have recognised the man he killed, then?'

'I...' What could she say? 'I did, and I saw him at least as often as Sam.'

'I see. He's another link to Lambourne.'

'You know his name?'

'Brendan Milne. Thirty-two. Breaking and entering, assault, petty theft.'

'No sexual offences?'

'Not per his record.'

'Did you ask me if I recognised him to see what I'd say? If I'd lie?'

'Yes and no. I want you to work with me, with Tim. We need to find the person who killed Ronnie Morgan. Then…'

'Then?'

Brady exhaled. 'I'm not sure. There are too many unanswered questions. Finding Glen Walker is a priority.'

'I can't see him killing Ronnie, it would be suicide. Lambourne will go after whoever did it, as Walker will know.'

'We still need to find him. We should have some results from forensics tomorrow. I want to know if Brendan Milne shot Ronnie Morgan. Either way, we need to find out why he was at Sam Clifton's house.'

'Will you want me to speak to Sam again?'

'I'm not sure yet. You'll need to direct me to your place from here.'

—

As they approached Caelan's building, Brady let out an appreciative whistle.

'Quite a place. How do you afford to eat?'

Caelan laughed, ignoring the dig of unease. This was why she rarely had visitors. 'I'm hardly here.'

'The rent must be ridiculous.'

'I… I own the flat outright.'

'At your age? Can't be bad.'

Caelan said nothing. She hadn't minded telling Ewan about inheriting the property, but she was reluctant to share it with Brady. She stared out at the night, wishing she'd stayed silent. It was none of Brady's business.

Brady brought the car to a halt under a street light. 'Be back at South Harrow early tomorrow.'

'Thought I was being arrested in the morning?'

'You might be. Pack a bag.'

Opening the car door, Caelan clambered out. 'Thanks for the lift.'

Brady looked up at her, green eyes glinting as the glow of the street light touched the gloom of the car's interior. 'Good to meet you, Caelan. You're not what I expected.'

'In what way?'

Brady took off the handbrake, eased the car into first gear. 'You're transparent. Not everyone is.'

She sped away. Caelan stood on the pavement until the car was out of sight.

Transparent.

Perhaps Brady wasn't as intelligent as she'd first thought.

–

The flat was cold, unwelcoming. Caelan locked the door, bolted it, slipped off her shoes. She hadn't contacted Ewan, but he would be asleep now. She would speak to Brady in the morning, ask if Ewan could tag along. Nasenby hadn't been able to protest, and she doubted Brady would either. Ewan worked for the Met; he'd been in the army. He might not be an investigator, but he would be an asset to any team, especially in a case where firearms were involved.

She went into the kitchen, filled the kettle, flicked it on to boil. Why was she so keen to have Ewan around? It was a question she knew Brady would want answering, that Nasenby had asked. She didn't know. He was solid, intelligent, and he knew when to keep his mouth closed. She had worked with officers who had placed personal glory before team success. You couldn't trust them, not with your cover story, your fake identity. Not with your life. Ewan had been a soldier, dependent on the vigilance of those around him for his survival.

She thumbed out a text: *Meet tomorrow, 7 a.m. outside South Harrow police station.* She sent it, hesitated. Sent another: *If you still want to work with me.*

With a mug of tea in her hand, she went into the living room, not bothering to turn on the light. She stood by the window, gazing down at the blackness of the Thames far beneath her. Across the river, lighted windows, street lights, traffic. Stepney, Shadwell, Limehouse. To the east, Canary Wharf. London had been her home for nine years, and she hadn't explored it anywhere near as much as she had expected to. She'd seen the shitty side of the city often enough, played her part amongst the gangsters, the drug dealers, the people traffickers. Many were serving time, more still free to ply their dubious trade.

Her phone chirped: *I'll be there. E.* Caelan smiled, relieved. She took a mouthful of tea, moved away from the window, perching on the arm of one of the sofas. She knew she should try to sleep, but her mind was fizzing through the events of the day. In Brady, she believed she had found an ally; in Achebe too. Did Nasenby know that Brady wanted Caelan on her team? He must. Penrith did, and he wouldn't keep the knowledge to himself.

She scrolled to Nasenby's number, stared at the screen. There were more reasons to avoid speaking to him than to do so, especially after what Brady had said about the Charlie Flynn case. Especially as Brady had said certain people wanted Caelan arrested.

He answered immediately, as if he had been waiting for her call.

'Do you ever sleep, Caelan?'

'About as much as you do.'

'Where are you?'

'At home, as instructed.'

Nasenby paused. 'How *is* Detective Chief Superintendent Brady?'

'She says Penrith wants me arrested.'

'I told you that myself. Caelan, listen. Can we meet?'

'Meet? When?'

'Now.'

She frowned, concerned. 'I was about to go to bed, Michael.'

'If you're going to work with Brady, I'd like to see you first. Privately.'

'Where?'

'Are you at home? I'll come to you. I know the address.'

He was gone, giving her no time to protest.

–

The tap on her door came thirty-five minutes later. Caelan checked through the security peephole before opening the door. Nasenby strode inside, watching as she bolted it behind him.

'You're a sight more security-conscious than your concierge down there.'

'Peter? I called down, told him to expect you.' Caelan waved him towards the kitchen.

'He didn't check my ID, opened the door as soon as I said my name.'

She held out a mug of coffee, strong and black. Nasenby took it with a nod of thanks. Folding her arms, Caelan leant against the worktop.

'Like I said, he knew you were coming.'

'Maybe you should have a word, ask them to tighten up. An amateur could get in here, never mind someone like Lambourne.'

'Lambourne?'

'Don't pretend it hasn't crossed your mind.'

'He doesn't know who I am.' Caelan concentrated on keeping her voice level, not wanting Nasenby to think she was rattled.

'After you were at the scene of his son's murder, I'd say it's a distinct possibility. Wouldn't you?' Nasenby lifted the cup, watching Caelan over the rim. She shrugged.

'Why should he? Karen Devlin helped Ronnie, Karen Devlin gave a statement. Tim Achebe never mentioned my real name when he arrived at the scene, neither did Richard.' She narrowed her eyes at Nasenby. 'Are you going to tell me what Richard was doing there?'

Nasenby gazed back, unconcerned. 'He should have kept out of sight.'

'Well, he didn't.'

Setting his mug by the sink, Nasenby pushed his hands into his trouser pockets. Still wearing a suit at three thirty in the morning, Caelan noted. Maybe he sleeps in it.

'Ian asked Richard to keep an eye on you when you went to Lincoln, supposedly without my knowledge. Richard phoned me, came clean. I decided he might as well stick around.'

'To keep an eye on me?'

'I wanted him to watch you, yes, but for your own protection. And...'

'And?'

'To protect Richard too. Ian seems determined to use him. I'm thinking of having Richard transferred out of the department. If Ian continues to persecute you, he'll be gone too, others brought in. We need a team to capture Lambourne, not a gaggle of bickering schoolkids.'

'Is Ian still saying I shot Ronnie?'

Nasenby waved a dismissive hand. 'Clutching at straws. I wanted to warn you, Caelan, remind you: be vigilant. Work with Detective Chief Superintendent Brady for now. Let her protect you. Remember, though, she's career-minded. Cross her, and she'll destroy you.'

'Another one? I'll keep it in mind.' Evidently Nasenby had changed his mind about Caelan working with Achebe and Brady, or had been overruled. Why?

'I'm serious,' Nasenby said. 'She's done it before. Where's Mr Davies?'

'Ewan? At home, I presume.'

'If you're determined to trust him, keep him close.'

'Brady said there's a possibility I'll be arrested.' Caelan didn't say she had begun to believe the same.

'Not if I can help it. We need you out here, not languishing on remand.'

'Thanks for that.'

Nasenby checked his watch. 'I've a meeting with Elizabeth Beckett in five hours. She'll want to talk about you and about Ronnie Morgan's death.'

'Probably regretting asking me to come back.' Caelan followed him to the door, opened it.

'Then find Lambourne. Prove that Beckett's confidence wasn't misplaced.'

18

It hadn't seemed worth going to bed. Caelan had spent a couple of hours curled on the sofa, watching the night sky and dozing. At five fifteen, she showered and dressed, and by six was back on the Underground. She wore a black suit and a smart coat, and carried a leather briefcase that had cost more than her outfit. It was another disguise. Physically, she appeared professional, capable. Ready for the day, whatever it hurled in her direction. Mentally, though… mentally, she was back on the floor beside Ronnie Morgan, beside Nicky Sturgess. She hugged the briefcase close to her chest, grateful that the train was quiet. Brady had suggested… what? Nicky couldn't be alive, Caelan knew for sure, but she wasn't comfortable with telling Brady how. Why would Brady, an experienced, respected officer of senior rank, dream up what amounted to a conspiracy theory? Why would she then share it with Caelan, someone she barely knew, someone who had seen what had happened to both Nicky and Charlie Flynn with her own eyes? It didn't add up. The problem was, nothing did.

Caelan allowed her head to fall back against the window as they hurtled towards Westminster station. The train was busier now; she was sitting between a man in a business suit and a girl wearing huge headphones. The girl had closed her eyes, and Caelan stole a glance at her. So many people rushing through the network of underground tunnels, beginning their day, knowing what to expect, where they were going. In contrast,

Caelan was a puppet, tugged this way and that by her superiors, her circumstances, her past. She had chosen this life, it was true – joining the Met after university, being shifted sideways into the murky world of undercover operations. She had loved it, at least at first. But constantly remembering who you were supposed to be took its toll. The deceit, the evasion, the need to keep everyone you met at arm's length. She had lied to her parents and her brother. She hadn't spoken to her sister in a few months, had spun her a web of evasions when she gently asked after Caelan's health, her work. Avoiding chatting at family occasions, living the legend. When she had handed in her resignation to Michael Nasenby, she had done so with relief. It had been a protest against their treatment of Sam, but also against the way of life she had been enduring – voluntarily, but no longer readily.

The girl beside her stirred, opened her eyes. Caelan turned away. If she could go back to her early days in the job, she wouldn't agree to go undercover, knowing what she did now. Living a lie left you vulnerable, open to being cast off, disregarded, rubbed out. Sam knew how ruthless they could be when you had served your purpose. Nasenby had warned her that Brady would do the same if she needed to, and Caelan could believe it. But Nasenby would too; Richard Adamson, Ian Penrith. Tim Achebe. If the choice was destroy or be destroyed, who wouldn't?

–

Caelan emerged from South Harrow Underground station, digging her hands into her coat pockets to protect them from the chill morning air, the briefcase tucked under her arm. She walked the short distance to the police station, relieved when she saw Ewan waiting outside. He smiled as she neared him, shoulders hunched around his ears despite his padded jacket.

'Seen anyone you recognise?'

Ewan shook his head. 'Not so far.'

They approached the main entrance, Caelan wondering if Nasenby was waiting inside. Worse, if Penrith was.

The desk sergeant was expecting Caelan, but furrowed his brow when she introduced Ewan.

'I'll have to phone upstairs,' he told them.

'We can wait,' Caelan smiled.

After a few minutes, Tim Achebe appeared. He was wearing a different suit and shirt, Caelan noticed, but looked as exhausted as he had the previous evening. Perhaps he kept a change of clothes in his office, knowing he might occasionally not get home. He frowned at Caelan and Ewan.

'Are we expecting you both?'

'We thought we'd surprise you,' said Caelan. Achebe didn't look convinced.

'We'll see what the Chief Superintendent says.'

The desk sergeant stroked his beard. 'They'll need visitors' passes.'

Achebe smiled. 'They're with me.'

The desk sergeant looked him up and down.

'Doesn't matter.'

–

In the office where Caelan had met with Achebe the previous day, Adele Brady sat on the desk, legs swinging. She raised her eyebrows at Caelan as Ewan followed her into the room. 'What's this, bring-your-boyfriend-to-work day?'

Caelan laughed, watched Ewan blush. 'Has no one told you about my new assistant?'

'Nasenby did, but I thought he was joking. When did you start being allowed to recruit your own staff?'

'Since I stopped trusting most of my colleagues.'

Brady stretched out her legs, climbed off the desk. 'Fair enough. Tim, are we ready for the briefing?'

Achebe nodded at Ewan. 'Does this mean he's staying?'

'I'm guessing if we don't accept Mr Davies, we don't have Detective Small. Correct?'

'I was going to ask if Ewan could join the team,' Caelan said.

'Ask or tell?' Brady beckoned to them, and they followed her out into the corridor. 'Either way, we don't have time to argue about it.'

–

The incident room was down the corridor. It was stuffy and already too warm.

'The post-mortem on Ronnie Morgan starts in an hour,' Achebe said as he closed the door behind them. Caelan suppressed a smile when she saw several of the officers inside scurry back to their desks or hunch further over their keyboards as they realised Detective Chief Superintendent Brady had entered the room. Brady herself looked around, hands on hips.

'Proper hive of activity.'

Achebe beckoned to a male uniformed sergeant, who hurried over. 'Has the search of the area around Northolt station resumed?'

'They started at first light, about fifteen minutes ago.'

'Any sign of the weapon?'

'Not as far as I'm aware. Not heard from forensics yet either. House-to-house is ongoing, but we've drawn a blank so far.' He looked from Achebe to Brady, clearly apprehensive.

Brady smiled. 'Thank you.' Beaming, the officer returned to his desk. 'So we've nothing? Not a lead, not a witness?'

'So far. Our crime-scene manager is back at the underpass. They haven't located the bullet, so we're assuming it didn't leave Ronnie Morgan's body. Hopefully after the post-mortem we'll know more.'

Lowering her voice, mindful of the tens of pairs of ears around them, Caelan said, 'What about the gun from last night? The one Sam Clifton's intruder, Brendan Milne, was armed with?'

'Forensics have it. They're getting their gun boffins involved, hoping they can help us track down where Milne got the weapon from,' said Brady. 'If the same gun was used to kill Morgan, things become clearer.'

'We need to know who Milne was working for,' said Caelan.

'We've asked for his mobile phone records, financial information; Ronnie Morgan's too. We're assuming Milne's our link to Lambourne,' Achebe said.

Brady raised a finger. 'We can't assume that, not yet. By lunchtime, I want to know everything there is to know about Brendan Milne, from his shoe size to what beer he drank. When's his post-mortem scheduled for?'

Achebe opened his mouth, closed it again. 'I don't—'

'Find out. We know how he died, but we want to know about gunshot residue, blood on his body or clothes that isn't his own, all the usual stuff. Have we applied for a search warrant for his home?'

'Yes. The search team is standing by.'

'Good. Let's find out what Milne was up to last night. I want the CCTV cameras around Clifton's flat looked at, the nearest Underground station, unless… Were car keys found on the body? Did Milne own a vehicle?'

'I'll check.'

Brady held up a hand, counting on her fingers. 'Priorities, Tim: forensics. Keep nudging them. We're fumbling around in the dark here. Also, find me some witnesses. Are we talking to Sam Clifton's neighbours?'

'We're going to,' said Achebe.

'We only have Clifton's word for it that he killed Milne in self-defence. I believe him, but let's be sure. Hopefully the neighbours will have heard arguing, fighting, whatever. The walls of those flats must be like tissue paper.' Brady checked her watch. 'And find Walker. Have we seen him on any CCTV footage?'

'We saw him hand Ronnie the Underground map, as Caelan described, but lose him soon after. We're checking to see if we can find him boarding the train at King's Cross St Pancras, but even if we do…'

'We won't know where he came from.' Brady pursed her lips.

'We've a decent image of his face; it's been emailed to you both. We could release it to the press and on social media?' said Achebe.

Brady shook her head. 'Not yet. He's not aware we know he saw Ronnie Morgan yesterday. When he finds out that Ronnie's dead, he'll panic.'

'Unless it was him that killed him.' Achebe folded his arms, catching Caelan's eye. 'Did you ever find out where Walker lived when he and Lambourne were working together?'

'Whitechapel.'

Achebe snorted. 'Fancy himself as Jack the Ripper, did he?'

'I doubt he would be stupid enough to go back there. He rented it, free to walk away at any time. It was a place to sleep, not a home,' said Caelan.

'So he could have had access to other properties?'

'If so, we never found them.'

'Where was Lambourne living?' asked Brady.

'He rented various properties in London at different times – Soho, Battersea. He stayed in hotels, guest houses. We never tied him to one particular address.'

'He didn't want anyone to know where he was living,' said Brady.

'Anyway, all the properties were searched and released to their landlords after Lambourne and Walker disappeared.'

'It's a dead end?'

Caelan shrugged. 'They'll have new tenants. We could speak to the owners and the letting agents, but I'd doubt we'll find anything.'

'Okay. There's no point asking if any of the official channels have current addresses. I doubt Walker and Lambourne inform the DVLA every time they move.' Brady drummed her fingers on her thigh. 'What about Ronnie's mother?'

'Suzanne Morgan used to live in Kentish Town, but when Lambourne disappeared, she and Ronnie had to keep moving. As I remember, they settled in Sidcup after Suzanne inherited a house from an aunt,' Caelan said.

'Inherited a property? All right for some,' said Brady.

Caelan's skin prickled as she tried to read Brady's expression. The Chief Super's face was impassive, and Caelan told herself she was being paranoid. Brady only knew what Caelan had told her, which was far from the full story.

Brady checked her watch. 'Tim, you need to get to Ronnie's post-mortem. I want us to focus on finding Glen Walker rather than Lambourne. At least we know Walker was in London yesterday. Lambourne could be anywhere.'

'I'll call you after the PM.' Achebe buttoned his jacket.

'As soon as you know anything. I want to know if the Underground map was still in Ronnie's pocket, and if so, whose fingerprints are on it.'

Achebe sketched a mock salute as he left the room. Brady turned back to Caelan and Ewan.

'I want you to find Walker. I know you don't have a magic wand, but you saw him yesterday, you know him from the Flynn case. You're our best hope.'

Caelan smiled. 'No pressure then.'

'I've a press conference shortly, followed by a meeting with my boss. You can hang around if you'd prefer?'

'No thanks.'

'Keep me updated, either via Tim or by calling me direct.' Brady dictated her mobile number, then turned away.

Caelan grinned at Ewan. 'Seems we're dismissed.'

He puffed out his cheeks. 'Where do we start?'

'Oxford Circus.'

–

Caelan marched up to the bored-looking customer service adviser who was skulking around the ticket barriers.

'Excuse me.' She identified herself, flashing her ID. 'Were you working yesterday?'

He rubbed his eyes. 'Sorry?'

Leaning forward, Caelan made a show of reading his name badge. 'Can I ask some questions, Dev?'

Scowling now, he took a step backwards. 'I—'

'What time did you start work yesterday?'

'What?'

Caelan raised herself onto her toes, getting in Dev's face. 'Have I said something that's difficult to understand, Dev? Aren't you supposed to help people?'

'Yeah, travellers, tourists. Not—'

'I'm a person, aren't I?'

He didn't look convinced. 'What's the problem?'

'I'm going to show you an image. I want you to look at it, tell me if you recognise the man in the picture. Were you here yesterday?'

'Yeah, all day.'

Caelan smiled. 'Didn't hurt, did it? Any reason you're being hostile?'

He dipped his head. 'Not supposed to speak to one person for too long. I've already had a warning about chatting to my mates.'

'Well, I'm not your mate, I'm a police officer. Tell me if you saw this man, then we'll be on our way.'

She held up her phone, a still of Glen Walker's face from the CCTV footage. 'Recognise him? He was in the station yesterday at one thirty in the afternoon.'

He took the phone, stared at it.

'You know how many people pass through this station each day?'

Caelan didn't miss a beat. 'Over a hundred and fifty thousand.'

'And you want me to identify one of them?' He handed back the phone. 'Sorry.'

'Have another look.' She thrust the device under his nose. He gave another cursory glance.

'Never seen him before. Why don't you try the CCTV?'

'We have. Where do you think we got the image from?'

'Look, I can't help you. There are other staff around – ask them.' He turned away, moved towards a group of teenagers bickering over a map.

'It was a long shot,' Ewan said.

'I know. Let's ask someone else.'

They spoke to four more members of staff, each of whom gave the same response: a smile, a lift of the shoulders, an apology.

'This is pointless, we're wasting our time,' Caelan said. 'Walker could be anywhere.'

'How did you find him before?' said Ewan.

'Before?'

'How did you know he was working with Lambourne?'

'I… don't know,' Caelan said slowly.

'I thought you worked on the case?'

'I was undercover, feeding information back. I wasn't involved in the investigation.'

'Who was?'

'Someone I don't want to have to speak to again.'

19

Ian Penrith laced his fingers over his belly as Caelan and Ewan entered his office.

'I didn't expect to see you, Caelan.' He waved them into the chairs that stood in front of his desk. Caelan told herself to relax as Penrith studied her. She was here to find answers, nothing more.

'Good morning, Ian,' she said primly.

Penrith swigged from a coffee cup. He set it back on the desk with a thump, the liquid slopping over the side and onto his fingers. He wiped his hand on his trousers. 'You're not at the meeting then?'

Caelan knew she was playing into his hands but responded anyway. 'What meeting?'

'Nasenby's having breakfast with Elizabeth Beckett. What do you suppose they'll be discussing?'

'I've no idea.' She didn't want to tell Penrith about Nasenby's late-night visit to her flat.

'Really.'

'Weren't you invited, Ian?'

He laughed. 'Plenty to keep me busy here. In case you haven't noticed, we're two officers down, expecting to lose another.'

Caelan narrowed her eyes. 'Do you mean me?'

'Not necessarily. What do you want, Caelan?'

'To talk about Glen Walker.'

'And you've come to me?'

'You headed the investigation into Lambourne's business activities. How did we know Walker was involved?'

Penrith leaned back, his shirt buttons straining over his gut. He tipped his head to the side, watching Caelan's face as he spoke. 'Adele Brady's got you scurrying around London searching for the invisible man? It's a good way to keep you out of the way, I'll give her that.'

Caelan said nothing, fought to keep her face blank. She would not give Penrith the satisfaction of rising to his bait.

'Why don't we stick to the facts?'

'A first for you, Caelan. Sam Clifton heard Walker's name linked with Lambourne's first. It was a whisper, but a persistent one. Lambourne had his legitimate businesses – some pubs, a nightclub – and Walker was brought in to manage one of them.'

'Not the Wheatsheaf?'

'The one where you kicked ten tons of shit out of the barman?'

'He wasn't the barman, he was…' Caelan hesitated. 'It was Brendan Milne.'

Penrith's eyes bulged as a huge grin split his face. 'Brendan Milne? The man Sam killed last night was, coincidentally, the bloke who assaulted you? Fucking hell. Another nail in your coffin, Caelan.'

'I'm surprised you didn't make the connection.'

'You didn't tell us at the time, if you recall, and Milne didn't report it. Strangely, he didn't want the world to know he'd had his balls bruised and his foot split open by a woman.'

'Might have ruined his image.'

'Whereas yours is as perfect as ever. Come on, Caelan, you must see how this looks.'

'What are you talking about?'

'Sam killed him because he knew who Milne was, what he'd tried to do to you.'

Her hands gripping the arms of the chair, Caelan forced herself to maintain eye contact with Penrith. 'Ian, you're delusional. The gun was found in Sam's flat, no doubt covered with Milne's fingerprints.'

'And? Sam's neck was bruised too. Doesn't prove Milne shoved a gun into it. There are so many lies around you, Caelan, you've forgotten what the truth looks like.'

'Oh fuck off, Ian. Your head's so far up your own arse, you can't see daylight.'

He picked up the coffee cup again, lifting it in a mock toast. 'But I can. Go to the Wheatsheaf, ferret around. Brady knows how to keep you busy. She's probably enjoying watching you and your little friend here chasing your tails.'

Caelan stood, placing a hand on Ewan's shoulder, feeling the tension in him. No doubt he was restraining the urge to smash Penrith's face in, as she was. Ewan got to his feet and Caelan stepped back, allowing him to leave the room first. As she reached for the door handle to slam it closed, Penrith muttered something.

'What?'

'I said, watch your back. From where I'm sitting, there's a fucking huge target painted on it.'

–

'He's a prick.' Ewan's face was red, his hands pushed into the pockets of his coat.

'Yeah, but we don't give him the satisfaction of telling him so.'

'I came across plenty like him in the army. Arrogant arseholes who knew it all until they were under fire.'

Caelan waited until they were out on the street before she said, 'And how were you when you had people shooting at you?'

'Me? Terrified, most of the time. If you weren't... Well, if you weren't, you were in trouble. You might get cocky, overconfident. Careless. Likely to be shot, or blown up.'

There was a catch in his voice as he said the final two words. Caelan glanced at him, but knew better than to ask. She understood that there were some memories you could only live with if you never spoke of them, never acknowledged they were in your mind at all. They might scar your brain, haunt your nights, follow you through your days, but if you kept pushing them away, you could convince yourself they were powerless.

'Where's the pub Penrith mentioned?' Ewan asked.

'Whitechapel. Rumour has it the Krays used to drink there, but I think every pub in East London claims the same.'

'Don't you mind going back?'

'Mind?'

'After what Milne did to you?'

'Tried to do. Not when he's lying in a pathologist's fridge, no.'

'What if someone else recognises you?'

'They won't. I didn't look like this when I used to drink there.'

They skirted around an elderly couple wandering along the pavement hand in hand. Caelan exchanged a smile with them as they passed, Ewan acknowledging them with a nod.

'What's it like, becoming different people?'

'Like? Difficult at first. Exhausting, because you can never relax, especially in deep cover.'

'Do you ever get confused? Forget who you're supposed to be?'

'Sometimes, for a second or two. I'm lucky to have an uncommon name – less chance of someone calling it and me forgetting and turning around.'

'Should we be talking about this on the street?'

'No, but there's no one listening.'

'Sure?'

She smiled. 'You know there's not. You're as watchful as I am. Another reason why I wanted you with me.'

He nodded towards a coffee shop. 'Can I buy you a drink? My sister has a new baby, I've not had much sleep.'

'Okay.' Caelan's phone began to ring and she pulled it from her pocket as they entered the shop. Ewan went to the counter, leaving Caelan to perch on a stool by the window.

'Where are you, Caelan?' Nasenby again.

'I can wear a GPS tracker if you're concerned.'

'You've seen Ian.'

'I have.'

'You're going to the Wheatsheaf?'

'I've no idea how to find Walker. It's a place to start.'

'You're going there alone, openly introducing yourself as a police officer?'

'I'm not alone, Ewan's with me.'

'I'd advise against it, Caelan. The place is a—'

'Sorry, Michael, I'm losing you. Crap signal.'

She turned the phone off, pushed it to the bottom of her bag. Bloody Nasenby, thinking he was her dad again.

–

Rain was beginning to fall as they left Aldgate East underground station.

'It's a five-minute walk,' said Caelan.

157

They turned onto Commercial Road, four lanes of thunderous traffic. Lining the street were shops of every description – bookmakers, takeaways, off licences, newsagents. The Wheatsheaf was sandwiched between a barber's shop and a place selling suits. On the pavement outside, several people were smoking, despite the rain. One man ducked back inside the pub as he saw them approach. Caelan frowned.

'Change of plan. We'll order drinks first, see what happens.'

'What are we looking for?'

'Honestly? I've no idea.'

'A couple of pints it is then,' Ewan smiled.

As they neared the pub, a figure stepped out of the barber's shop and grabbed Caelan's arm.

'Fuck's sake, Michael,' she hissed. 'What the hell are you doing here?'

Nasenby let go of her. 'I'm coming in too.'

Caelan looked him up and down, taking in the scruffy jeans, the faded sweatshirt. 'Dressed to impress, I see.'

'I'm not mad enough to introduce myself as a copper around here, unlike some. I'll go in first; give me two minutes to—'

The first shot shattered the barber's window, the glass cobwebbing as Nasenby fell to the ground. Caelan spun around, searching for the shooter as a woman screamed, long and loud. People began to run as the second shot was fired, the sound echoing, ricocheting. Caelan seized Ewan's arm, shoved him into the nearest shop.

'Call it in,' she told him. She crouched, crept forward, taking cover behind a parked car. She reached out to Nasenby, called his name. He lay face down, arms wide, legs splayed. Not moving.

A third shot, pinging into the vehicle Caelan was hiding behind. She shook her head, touched her face. Still here.

Another shot. Screams, shouts, running feet. The screech of brakes.

Silence.

20

Adele Brady looked exhausted, Caelan noted as she watched the Chief Superintendent pace the carpet in front of them. Six hours after the shooting in Whitechapel, Brady had called Caelan and Achebe into a meeting. Achebe sat behind his desk, Caelan taking a spare chair.

'The road has been reopened,' Brady was saying. 'The armed response vehicle arrived within a few minutes, other firearms officers joining them soon after, but they found no trace of the gunman. I don't need to tell you the media are hysterical, as are the public.'

'They're saying the shooter was a terrorist,' Achebe said.

'Of course they are. We can't talk about Michael Nasenby or Caelan, or what they were doing at the Wheatsheaf.' Brady glared at Caelan. 'By the way, why did Nasenby show up?'

'I don't know. I wasn't expecting him.'

'But our gunman was. He knew you'd be there. How?'

'No idea. You think he deliberately targeted Michael?'

Brady's face looked grey. 'I don't know.'

'But how could he know Michael was going to be there? I didn't until I saw him; how would anyone else?'

Brady sighed. 'He was shooting at you, or he was aiming for Nasenby. Either way, shots have been fired on the streets of London. People are understandably terrified. We've released a statement saying it was a lone gunman with a grudge, no links to terrorism, but people are sceptical, and who can blame them?'

'We don't have a clue who fired the shots,' said Achebe. 'We now have more CCTV footage to go through, more witness statements. We've been allocated extra officers, but it's all going to take time.'

'We've contained the story as much as we could, but there are eyewitnesses. People are talking about it on social media, and we're appealing for anyone who saw anything to come forward. Some wanker probably recorded the whole thing on their phone.' Brady came to an abrupt halt, leaning against the wall, running her hands through her hair. 'We need to find Glen Walker, even more so now than before. Tim, tell us about the post-mortem.'

Behind his desk, Achebe picked up a notebook, flicked through the pages. Caelan watched, surprised that he hadn't used a tablet computer to record his observations. He could be a poster boy for the modern police force, with his smart suits and obvious ambition, someone comfortable with technology, eager to adopt new ways of working. She watched him run his finger down a page, frowning.

'Ronnie Morgan was killed by a single shot to his abdomen. The bullet caused a rupture in an artery.' He squinted at the page. 'The abdominal aorta.'

'Simply put, he bled to death?' said Brady.

Achebe nodded. 'He was shot at point-blank range. In other words, the shooter was close to him, but it wasn't a contact shot.'

'The gunman was facing him when he shot him?' Brady glanced at Caelan as she asked the question. Caelan said nothing, knowing that Brady needed confirmation of the facts, but angered all the same. She had told them what had happened. If the gunman had been behind Ronnie, she would have seen him, wouldn't she? Unless he was already in the underpass when Ronnie entered it, had allowed Ronnie to pass him in the darkness, before rushing past him and firing the shot…

'The shooter was directly in front of him when the shot was fired,' Achebe confirmed. Caelan opened her mouth, took in some air. She should have been there, been closer. She should have prevented this. Brady's eyes were on her again. Achebe hesitated, his gaze moving between the two women.

'Carry on, Tim,' Brady said softly.

'There's not much more to say. The Underground map Walker gave Ronnie was found in his back pocket, and it's being examined. They're still looking at the bullet, which was removed from Ronnie's body, and they're still processing the underpass. The fingertip search has turned up nothing.'

'We don't have a weapon, don't have a suspect.' Caelan's face was grim.

'What about Walker?' said Achebe. Brady spread her hands.

'We have to consider the possibility. Why would he shoot at Michael Nasenby, though?'

'He might not have been.' Achebe looked at Caelan. 'Nasenby wasn't the only person outside the pub.'

'We've taken statements from the four people outside the Wheatsheaf, as well as the half-dozen inside,' said Brady. 'Some have records, none for gun crime. Mainly petty theft.'

'Do we know where the gunman was standing?' said Caelan. 'I didn't see him, couldn't tell where the shots were coming from.'

'We've an idea.'

Caelan waited, but Brady was silent.

'How many shots were fired, Caelan?' Achebe said.

'As I said in my statement, I heard four.'

'The first shattered the barber's window, two hit a parked vehicle and the fourth bullet was found embedded in the wall of the Wheatsheaf public house.' Achebe folded his arms. 'All extremely close to where the three of you were standing.'

'But none of you were hit.' Brady stared down at Caelan. 'Nasenby cracked his head as he threw himself to the ground, but a mild concussion doesn't compare to having your brains blown out.'

'If the shooter was using a handgun, it would have been easy to miss us at that range,' said Caelan.

Brady's head snapped up. 'What range?'

Caelan shrugged. 'I couldn't see him. He must have been in the shadow of a building, or... Out of sight, anyway. At least ten metres away, probably more.' Brady and Achebe were both staring at her, and she felt a flicker of panic. 'At least you can't suspect me this time.' She forced a laugh as she spoke, but nausea welled in her stomach. Brady pushed away from the wall.

'Caelan, I want you to go home. This has been a difficult day for us all, and we need to focus on our next steps. I'll speak to you in the morning.'

Caelan stared at her. 'You're dismissing me?'

'You were shot at today. Yesterday, a murder, another shooting, happened a few feet away from you. Are you beginning to see a pattern?'

'But—'

'For your own safety, Caelan, please. Go home.'

Caelan looked at Achebe, who was studying his notebook, his shoulders hunched. Knowing she had no choice, she got to her feet.

'And if the gunman comes to my door?'

Brady shrugged, already turning away. 'Don't answer.'

Ewan waited outside South Harrow police station for Caelan to emerge from her meeting. He had given a statement about the incident at the Wheatsheaf and knew from the questions he had been asked that they hadn't captured the gunman. Had Ewan seen him? Seen a vehicle he might have arrived in? Had he heard the shots, seen where they came from? Each time, he had to say no. All he knew was that shots had been fired. The churning in his gut, the sweat still dampening his shirt told him so, as well as his eyes and ears. If he closed his eyes, he'd feel the heat of the sun on his back, the sand in the breeze, the fear. Relentless and brutal – always the fear. The constricting band of pressure tightening around his chest each time he was sent on patrol. Senses hyper-alert, the tension increasing as the armoured vehicle trundled along. Trying to switch off long enough to sleep when you got back to base. The anxiety, the responsibility. Knowing that each minute could be your last, or worse, bring the death of those around you. Then, the day it happened. The building, the stench of human waste, of decay and despair.

The boy's face.

Wide brown eyes staring, pleading. A second to decide. Death sentence, or suicide? No real choice, not with your men behind you and death tapping you on the shoulder.

Seeing his eyes in the face of everyone you met as punishment, even your newborn nephew.

Forever.

'Ewan?' Caelan's hand on his shoulder startled him. Her expression told him how he must look, and he rubbed his face. 'Ewan, listen. After this morning… I think you should go back to your own job. I've been sent away again, and this time I'm going to do what I'm told.'

He looked at her face, saw the exhaustion. They were shutting her out, and it angered him. She was as confused as they were about the events of earlier. He could see it; why couldn't they? They were her colleagues, they'd known her a good deal longer than he had. She didn't know what had happened, really happened, the day Charlie Flynn died either, Ewan would swear on his life. He'd heard her speaking to Ian Penrith, to Sam Clifton – no one was that good an actor, not even Caelan Small. She'd been bemused, horrified.

But then this was nothing to do with him. She wasn't one of his men. He could walk away. You never left a man behind, even if you had to carry him on your back, but Caelan wasn't a soldier.

He looked down at her. Her hands were loose by her sides, her face blank. She was waiting for him to reply, and he wondered why he couldn't walk away from her. His army mates would laugh: *Because you fancy her.* But Ewan knew it wasn't that simple, not at all. She was attractive, there was no doubt, but there was more. He admired her, was drawn to her. When she had insisted on him accompanying her on her assignment in Lincoln, he'd been flattered, though he had also wondered whether she had an ulterior motive. She had given Nasenby no option but to allow her to have her way, and Ewan knew Nasenby had been annoyed, even angered. But he had also protected her, defended her.

Caelan touched his arm, repeated his name.

He smiled. 'Sorry, miles away.'

'I said I think this is the end of our partnership.' She looked up at him, eyebrows raised. 'Thanks for everything.' She lifted a hand, took a step backwards.

'Caelan, wait.'

'I'm going home, Ewan. You should do the same.'

'Why?' It came out whiny, and he moderated his tone so he sounded less like a six-year-old. 'You're letting them win.'

She narrowed her eyes, hands moving to her hips. 'Pardon?'

'They're trying to sideline you, have been from the beginning.' Ewan held his breath, waited for her to explode.

She put her hands in her trouser pockets, rocked back on her heels. 'Maybe. But earlier today, we were both shot at. You wouldn't have been there if you hadn't been working with me. If you'd been hurt, or killed—'

'I wasn't.' He had been terrified, catapulted back into a life he had walked away from, but he was safe.

'Ronnie Morgan was, though.'

'His dad's a career criminal. My parents run a post office. They're more likely to be robbed than arrested.'

'We don't understand yet why Ronnie was killed. The attack on us today could have been unrelated to his death.'

'You don't believe that.'

She smiled then. 'No, I don't.'

'Have they told you to stay away from the investigation?'

'Not exactly.'

'So we keep trying to find out what happened.'

'I reckon you just fancy a pint in the Wheatsheaf.'

He laughed. 'Maybe. How about a drink somewhere safer?'

She checked her watch. 'Go on then.'

–

Caelan leaned back in her chair and watched Ewan cross the room to the bar. The pub wasn't busy and they'd managed to grab a table by the stone fireplace, where flames were beginning to build. She closed her eyes, enjoying the warmth on her face. She saw Ewan exchange a few words with the young woman

166

behind the bar, who didn't take her eyes from his face as he ordered their drinks. Caelan smiled to herself.

When he returned, she said, 'Did you ask for her number?'

He blushed. 'No. Why?'

'Because I think she wanted you to.'

'It's her job to be friendly.' He took a mouthful of Guinness. 'Though she did ask if you're my girlfriend.'

'There you go,' Caelan grinned.

Ewan dipped his head, lowered his voice. 'Can we talk about the case here?'

'Quietly.' Caelan's eyes scanned the room. The bartender was now staring at her phone, and a couple sitting near the door were gazing at each other, forgetting there was anyone else in the world. Safe to talk.

'Do you think the person who shot at us today was the same person who killed Ronnie Morgan?'

Caelan leaned her elbows on the table, resting her chin on her hands. 'I've been assuming so. Why?'

'Ronnie's death was quick, quiet. You didn't hear a shot, did you?' Ewan lifted his pint.

'No, but there was a lot of traffic noise.'

'You've used firearms, you'd know if a gun had been fired close by. They're not exactly quiet, even with a silencer…'

Caelan chewed her bottom lip, considering it. 'Yeah, but I didn't hear it. I thought he had been stabbed at first.'

'Yet today, the shots were loud and clear. No silencer, no attempt to disguise what was happening.'

'You think it's significant?'

'I don't know. I thought it worth mentioning.'

'The gun Brendan Milne brought to Sam's flat had a silencer.'

Ewan was nodding. 'Makes sense. Even if he was only planning to threaten Sam with it, Sam would see the silencer and think Milne meant business. Less chance of someone hearing the shot and running to help him. But today...'

'Today was different. Are you saying you think the shots fired outside the Wheatsheaf were a warning?' Caelan picked up her bottle of lager, her eyes on Ewan.

'That makes sense to me. Or it was someone else, not the person who killed Ronnie. Or...' He paused, frowning. 'If he'd really wanted to kill one of us, or all of us, why there? Why then?'

'A busy London street isn't the easiest place to get away with murder.'

'Unless you use a sniper rifle and stay away from your target. Not likely. We were out in the open, not expecting an attack, but none of us were hit.'

'I'll mention it to Brady, if I ever hear from her again.'

'Don't you think you will?'

'Who knows? She's suspicious of me, like Ian Penrith. I think even Michael is having his doubts.'

'You couldn't have fired the shots today.'

'No, not this time.' She rubbed her forehead, an ache beginning to push against her eyes. 'It's difficult to get hold of guns in this country, whatever the newspapers tell you about gangs running around constantly shooting each other. Most people would have no idea how to use a gun even if they had access to one.'

'But Lambourne had one?'

'Yeah, and Walker. Lambourne had the right connections, though. Your average criminal wouldn't, and they wouldn't want a gun anyway. There are plenty of other weapons, easier to obtain and with less of a prison sentence if you're found in possession of one.' Caelan took another mouthful of lager. 'And if you're armed with a gun, you're likely to be shot yourself before you have a chance to use it.'

'True, especially after the recent terror attacks. People are more aware of the possibility of guns being used, even here.'

'You'll be used to firearms, of course.' Caelan watched Ewan's face as she spoke, wondering how he would react. She had seen him freeze as the first shot had been fired, his face a mask of fear and panic. Not what she would have expected from a former soldier. She had deliberately not dug around in his past, wanting to trust her instincts. He was someone she wanted by her side, and she knew now that she would trust him with her life. The fact that she had remained calmer than he had under gunfire had intrigued rather than worried her. She'd rarely been shot at before, but since the shooting had stopped almost before they had realised what was happening, she'd had no time to worry about her safety. Her instinct had been to call for backup and to ensure her colleagues were out of the firing line.

Ewan blinked, lifted his pint. 'I used to be. I've not been around guns or weaponry for a long time, thankfully.'

'What did you do in the army?'

'You don't know?'

She smiled. 'I've no idea. No doubt Michael's scrutinised your service record, but I haven't.'

He studied the tabletop. 'Lucky you.'

'Ewan—'

He drained his drink, got to his feet. 'I'm going to head off.'

'Ewan, wait.' Caelan pushed back her chair. 'Whatever happened when you were in the army, it's in the past.' His face twisted, and she held up her hands. 'All right, I'm sorry. I'm talking crap. It's not in the past, it's in your head.'

She pressed her lips together, waiting for the images from her own nightmares to appear and start dancing. *Sitting behind your eyes every minute of every day, poking and prodding like indigestion.* She didn't say the words, but as she stared at Ewan, saw his hands tighten around the back of the chair, watched his lips tremble, she knew she was right.

'We all saw things…' He swallowed, passed his hand over his eyes. 'It's not as though I'm the only one. People have been through much worse than me.'

'I don't think it's a competition. Why don't you come to my flat? We can have some food.'

He attempted a smile, but it wasn't convincing. 'Thanks, but I'm going to go back to my sister's. I should speak to my boss, too.'

Caelan stood, held out her hand. He took it, squeezing it between both of his own before releasing it.

'I'll see you, Caelan.' The bartender frowned, her eyes following him across the room and out of the door. She looked at Caelan, who smiled, picking up Ewan's empty glass and her own bottle. She went to the bar, set the empties down.

'Cheers,' the bartender said. 'Your friend gone?'

Caelan shrugged. 'He's a colleague.' The other woman's face lit up, and Caelan laughed. 'I told him he should have asked for your number.'

'Is he single?'

'Think so. Write down your details and I'll pass them on.'

The bartender grabbed a pen from the bar and scribbled on a beer mat. 'Thank you. I usually try not to go out with people I meet here – too awkward if it goes wrong and they've become a regular.'

Caelan shoved the beer mat in her pocket. 'I can imagine.'

'I'll make an exception for him, though. What's his name?'

'I'll let him tell you,' Caelan smiled.

On the pavement outside, a cold wind bit at her hands and face. She shivered, pulling out her phone, texting the bartender's name and phone number to Ewan before tearing the beer mat into pieces and dropping them into a litter bin. She had no idea whether he would contact the woman, but why not give them the chance? Huddling deeper into her coat, turning to walk towards the Tube station, she thought about her flat – empty. Her career had left little room for socialising. There had been flings: short and intense. Spending most of your time living as someone else wasn't conducive to a long-term relationship. There were mates she could call if she wanted company; some she'd worked with, a couple from school…

Caelan stopped, ducked into a doorway. She didn't want to go home, didn't want to open the door and feel the press of shame, of guilt. Her black suit and coat weren't the outfit she would have chosen to go out in, but what did it matter? She'd learnt soon after moving to London not to worry.

She knew this mood, though. The urge to go out, get drunk, go home with someone. Anonymous, meaningless and, occasionally, reckless. It usually happened when she'd finished an operation, been recalled or told to stand down. It was as if she was rediscovering herself, the woman who hid behind all the personas, then finding that pretending to be someone else was easier after all. She remembered talking to Nicky Sturgess about it, discovering she had done the same on occasion. Their way of life was fluid, most relationships they built based on lies and deceit. Allowing someone close to the real person seemed impossible, and pointless. Asking a partner to live with months of unexplained absence would be too much.

Most of her colleagues were single, intentionally so. People like Nasenby, who had done his time in the field and was now dreaming of retirement, had been married for years, but they were a minority. Partners learnt early on not to ask questions; to expect their loved ones to disappear for days, even months. In some cases, forever. Maybe absence did make the heart grow fonder, but Caelan hadn't had the chance to test the theory. She had imagined a happy future, a partnership, the smell of a meal cooking when she opened the door to her flat. A warm, happy home to return to after wading through the shit she dealt with every day. It had only ever been a dream, though. There had been someone who might have made a difference, but not any more. She been dragged back into this world, and the sacrifices she would have to make would at least be familiar.

She scrolled through her contacts, selected a name. She listened to it ring, heard music and laughter when she eventually answered.

'Caelan? You *must* be bored.'

'Bored?'

'Well, you never phone to see how I am, do you?' Laughter. Caelan gripped the handset, knowing Lucy was right. They'd known each other since secondary school, had met again when they discovered both were living in London.

Caelan cleared her throat. 'How's the bank?'

More laughter. 'The bank's the same as ever. Listen, Caelan, we're in Lulu's.'

'Which is?'

'Soho.'

'Right.'

'Join us if you want to. We'll be here until closing time.' Caelan wrinkled her nose. Did she want to spend her evening in a sweaty bar drinking warm beer?

'Well, I'll—'

'Come on, you miserable cow.' Another round of guffaws, and Lucy had gone. Caelan checked her watch. It would take her an hour at least to make her way to Soho. The alternative was eating toast, having a bath and watching mindless TV until she fell asleep.

She headed for the train.

—

Five hours later, the dance floor lurching and tilting beneath her feet, Caelan grinned as the woman she'd been dancing with grabbed her hand and led her to a dark corner. She hit the wall with a thud as her partner grabbed her backside with one hand, the other stroking her cheek and then moving to caress the back of her head. Their teeth clashed, Caelan wincing as the other woman, whose name she'd been told but had immediately forgotten, leant back and laughed.

'Sorry, darling.'

Caelan shook her head, wanting to say it didn't matter. As the other woman lurched towards her again, she saw the glint of a ring on her left hand, and froze.

'What?' She followed Caelan's eyes, and laughed. 'This? Don't worry about it. I never do.'

Caelan took a step away. 'You're married.'

She smirked. 'You're not.' Making another attempt to grab Caelan, she saw the expression on her face and stopped, scowling. Caelan pushed past her, marching across the dance floor to Lucy and her gang of friends, loitering by the bar.

'Changed your mind?' Lucy held up a gaudy cocktail in a mock toast. 'Long live St Caelan. Didn't you see her wedding ring when you were dancing?'

'No. I don't understand how—'

'People are here to have a good time, forget themselves for a while. Some prefer to forget they have partners too.'

Caelan ordered a beer, held the ice-cold bottle against her cheek. She turned, gazing at the people on the dance floor, bodies writhing, hands waving, and hated them. Suddenly sober, she put the bottle back on the bar.

'You're off then?' Lucy had been watching.

'Work in the morning,' Caelan lied. Lucy nodded, opened her arms. Caelan felt her body respond to the press of Lucy's breasts, the curve of her hips, the smell of her hair. Involuntarily she tensed, and Lucy pulled away, her mouth turning down at the corners.

'See you in another six months then.' Waving a hand, she turned back to her friends leaving Caelan to walk away, desolation rushing through her.

21

Dry mouth, heavy head. Stomach on a spin cycle.

Caelan rolled onto her back. Gone were the days when she could drink until the early hours and wake feeling fine. She covered her eyes with her hands, the wooden blind and heavy curtains failing to prevent the sunlight from leaking into the room. What time was it? Had Brady tried to call?

She pushed back the duvet, grabbed a pair of pyjamas from the foot of the bed. She showered, scrubbed at her teeth. In the living room, she paused by the window, watching the sunlight dance over the surface of the Thames. The sky was cloudless, the air sharp. Bright and cold, her favourite winter weather.

She made tea, poked around in the cupboard for breakfast, found nothing she wanted. When the entry phone buzzed, she was back by the window, tea in hand, watching one of the Marine Policing Unit's vessels skip across the water. She yawned as she picked up the handset, greeted Jitesh, who was the youngest of the three-man concierge team. She asked how he was, how his course was going. Jitesh spent his hours behind the reception desk covertly reading textbooks and trying to stay awake.

'I have a visitor for you, Caelan,' he said.

Caelan raised an eyebrow. Whoever it was could wait until she was dressed. 'Did they give their name?'

'Detective Chief Superintendent Brady.' Even Jitesh sounded nervous.

'Thank you. You can send her up.' Caelan grinned, deciding to receive Brady as she was – barefoot, with wet hair, and in her oldest pyjamas. Let Brady come into the apartment, and look around, wonder how Caelan had afforded to buy it.

In the kitchen, she filled the kettle again. Four knocks on the door. Caelan took her time, not rushing. She peered through the peephole. Brady was there, briefcase in hand, chin up, staring back as if she could see Caelan looking at her.

'Good morning, ma'am.' Caelan opened the door wide, smiling as though Brady arriving unannounced first thing in the morning was the perfect surprise.

Brady stomped inside, took off her boots, carefully set the briefcase on the floor. She looked Caelan up and down, though her expression didn't change. 'Late night?'

'Early morning.'

'You'll be wondering why I'm here?'

'It had crossed my mind. Tea?'

Brady smiled. 'Please. Milk, no sugar.'

Caelan led the way to the kitchen, knowing Brady was watching her while absorbing the details of her home.

'You live alone?'

'Yep,' Caelan replied, grateful that she hadn't brought the woman from the bar home the previous evening. This unexpected visit was going to be awkward enough already. 'Have you heard how Michael is? I sent him a text, but he hasn't replied.'

'Nasenby? He's fine, back at work.'

Brady's eyes settled on Caelan's face, but Caelan turned away, reaching to take two mugs out of an overhead cupboard. She dropped tea bags into them, poured on the hot water. Brady folded her arms, and Caelan knew she was taking in the bespoke kitchen cabinets, the expensive appliances. In her place, Caelan would be doing the same. The kettle alone probably cost more than the whole kitchen in Caelan's family home. Her mum would be afraid to use it.

Caelan handed Brady one of the cups and waved her through to the living room. Caelan sat at the dining table, her back to the window, and Brady followed, pulling out one of the heavy oak chairs on the opposite side and settling into it. The sun was warm on the back of Caelan's neck. She watched Brady squint and realised she would be dazzled if she stayed where she was. She hid a smile as the Chief Superintendent moved to the seat at the head of the table, to Caelan's right.

'It's a lovely place,' said Brady.

'Thank you.'

'Though not if you're wary of heights.' Brady eyed the windows, her face paling.

'We can sit on the sofa if you'd rather.'

'No, this is fine.' Swallowing, Brady lifted her head, avoiding looking down. 'Caelan, we've had some results from the lab.'

'Already?'

'Fast-tracked. Cost a bloody fortune.' She sipped her tea. 'If you were anyone else, I'd be arresting you.'

'Or ordering some uniforms to.' Ignoring her churning stomach, Caelan took a mouthful of tea, wincing as it scalded the roof of her mouth. 'I presume we're talking about the murder of Ronnie Morgan?'

'We are. You had the opportunity, you had a motive, we have physical evidence. Then I come to your home and find you living in a palace.'

'A palace?'

'Your take-home pay is what, about three grand a month? You told me you own this place outright. The least these apartments sell for is between six hundred and nine hundred thousand, and it's often considerably more. Even with a mortgage it would be impossible. The sums don't add up.'

'What are you saying?' Caelan thumped her cup onto the table.

'How do you afford to live here?'

'You mean, does Seb Lambourne own the place, let me stay if I continue to work for him?'

'This isn't the time to be stubborn. People are already asking questions.'

Caelan touched her index finger to her lips, giving herself a second to gather her thoughts. It was pointless to lie. Brady wouldn't need to do much digging around to uncover the truth.

'I inherited the apartment,' she said finally. Brady's eyes widened.

'Someone left it to you?' She whistled. 'Bloody hell. Who?'

'I'm surprised you don't already know.'

Brady narrowed her eyes. 'I'm not going to like this, am I?'

Caelan laid her hands on the table, palms down. 'It came as a huge shock to me. I didn't want it, tried to refuse, but I couldn't. Legally, the place is mine.'

Leaning forward, Brady cradled her mug between her hands. 'Tell me who left it to you.'

Caelan licked her lips, unwilling to say the words. 'It was Nicky. Nicky Sturgess.'

Brady took a second, opened her mouth. Closed it. 'Your colleague left you this property? Nicole Sturgess, the officer Seb Lambourne killed?'

'She hated being called Nicole.' Caelan lifted her hands to her cheeks, her chest aching. 'I didn't even know she'd made a will; certainly never expected to be the beneficiary.'

Brady put down her mug, her eyes never leaving Caelan's. 'What was your relationship? I assume you were more than colleagues? If not, Nicky was the most generous workmate on earth.'

Caelan shoved back her chair and staggered to her feet, wrapping her arms around her body. Blindly, she made it to the window, her cheeks already wet. She knew Brady was watching her, could feel her concern, her curiosity. Let her wait. She hadn't yet had to say the words out loud, and once she did, the wall she had built around herself would come tumbling down.

She scrubbed at her eyes, her throat raw. Far below, one of the boats that provided sightseeing tours up and down the Thames was cruising past. Caelan gazed down at the people on board, well muffled against the cold air. At the front of the vessel stood a young couple, arms around each other's shoulders, heads close. How would it be to view London through their eyes? To explore, admire the sights, absorb the history holding hands with the person you loved? She blinked, pressing her lips together. It was a dream. Once she had agreed to go undercover, she had turned her back on the chance of casually wandering the streets of London.

She heard Brady get to her feet and move to stand beside her. A touch on her shoulder. 'Caelan?'

Slowly, she turned. She lifted her hands, covered her face. Brady was silent, waiting. Caelan allowed her hands to fall to her sides, her eyes meeting the other woman's.

'Nicky and I... We were together.'

Brady stared. 'Together. You mean...?'

'Yes. Partners, lovers, whatever you want to call it.'

'You were a couple.'

Caelan managed a nod. Telling Brady felt like a betrayal of Nicky, of their time together, but what choice did she have? It would come out in the end; better to be honest now. 'We

179

hadn't been together long; it was early days. No one knew, at least no one we worked with.'

Brady moved back to her chair, shaking her head. 'But you were there. When she…'

The memories hitting like punches. 'When she was murdered. Yes, I was.'

'You saw it happen.' Brady's voice was flat, devoid of emotion.

'Saw it, heard it. Tried to help. Watched her die in my arms.' The room blurred as Caelan fought to maintain some semblance of composure. 'I know that as colleagues we shouldn't have, but…'

Brady shrugged. 'These things happen, as we all know. God, Caelan, I can't imagine.'

Caelan took a shuddering breath, straightening her spine. 'It's okay. I'm okay. I've had some time to try to live with it. It just… It's so fucking unfair. Nicky shouldn't even have been there. It wasn't her case.' She sat back down, her arms hugging her body again. Brady allowed a silence to develop.

'How had Nicky managed to buy this place?' she asked eventually.

Caelan sighed, not wanting to talk about it, knowing she must. 'She hadn't. It was part of her divorce settlement. She was married briefly, to the son of a stupidly wealthy businessman who treated her like crap. I don't know many of the details, but to them, a place like this was little more than a cupboard. I think they thought Nicky was getting the shitty end of the deal.'

Brady puffed out her cheeks. 'I wouldn't complain.'

'He beat Nicky, kept her locked in their bedroom. Hand-cuffed her, tied her up. Did what he wanted to her, took photographs for his mates to laugh at. Believe me, you wouldn't have wanted to be in her shoes. No one would.'

'Why did she marry him? Especially if she was gay.'

'She was young, didn't know herself. He was charming at first, dazzled her with presents and holidays. She was impressed, flattered.' Caelan looked up at Brady. Smiled. 'We all make mistakes.'

'What happened to him?'

'His mother found out how he was treating Nicky, got her out of the house.'

'Did she press charges?'

'What do you think?'

'They paid her off so she kept her mouth closed.'

'They gave her a settlement, yes.'

'What about him?'

'His parents packed him off to the US.'

Brady stared. 'He got away with it?'

Caelan shook her head. 'One of Nicky's brothers and a few of his mates paid him a visit before he left.'

'And what, they sorted him out?' Brady's tone made her distaste clear. 'Wouldn't it have been better to let the law deal with him?'

Caelan got to her feet again, turned away, gazing out over the Thames. The sun was hidden now, grey clouds queuing across the sky. 'What does it matter? Nicky's gone.' She went to the window, touched a fingertip to the cool glass. 'Lambourne saw to that.'

Brady was on her feet, standing beside Caelan. 'And you decided to punish him.'

Caelan's head jerked up. 'What?'

'Come on, Caelan. You've been gunning for Lambourne since Nicky died. You tracked him to Egypt, but couldn't find him there. You made new plans. You killed his son, partly as revenge for Nicky's death, partly to attempt to draw Lambourne out of hiding. You planned to capture him, have the satisfaction of knowing he'd die in prison, still mourning his son.'

Caelan's heart thumped, her skin prickling. 'You should write fiction.'

'I don't need to make it up. We have all the evidence we need. We have proof, Caelan.'

'I'm sure you can manipulate the facts to suit your theory. You knew about the flat, didn't you? Knew when you gave me a lift home. Guessed about me and Nicky.'

Brady didn't deny it. Caelan was silent, knowing she would have to fight.

'You were clever.' Brady's voice was soft. 'Who are you working with?'

'What?'

'You couldn't have shot at yourself yesterday.'

Caelan sighed. 'We agree on that, at least.'

'Is it Walker? Where is he?'

'Fuck off.'

'Tell me, Caelan. If you want to help yourself…'

'Are you wearing a wire?'

Brady blinked. 'A wire?'

Caelan flapped an impatient hand. 'You know what I mean. Are you recording what I'm saying, broadcasting it to someone?'

'You and I are talking. No one's listening.' Brady sounded sincere, but Caelan shook her head despairingly.

'No, not even you.'

'Then tell me. I'm your last chance, Caelan. Make me understand.'

'How can I? I don't understand myself. You were the one who suggested Nicky hadn't died, hinted that you had suspicions about Charlie Flynn's death and Lambourne's escape. You told me people were out to get me.'

Brady's eyebrows flickered. 'The evidence—'

'Where's the gun?'

'What?'

'If I shot Ronnie Morgan, what did I do with the weapon? It wasn't discovered in the underpass, or the surrounding area. It wasn't found on my body when I was strip-searched and swabbed.' Caelan knew her voice was shaking, her fury barely contained. 'How did I make the gun disappear in less than a minute? Richard Adamson was behind me; he'd have seen if I'd left the underpass to dispose of it. Even if I had, it would have been found.'

Brady said nothing, and Caelan knew she was here on a fishing trip. She knew Caelan wasn't guilty but had no idea who was.

'We're wasting time,' Caelan went on. 'Standing here playing guessing games when we could be finding Walker.'

'Do we need to?'

Caelan bit back a scream. 'Yes. It was no accident, no coincidence that he was on the train. He wanted to speak to Ronnie Morgan. Someone wants me out of the way, is working hard to ensure I'm convicted of murder. I want to find out who.'

'We've released a still of Walker's face from the CCTV footage this morning, asking anyone who's seen him to come forward.'

'I thought you wanted to wait?'

'I did, but now we need to act.' Brady rubbed the small of her back, moved over to her chair. 'If we want to find him, we need help.'

'You mentioned evidence. What is it?'

Brady laughed as Caelan sat back beside her. 'The gun Brendan Milne threatened Sam Clifton with was not the one used to kill Ronnie Morgan. The striations on the bullet don't match Milne's gun, which hadn't been fired recently anyway. We're still missing a weapon.'

'What about the shots fired at us yesterday?'

Brady's face was grim. 'From the same gun used in the murder of Ronnie Morgan.'

'Fuck.'

'That was my reaction.'

Caelan crossed her legs. 'And you still think I shot Ronnie?'

'Or your accomplice did.'

'The one who deliberately missed me yesterday?'

'That's him. Or her.'

'Is there evidence from the underpass?'

'Loads, as you'd expect from a public area. Hairs, threads of fabric, vomit, blood, saliva…'

'Lovely.'

'Semen.'

'Well, it's a romantic location. Any matches?'

'Not yet.'

'Not even to me?'

'As I said, not yet, but we know you were there.'

'If you're not going to arrest me, why are you here?'

'I was passing, heard you were in your pyjamas.'

'I'm supposed to be off duty.'

Brady stretched her neck, wincing as she tilted her head. 'I don't want anyone to know we're having this conversation.'

'Really?'

'Haven't even told Tim. The boss knows, mainly because I had to explain why I wasn't arresting you.'

'Beckett?' Brady nodded. 'Why the secrecy?'

'Come on, Caelan, you already know the answer. Someone is doing their best to set you up. In my mind, there are only a few people with the knowledge and opportunity to do so.' Brady held up a hand, counting on her fingers. 'Richard Adamson, Michael Nasenby and Ian Penrith. Sebastian Lambourne, Glen Walker.'

Caelan blinked. It was the obvious conclusion, one she had drawn herself, but hearing Brady say the names made it real. 'Penrith has been wanting me sacked and prosecuted for weeks.'

Brady held up her other hand and made a fist, extended her thumb. 'Elizabeth Beckett.'

'No way, she—'

'I don't care how high up the ladder she is, whether she's the Commissioner's right-hand woman. She lost credibility when Lambourne escaped. She's powerful and influential. We'd be stupid not to include her.'

Caelan had to admit it made sense. 'You think I'm being naïve?'

'These are people you work with, have had to trust. It can't be easy to think about one of them potentially trying to destroy you.'

'Elizabeth Beckett wanted me back in the fold, asked Adamson to talk to me.'

Brady spread her hands. 'And?'

Resting her elbows on the table, Caelan allowed her head to fall into her hands.

'Adamson couldn't have shot Morgan,' she said.

'I think he could. We've only his word for it that he was behind you all the time. He could have left the station before you, gone to the far end of the underpass, shot Ronnie, gone back across the road and then run up behind you.'

'There wouldn't have been time.'

'There would. Three of my officers did a reconstruction.'

Caelan lifted her head. 'Seriously?'

'Wouldn't have said so otherwise. Adamson's not off the hook. Gunshot residue was found on his clothes, his hands.'

'We knew it would be; he was there. It's not conclusive.'

'He was in Lincoln too.'

'At Penrith's request.'

'And Nasenby's.'

'Can I ask a question?'

'You don't usually ask permission.'

'How do I know I can trust *you*?'

Brady had her phone out, her finger swiping across the screen. 'Honestly? You don't.'

'But you're not sure you can trust me either.'

'True.'

Picking up their empty mugs, Caelan took them through to the kitchen, set them in the sink. Brady had followed her. Caelan leaned against the worktop, the ceramic tiles cool under her bare feet.

'What about Tim Achebe?'

Brady looked up from her phone. 'What about him?'

'Can I trust him?'

'Yes, but you're working for me. Speak to me directly, no one else. As far as Nasenby and the others are concerned, you're out of action.'

'How are you going to continue the investigation if everyone thinks you've arrested me?'

'They won't, because we can't. Our evidence is circumstantial.'

'But you said—'

'I know.' Brady grinned. 'Like I said, you don't know if you can trust me.'

Anger erupting again, Caelan clenched her fists. 'You lied to me.'

'No. We *could* arrest you, based on the evidence. Doesn't mean we will.' Brady left the kitchen, reappeared holding the black briefcase she had brought with her. Setting it on the work surface, she opened it. 'Here you go.' She stood back, allowing Caelan to see what was inside.

'A gun? I don't want it,' Caelan said immediately.

'Tell me that when you're being shot at again. Brendan Milne asked Sam for your name. They want to find you, Caelan.'

'I don't want the gun. I don't like them.'

'Me neither, especially when they're being pointed at my officers, used in my city. Take it.'

Caelan stared down at the weapon, squat and ugly. She hated firearms, had done all the time she was being trained to use them. The noise, the smell, the responsibility. Guns were still so rarely used in the UK, she had only occasionally been ordered to carry one...

'Why didn't you shoot him?' Brady said, as if reading her mind.

'Who?'

'Lambourne. You knew he was armed; it would have been justified. If you'd shot him dead, you'd have been a celebrity.'

'My life's ambition. I wouldn't. I'd have been hated.'

Brady nodded. 'Destroyed by our glorious press.'

'And by social media, like Sam was.'

'We're trained to preserve life. If you thought Charlie Flynn was alive, killing Lambourne would have saved him for sure.'

'We didn't want to start shooting with Charlie there. We thought, we all thought Lambourne and Walker would be captured as soon as they left the house. There were enough people around.'

'That's why you let them go?'

'Why I did, yes. I can't speak for Sam or Nicky.' She touched the gun with a fingertip. 'I could have killed Lambourne. I wanted to, seeing him grab Nicky, raise the knife…'

'Why did he kill Nicky? Why not you, or Sam?'

'I was on the left, Sam on the right. Nicky was in the centre, blocking their path.'

'And she didn't shoot either?'

'It happened so quickly. No. None of us fired a shot.'

'I'm struggling to understand why.'

'I told you. We believed Charlie was alive. If we'd starting shooting in a space so small, we could have killed him ourselves.'

'And when you discovered he was dead?'

'What do you mean?'

'Quite a thing to come to terms with.'

Caelan lifted the gun, felt the weight of it. She looked at Brady, wondering. Why had she brought the weapon here? Deliberately, watching Brady's eyes, she slid her finger onto the trigger. Her prints would be all over the weapon now. Brady didn't react, and Caelan frowned. 'You think?'

'I'd imagine it would be devastating.'

'You'd be right. But we had no choice, we were sent in there blind. If we'd known Charlie was dead, we could have killed Lambourne and Walker, and Nicky would be alive.'

'Alive and living here.'

Ignoring the tightening of her throat, Caelan nodded. Why hadn't she brought the woman from last night home? Why hadn't she downed drinks until she could barely stand? She remembered Lucy hugging her goodbye, the reaction of her body to her friend's touch. On her way home, she'd decided the chemistry was because of the alcohol she'd indulged in, and the black veil of loneliness she'd been shrouded in since Nicky's death. Since agreeing to work undercover, if she was honest. She and Lucy had known each other for years, though they'd never been close. Lucy was the person she contacted for a drink, a night out, when she needed to escape. The problem was, all the shit in her head came along for the ride. No matter how much you drank, how hard you danced, the memories remained. *Blood on your hands, Caelan,* Ian Penrith had said. He was right. Blood everywhere – on her hands, and staining her career.

She looked down at the gun, still in her hand, hanging by her side. Maybe she should take it. She didn't have to use it, after all. Unless Brady had been told to bring it here, to plant it…

Brady's phone was ringing, the sudden chiming startling Caelan out of her reverie. She watched Brady's face as she listened to the caller speaking.

'This is definite?' She paused. 'Okay. Okay, I'll call you back.' Slowly she put the phone back in her jacket pocket. She stared at the gun in Caelan's hands, her mouth working.

Concerned, Caelan put the weapon back in the case. 'What is it?' Brady didn't move, didn't respond. Caelan reached out, touched her sleeve. 'Ma'am?'

'Get dressed.' Brady locked the briefcase, pushed it into a cupboard. Caelan wanted to protest that she didn't want the weapon in her home, but Brady's expression persuaded her to reconsider as she handed over the key.

'I have a gun safe. I need to—'

'Later. It'll be okay there for now.'

Caelan hesitated, knowing the gun should be locked away more securely. What was Brady up to?

'Have I got time for a shower?' she said.

'Five minutes.'

Under the steaming water, Caelan soaped her body, tipping back her head and allowing the warmth to ease away the last of her hangover. Where was Brady intending to take her? And did she want to go?

The café had a murky tiled floor and a queue of defeated-looking customers. Brady pushed open the door, the smell of burnt cooking fat greeting them. Behind the counter, a thin woman scurried between customers and the till, dodging around a scowling man whose sole task seemed to be to operate the coffee machine.

'Why are we here?' Caelan looked around, expecting to see Glen Walker tucking into a fry-up or Seb Lambourne swigging coffee. No one had noticed their arrival, no smiles, waves or shifty glances of acknowledgement.

Brady grimaced as a middle-aged waitress hurried past bearing a plate of food, grease already pooling around two watery fried eggs and rashers of bacon. Remembering the breakfast she and Ewan had enjoyed in the café in Lincoln, Caelan wished herself back there. Her task had been simpler then. Now, she was halfway between disgrace and the country's most-wanted list.

'We've a possible sighting of Glen Walker. The woman who phoned it in works here.' Brady spoke quietly.

'Shouldn't you be at the station, doing… whatever chief superintendents do?'

Brady sniffed. 'Tim can handle it. I felt like getting my hands dirty.'

'You're certainly doing that. This place is a shit tip. Who says they've seen Walker?'

'The woman taking the orders, I assume.'

'Are we going to talk to her?'

Brady stared at the surly man, now glaring in their direction. 'Maybe we should order something.'

'I'll risk a coffee, but no food.'

'Did I offer any?' Stomping to the back of the queue, Brady left Caelan to search for an empty table. There were several, so she chose the cleanest-looking. She watched Brady exchange a few words with an elderly man who leaned on a grey metal walking stick as he waited. He waved a spindly hand towards the counter, Brady smiling, nodding.

The queue moved quickly, and Brady was soon at the table. She sat beside Caelan, took out her warrant card and left it face up in front of her. Caelan watched with interest.

'What are you doing?'

'She's bringing our coffees over. I want her to know who we are.'

'What did the old man say?'

'Nothing relevant. Passing the time of day. Weather, the evils of immigration. The usual. Here she comes.'

The woman was hurrying towards them, two white mugs in her hands. Brady sat back in her chair as she approached and put the cups down. Coffee slopped onto the table, and the woman shrank back.

'Oh, I'm sorry… I'll get a cloth.'

The hint of an accent was hard to place. Eastern European, but which country? Caelan watched the man behind the counter speak harshly to the woman. Was he her partner, or her boss?

As she wiped the table, the woman's eyes flicked to Brady's warrant card, her head darting from side to side as she read it.

'Do you have information for us?'

'The man on the news…' She hesitated, looking around the café without moving her head. 'He's been here. Two times, maybe more. Buys coffee to take away.'

'Do you know where he lives?'

'No. He came in with another man.'

Brady had her phone on the table, pushing it towards the woman. 'Was it him?' On the screen was Brendan Milne's mugshot.

She stared. 'Yes.'

'You're sure?'

'Yes.'

'When?'

'Yesterday. The day before also.'

Brady thanked her. 'We'll need you to make a statement.'

The woman licked her lips, her eyes straying to the counter. 'Not today. I have to work. He won't let me…'

'We have your name and address. Officers will come to your house later. Okay?'

She nodded, turned away. Brady looked down at the drinks, picked one up, took a mouthful.

'Not bad. He might be a miserable bastard, but he can make a decent cup of coffee.'

'Milne and Walker knew each other.' Caelan risked the coffee. Brady was right, it was good.

'Not a huge surprise, is it? It's a point in your favour, Caelan.'

'What is?'

'Brendan Milne trying to find out who you were. Walker can't know either, or why would they be asking?'

'Walker saw Kay Summers, not me.'

'We were lucky your identity wasn't exposed by the media. Listen, Caelan. Do you think Lambourne knows your real name?'

'How can I know?'

'Why did you go to Egypt using your own passport?'

'Why not? I wasn't working; it would have been wrong to use a different identity. I'd resigned.'

'Yet while you were there, you made some enquiries.'

'Sam had said Lambourne had property in Egypt. It was gossip, no more, but I thought I could make myself useful.'

'How public-spirited. And you discovered…?'

'Nothing. As you know.'

Brady stood. 'Lambourne does own property in Egypt. He's not there, though, hasn't been for a long time. Come on.'

—

Tim Achebe stood to greet Brady, glanced at Caelan, then looked away. He sat behind his desk, flicking through a pile of paperwork, clearly tense. Caelan couldn't blame him. Brady was placing him in a difficult position by bringing her here.

'Did you see the email?' Achebe said.

Brady was casual. 'Which one?'

'About the meeting this afternoon.' He glared at Caelan. 'Detective Small wasn't included.'

'Are you surprised?' Brady stepped closer to Achebe's desk, picked up the top report from his pile, glanced at it. 'She's supposed to be in custody by now.'

Achebe set his jaw. 'Then why is she here, ma'am?'

Brady placed her hands on his desk, leaning forward, her face inches from his. 'Do you trust me, Tim?'

He recoiled. 'Yes.'

'Caelan is as clueless as we are about what's going on here. She's killed no one, but she's going to help us find out who did. I don't want another word about her alleged involvement. Clear?'

Achebe bowed his head. 'Yes, ma'am.'

Brady threw herself into one of the chairs opposite him. 'Now, I want an update.'

Leaning against the wall, Caelan silently cheered as Achebe frowned, then relaxed his shoulders.

'We found no trace of Glen Walker in Brendan Milne's flat.'

'Which is close to the café Caelan and I have been to?' said Brady.

Achebe nodded. 'But we don't know where Walker's living.'

Brady scowled. 'What *do* we know? You've a million officers at your disposal; what have they found out?'

'Milne doesn't have a car. He travelled from his home on Ealing Broadway to Sam Clifton's flat by bus and tube. The mobile phone found on his body gave us a list of contacts, but we've traced them all. None were people you'd want to be friends with, but none were Walker or Lambourne either.' Caelan could see Achebe was frustrated. 'The lab was able to give us some results quickly, for a change. Top priority. No fingerprints on Milne's gun, except his and Clifton's. As you know, it hadn't been fired recently. No gunshot residue on Milne's hands, body or clothes.'

'Not conclusive, but I think we can count him out of Ronnie's murder. I dread to think how much fast-tracking the results of all that cost,' said Brady. She glanced around. 'Tim, I'm assuming we can speak freely in here?'

He stared at her, uncomprehending. 'Yes, of course.'

'Who's invited to this meeting later? I'm guessing Nasenby, Penrith?'

'And someone called Richard Adamson.'

'Who called it?'

'Michael Nasenby. Elizabeth Beckett will be there as well.'

Brady whistled. 'The organ grinder too. Why are we having it?'

'Sharing information, ideas.'

'Checking up on us, in other words. Have you spoken to any of them today?'

'No.'

Brady pulled a face. 'Listen, Tim. What about the phone call made to Ronnie Morgan while he was at the restaurant? Have we traced it?'

'Yes. Pay-as-you-go SIM, used for the calls to the restaurant and Ronnie's mobile only.'

'Where was the call made?'

Achebe held out a sheet of paper. 'To the restaurant? Near Brendan Milne's flat.'

'CCTV?'

'To verify whether Milne himself made the call? No, no cameras nearby.'

'Shit. And the handset wasn't found in Milne's flat?'

'Nothing was found in Milne's flat except takeaway cartons and beer cans.'

'Do we know where the SIM was purchased? The handset?'

'Not yet.'

Brady ran a hand through her hair. 'Any more calls about Walker? Any sightings?'

'Not as far as I know.'

'Let's concentrate on Ealing. Walker may not have been in Milne's flat, but he was in the café.'

'Will you be at the meeting?' Achebe asked.

'I suppose I'll have to be. Tim, finding Walker is our top priority.'

'I know; it has been since we knew he was in London.'

'Do we have a DS or DC we can depend on to keep their mouth closed?'

Achebe frowned. 'I'd vouch for any of them.'

Brady shook her head. 'I have a job for someone, but it has to be the right officer.'

'If you tell me what you want them to do...' Achebe's mobile began to ring and he muttered an apology. He greeted the caller. Caelan watched his face. Whatever he was hearing was clearly causing him concern. Brady mouthed, *What?* Achebe held up a hand, thanked the caller, put his phone down on his desk.

'That was the lab,' he said.

'And?' Brady's eyebrows were up by her hairline.

'The bullet removed from the body of Ronnie Morgan has flagged up a match on their system.'

'Meaning the weapon that killed him had been used in a previous crime?' Caelan wanted to make sure.

'They say so.'

'Which one?' Dread had gathered in Caelan's stomach.

Achebe nodded, his face clenched tight. 'The Charlie Flynn case.'

Brady opened her mouth, said nothing for a second. 'Are they sure?'

'Certain. The gun that killed Ronnie Morgan also killed Charlie Flynn.'

22

Nasenby poured water, passed the glasses around while Ian Penrith stared at nothing, his arms crossed, white shirt tight across his shoulders. Brady smiled at Nasenby as he handed her a glass. Beside her, Achebe took his notebook from his jacket pocket and uncapped his pen.

'This latest development was unexpected,' Assistant Commissioner Elizabeth Beckett was saying, 'but I'm not sure it should have been.' She looked at the faces of the people sitting around the conference table. 'Where's Caelan Small?'

Nasenby cleared his throat. 'We thought it unwise to involve Caelan when questions have been raised about her suitability, her—'

'Call her in immediately.' Beckett pushed her glasses up her nose, glaring at Nasenby. 'What were you thinking, Michael?'

'With respect, Caelan lost Ronnie Morgan, giving his murderer a chance to kill him,' he said. 'If she'd kept him in sight—'

'She could be dead too.' Beckett took out her phone, tapped out a text. 'I've asked her to join us. You can't believe she killed Morgan?'

'She had the opportunity, a motive,' said Penrith.

'Ridiculous. Richard, you were close behind Caelan. What do you say?' asked Beckett.

Adamson moistened his lips. 'I think Caelan's version of events is the truth. I've worked with her long enough to know she's honest, and,' he looked at Penrith, 'I can't understand anyone who knows her thinking otherwise.'

Penrith curled his lip. 'You're blind, Adamson, as usual where Caelan's concerned. She's a loose cannon. Running off to Egypt, trying to track down Lambourne herself. When her plan failed, she shot his son. I'm not saying she meant to kill him, but...' He took a sheet of paper from his shirt pocket, unfolded it, pushed it towards Beckett. 'You might find this interesting.'

Beckett narrowed her eyes. 'What is it?' She took the sheet, frowned over it. 'Ian?'

Penrith leaned back in his chair, smiling as Beckett unfolded the paper. 'A photo Caelan wouldn't want you to see. Here's another.'

Beckett smoothed out the second sheet, then pushed both into the centre of the table. In the first, Caelan had her arms around Nicky Sturgess, both women smiling, bodies pressed close. In the second, Nicky and Caelan were pictured leaving a solicitor's office. Brady's stomach dropped.

'This isn't a secret,' she said. 'Caelan told me about Nicky's will and her inheritance herself.' *Though she also said she hadn't known about the will before Nicky's death, and here she is coming out of the solicitor's with her.*

'Did Caelan tell you that Nicky was cut down beside her, that she did nothing to help?' Penrith stabbed his finger on the first photograph, covering Caelan's face. 'People don't bleed to death instantly. We had an ambulance outside, a helicopter.' His face twisted. 'Nicky shouldn't have died.'

Beckett pushed the images away. 'We're not disputing it, but the operation was a disaster, Ian, and Caelan wasn't in charge.'

Penrith gave a bark of laughter. 'No, I was. Me and Sam Clifton. What a team. Incidentally, can we talk about Sam for a moment?'

Beckett sighed. 'Is it relevant?'

'I'm worried about him. He's drinking, he killed a man.'

'In self-defence.'

'That's his story. He was drunk, absolutely pissed out of his mind. And he fought off a man with a gun?'

'Ian, listen to me.' Beckett had clearly lost patience. 'As you know, we work in grey areas. Nothing about our world is black and white. I'm not sure what you're trying to achieve by constantly questioning and undermining your colleagues, but I'm tiring of it.'

Penrith's cheeks blazed. 'I apologise, ma'am. All I want is the truth, and justice. I recognise my approach may have been... misguided.'

'As I see it, we need to work together, not destroy each other,' Beckett continued. 'I won't ask how you obtained these photographs, but I hope you understand that they change nothing. I have faith in all of you, Caelan included.'

As she said the name, there was a tap on the door and Caelan herself appeared.

Penrith scowled at her, then at Beckett. 'That was quick.'

Caelan smiled, pulled out the chair beside Brady. 'I was in the area.'

Brady flushed and kept her eyes fixed on the tabletop, hoping no one would notice. She had told Caelan to stay close by, hoping to appeal to Beckett after the meeting about the lunacy of closing her out of the investigation. She watched as Caelan spotted the photographs of herself on the table between her colleagues, colour rising in her cheeks. The look she gave Ian Penrith was venomous. Penrith pretended not to have noticed, reaching out to scoop them up. Caelan got there first, slamming her hand onto the sheets.

'Been doing some unauthorised surveillance, Ian?' Her voice was quiet, the fury held in check. Anyone hearing her but not able to see her expression would think she was being friendly. Brady watched as Penrith squirmed.

'Not exactly,' he said.

'Or asking other people to do it for you?' Caelan shot a glare in Richard Adamson's direction. 'No, Nicky and I didn't broadcast the fact that we were seeing each other, mainly because it was no one else's business. You all know the shit she'd been through. It didn't affect our work, and since she's dead, I'm not sure why we're still talking about it.' She snatched the photographs up and thrust them at Penrith, who took them and screwed them up.

Beckett sat impassive. 'If you've finished, we'll continue.' Caelan smiled at her, while Penrith looked thunderous. 'I know you've been focusing on finding Glen Walker, but I think we need to track him down immediately. How can we do that?'

She waited, but there was silence. Brady knew that Beckett was looking at her and Achebe for ideas. This was their case, after all.

'I could go back to the Wheatsheaf,' said Caelan.

'No,' said Nasenby.

'You could have been killed there yesterday.' Achebe finally lifted his head.

Caelan folded her arms. 'It's a link to Walker.'

'You think he'll go back there? But he knows we're aware he used to visit the place.' Beckett tapped a fountain pen on her notepad. 'I'm not sure it's worth the risk.'

'And someone knew we were heading there yesterday,' said Nasenby. 'It's dangerous.'

Beckett turned to him. 'Why did *you* go to the Wheatsheaf, Michael?'

Nasenby smiled. 'I knew Caelan would march straight in, not worry about the risks. I didn't want her doing it alone.'

'She had,' Beckett consulted her notes, 'Ewan Davies with her.'

'I'm sure he was excellent in the army, but in our line of work, he's inexperienced, untested. Unarmed.' Nasenby risked a smile at Caelan, who ignored it.

'You were all unarmed. A shame the person who attacked you wasn't.' Beckett looked over the top of her glasses at Achebe. 'Any news on the bullets recovered from the scene?'

'I received a call on the way over here. Again, the bullets were fired from the same gun.'

'The weapon used to kill Charlie Flynn and Ronnie Morgan?'

'Sorry. Yes.'

'In my mind, this adds weight to the theory that Glen Walker is behind the shootings.' Beckett looked around the table. 'Thoughts?'

'Why would he kill Lambourne's son?' Penrith said immediately.

'We don't know their history, we don't know what's happened since Charlie Flynn's death and their escape. Lambourne killed Nicky Sturgess and we assume Charlie Flynn – Walker could blame him for events escalating, meaning he had to go on the run.'

'We can't be sure, and I know we've all spent lots of time thinking about it, discussing it. I agree we should concentrate on finding Walker. He could lead us to Lambourne,' Nasenby said.

'Have we spoken to Ronnie Morgan's mother again?' Caelan asked the question of Achebe, who shook his head.

'There's a family liaison officer with her, but since breaking the news of Ronnie's death, no. We searched his bedroom at her house, but came up with nothing.'

'Go and speak to her, Caelan,' Beckett ordered. 'Then tonight, go back to the Wheatsheaf. Not as yourself, of course.'

Nasenby was frowning. 'Ma'am, I—'

Beckett held up a hand. 'I understand your concerns, Michael, but the time for caution is over. Caelan knows the risks, and I'm sure she is as capable of looking after herself as ever.'

Brady met Caelan's eyes, gave a tiny nod. Beckett knew about the gun she had taken to Caelan's apartment, but she hadn't mentioned it. Why?

Half an hour later, after more largely pointless discussion and coffee, the meeting broke up. Caelan remained in her chair, watched Ian Penrith stalk out of the door without speaking to anyone. Achebe hurried off too, eager to get back to his team, while Brady remained in her seat, took out her phone. Elizabeth Beckett rose, collected her glasses and briefcase. Her chauffeur would be waiting.

Richard Adamson approached, flashing a hopeful smile.

'How are you, Caelan?'

She stretched her spine, not wanting to speak to him. 'Fine. How are you? What's Ian got you doing today?'

The smile vanished. 'Caelan, listen. I was—'

'Obeying orders? I know. Not a defence, though, is it, as proven many times before.'

He blushed. 'You think I wanted to follow you? I knew you'd see me.'

'I didn't when you took the photographs.'

'First time for everything.'

'Maybe Ian wanted me to notice you.'

'What do you mean?'

'He's trying to end my career, Richard. Haven't you realised?'

'I...'

'And you're helping him, whether you're intending to or not.'

Adamson lifted his chin. 'I told him you were the best officer we have. I stand by that.'

Caelan laughed. 'Well thank you. I'll be sure to add it to my CV. Might come in handy when I'm in the queue at the job centre.' Adamson scowled, turned away. Caelan felt a pang of guilt, and called him back. 'Look, Richard, I'm sorry. I know you were in an awkward position. But how would you feel if I'd been told to keep tabs on you?'

His smile was rueful. 'There's a difference, Caelan.'

'Why?'

'Because I wouldn't have known you were there.'

He walked away, left the room. Nasenby had been listening. 'I meant what I said about the Wheatsheaf,' he said.

'I know. Please don't turn up again, Michael.'

'I won't.' He laughed. 'Didn't help yesterday, did I?'

'None of us expected what happened. I doubt it will happen again.'

'Stay in touch and—'

'Don't get killed?' She smiled.

'If you can help it.'

When Nasenby had gone, Brady finally moved in her seat.

'They're afraid of you,' she said.

'I doubt it. Nasenby and Penrith both outrank me, Richard has several years' more experience.'

'They know Beckett's relying on you, and they don't like it.'

A cough came from the doorway. A man stood there, unfamiliar, wearing a dark suit and an earpiece, the wire from it disappearing under his clothes. 'Could you follow me, please?'

Caelan stared at him. 'Where to? Who are you?'

He walked over, smiled, handed her a square of paper. 'She said you'd be wary.'

Caelan unfolded the handwritten note, read it, handed it to Brady.

–

The chauffeur opened the car door. Elizabeth Beckett was waiting inside. She smiled, waved them in. When the door was closed behind them and the chauffeur had started the engine, she finally spoke.

'I'm sorry for the cloak-and-dagger approach, but I needed to ensure we weren't overheard. You have the gun, Caelan?'

'It's at home.'

'I'd suggest you carry it. No, I'm ordering you to.'

Caelan cleared her throat, concerned. 'Ma'am…'

'Allow me to explain, then you can ask questions. Detective Chief Superintendent Brady came to me yesterday, voicing concerns about the Charlie Flynn case. About Nicky Sturgess's death, about Sam Clifton. About you.' Caelan glanced at Brady, who resolutely kept her face turned away. 'As you know, Ian

Penrith has been extremely vocal about his belief in your failings. Why?'

Caelan stared out of the window, watching the street whip by. 'I don't know. Because he needs someone to blame for Charlie's death?'

'Tell me, Caelan, what were you expecting to find when you arrived at the house with Sam and Nicky?'

Caelan felt as though she'd been punched in the stomach. 'Charlie, held captive but safe. Sam and I had been undercover for months, creeping closer to Lambourne. Nicky had been working on a different assignment, unrelated.'

'She was infiltrating a drug-dealing network,' said Beckett.

'Yeah, though I didn't know that at the time.'

'Why did Nicky go into the house with you? Why was she part of the team detailed to rescue Charlie Flynn when she hadn't been involved in the case before then?'

'She'd worked on other kidnappings. We didn't know Lambourne and Walker were waiting for us.'

'No, you didn't.'

'You're telling me someone else did? It was a set-up?'

'We think so.'

'You think so? It's a hell of an accusation to be throwing around. There were teams of officers, dogs, the helicopter, all on standby. If what you're saying is true, why do it so publicly? Why not turn up with Charlie safe and well, and take the plaudits?'

'Charlie couldn't live to tell the tale.' Beckett's voice was cold. She was discussing the death of a child with no more emotion than if she were talking about swatting a fly.

'Why?' Caelan managed to say.

'Because he knew Lambourne and Walker hadn't snatched him. They weren't his kidnappers.'

'Who was?'

Beckett smiled, lifted her shoulders. 'We don't know.'

'You… what?'

'Lambourne dabbled in extortion, owned successful pubs, nightclubs, had a profitable drug-dealing operation. Walker didn't have much in the way of brains, but he could do as he was told. Why would they suddenly decide to kidnap a child? A ten-year-old, remember, not an infant who would be easy to snatch and conceal. A child old enough to understand what was happening, old enough to talk, to describe people.'

'What are you suggesting?'

'Why take Charlie Flynn?'

'I've no idea.'

Beckett pursed her lips. 'His mother was reputed to have inherited a fortune from her grandparents.'

'And had she?'

'Depends what you call a fortune. A couple of million.'

Caelan snorted. 'Sounds like a fortune to me.'

'More than Nicky Sturgess left, for sure.' Beckett gave her a sidelong look, and Caelan flushed. 'The problem was, Charlie's parents had blown the lot on a house, holidays, cars and coke. No one realised it, but they had no money left.'

'You're suggesting they were involved?'

'No.' Beckett exhaled, a sign of frustration. 'It makes no sense, none of it.'

'These questions were asked at the time.' Brady spoke up for the first time since getting into the car. 'The consensus was that Charlie's kidnappers had expected his parents to be able to pay a hefty ransom. When they couldn't, Charlie was killed.'

'But the Flynns denied the kidnappers had made any contact,' Caelan said.

'Doesn't mean they told the truth,' Brady pointed out. 'Maybe they were told that Charlie would be punished if they rang the police.'

'Then why would they not say so afterwards, when they knew Charlie had been killed?' Caelan rubbed her eyes. 'Would they really stay silent? What happened to them anyway?'

'The press turned on them, as you know. The longer Charlie was missing, the more rumours circulated. They were suspected of killing him, or of hiding him away themselves. They wouldn't have been the first to try it. In the end, they sold everything, moved away.' Beckett glanced at Caelan. 'They're both dead.'

It was another hammer blow. 'What?'

'It's never been reported in the press, not acknowledged. They changed their names, but we kept track of them. Their bodies were found in the garage of their new house. They'd hanged themselves.'

'Jesus.' Caelan's hands trembled. She folded them together, clenched them between her knees.

'I know I'm raising more questions than I'm answering, but you need to understand the depth of this…' Beckett fumbled for the word. 'This tragedy. We need to determine who's involved, and to what extent.'

'And we know you're not.' Brady managed a smile, though Caelan couldn't return it.

'How?' she said.

'The way you've behaved since Charlie's death. Your anger, your resolve.' Beckett lifted her hands. 'We know you.'

'I resigned.'

Beckett was nodding. 'As we expected. And if you'd been involved, you would have stayed away, kept your head down. You wouldn't have come back, especially not to tail

Lambourne's son. And then Ronnie Morgan was shot with you a few metres away. The spotlight was firmly centred on you.'

'Because someone was trying to set me up.'

'Precisely.'

'I…' Caelan felt overwhelmed. She had begun to have suspicions, but this was beyond belief. 'Who's doing this?'

'We don't know,' Beckett said. 'It could still be Walker and Lambourne, or Walker working alone. We need proof, evidence, and it's so far proved impossible to obtain.'

'Who else are you looking at?'

'You already know. Detective Adamson. Deputy Assistant Commissioner Nasenby. Commander Penrith.'

Caelan closed her eyes, nausea rising. Three men she had worked with for years. Hearing Beckett use their ranks made the situation even more unbelievable. 'What about Achebe?'

Brady turned sharply. 'Tim?'

'He was involved in the Flynn case, wasn't he?' What had he said at the meeting the day she had returned from Egypt? *I'm only involved because the Charlie Flynn kidnapping and murder was on my patch.*

'Tim was seconded to the case at a late stage,' Brady said. 'We both were. It felt like the whole Met was on it by then.'

Caelan nodded, remembering. She had been on the periphery, detailed to gather what information she could, but Charlie Flynn's face had beamed out of every television, every newspaper front page for days. *Brady worked on the case too.* Caelan shivered. Was this how it was going to be? Suspecting all, trusting no one? What about Beckett? Who could vouch for her?

'Why haven't you arrested me?' she said, pushing down her doubts. She would examine them later, when she was alone. Now was the time to keep her head. Her freedom, her life, could depend on it. 'Whoever's behind all this, if they thought their plan was working and I was out of the way…'

Beckett shuffled, stretched her legs as far as she was able. There was a glass screen between them and the driver, and as her feet touched his seat, he glanced over his shoulder. Beckett smiled, and he focused on the road ahead. Calean realised they were circling around the same streets, with no destination in mind. They were in the car so they could speak freely, with no witnesses. The thought gave her no comfort.

'We will arrest you,' Beckett said, with a glance at Brady.

'What do you mean?'

'Later today, you'll be arrested.'

Caelan stared at her. 'What?'

'Once you've spoken to Ronnie Morgan's mother and been to the Wheatsheaf, officers will be waiting at your flat. We'll have to make it look real, of course. Discreet but convincing. No publicity, no press. You'll be taken to a local station for the night, then spirited away in the morning to a secure location.'

Caelan swallowed. 'Where?'

'A hotel room. It's a charade, Caelan. We want you to continue tracking down Walker and Lambourne.'

'Secretly?'

'It's what you're good at, isn't it?'

'What about the others? Richard, Michael, Ian?'

'We'll be watching them.'

Caelan considered this. 'You don't trust me, do you?'

Beckett turned her head. 'Yes we do. *I* do.'

'From the day Richard Adamson came to me in Egypt, I've felt someone behind the scenes, pulling the strings. I thought it was Lambourne.'

'It could still be, but why kill his own son? And why would Walker do it, regardless of whether he was working with Lambourne or not?'

'But why would any of my colleagues, *your* colleagues, risk everything for money? A ransom they didn't even receive? The only person who profited from the whole mess was...'

'You,' said Brady.

Caelan nodded. 'Me.'

There was a silence.

'You told me you didn't know Nicky had left you her apartment.' Brady's voice was soft.

'I didn't.'

'The photograph...'

'Ian's photograph?' Caelan sneered. 'I agreed to pick Nicky up from the solicitor's. She was giddy when she came out, laughing, wanted us to book a holiday together. I didn't know what she'd been doing in there.' She met Brady's eyes. 'That's the truth.'

Brady held up her hands. 'Okay. My point is, there's no one involved in this case we can't consider as a suspect.'

Caelan nodded. *Even the three of us.* 'How did Ian know about Nicky and me? How did he know where to find us? Her past wasn't a secret, especially at work, because there were concerns about how she would cope with what had happened, but...'

'Who knew about Nicky's abusive marriage?' said Beckett.

Caelan paused. 'Adamson, Nasenby and Penrith again. Her family. Whoever did her psych assessments.'

'Friends?'

'Possibly. I never met any of them.'

'She didn't introduce you to her friends?'

'There wasn't time.'

'You didn't seem to know her very well,' said Brady.

Caelan stared out of the window. 'I thought I did. We were both other people most of the time.'

'You don't think…' Brady hesitated.

'What?'

'You don't think Nicky could have been involved?'

'Involved? How?' But Caelan knew.

'Working for Lambourne. Helping him.'

'Then he killed her to protect himself? That's ridiculous, you know. You're throwing accusations around like…' Caelan paused, unable to think of a simile. 'You haven't got a clue.'

Beckett laughed. 'You're right.' She leaned forward, tapped on the glass partition. The driver nodded, indicated. 'Thank you for your time, Caelan.'

The car neared the kerb, stopped. Caelan looked at Beckett. 'Am I to report back to you, or…?' Beckett might have overall responsibility for the Specialist Crime & Operations directorate, but Michael Nasenby was in charge of Intelligence & Covert Policing within it. Caelan had reported to both Nasenby and Ian Penrith during recent operations, but she saw Nasenby as her boss. Adele Brady had told her not to report to anyone but herself, but as a chief superintendent, Brady was outranked by Beckett, Nasenby and Penrith. Her impartiality and Beckett's apparent faith in her was clearly placing her temporarily at Beckett's right hand.

'I'll be in touch. Speak to me or to Adele. No one else.' Beckett slid a tiny phone out of her pocket and handed it to Caelan. 'Contact me using this. Do you have the note?'

'Note?'

Beckett nodded towards the chauffeur. 'The one he gave you, asking you to come to the car.'

Caelan pulled it out of her pocket, handed it over. Beckett scrunched it into a ball, tucked it in her bag. 'We'll speak later.'

Caelan took the hint, opened the car door.

'Caelan,' Beckett called. She turned back. 'Ewan Davies.'

'What about him?'

'Take him with you.'

23

Ewan smiled from the driving seat as Caelan crossed to his car. She'd come home to change, and would need to do so again before venturing to the Wheatsheaf.

'I wasn't sure I'd see you again,' he said as she fastened her seat belt. 'Where are we going?'

'Sidcup.' She gave him the details as he joined the traffic. 'Did you phone her?'

'Who?'

'The woman from last night, the bartender.'

His cheeks flushed. 'Well, I sent her a text.'

'Good for you.' Relief coursed through Caelan as she realised that Ewan had picked up on her unspoken message. She wasn't arrogant enough to believe that everyone she met fancied her, but she didn't want to give him the wrong impression either. His reluctance to share a bed with her had been excruciating enough.

'When are you seeing her?'

'Don't know. I told her I'd let her know, said my working hours are irregular.'

'People love to hear that.'

'Sounds like you're speaking from experience.'

Caelan was quiet. Beckett hadn't forbidden her from confiding in Ewan, but she would be expecting her to keep her mouth shut. Caelan wouldn't know what to tell him in any case. Now that she had begun to talk about Nicky, about their relationship, she found she wanted to continue after weeks of remaining silent. She had attended Nicky's funeral as a colleague, sitting dry-eyed in the last row of pews between Nasenby and Adamson while Nicky's parents and sister sobbed at the front. Brady had suggested that it might not have been Nicky in the coffin, but Caelan wasn't going to allow that possibility to enter her head. Why had Brady suggested the idea? Simply to observe Caelan's reaction, or did she actually believe it? Beckett hadn't mentioned it, and Caelan wondered again about Beckett and Brady. Did they trust each other, or were they being forced to compromise through circumstance? Either way, it seemed an uneasy partnership.

She put the thought out of her mind, focused on Ewan. They were going to be in the car for at least an hour, and she couldn't sit wrestling with her thoughts and memories while ignoring him.

She cleared her throat. 'Did you speak to your boss?'

'No. I had an idea you'd contact me again.'

Caelan laughed. 'Predictable, aren't I?'

'It was more that I hoped you would. When I met you at the airport and then asked me to work with you, I realised I missed… I don't know.'

'Being shot at?'

He laughed. 'I can live without that. I mean working together, depending on colleagues. Being a team.'

Caelan was silent, touched by his admission. 'Don't you see your army mates now?'

'The ones who made it home? No.'

'I'm sorry. I won't ask.'

He glanced at her. 'No, I should apologise. I loved the army, but my career ended badly, as you've no doubt guessed.'

'Don't tell me if you don't want to.' She turned her head, staring out at the traffic. He was quiet for a moment, the only sounds from the vehicles around them.

'We were on patrol. We were wary of IEDs – you know what they are?' Caelan nodded. 'Well, we hit one. Three men were killed, our vehicle was fucked. I was okay, me and two others. I don't know why they died and we survived – I try not to think about it.' He licked his lips. 'There was a building at the side of the road. We were stupid, we thought it was empty.'

'It wasn't?'

'No. No it wasn't. They killed my mate as he walked through the door in front of me. There were three of them in there – Taliban fighters. We… we shot them all.' Caelan was silent, hardly breathing. 'I'd killed before, but the third, he was just a boy. He ran upstairs after he saw his mates go down. I followed him. He was in a corner, cowering, but he still raised his gun. I looked at him, saw him pleading – and shot him dead.' He lifted a hand, scrubbed his eyes. 'We were trapped there for three days with their bodies, surrounded by Taliban. In the heat – you can imagine.'

'No one came for you?'

'Eventually. It was a fuck-up.' The ghost of a smile. 'Bet they didn't show that on the news. I see his face, his eyes, especially at night, sometimes even during the day. Aiming the gun, knowing he wouldn't fire. I couldn't… I didn't know what to do. And I killed him.'

'You had no choice.'

'But I did. I didn't have to be there at all, I wasn't conscripted. They were little more than kids, especially him. I think about his family, his mother. I lost four friends, not for the first time. I didn't see the point any more.'

'You left?'

'Discharged, in the end. Went a bit…' He made a fluttering motion with his fingers. 'Struggled mentally.'

'Not surprising.'

He shrugged. 'One of my old COs joined the Met after he retired from the army. He had a word in the right ear, and here I am.' He glanced at her. 'They even let me near guns again.'

'And now you're stuck with me.'

A laugh. 'Getting shot at.'

'I don't know what to say.'

'It helped to go home, walk in the fields, go out with the dogs. My mum's cooking, a few beers in my local. Normal stuff.'

'Thank you for telling me.'

'I let my mates down. Why should I have lived when they didn't? If I'd gone into the building first…'

'But you didn't.'

He changed gear, glanced in the rear-view mirror. 'There's a van behind us, been there since we left your road.'

'Following us?'

'I don't know. Seems a coincidence they're turning the same way as us each time we reach a junction.'

Resisting the temptation to look behind, Caelan leaned forward, trying to glimpse the vehicle behind in the wing mirror. 'Can't see. How many people are in it?'

'Only the driver, I think.'

'Male?'

'I'd say so. Hard to be sure.'

'He's obviously not worried about us seeing him.' Caelan took out her phone.

'Who are you calling?'

'The person who sent us out here.'

Brady answered on the third ring. 'Caelan? Is there a problem?'

'I don't know. Have you asked someone to follow us?'

'No, why would I?'

'I've no idea.' Caelan waited, wondering if Brady was being truthful. The man behind was either an amateur, or he wanted to be seen.

'Text me the details of the vehicle. I'll call you back.' She was gone.

'Can you see the reg, Ewan?'

He glanced up. 'No. The number plate's filthy.'

Caelan turned her head, moved in the seat. 'See what you mean. I can barely make it out. I'll have to guess the final letter.' She sent the text, glanced behind them again. 'Can't see his face, he's wearing a cap.'

Ewan gritted his teeth. 'Any closer, he'll be in our boot.'

'Touch the brakes.'

'He'll hit us.'

'He won't.'

The car slowed for a second as Ewan did as she asked. Caelan turned again, lifting a hand to the man driving the van.

'He's dropped back,' said Ewan.

'For now.' Facing forward again, Caelan checked her phone. Nothing.

'We're going to lead him to Suzanne Morgan's house,' said Ewan.

'I know. If he's still with us when we're closer, we'll have to make a detour.'

Risking another glance in the mirror, Ewan changed down a gear. 'He's put his sun visor down. I think he's on the phone. His hand's up by his ear.'

Caelan swivelled in the seat. 'Could be coincidence, could be speaking to his boss.'

'Lambourne?'

'I don't know.' She turned again, wanting him to see her staring. Was it Walker? Impossible to tell. A shadowy figure, the shoulders bulky enough to suggest a man, but there was no guarantee.

Ewan was forced to brake again as the vehicles in front of them slowed. The van came to a halt too, leaving a generous gap between them. Caelan's phone pinged. 'The van's registered to a business up in Edinburgh.'

'Stolen?'

'Or the plates have been cloned. Dodgy, if nothing else.' She looked through the windscreen at four lanes of solid London traffic. 'Not like we're going to be able to lose him.'

'What do we do?'

'Keep going. We have no choice.'

'Who do you think it is?'

'At a guess, Glen Walker.'

'Isn't he taking a huge risk?'

'I don't think he's too bothered.'

'Doesn't want you to see his face, though.'

'We're assuming he knows who he's following, but it's possible he doesn't. He could just have been told where to go, which vehicle to tail. Either way, he knows where I live and what car you're driving.' Caelan paused, allowed the statement to sink in as her phone rang.

'Did you get my text?' said Brady.

'Has the vehicle been reported stolen?'

'No. The registered keeper's a plumber, been working in and around Edinburgh for thirty years. Safe to say it's not him following you.'

'You're sure he's not one of ours?' Caelan detected a moment of hesitation before Brady replied.

'No.'

'You mean not that you know of.'

Brady sighed. 'Okay, no one I've sent, no one Tim has sent. Better?'

'Yeah, I'm completely reassured.'

A tiny chuckle. 'At least you haven't been shot at today.'

'Not yet.'

'We've a squad car nearby, another a few miles away,' said Brady. 'We're going to pull him over, give you some room. If it's Walker, we've hit the jackpot.'

'And if it's not?'

'He's still got some explaining to do. Stay safe, Caelan.'

Brady was gone. Caelan left her phone on her lap, wanting to have it to hand.

'Keep driving, Ewan,' she told him. She decided not to mention the cars Brady was sending, reasoning that he would be better concentrating on the road rather than on what was happening behind them.

'Hang on, he's gone.' Ewan's eyes were fixed on the rear-view mirror. Caelan whipped her head around, saw he was right. She grabbed her phone again.

'Where did he turn off?'

'Didn't see.'

'Ewan!'

They were speeding towards the back of the car in front, which had stopped again, brake lights glowing red. Ewan's hands gripped the wheel, his arms straight. Caelan braced herself, ready for the impact, as Ewan stamped on the brake. The back wheels shuddered, the nose of the car weaving as they came to a halt within touching distance of the car in front.

Ewan's hands were still tight around the wheel, his mouth open. Caelan forced a laugh.

'You've done the advanced driving course then?'

'Luckily. Fuck. I'm sorry.'

Caelan had already lifted her phone again. 'We've lost him,' she told Brady. 'Didn't see where he went.'

There was some muffled cursing. Eventually Brady said, 'Okay. We'll find him.'

Ewan flashed Caelan a tiny smile. 'Close call.'

She nodded, not laughing. Had Brady called off the man tailing them, given him a rollicking for being spotted? Or had he been sent by someone else? She had no idea what to believe. When she had agreed to speak to them about finding Lambourne, she had felt herself snared, trapped by her determination to track him down and make him pay. How she was going to do so, who was going to help or hinder her quest, she hadn't considered. Now the net was tightening, but around herself, not Lambourne. Could Brady be right about Adamson, Nasenby and Penrith? Was one of them behind the whole mess? Behind the scenes, someone was watching. Caelan knew she was vulnerable.

Maybe she should have brought the gun.

–

Suzanne Morgan's house was semi-detached, well maintained, with a neat front garden. It was an ex-council property, separated from the house next door by a shared concrete driveway, joined to the neighbour on the other side.

As they approached the house, Caelan saw the curtains in what she presumed was the living room twitch. There were two cars in the drive, and Caelan guessed the family liaison officer was still present. Sure enough, the door swung open and a woman stepped out, hurrying towards them.

'Ms Morgan has no comment to make. Now, you need to leave.'

Caelan took out her identification, held it up. 'You're the FLO?'

The woman nodded, blushing. 'DC Lonergan. Sorry, I wasn't expecting anyone. Is there news?'

'No problem. No, but we need to talk to Ms Morgan again. How is she?'

'Surviving, I'd say. You can imagine, it's been a massive blow.'

'We understand.' Caelan watched as another woman appeared in the open doorway.

'Who is it, Lorna?' she called. She rested a hand on the door frame, leaning against it as if the walk to the front door had tired her. No doubt it had. Grieving was an exhausting business, as Caelan knew. She shrugged off the pang that thumped her in the gut, raising an eyebrow at the FLO.

'Lorna Lonergan?'

Lonergan tossed her hair. 'Sounds like a character from Harry Potter, doesn't it?'

Suzanne Morgan was on her driveway now, stepping carefully, clutching the shapeless woollen sweater she wore tighter around her body.

'She's barely eating,' Lonergan confided in an undertone. 'Her mother wanted to come and stay, but Suzanne wouldn't hear of it.'

'Anything else to report?' Caelan asked. Lonergan shook her head.

'She cries a lot, won't speak to anyone apart from her parents.'

'No contact from Ronnie's father?' Caelan deliberately didn't say Lambourne's name.

'None that I'm aware of.' Lonergan turned away, took Morgan's arm. 'Come on, Suzanne, let's go inside, where it's warm. I'll make you a drink. These two officers need to ask you some questions.'

The living room was pleasant, with cream walls and an oatmeal carpet. There were two bookcases, one either side of the wall-mounted TV, each crammed with paperbacks. A blanket and a teddy bear were bundled in the corner of the sofa. Suzanne Morgan waved a listless hand towards two armchairs and said, 'Please, sit down.' On the settee, she tucked the blanket around her thighs, folding her hands in her lap. The teddy looked on, old and well loved. It had no doubt been a favourite of Ronnie's in his childhood, and was now bringing comfort to his mother.

Caelan took the chair furthest from Suzanne Morgan, unbuttoning her coat, relaxing her posture, wordlessly sending the message that she wasn't a threat. Ewan was silent, his face grave, his eyes on his shoes. Caelan knew she had to tread carefully. Although Suzanne Morgan appeared reasonably composed, one badly chosen word and the facade would crack. She had seen it happen many times.

'I'll put the kettle on,' said Lonergan.

Watching the FLO leave the room, Suzanne said, 'I'm sorry, I should have offered.'

Caelan shook her head. 'Don't worry, Ms Morgan.'

'Please, call me Suzanne.'

'Thank you.' Caelan introduced Ewan, then herself. 'I'm part of the team working to find the person who killed your son, Suzanne.' However gentle her voice, she knew the words would be hitting Ronnie's mother like hammer blows. Every nerve would be stretched to breaking, every sense fighting to deny the truth. Suzanne Morgan's son was dead, and her world was ending – Caelan could see it in her eyes, in her trembling lips and fluttering hands. She waited, giving the other woman a moment. 'We need to ask you some questions. Is that okay?'

A nod. 'Find the person who killed him, that's all I care about now.'

'We'll do everything we can.'

Suzanne lifted her gaze, met Caelan's for the first time. 'I know you will.'

Caelan nodded, the naked emotion in the other woman's eyes knocking her off balance. She took a breath, steadied herself. *Don't think about Nicky.*

'Firstly, I know this will be painful and I'm sorry to have to ask, but has Ronnie's father contacted you?'

The impact was immediate. Suzanne's nostrils flared, her hands clenched around the blanket. 'No. No, he hasn't. You know who he is, what he did?' Caelan nodded. 'Well then. Why would he? If there's one thing Seb knows how to do, it's look after himself. Ronnie's...' She choked on the name, tried again. 'Ronnie's death won't change that.'

Suzanne's words were understandably bitter, but her tone was resigned. Her ex-husband was irrelevant to her, no more worthy of her attention than a housefly. Her son and his death was all she could see, and who could blame her? Her grief had a presence in the room so urgent and real that Caelan almost believed she could see it. A grey haze, all-consuming. She had to ask her questions, and she knew they were going to hurt. No amount of empathy was going to ease Suzanne Morgan's pain. Finding the person responsible for her son's death and bringing them to justice was the only comfort Caelan could offer.

'Do you know if Ronnie's father had contacted him recently?'

Suzanne's eyes widened, her hands worrying a thread on the edge of the blanket. 'I don't think so.'

'Would Ronnie have told you if he had?'

'Well, I… Ronnie was at an age where he didn't tell me everything. When he went to uni, had girlfriends… I wouldn't have wanted to know.'

'You're saying it's possible he *had* spoken to his father?' Caelan didn't allow any impatience to colour her tone.

'I'm saying… I'm saying he might have done, but I doubt it.' Suzanne pressed her lips together, clearly unhappy with the idea.

'Did Ronnie have accounts on Facebook or Twitter? Instagram? We couldn't find any.'

'Do you have his phone?' Suzanne asked. Caelan nodded. 'Need it to find who he's been speaking to, I suppose. No, he didn't have Facebook, or any of that.'

'Because he changed his name, his identity?'

'Can you blame him? After the child died, people hated us. We had to move, more than once. Ronnie was beaten up every time he left the house; my car was vandalised. Bricks through our windows, threats. Then the fire… We were lucky to escape with our lives. And where was Seb? Not here protecting us, that's for sure.' She stifled a sob. 'Seb's to blame for Ronnie's death. I told him he'd kill us in the end.'

Lonergan came back into the room with a tray. She went to Suzanne first, held out a mug and wrapped the other woman's fingers around it. Caelan and Ewan smiled their thanks as Lonergan gave them their drinks, then sat unobtrusively in the corner.

Caelan waited until Suzanne had composed herself and was sipping her tea before asking, 'How do you mean, Seb would kill you?'

'His friends, the people he knew. When we first met, he had a job, a real job. Then he started turning up with loads of cash, a new car, expensive jewellery for me. I'm not stupid, I knew he couldn't be buying all that on a labourer's wage. He laughed at me, told me no one was getting hurt. Then... Well, someone did.'

Caelan nodded. 'His GBH conviction.'

'When he came out of prison, he wanted to see Ronnie, though I'd told him our relationship was over. I didn't want Seb in Ronnie's life, not really, but he wanted to see his dad. You might not believe me considering what's happened, but Seb was wonderful with Ronnie when he was around.'

'I do believe you,' Caelan said softly.

Suzanne gave a tremulous smile. 'Bless you. I begged him to change his ways, for Ronnie's sake. He couldn't – he was in too deep, liked the lifestyle too much. I never saw him as a kidnapper, though.' She attempted a laugh. 'Shows what I know.'

Caelan had to ask. 'Were you surprised to hear what he had done?'

'That he'd murdered an innocent boy? I was horrified. I couldn't... There's a part of me that still doesn't believe it. And yet... he did, didn't he?' She stared at Caelan, her eyes wide. 'Kidnap, murder. A ten-year-old child. They said he killed a police officer too.'

Caelan swallowed. 'He did.'

Suzanne frowned. 'I'm sorry. Did you know her?'

'We'd met. Suzanne, why do you think Ronnie was in London? Did he tell you he was coming home?'

Her lips trembled. 'No, he didn't. Never breathed a word.'

'Is it possible he'd arranged to meet his father?'

'Like I said, I don't know, he wouldn't have said. He knew how I felt about Seb, but... Seb and I were divorced. I'd removed him from my life completely, and I've never regretted it. Ronnie, though, he couldn't do that. Seb was still his father, however much Ronnie might want it not to be the case. Their bond would always be there.'

Caelan crossed her legs, drank some tea. 'There were no traces of any contact in Ronnie's emails, his phone records. What about a letter? Did Seb have this address?'

'Not as far as I know, but Seb knows so many people, he might have heard Ronnie had gone to university up in Lincoln, and traced him there. I don't know where Seb's been hiding, but I'm sure some of his old friends stayed in touch.'

Making a mental note to ask Brady if Ronnie's flat in Lincoln had been searched, though she knew it should have been, Caelan asked, 'Can I see Ronnie's room, please, Suzanne?'

She sniffed, gave a faint nod. 'Though I'm not sure what you're expecting to find. It's already been searched.'

'Thank you.'

As Caelan stood, Ewan met her eyes, and she nodded. Leading the way up the stairs, she heard Lonergan talking to Suzanne, her voice quiet, soothing.

'You didn't ask her about Walker,' said Ewan.

'You think I should?'

'I suppose she'd have mentioned it if he'd contacted her.'

'I should check. Thanks, Ewan.'

He beamed, and Caelan grinned back. She'd intended to ask, had more questions for Suzanne Morgan, but why not let Ewan think he'd helped?

They reached a square landing with three doors leading off it. One door stood ajar and Ewan, standing nearest, poked his head around it. 'Bathroom.'

Caelan reached for the handle of the door closest to her. Double bed with a white duvet cover patterned with embroidered red hearts. Suzanne's room. Quietly Caelan closed the door, opened the next.

Ronnie's room was square, the pale grey walls dotted with specks of Blu Tack where posters had been removed. The double bed had been stripped to the mattress; a pair of smart black shoes were gathering dust beneath a battered desk. Caelan stood in the doorway, searching for details. The sleeve of a white shirt caught in the door of the wardrobe. The corner of a photograph frame visible behind one of the navy-blue curtains. She moved closer. Sebastian Lambourne grinned up at her, Ronnie, aged about eight laughing in his father's arms. She picked up the frame, studied the photograph. She remembered Lambourne as she had last seen him, running past her, Nicky's blood dripping from his sleeve. The father. The killer. Could he be both? Many people were.

Ewan stepped towards her. 'Is that him?'

'Lambourne, yes.'

'He looks… ordinary. Normal.' He screwed up his face. 'I mean…'

Caelan replaced the photograph. 'He is.' She turned, her eyes scanning the room again. A flat pillow under the bed. Euro coins heaped on a bookshelf. It felt empty, forgotten, as though Ronnie had been absent for years. What was she looking for? She had no idea. All the obvious places would have been searched already.

'I've been sitting in here sometimes.' Suzanne Morgan was in the doorway, Lonergan pulling an apologetic face over her shoulder. 'Ronnie didn't spend much time in this house, but this was still his room. I know it sounds stupid...'

'It doesn't.' Caelan stepped closer, touched Suzanne's shoulder. The woman gave a faint smile, wrapping her arms around her body. Tears filled her eyes as she crossed the room and picked up the photograph of Lambourne and Ronnie.

'He had a picture of me in his room at uni, one of my parents, but not his father. He left this one here.' She touched a fingertip to her son's laughing face. 'Seb was stupid. He threw all this away.'

'Did you know Glen Walker?' Caelan asked.

'Glen?' Suzanne moved to the bed, sat, dropped the photograph onto the mattress beside her. 'I met him, yes. He came to the house occasionally when Seb lived with us.'

'What did you think of him?'

'Honestly? He made me uncomfortable.'

'How do you mean?'

'He was polite, pleasant, but as though it was a huge effort. As if he was playing a part, putting on a mask.'

'He frightened you.'

Suzanne met Caelan's eyes. 'Yes. I told Seb I didn't want him in the house, especially not near Ronnie. He was never violent, never lost his temper, but the threat was there, if you know what I mean.'

'Thank you. Do you know where Glen lived?'

'Back then?' Suzanne's brow wrinkled. 'I can't remember, but I've an old address book in my room. I'll have a look if you think it's important.'

'We're trying to find him.' Caelan hesitated, wondering if she should continue. 'Glen Walker was seen speaking to Ronnie recently.'

Suzanne stared. 'Ronnie saw Glen? I don't understand.'

'We think it was a chance meeting, not prearranged.'

Suzanne stood quickly, seized Caelan's arm. 'He's dangerous. Find him.'

'We don't know if—'

'Glen hurts people, you understand? He enjoys it. He used to fight, bare-knuckle boxing. Even Seb was wary of him, GBH conviction or not. He used to say Glen was like a vicious dog, needed keeping on a chain.'

Caelan looked down at Suzanne's hand clutching her arm. 'When was the last time you saw him?'

Suzanne moved away. 'Years ago. I don't understand why Ronnie would talk to him.'

'You've been very helpful, Suzanne. Thank you.'

'You'll keep me informed? If Glen's involved…'

'We will, through DC Lonergan.'

'I'll have a look for that address. I'm not sure why I kept it; it's not as though I wanted to send Glen a birthday card.' She looked at Caelan, her mouth twisting. 'Maybe I guessed that one day someone would come looking for him.'

24

Brady's phone went to voicemail, but she called back a few minutes later. 'Those clowns who were supposed to intercept the van driver? They lost him. No idea how, but they managed it. Bloody useless.'

'He probably switched the number plates again,' said Caelan. 'It doesn't matter.'

'We're trying to track him through various cameras, but as you can imagine, we're stretched pretty thin. Have you seen him again?'

'No. Listen, we have an old address for Glen Walker.' Caelan dictated it.

'We'll do some digging,' said Brady.

'Are you still focusing resources on Ronnie's murder?'

There was a pause. 'Why wouldn't we be? We don't know who did it.'

'I thought after our conversation with Elizabeth Beckett...'

Caelan heard a door close on Brady's end of the line. When she spoke again, Brady's voice was little more than a whisper. 'We're continuing to run the investigation exactly as we were before, regardless of who we might or might not suspect. One, we need evidence, and two, we need to keep our suspicions to ourselves, as you know.'

'But if one of the people we discussed earlier is involved...'

'You're continuing your investigations, as are myself and DCI Achebe. We'll get them, Caelan.' She cleared her throat. 'Are you heading to the Wheatsheaf now?'

'When I've been home. When I'm ready.'

'Time for one of your disguises?' Caelan could hear the smile in Brady's voice.

'When I went there as myself, I was shot at, so yeah, I thought it'd be a good idea.'

'Don't forget your appointment tonight.'

'With some burly uniforms?'

'That's the one. Remember, we need it to look real.'

'Fine.'

'And Caelan?'

'Ma'am?'

'Take the gun.'

–

Caelan Small walked into apartment 135, but the woman who exited her bedroom an hour later was a different person. Her blonde hair fell past her shoulders, her make-up carefully applied to highlight blue eyes and full lips. Her cheekbones were sharper, her eyebrows pencilled to appear a different shape, her face seeming longer, wider. As she entered the living room, Ewan gaped, his eyes wide.

'You look…'

'I hate these clothes,' said Caelan, tugging on the waistband of the tight denim jeans she wore. Under a leather jacket, a loose black T-shirt hid the gun at her hip. 'Are you ready?'

Ewan was still staring. 'I wouldn't have recognised you.'

Caelan laughed. 'That's the idea.'

'Until you spoke… It's amazing.'

'It's my job. When we get to the Wheatsheaf, I'll change my voice too.' She heaved an oversized PVC handbag onto her shoulder, pushed her feet into a pair of black spike-heeled boots. 'God, these shoes are a nightmare.'

'Difficult to run in.'

'I'm hoping I won't need to. Anyway, I have these.' Caelan opened the bag to reveal a pair of canvas pumps. 'Here.' She handed Ewan a beanie hat and a pair of glasses. 'Clear lenses. It's not much of a disguise, but it'll have to do.'

Ewan took them, put them on.

'You want me to come into the pub then? I wondered if you'd want dropping off nearby.'

'No, come in with me, please. You're going to be my boyfriend, but don't be surprised if I talk to everyone but you.'

Ewan grinned. 'I'm hurt.'

Caelan's face was serious. 'Hopefully not.'

–

They left the car a few streets away, making it to the pub without incident. Caelan took Ewan's hand as they walked. She squeezed, feeling the tension in his body. 'Don't worry. We won't stay long.' He looked down at her with a smile. Guilt rose in her throat as she remembered the previous day, the danger she had exposed him to. 'You don't have to come in, Ewan.'

'We're here now.'

'We'll have a row, you can storm off. I don't mind.'

'No way.' As they neared the pub, one of the men standing outside dropped his cigarette end into the gutter and disappeared through the door. 'Do you think he's a lookout?'

'Possibly. Don't worry.' Anxiety clawed at Caelan's belly. 'Remember, we're a couple calling into a pub for a drink.'

As they passed, the other men stared, their eyes hardening. Regretting coming here already, Caelan pushed open the door and stepped onto the dark wooden floorboards inside. As she remembered, the bar ran the length of the room, with tables, chairs and a couple of booths on the opposite wall. Two ornate chandeliers hung from the ceiling, doing little to cheer the place or lighten the oppressive atmosphere. At the bar two men stood, their heads close together, deep in discussion. One was the man who had been outside as they approached. At a table in the far corner, two more men sat with pints of beer, their eyes on a TV fastened to the wall above their heads. Behind the bar, a young man with slicked-back blond hair was polishing glasses with a white cloth. Other than Caelan, there were no women in the place.

'Shall we sit down?' Her heart thumping, Caelan led Ewan to the booth nearest the main door, knowing it was the only easily accessible way out of the building. There was a back door, but to reach it they'd have to venture behind the bar.

'I'll get the drinks.' Ewan strolled to the bar, Caelan pleased that his nervousness wasn't obvious. The barman looked him up and down, his expression bordering on a sneer.

'Not seen you in here before,' he said.

'We were passing, fancied a drink.'

The barman's face didn't change. 'Right. What can I get you?'

Ewan scanned the beer pumps. 'Pint and a half of Christie's, please.'

'Christie's is off.'

'Mackay's then.'

'That's off too.' Folding his arms, the barman curled his lip. 'Maybe you should find another pub.'

Caelan got to her feet, approached the bar, pressed herself against Ewan's side. 'How about spirits?' She smiled at the barman, who sniffed.

'We've a single malt. It's expensive, though.'

'My favourite kind. Thank you.'

The barman inclined his head. Caelan poked a finger into Ewan's ribs and he moved away to sit in the booth. Caelan hoped he'd keep his mouth shut. A wrong word could get them both beaten up, or worse. Her gaze strayed to the closed door on the back wall, between the doors leading to the toilets. The storeroom. She had no desire to see the inside of it again.

The barman plonked two shot glasses in front of her. 'Twenty quid.'

'Twenty? For two drinks?'

He leered. 'Is there a problem?' The two men at the other end of the bar sniggered.

Caelan turned to Ewan. 'No. No problem.' He hurried over, handed her a folded note. She smoothed it out, passed it to the barman, who grinned, exposing perfect teeth. 'Cheers, darling.'

Caelan lifted one of the glasses, the smell making her stomach somersault. She couldn't bear whisky, but she knew she had to drink it. She took a sip, swallowed, then threw as much down her throat as she could. The barman laughed. 'Hope you've brought plenty of money, mate,' he called to Ewan, who smiled, took his own drink, said nothing.

'Nice place,' Caelan said.

The barman picked up his cloth again. 'No it isn't.'

Another sip of whisky, her stomach readying itself to force the lot back up. She held her breath, praying it would stay down. The barman watched her closely, one corner of his mouth lifting.

'Enjoying your drink?'

'Yes thanks.' Fluffing her hair with one hand, Caelan set the other on her hip. 'Brendan said the Wheatsheaf was worth a visit.' It was a guess, a shot in the dark, but it got a reaction. The two men sitting at the table fell silent, while the barman glared at her.

'Brendan?' he said.

'Brendan Milne.'

'Never heard of him.'

'Really? I'm sure he said the Wheatsheaf.' Caelan lifted the glass again. Waited.

One of the men from the end of the bar sauntered up, pint in hand. He wore a slim-fitting suit, his hair clipped close to his head, his beard neatly trimmed. He narrowed his eyes at Ewan, treated himself to a gawp at Caelan's cleavage before saying, 'How do you know Brendan?'

Caelan thought quickly. 'Friend of a friend. You?'

He bared his teeth. 'Prick owes me five hundred quid.'

'Wouldn't count on getting it back.'

He set his empty glass on the bar, his movements slow, deliberate. Taking a pace closer to Caelan, he pushed her face towards her. 'Where is he?'

Feeling Ewan tense beside her, Caelan trod on his toe. 'Where's who?'

'Brendan. Brendan fucking Milne.'

Caelan fought the urge to step back, to run. 'Brendan's dead.'

The man laughed. 'Fuck off.'

'If I were you, I'd wave goodbye to my money.'

He stared at her, then at Ewan. 'This true?'

Ewan lifted his shoulders. 'It's what we've heard.'

The barman said, 'Fucker. He owes me too.'

'Never lend Brendan money.' Caelan forced down another sip of whisky, the burn of it hitting her throat, triggering another wave of nausea.

'Lend? Gambling debts the bastard never paid,' the barman spat. The other man frowned a warning at him.

'Another mate of his used to drink in here too,' Caelan said. Her stomach churned, a combination of whisky and fear. 'Glen Walker. Heard of him?'

There was a silence. Caelan worried she'd pushed too far, too soon. The door opened and three more men walked in, trailing the smell of cigarette smoke. They grouped behind Caelan and Ewan, effectively preventing them from leaving the bar.

'We might recognise the name,' said the barman. 'Doesn't mean we know him.'

One of the newcomers moved close to Caelan, his breath hot on the back of her neck. 'Why are you asking?'

She stood her ground, knowing that if he lifted his hand, if he touched her, he would find the gun. Her cover would be blown, and she and Ewan would be lucky to escape with their lives.

Or she would have to use the weapon herself. It would be eight against two, and unarmed, she didn't fancy their chances.

She relaxed her body, seeing Ewan clench his jaw as another man stood nose to nose with him.

'Walker killed my friend's kid,' Caelan said. 'Bet he didn't tell you that.'

The man behind her grabbed her chin and yanked her head back. Caelan held her ground, not giving him the satisfaction of seeing her flinch. A quick sideways glance showed her that Ewan was surrounded by sneering, mocking faces. Her breathing quickened, adrenalin coursing through her. She could escape the man's grasp easily, have him in a heap on the floor immediately, but then the rest of them would be on her. They might have knives, other weapons. There were plenty of glasses and bottles to hand.

'What kid?' His mouth was beside her ear, his lips brushing her skin. Caelan was aware of his other hand moving, and panic rose in her throat. If he touched her breast, her skin, she would have to act. His fingers dug into her face. 'Did you hear me? What kid?'

'His name was Charlie Flynn. It was all over the news.'

His right hand brushed her arm, the side of her face. He tightened his grip on her jaw, turning her head so she was forced to look at him. His breath was hot, stinking of beer and fags, his groin pressed against her backside. Two of the others moved forward, circling like sharks. Their smiles, the blankness of their eyes – she could read their minds. She had entered their territory, spoken to them as an equal, and now she would pay.

There were rules about using firearms. In this situation, however, Caelan was going to ignore them. Her left hand flew up, breaking the hold the man behind her had on her hair. He snarled, leaping forward as she pulled the gun out, only to fall back, stunned, as he realised what she was holding. Scowling, she turned on them. She didn't raise the gun. She didn't need to. The men were frozen, still as children playing musical statues. They stared at her, the shock so transparent she had to laugh.

'Not so clever now, are you? Not such big men.' She stood, one hand on her hip, the gun pointed at the floorboards. 'Still going to grope me, push me around?' She marched up to the man who had taken hold of her, chin jutting. 'Well? Are we still talking? Maybe I should grab you by the bollocks, mate. See how you like it.'

He swallowed. 'I'm sorry, love, it was—'

'It was you thinking you could do what you wanted to me, thinking you have a right to touch me, to speak to me like shit. Well, now we're equal.' He stared at her, his brown eyes wide, lips pressed together. 'Answer my question. Do you know Glen Walker?'

He glanced at the barman. 'Like he said—'

'He? What's his name?'

His tongue came out, moistened his lips. 'I don't know.'

Caelan smiled. 'And I don't believe you. Tell me.'

'Kane. Like Kane said, we've heard the name. He's been in here.'

The man he'd called Kane groaned, shutting up when Caelan turned her glare on him.

'When? When was he here?'

'Couple of years ago?'

Caelan took a pace towards him. 'Try again.'

Another anxious look at the barman. 'Last week.'

'Better. Do you know where he lives?'

'No. Honestly, I—'

'Near King's Cross,' the barman, Kane, whispered. Caelan looked at him. He gave a quick nod of his head. 'He mentioned the trains waking him early in the morning.'

'Address?'

'No idea. I swear.'

Caelan nodded, believing him. 'Now, my friend and I are going to leave. I want you all to forget we were ever here. If you don't, if you speak to anyone about what happened here tonight, I'll make sure Glen Walker knows you were the ones who told us where he lives. I'm not sure he'll be pleased, are you?' Shaking heads. 'If you try to discover who we are, if you seek us out, Glen Walker will be told who grassed, I promise you. Forget our faces, and our voices. Forget I had a gun.' She smiled at Ewan, led the way to the door. 'And next time you have strangers in your pub, I'd advise you to remember your manners. Have a good evening.'

–

'That was...' Ewan managed to say as they ran for the car.

'Fucking scary?'

'Amazing, I was going to say.'

'No, it was unforgivable.' Caelan's hands were clammy, the enormity of what she'd done hitting her as she limped along in the high-heeled boots.

'You had no choice.'

'I had the option to withdraw. We should have left as soon as we realised what sort of place it was. Nasenby did warn me.'

'I'm sorry I was no help.'

'Help? What were you going to do, take seven of them on?'

'Well, no.'

'No.'

As they reached the car, Ewan popped the locks with the remote. They threw themselves inside, Caelan tearing off her blonde wig as Ewan started the engine.

'Where to?' He wrenched the gearstick, flicked on the head-lights.

'Let's get away from here. I don't know after that.'

'I thought you'd say King's Cross.'

She shook her head. 'Not tonight.'

'Those lads won't say anything.'

'I hope not. I'd be in shitloads of trouble if Nasenby found out I'd drawn my gun on a gang of civilians.'

'But you didn't, or not really. You didn't threaten them with it.'

'Not how he'll see it. I had a firearm; the threat was there, regardless of what I did with it.' They were speeding towards the City. Caelan rubbed her eyes, forgetting the thick make-up she wore. What should she do? Brady would need to know what the barman had said about where Walker was living. He might have been lying, saying anything to get her and the gun out of his pub, but they needed to follow it up.

'Let's head for Southwark,' said Caelan.

'Why?' Ewan indicated, changed lanes.

'Taking the long way home.' She allowed her head to fall against the headrest, closed her eyes. They were going to arrest her tonight, and after her actions in the Wheatsheaf, they should. A headache pushed against her temples, exhaustion clouding her brain.

'Caelan.' Ewan nudged her. 'Caelan, your phone.'

She forced her eyes open. Had she been asleep? Blinking, she stared out through the windscreen, trying to get her bearings. Fumbling in her bag for her phone, she dropped it in the footwell, had to bend to retrieve it, the gun digging into her side. She checked the screen.

Sam Clifton.

The phone stopped ringing. Caelan stabbed at the screen, listened to Sam's cheery recorded message.

'Change of plan, Ewan. We need to go to Sam's flat.'

'Sam's? In Battersea?'

'Please.'

Responding to the urgency in her voice, he stamped on the accelerator. 'What's the problem?'

'I don't know, but Sam never calls me, not any more.'

'You're worried?'

'After Brendan Milne turned up with a gun?'

'You think—'

'Let's just get there, Ewan. Please.'

He nodded. 'Wouldn't it be better to see if they can send someone else? There must be officers closer than we are.'

'Sam called me.'

'Or someone else did, using his phone. What if it's a trap?'

'It's a risk I'll have to take. Please, Ewan.'

'All right.'

The roads were quiet, allowing them to make decent time, cutting through Southwark and Vauxhall, arriving in Battersea in little more than half an hour. As they approached Sam's building, Caelan sent Brady a text explaining where she was. If there were officers waiting at her flat to arrest her, they would have to wait.

Rain was falling, had been for some time judging by the puddles. Caelan swung out of the car, the canvas pumps she'd changed into soaked as soon as her feet hit the gutter. Ewan had parked around the corner from Sam's building so they could approach quietly, on foot.

The grassy area between the blocks of flats was deserted tonight, most of the windows in the surrounding buildings in darkness. Caelan's hand strayed down to her hip, touched the handle of the gun. She lifted her face, rain hammering her cheeks, a biting wind cutting through her leather jacket, her black T-shirt already soaked.

'No lights on,' said Ewan.

'Let's go. Stay behind me.'

Moving quickly, they climbed the stairs to the third floor, treading as softly as they could on the concrete. The thump of Caelan's heart echoed in her ears. Sam's front door was closed, the hallway beyond it dark. Tugging her sleeve over her fingers, Caelan reached for the door handle with her left hand, gripping the gun in her right. Silence. The door wasn't locked, opening easily, without a sound. She peered into the murky hall. No sound, no movement. Ewan was close behind her, and she reached out, laying her hand on his arm, asking him to wait. She took a breath, stepped forward. Her damp shoe squeaked on the laminate floor, the sound as shocking as a gunshot in the silence. She froze, waited. No one moved. The flat was cold, quiet. A smell in the air – not blood, but familiar. Caelan shut it out, fear hurtling through her veins.

'Sam? Sammy?'

No reply. Caelan cursed, strode forward, all attempts at stealth forgotten.

The kitchen was untidy, the sink filled with unwashed pots, the bin ready to overflow. No Sam. At the end of the hallway, the living room was empty too, the TV turned off, a half-drunk bottle of beer on the windowsill. Caelan saw it, frowned.

'Where the hell is he?'

She turned, retraced her steps. There were two more doors leading off the hallway, both closed. Caelan pushed open the nearest. A tiny bathroom, with a shower cubicle, a sink and a toilet.

No Sam.

She stared at the final closed door, gave a shuddering sigh. Ewan touched her sleeve.

'Do you want me to go in first?'

'It's okay.' She glanced up at him. 'Thanks, though.'

A step forward. The dread coiling in her stomach climbed higher, knotting around her throat. Slowly she took hold of the handle.

The stench hit her like a punch, the sight of Sam's ruined body smashing into her brain a second later.

He hung from the light fitting, his tongue protruding from his mouth like a hideous swollen tumour. A pool of urine and other stinking fluids soaked the carpet beneath him, his bare feet a couple of inches from the floor. A wooden chair lay on its side nearby, his mobile phone face down by the puddle of waste.

'Sammy,' Caelan heard herself say. She hadn't known she was going to speak, the sound escaping involuntarily. She was aware of Ewan moving to stand behind her, his hands gripping her shoulders. 'Jesus, Sam.'

'Come away, Caelan,' Ewan urged. 'Please. We can't help him now.'

She made a sound between a sob and a shout. 'I didn't know...'

Ewan gently pulled her arm, and Caelan allowed him to lead her away.

25

South Harrow police station was quiet, offices empty, computers left to idle for the night. Tim Achebe met them at the front desk again, holding his hands out to Caelan, grasping hers for a second before releasing them.

'They're upstairs,' he said, turning to lead the way.

'How could this happen, Tim? Why wasn't Sam protected?'

'He refused to leave his flat. We didn't realise…'

'Wasn't it being watched?'

'Yes, but…'

'But?'

'We're still trying to determine what happened.'

'In other words, someone fucked up.'

Achebe was silent. Their footsteps clattered, echoing in the wide, empty corridor. Caelan's hands were bunched into fists, her chest tight as she marched along. Another death, another wasted life. Sam had been floundering, lost in a mess he was not responsible for, blamed and ostracised. Caelan knew she could have reached out to him, offered help or a place to stay. Once again, she was too late.

The incident room was silent, the blinds closed, the lights turned off except for in one corner, where Elizabeth Beckett and Adele Brady stood waiting. Brady's arms were folded, Beckett's face grim.

'Do you want to explain what the fuck's been happening?' Caelan heard herself bellow as she approached them. The fury that had been building since she'd received Brady's call erupted, the fear and frustration of the past few days raging.

Brady uncrossed her arms, took a step forward. Held up her hands. 'Caelan, we understand you're upset—'

'Upset? Fucking upset? Sam had already been attacked; now you've allowed him to be killed.'

'Calm down,' ordered Beckett. Her words, her demeanour infuriated Caelan further.

'Let me guess – no one saw who went into his flat. We've no idea who's behind this, or who's going to have a bullet in their head this time tomorrow.' She glared from Beckett to Brady, wanting to grab them by the shoulders and shake them, to scream in their faces.

'You're right, Caelan,' Brady said gently. 'We're struggling.'

Caelan's legs were weak, tears blinding her. She turned away, scrubbing her eyes again with her fingertips, her cheeks wet, the make-up she had applied so carefully smudged and ruined. She rounded on them. 'You can't believe he killed himself?'

Beckett and Brady exchanged a glance. Caelan saw it, wondered what it meant. 'We're keeping an open mind,' Brady said neutrally.

'There's no need. It's another murder.' Caelan tried to match Brady's bland tone, but found it impossible. She wanted to rant, to rail against their passivity, their ineptness. Brady's face reddened, but her voice was measured.

'Scene-of-crimes officers are at Sam's flat, collecting what they can for—'

'Analysis. Because forensics have been so helpful so far.' Realising her fists were clenched, Caelan relaxed them. 'What about Walker, the address Suzanne Morgan gave us?'

'He's not there,' said Achebe, stepping forward to stand beside Brady. 'We've had no more calls from people claiming to have seen him, though we'll put the appeal out again, mentioning that he might live in the King's Cross area.'

Caelan nodded. She'd told Brady on the phone what she'd found out in the Wheatsheaf, leaving out the part involving the gun.

'Walker's wandering around London and you believe Sam's death was suicide?' She couldn't keep the bitterness out of her voice. Beckett frowned a warning, her eyes on Achebe.

'Tim, let's go to your office,' said Brady. 'We need to discuss tomorrow's press conference.'

Achebe looked like he might protest, but then followed Brady out of the room. As the door closed behind them, Beckett turned to Caelan.

'You need to calm down,' she repeated. 'This situation can only be resolved if we work together.'

'I thought you were arresting me?'

'We've had a rethink, in light of this evening's events.'

I bet you have. 'Another body, you mean?'

Beckett nodded. 'You know as well as I do that if Sam was murdered, whoever did it will have left no trace of themselves. This is a professional, someone with access to firearms and information, someone who Sam would open his front door to.'

'Unless they forced their way in.'

Beckett waved a dismissive hand. 'I'm talking about one of Sam's former colleagues, Caelan, as you know. One of *your* colleagues.' She looked at Ewan. 'I'm going to trust you, Mr Davies. Caelan will need your help.'

Ewan moved closer to Caelan. 'I'll do what I can,' he said.

'Good. I'll speak freely. We've been conducting extremely discreet investigations into the finances and communications of your three friends, Caelan. We've found nothing untoward.

As you'll appreciate, being allowed to do so hasn't been easy.' Beckett reached behind her, held up a thick sheaf of papers.

'You've found nothing to suggest that Richard, Michael or Ian is involved?'

'Not so far.' Beckett frowned, frustration clear on her face. 'Detective Chief Superintendent Brady and I have also reviewed the financial records of Charlie Flynn's parents, to see whether a ransom payment could have been made that they didn't tell us about. Again, we found nothing. The Flynns had plenty of debt but no cash, at least not until they sold their house, which as you know was after Charlie died.'

'What happened to their assets after their deaths?'

'There were still debts outstanding, credit cards and so on. Their parents inherited the rest, but there wasn't much.'

'We're sure they killed themselves?'

Beckett pursed her lips. 'As much as we're sure of anything.'

'In other words, no.'

There was a silence. Beckett lifted a hand to her throat, straightened the collar of her blouse.

'We're going to follow Ian Penrith and Michael Nasenby. I won't tell you who's on board, but rest assured, if they blow their nose, we'll know about it.'

'How reassuring. What about Adamson?' Caelan waited, soon realising what Beckett was going to ask. She shook her head. 'No.'

'You're the best we have.'

'I'm not doing it. I thought my job was to look for Walker and Lambourne?'

'It was. Now Sam Clifton's dead. Even if Walker killed him, he isn't acting alone. He has no reason to kill Sam.'

'Unless he's destroying everyone who was part of the Charlie Flynn case.'

'You're not even convincing yourself.'

Caelan was quiet, conceding the point. 'I've worked with Richard before. He'll know I'm there.'

Beckett shook her head, unconcerned. 'No he won't.'

'I've tracked Walker as far as King's Cross. Let me find him.'

'You'd be wasted.'

'No, I'd be wasted following Richard. You involved him, asked him to come to Egypt. You trusted him.'

'Before this, yes, I did.'

Beckett went to the nearest desk, pulled out a chair. Ewan hurried over to help, passing Caelan a seat before settling into one himself. Beckett laced her fingers together on the tabletop, looking at Caelan over her glasses.

'Who briefed you before you went into the house where Charlie Flynn was being held?'

'Ian Penrith.'

'Because it was Ian's operation,' Beckett said slowly. She allowed her hands to fall onto her lap, frowning, considering the possible implications.

'Ian who's been trying to get rid of me since I landed back in the UK.'

'Who had you been reporting to during your time hunting Lambourne undercover?'

'Michael. We'd known for a while that Lambourne was controlling parts of London. The idea was to find people we could turn, who'd be willing to testify against him.'

'But you never found any.'

'No. People didn't want to talk about him at all.'

'Because they were frightened?'

'Possibly. He never visited any of the places he owned, left the managers to run them. It was like his staff knew nothing about him. As though he was a myth.'

'A myth,' Beckett repeated thoughtfully.

'If you're serious about investigating Ian, Michael and Richard, why aren't we looking into their movements properly? Finding out where they were when Ronnie was killed, where they are tonight?'

'You know why. We've got to be careful.'

'But people keep dying.'

Beckett ignored her. 'It was difficult enough to access the information we have already. If we start running the number plates of our senior officers, asking them to provide alibis, it'll soon become obvious what we're up to.'

'Not if we're careful, if we cover our tracks.'

Beckett barked out a laugh. 'Caelan, we're not MI5.'

'No, but sometimes we're not far off. Our work is clandestine, our operations hidden. We keep secrets.'

'Granted. That doesn't mean we can now come out all guns blazing. Discretion is imperative if we don't want to alarm the person we're looking for.'

'Yeah, because they've only killed three people so far. Who knows what rampage they'd go on if they were alarmed?'

'I understand you're frustrated—'

Caelan slammed her hand on the table. 'Frustrated? I knew Sam, had worked with him for years. I watched while he was destroyed, both by the media and by the passivity of the people who should have protected him.'

'People like me and Chief Superintendent Brady?'

'You said it, not me. You could have released a statement, said Sam was blameless. You didn't, and the media ripped him to shreds. He could have been given a new identity, a new start. Instead you left him in a shitty flat, drinking himself to death.' As Caelan said the words, they triggered a memory.

'What are you thinking?' Beckett was watching her face.

'The first meeting, when Michael asked me to follow Ronnie.' Caelan stared past Beckett, seeing nothing. 'Ian said something about Sam.' She looked at Ewan. 'Can you remember?'

'About falling in front of a bus?'

Caelan snapped her fingers. 'He said, "if he stumbles in front of a lorry or a train one day, well, wouldn't that be tragic".'

Beckett had pulled a notepad out of her bag and was scribbling in it. 'You're sure he meant Sam?'

'Definitely.'

'Ian was saying he believed Sam to be at risk?'

'I don't know. At first I thought he was saying anything he could think of to provoke a reaction. Now, though… I told Sam that Ian had implied I was to blame for Charlie's death. Sam said Ian was full of shit.'

Beckett looked up from her notes. 'When was this?'

'The day Ronnie was killed. I went to tell Sam, to warn him.'

'So you thought he was in danger too?' Beckett's eyes burned into Caelan's.

'I didn't know. Now, when I look back at the conversation… Sam's reaction when I told him Ian had accused me of working for Lambourne was strange.'

'Strange? In what way?'

'He hunched his shoulders, curled up as though he was trying to protect himself. As though he didn't want to hear.'

'Not surprising. Who would want to hear a colleague being accused of corruption?'

'But he wasn't surprised. It was as though he was already aware of what I was saying but had deliberately put the knowledge out of his mind.' She hadn't considered it before, but now she replayed the scene with Sam in her head and knew she was right. Sam had known more, much more, than he'd admitted.

And now he was dead.

'Do you think Ian had spoken to Sam about you?' Beckett asked.

'I don't know.' Caelan pushed back her hair, frustrated. 'There's nothing concrete, it's all guesswork. What about Richard?'

'Adamson? Same as the others. No suspicious amounts of money received or any spending beyond his means, which would obviously be a bigger giveaway if he'd received cash illicitly. Why do you ask?'

'Because Penrith told him to follow me. I thought they could be working together. Adamson was on the scene when Ronnie was killed, and Brady said she thought he could have had time to do it. I'm not convinced, but...'

'It's been proved. Adamson did have time, if he was quick.'

'He wasn't out of breath when he...' Caelan closed her eyes. 'No, he was, slightly, but then he'd run the length of the underpass.'

Beckett sniffed. 'A matter of what? Twenty-five metres? Were you out of breath, having done the same?'

'No, but...' There was something else. How had Adamson seen her at the end of the underpass? She hadn't seen Ronnie lying there herself until she'd switched on her phone's torch. Adamson could possibly have seen a silhouette, and he'd known Caelan was heading that way, but... She lifted her chin. No. She wouldn't mention the thought to Beckett. She would speak to Adamson herself.

Beckett and Brady didn't have to know.

'I assume you're keeping the news of Sam's death quiet?' she asked instead.

'Trying to, though no doubt it'll come out soon enough. The press will have a field day when they find out someone's killed Sam. They'll probably be queueing to shake his murderer's hand.'

'What if I go and break the news to Michael, Ian and Richard?'

'See how they react, you mean? If anyone looks guilty?' Beckett thought about it, rubbing her chin. 'Okay. I could be making a mistake, but okay.'

'We're not able to follow normal lines of investigation, we can't find Glen Walker, especially since you won't let me go and look for him…'

Beckett sighed. 'How do you expect to find him, even if did I permit you to go to King's Cross?'

Caelan wrinkled her nose at Beckett's choice of word. 'Ask around, talk to people.'

'We don't have the time. We're going over the CCTV footage from both inside and outside King's Cross St Pancras Underground station again, now that we know Walker's living in the area. I'm hoping we spot him, get some idea of the direction he came from.'

'Which will also take time, lots of time.'

'A fact I'm only too aware of.' Beckett leaned back in her chair. 'Truth is, we've no idea how else to approach this. Walker knows how to disappear.'

'We could go back to the café. Walker may live in King's Cross, but we know he's spent time in Ealing,' Caelan said.

'We've had officers posted inside and around the café all day. No one's seen him.'

Caelan pursed her lips. 'What about Milne's flat?'

'What about it?'

'Is it empty?'

'There was a uniformed officer there earlier. I'm not sure. Why? Walker's never been there.'

'But we know he's spent time with Milne. He must know that Milne's dead, or at least missing. What about Milne's phone?'

'He didn't have one, at least not when he went to Sam Clifton's flat.'

'Which is impossible. Every small-time villain needs a mobile, don't they?'

'You'd think, but where is it?'

'Can I go to Milne's flat?'

'Why? Do you think the search team missed something?'

'No, but it makes no sense. Have we checked if Milne owned or rented any other property? A garage, another flat? A vehicle?'

'We have, but found nothing. He probably dealt in cash transactions, though, leaving no paper trail.'

'Someone was paying him to go to Sam, to ask about me. Where's the cash?'

'Maybe he was going to be paid after he'd done the job.'

Caelan blew out her cheeks. 'It's like searching for the invisible man. Invisible men.' Hadn't Penrith said the same?

'Which is no doubt the point, exactly what they were aiming for.'

'It doesn't tie in with Adamson, Nasenby or Penrith being involved either. Why would they pay Walker to talk to Sam?'

'To cover their tracks? Caelan, we can discuss this all night. The truth is, we're no nearer knowing who killed Ronnie Morgan. Let's focus on that crime first.'

'Which means we're back to finding Walker.'

Beckett gritted her teeth. 'I think I'll scream if I hear Walker's name again, unless it's followed by the words "is in custody".'

'So let me go and look for him. Let me do it my way.'

'Fine. But Caelan...' Beckett seemed to run out of steam. 'Never mind. Stay in touch.'

'Using the phone you gave me?'

'The safe phone, yes.'

Caelan pushed back her chair. 'I'll speak to you in the morning.'

'You're going home?'

As she and Ewan reached the door, Caelan turned back with a smile.

'I didn't say that.'

26

Richard Adamson lived in Kentish Town. Caelan stood on the pavement outside his building, hands on hips. It was long past midnight, but a light glowed in one of the windows of his flat.

'Are you sure you don't want me to come in?' said Ewan.

Caelan looked down at him in the driver's seat.

'No, it's fine. I won't be long.' He said nothing, obviously disappointed. She smiled. 'I need to speak to him alone, Ewan. You can go home if you want to.'

'What about the others? I bet you're not planning on waiting until the morning to speak to them?'

'I can get a taxi.'

'I'll wait.' He closed the window, giving her no opportunity to argue further.

Adamson's flat was on the ground floor of a shabby terraced property. Caelan approached the front door quietly, noting the four doorbells. Beside each one was a label with a name printed on it. She considered pressing Adamson's, but instead stepped away from the door, towards the window with the light on. She stood in the shadows, able to see in if she crouched. Inside, Adamson slumped on a brown leather sofa, his eyes closed. He wore pyjama bottoms, a white T-shirt and huge headphones, a bottle of lager cradled close to his chest. Caelan counted to three then hammered on the glass with her knuckles. Adamson leapt into the air, his headphones and beer bottle going flying.

He glared at her as he retrieved the bottle from the carpet. He approached the window and opened it a fraction.

'Good thing the bottle was empty. What the hell are you doing here, Caelan? Couldn't you have rung the bell?'

'I did, several times,' she lied.

Adamson sighed. 'What do you want?'

'To talk to you. I have news.'

He stared, realising she was serious. 'Give me a second.' He left the room.

The front door opened quickly and Adamson stood back, his eyes never leaving Caelan's face. Was he rattled, or concerned? She couldn't say.

In the living room, he hovered, shifting his feet as though nervous.

'Coffee?'

Caelan shook her head. 'Sit down, Richard. Let me tell you what's happened.'

He frowned, setting the headphones on the floor and curling into the corner of the sofa.

'What's going on, Caelan?'

She sat on the floor, her back against the wall, the window she'd watched him through above her head. Stretching out her legs, she kept her eyes on his.

'Richard, there's no easy way to say this. Sam died tonight.'

She watched his face working as he absorbed what she had said. She saw shock, disbelief, horror. If he'd known about Sam's death before she'd arrived, he was the best actor she'd ever seen.

'But…' he managed to say. 'How?'

'Depending on who you ask, suicide or murder. I found him hanging from a light fitting.' Caelan had to work hard to keep her voice level. She was being brusque, but she had to see how Adamson reacted. She had to push the image of Sam's body from her mind, get on with her job. There would be time later to think, to feel. She pushed herself to her feet, sat on the sofa, leaving a cushion free between herself and Adamson. He stared at her, hunched over as though he had stomach ache. He rubbed the palms of his hands over his cheeks. 'You found him? Was he at home?'

'Yes.'

'Why did you go there?'

'To ask what he's been hiding.'

Adamson screwed up his face. 'I don't understand.'

'Good. Then you're probably safe.' Caelan pushed off her shoes, pulled her legs up onto the sofa. 'Richard, listen. Ian's been accusing me of being corrupt, hasn't he? To you, to Nasenby, to anyone who would listen.'

'Like I said, I told him it was nonsense. I *know* you, Caelan.'

'I want to talk to you about Ronnie Morgan's death. We're both under suspicion.'

He raised his eyebrows. 'Both?'

Caelan explained what Brady had said. 'They've proved that if you ran—'

Adamson snorted. 'Do they think I'm an Olympic sprinter? Why would I kill him?'

'The same reason any of us would. To draw Lambourne out of hiding, or to teach him a lesson.'

'Isn't it more likely one of Lambourne's enemies did it? Charlie Flynn's family? Have they looked at Ronnie's friends, what he was up to? He could have been into drugs or… And we still haven't found Walker.'

'We will.' Caelan spoke with more certainty than she felt. 'Richard, I'm going to trust you, because I think I can. I *know* I can. Elizabeth Beckett suspects you, Nasenby and Penrith. She thinks one of you killed Ronnie Morgan, and Sam. Charlie Flynn too.'

Adamson blinked. 'Everything Penrith is accusing you of, in other words? She thinks he's trying to set you up?'

'It's a possibility.'

'What about Nasenby?'

'What about him?'

'He told me he wanted you to look for Lambourne so he could keep you close. Save you from yourself, he said.'

Caelan laughed. 'He knows I was looking for Lambourne in Egypt.'

'Were you?'

'In a way.'

'And you didn't care if Lambourne knew it. That's what Nasenby meant. He thought you were being reckless.'

'Because Nicky had died, and I didn't care what happened to me? He didn't know about us. Spare me the amateur psychology.'

Adamson said nothing. He tipped back his head, staring up at the ceiling.

'Why did you come here tonight?' he said eventually.

'To tell you about Sam.'

Now he looked at her. 'And to see how I reacted?'

'Yes.'

'And? Did I pass?' His tone had changed, anger biting off the ends of his words. 'You're my judge and jury, is that it?'

'Don't be stupid. I want you to help me.'

'How magnanimous.'

'There's more to this than we thought, Richard. More to Charlie Flynn's death, to Nicky's.'

'What do you want me to do?'

'I don't know.'

He laughed. 'Then it's going to be a long night.'

'Walker's living in King's Cross.'

'How do you know?'

'Someone in the Wheatsheaf told me.'

'How did you manage that?' Caelan drew back her T-shirt, allowed Adamson to see the gun. He shook his head. 'You threatened them?'

'I didn't say that.'

A pause. Caelan studied Adamson's face, the man she had shared a bed with for half a year. It had been work, yes, but you couldn't live in such proximity to someone without seeing through the disguise. Adamson was genuine, she'd bet her life on it. She could trust him. She had to.

'Whoever's behind this, they can't be working alone,' she said softly. 'Sam didn't hang himself, and one person couldn't have lifted him up there.'

Adamson flinched, no doubt visualising the horror of Sam's last moments. 'Who, then? Walker and a partner?'

'I see Walker as a follower, not a leader.'

'Lambourne wouldn't kill his son.'

Adamson was definite, and Caelan wondered why. He hadn't worked on the Charlie Flynn case, not closely. He shouldn't know what Lambourne would do, unless... Adamson saw her staring, raised a hand to his mouth.

'Even Seb Lambourne wouldn't kill his own flesh and blood,' Adamson said quickly. Caelan was quiet, and he gave a nervous laugh. 'If you're trying to unsettle me, Caelan, it's working.'

'How did we know that Lambourne was back in the country?' she said.

'I don't know. Elizabeth Beckett told me when she asked me to find you.'

'And I'm wondering who told her.'

Fifty minutes later, Caelan was outside Michael Nasenby's home in Fulham. The house was in the centre of a block of terraces, but Caelan knew that Nasenby and his wife had extended and improved the property extensively in the thirty years they had lived there. The surrounding houses were well maintained, the area having an air of prosperity. Exactly the kind of street Caelan would expect Nasenby to call home. She decided to ring his mobile rather than knock on the door and set the neighbour's curtains twitching. Nasenby answered on the fourth ring, his voice heavy with sleep.

'Caelan?'

'Morning, Michael. I need to speak to you.'

A yawn, some muffled conversation. Nasenby's wife had woken too. Caelan waited.

'I was asleep.' The note of reproach in his voice was subtle but unmistakable. Caelan noted it with interest. Nasenby had encouraged her from the first day she'd met him to phone if she needed to, no matter the time of day. Another sign that she was on Brady's team now, not his own?

'I'm sorry, Michael, but this is important.'

A harrumph from Nasenby's wife, his voice placating her.

'Can't it wait until the morning?'

'No.'

He sighed. 'Fine. Where do you want to meet?'

'Your living room?'

A pause. 'What?'

'I'm in your driveway.' Caelan looked up at the windows above her. Sure enough, the curtain moved aside and Nasenby's face appeared.

'Christ, Caelan. What are you doing here?' He sounded appalled. Caelan beamed up at him with a wave.

'Wanted to save you the trouble of getting your car out. Are you going to let me in?'

She had to appear normal, not give him any idea of the grey desolation she had been shrouded in since finding Sam's body. The horror of witnessing Nicky's death, never far away, was back within touching distance. She had to keep going, keep fighting. Nicky and Sam both deserved justice. Ronnie Morgan, Charlie Flynn. Suzanne Morgan.

'I hadn't… I mean, we weren't expecting visitors,' Nasenby said quickly.

'I need a word, then I'll be on my way.'

A sigh. 'All right, give me a moment.'

Remembering their last conversation, when Nasenby had arrived at her door in the early hours, Caelan smiled to herself. Serve him right.

When he opened the door, Nasenby wore a pair of navy chinos, an England rugby shirt, and slippers. Caelan smiled.

'You don't, then.'

He stepped away from the door, bemused. 'Don't what?'

She followed him inside. 'Sleep in a suit.'

'Never off duty, Caelan. You know how it is. We can talk in the kitchen.'

He led her towards the back of the house. The room they entered was dark, but when Nasenby flipped on the lights, Caelan took a step back.

'Wow.'

The ceiling was double height, the room an expanse of glass, stone and exposed brickwork. The cupboards were a glossy grey, a stainless-steel range dominating one corner. Nasenby smiled.

'I'm glad you approve.'

At the back of the room, the windows looked out onto the darkened garden. Caelan watched a white cat flit past the glass, ghostly in the shadows. The room was perfect, but clinical, resembling an operating theatre more than a room in a home.

'Coffee?' Nasenby raised his eyebrows.

'No thanks.'

'Then come and sit down.'

The dining table was made from polished black granite, reminding Caelan uncomfortably of an oversized headstone. Nasenby pulled out a chair, waved her into it. Caelan sat gingerly. The chairs were angular, designed for aesthetic appeal, not comfort. Nasenby settled opposite her. He smiled, totally relaxed, waiting for her to speak. Caelan leaned forward, setting her elbows on the cold glossy surface of the table.

'Michael, Sam's dead.'

The reaction was instantaneous. Nasenby shoved back his chair, blundered to his feet. He turned away, his eyes half closed as though he had taken a physical blow. Caelan watched as he straightened his back, took a few heaving breaths. When he turned back, his face was calmer, though his hands were shaking as he gripped the back of his chair.

'How do you know?'

'I found him.'

'Shot?'

'Hanged.'

'Suicide?' Nasenby gave a violent shake of his head. 'No, not Sam. Not now. If he was going to kill himself, he'd have done it before.'

'Nothing's been confirmed.'

'But you've made up your mind.'

She nodded. 'He was murdered.'

'Disguised as suicide.' Nasenby was nodding. He sat again, ran his hand around his jaw.

'Like Charlie Flynn's parents.' Caelan sat back, waited. Nasenby didn't react.

'You know they're dead?' he said.

'Hanged too. Quite the coincidence.'

'The Flynns' deaths *were* suicide, Caelan.'

'Because the coroner said so?'

'And the pathologist, and the evidence.'

A silence stretched, Caelan unwilling to break it, wanting Nasenby to speak first. She was treating him as she would a suspect. The trouble was, he knew how to play the game too. A minute passed. Eventually he smiled.

'I wouldn't mind going back to bed.'

Caelan stood. 'I'll see myself out.'

He followed her to the front door, opened it wide. As she stepped onto the gravelled path outside, he cleared his throat.

'Who told you about the Flynns?'

She turned back. 'Why?'

'The list of people who know about their deaths is exclusive. I understood it was to stay that way.'

'Must have been one of the people on that list then.' Caelan smiled.

Nasenby was unamused. 'Brady?' Caelan didn't reply. 'Beckett?'

'Why don't you ask them? Goodnight, Michael.'

She walked away, not looking back until she reached Ewan's car. Nasenby stood watching her, leaning against the door frame. Their eyes met, and Caelan knew that their easy relationship, that of pupil and mentor, had changed.

–

Back in the car, Caelan rubbed her eyes. She wanted to go home to bed, but she had to speak to Penrith before the news of Sam's death became public. She knew it would, no matter how careful they were. Sam Clifton had been blamed for Charlie Flynn's death as much as Seb Lambourne himself. The press would delight in reporting his suicide to the nation. Sam's parents lived in Canada, and had escaped much of the furore. Caelan hoped they would be left alone now to grieve for their son. Somehow she doubted it.

'Where does Ian Penrith live?' asked Ewan.

'Hammersmith.'

'Not far.'

'No, but…' She gave him the address. 'It's a huge block of flats next to a dual carriageway.'

'Not in the same league as Nasenby's place, then?'

'I prefer Penrith's, they're lovely apartments. I've only been there once, to pick him up. We were on a job he hated.'

'Why?'

Caelan laughed at the memory. 'He had to pretend to be my dad.'

'Your dad? Is he old enough?'

'Nasenby thought so. Ian didn't find it as funny as the rest of us.'

'How was Nasenby?'

'Shocked to hear about Sam.'

'I'm sure. Listen, Caelan, I can't imagine what it was like for you, finding your friend like that.'

'You can, Ewan. We've both seen worse, had friends killed in front of our eyes. Heard the screams, felt the blood spattering your face. The guilt when you realise you're still alive.' She rubbed the back of her hand over her mouth. 'You know.'

They didn't speak again until they arrived outside Penrith's home. Caelan climbed out of the car, looked up at the twelve storeys in front of her. Gathering herself, she blinked back the exhaustion.

'I'll get a taxi home,' she said again. 'Get out of here, Ewan.'

'No, I'll wait.' He didn't look at her, kept his head turned away. Caelan slammed the car door, annoyed, knowing she was being unfair. Ewan was doing what she had asked him to. She couldn't punish him for his loyalty.

Should she ring Penrith, or hammer on his door? Marching into the building's lobby, she decided on the latter. No concierge here, though a security camera blinked in the corner. She glanced at the lifts, headed for the stairs. Penrith's apartment was number 610 – the sixth floor. One final treat after a long and difficult day.

Penrith's floor was silent, Caelan's steps muffled by the navy-blue carpet. The doors were a lighter blue, the air a pungent mix of air freshener and curry. Maybe someone had been having a late-night takeaway.

She halted outside Penrith's door, saw the peephole. She had no fear he wouldn't open the door. He would relish seeing her, would enjoy having the chance to needle her again, even at this hour. She tapped on the door. When he didn't appear, she thumped it.

Footsteps.

'Caelan? Is it Hallowe'en again?'

'Ha bloody ha. Open the door, Ian.'

It swung open to reveal Penrith bare-chested, his belly hanging over the waistband of a pair of baggy blue boxer shorts. 'To what do I owe the pleasure?'

'Sam Clifton's dead.'

Penrith's eyes bulged. 'Sam? Jesus. Tell me you're joking!'

'No, Ian, I'm not.'

He lunged forward, hauled her inside. As the door slammed behind her, Caelan said, 'You'll wake your neighbours.'

'I don't give two shits about my neighbours. Tell me what happened.'

Caelan explained how she'd discovered Sam's body. Penrith listened, hands on hips. When she fell silent, he pointed to his left.

'Kitchen's through there. In case you've forgotten: tea, no sugar, splash of milk. I'll get dressed.' He stomped away.

Mechanically, Caelan did as she'd been asked, too tired and empty to take umbrage. Penrith's kitchen was spotless, with a pristine white cloth on the table and a teapot by the kettle. When he came in, now dressed in jeans and a polo shirt, she said, 'Do you live with your mum?'

'My mum?'

Caelan nodded at the teapot. Penrith smiled.

'Only way to make a decent brew.'

'I'm afraid I didn't use it.'

He tutted. 'Tea'll be awful then.'

'I'll take the risk.' Caelan picked up a mug, wrapped her hands around it, savouring the warmth. Penrith picked up his own cup and peered inside, wrinkling his nose at the contents.

'Worst cup of tea I've ever seen. Shocking.'

Caelan drank. 'I thought you'd be more upset that one of our colleagues is dead.'

Penrith heaved his bulk into a kitchen chair, ignoring her comment. 'Sit.'

She did as she was told. 'I must admit, I'd expected you to have accused me of killing him by now.'

He studied her face, took a cautious sip of tea. Winced as he tasted it. 'Would you blame me? You're as common as blood spatter at crime scenes these days. Have they found Walker yet?'

'No.'

He bared his teeth. 'No. Why did you come here at this hour to tell me about Sam?'

Caelan was thrown. Adamson had asked the same question, Nasenby hadn't. She'd told Adamson the truth, but she couldn't do the same with Penrith.

'I wanted you to hear it from me, rather than in the news tomorrow.' It wasn't a total lie, but Penrith's sharp glance told her he wasn't fooled.

'Who told you to tell me?' he said.

'No one.'

'Not dancing to Brady's tune tonight?' He watched her over the top of his cup. Caelan stared back, unfazed. 'Who else knows? Michael?'

Caelan nodded. 'And Richard.'

'I'm your last visit? I'm hurt.'

'No you're not. And I didn't say I was the one who told them.'

'You did, though, didn't you? You went and knocked on their doors, disturbed their sleep.' He tapped the side of his chin with his forefinger, making a show of considering what Caelan had said. 'Interesting. Sam's flat is in Battersea. If I'd found his body then decided to break the news to his former colleagues, I'd have crossed the river to Fulham to talk to Nasenby first. Geographically, it makes sense. Then a quick stop here before travelling on to Adamson in Kentish Town. But you didn't.'

Heat was rising in Caelan's cheeks, but she was damned if she was going to allow Penrith to see it. 'No, I—'

'Which either means,' Penrith interrupted, 'you went else-where before going to see Nasenby, or you left me until last deliberately. Which?'

'Ian—'

'Or is it both?' Caelan said nothing, and Penrith chuckled. 'Both then. Shall I keep guessing, or are you going to tell me what's really going on here?'

'What do you expect me to say?'

'The truth would be nice.'

'When you've spent the past few days spouting lies about me to anyone who'd listen?'

'Tit for tat, is it? Very professional.'

'Takes one to know one.'

'And you'll get me at playtime? Come on, Caelan.'

She stared at him. 'What, you expect me to forget what you've said, the accusations you've made? You want me to confide in you?'

He pounced. 'So you *do* know more than you're saying.'

'About what?' Fury rose in Caelan's chest. The secrets, the lies, the two-faced deceit of it all. Now Penrith had the gall to suggest she was concealing information from him?

'Can I ask a question?' He took another swallow of tea, creasing his face theatrically as he swallowed it.

What was he up to now? 'Go on.'

'Do you trust me?'

She shrugged. 'About as far as I could throw you, as the saying goes.'

'Which, I think we'll agree, wouldn't be far.' Penrith looked down at his belly. 'Why?'

'Why don't I trust you? Because you've lied about me, about Nicky, about...' She shook her head. 'You've suggested I'm unprofessional, corrupt, both to my face and behind my back. Tell me why I should trust you.'

He stood, went to the sink, set his empty cup in it. 'Biscuit?'

'It's four in the morning. No thank you.'

Penrith shrugged, opened a cupboard. Found a packet of chocolate digestives, held them up like a gleeful child. 'What has the time to do with it?'

'Ian…'

He removed three biscuits, bit into the first. 'You should trust me, Caelan, because I've been telling the truth.'

Caelan shoved herself away from the table, stood, and strode towards the door. 'Goodnight, Ian.'

'Come back.' His voice was steel, all pretence at light-heartedness gone. 'If you value your career, your *life*, you need to listen.'

She paused. 'I took you seriously there for a second. You sound as though you're in a TV show.'

'If I was, I'd be five stone lighter and you'd be six inches taller. And we'd probably be in bed by now.'

Caelan couldn't help laughing, despite everything. Let him say his piece. What harm could it do? She dropped back into the chair.

'I need you to trust me,' Penrith repeated.

'I can't. I did, but not anymore.'

'Because of what I said about Charlie Flynn?'

'And about Nicky. You had Adamson follow us, follow me. He took photographs, for Christ's sake.'

'I know.'

'And now you're going to tell me you were trying to protect me? It wasn't about collecting evidence to discredit me and to raise suspicion against me?'

269

He shoved a whole biscuit into his mouth. Chewed, licked the chocolate from his fingers. Sat back down. 'No, that's exactly what I was trying to do. And it worked.'

Caelan sneered. 'Yeah, well good for you. Hope you're happy.'

'Why do you think I did it?'

'Because you're a twat?' Caelan didn't miss a beat.

Penrith laughed. 'That too.'

'Is there another reason?'

He ate the final biscuit, his eyes on her face. 'No, there are several. One being because I wanted to be free to do some poking around while everyone's attention was diverted.'

Caelan rubbed her forehead, a headache gathering momentum behind her eyes. 'Don't tell me. Another conspiracy theory.'

Penrith's eyes narrowed. 'For the best undercover officer we're supposed to have, you're giving away a lot of information tonight.'

'Yeah, well, I'm tired.' She looked at him from beneath her eyelashes. He grinned.

'As if you'd tell me anything you didn't want me to know.'

She ignored him. This conversation wasn't going as she had planned. Penrith in this mood was slippery, and she was exhausted. He would outwit her at every turn. She held up her hands.

'I don't understand what you're saying, Ian.'

'Me neither, not all of it. The accusations I made against you were true, but I know you're not the guilty person.'

She stared, uncomprehending. 'What does that mean?'

'It means someone in our merry band knows more than they're letting on. The question is, who? I know you've been thinking the same. No doubt Elizabeth Beckett is too. Have you seen her this evening?'

What could she say? 'Yes.'

He smiled, triumphant. 'And Brady? Achebe?'

'Yep.'

'All wondering who the bad apple is. Do they think it's me?'

'You've been making a lot of noise. People tend to notice.'

'And I'm going to continue to do so. It's a smokescreen.'

Caelan looked at him – the self-satisfied eyes, the smirk. Could she believe him? After all he'd said, all he'd done? From the beginning, the first meeting on the day she had arrived back in the country, he'd done his utmost to poison the minds of her colleagues against her. That he hadn't succeeded was not down to lack of effort on his part. Caelan had to admit, he'd been persuasive, even convincing. She hadn't been able to defend herself, because there were unanswered questions, doubts and regrets. Nicky shouldn't have died, Caelan shouldn't be living in her apartment, at least not alone. As fall guys went, she was perfect.

Perfect, but innocent.

And now Penrith was saying he knew it too.

Caelan rubbed her eyes, attempting to gather her thoughts. She needed to get out of here. Penrith might say he wasn't a suspect, but she had no proof. She did have questions, but if she asked them, she would be showing him where her thoughts were leading, and she had already told him too much. Perhaps unconsciously, she realised she had decided to trust him again.

'Ian, how did you know Seb Lambourne was back in the country?'

He gazed at her, brow wrinkled, mentally scrambling after her. 'What do you mean?'

'An informant? A tip-off? A full-page advertisement in the *Times*?'

Penrith's mouth opened, but he didn't speak. He closed it again. Frowned. 'I don't know.'

'What about when we found Charlie? How did you know where he was?'

He brightened. 'That *was* an anonymous tip-off. A call to the main switchboard. Wouldn't leave a name or address. We never traced them.'

'Them?'

'We couldn't tell if the caller was male or female, there was no discernible accent… The call was made from a pay-as-you-go number.'

'And the SIM was used to make only that one call?'

'Naturally. Then no doubt destroyed.'

'Where was the call made?'

'Where? Ealing.'

The back of Caelan's neck prickled. 'Really?'

'Significant because Glen Walker has been sighted there?'

'Well—'

'One possibility being that whoever's behind this wanted us focusing on Walker, even back then.'

'Which would mean they knew he had associations with the area.'

'You mean he visited a greasy spoon there once or twice?'

Caelan's head was thumping. 'Yes. But we've only one person's word for it.'

'I assume her background has been examined, her statement verified?'

'Yes. Her boss also confirmed that a man resembling Walker has been in there, but he couldn't say for sure it was him. It's a busy place, with a high turnover of customers.'

'But your witness was certain?'

'She said so. She seemed it.'

'You went there with Brady?'

'If you know I was there, you also know who was with me.'

Penrith nodded, conceding the point. 'I hope you're being cautious.'

Caelan snorted. 'With Brady? You've got a cheek.'

'I'm serious. She's a ball-breaker.'

'Lucky I don't have any then.'

'What about Achebe?'

'I like him.'

'And? Not what I meant. He was involved in the Charlie Flynn case.'

'I've heard.'

'He was outside the house when you went in. Did you know that?'

Slowly, Caelan shook her head. Achebe hadn't mentioned it. Neither had Brady. 'I hadn't realised.'

'He was there. And he was armed.'

'Ian...'

He held up a hand. 'I know, so was everyone else. You should go back and review the file, Caelan. It's interesting.'

'Interesting?' Caelan spat the word. 'It'll raise more questions. I've seen most of it before. The anonymous tip-off obviously checked out, though?'

'We watched the place, spoke to the neighbours. We saw nothing suspicious, so in the end we had to take the chance and go in. No one saw Charlie arrive, or saw anyone coming to care for him.'

'Because they didn't.'

'No, his captors left him with plenty of food and water.'

'You don't believe it was Lambourne and Walker?'

Penrith was shaking his head. 'Do you?'

'I don't know.'

'Come on, Caelan. It makes no sense.'

'They were there. Lambourne killed Nicky. I saw him.' Penrith said nothing, staring down at the table between them. Caelan watched him, anger coursing through her again. 'What, you're going to suggest I imagined it?'

'No, Caelan. Why would I?'

She allowed her head to slump, her chin close to her chest. 'No reason.'

'Have others?' His voice was soft, as gentle as she'd ever heard it. She lifted her hands, touching the corners of her eyes where tears were gathering.

'Yes.'

He reached for her empty cup, took it to the sink. Caelan swallowed, blinked. Closed down the memories. Penrith stood looking at her, his arms folded.

'I've been asking myself the same questions since Charlie died,' he said. 'I don't have any answers.'

'Me neither. Everyone I speak to confuses me more.'

'Perhaps intentionally.'

Caelan threw back her head. 'There you go again. I need to get some sleep.'

'Before you leave, let me make one more point. I'm not your enemy, Caelan.'

She stood, limbs heavy, eyes gritty. 'So you've said. Forgive me if I struggle to believe you.'

27

Caelan stood under the shower, the scalding water pounding her shoulders and head. With her eyes closed, falling asleep where she stood, she soaped her body and hair. The dull thump of her headache had evolved into piercing pain on the journey from Penrith's flat to her own, jabbing at her eyes and temples. Ewan had been quiet as he drove, and Caelan hadn't felt like talking either. She had wanted to use the time to mull over what Penrith had said, but instead found herself dozing, jerking awake whenever Ewan had to stop for red lights. They'd hardly spoken for the hour it had taken to drive back to Rotherhithe. She'd apologised for treating him like a chauffeur, and he'd smiled, waved as he'd driven away. Caelan had stared after the car as it rounded the corner, wondering if she would ever see him again.

She dried herself quickly, pulled on an old pair of Nicky's pyjamas. Wrapping her arms around herself, she remembered Nicky wearing the same pair one long, lazy Sunday. There hadn't been many occasions when they were both off work, free to be themselves, but the few weekends they'd spent together had been memorable.

In the kitchen, she took a beer from the fridge. Not advisable given her headache, but one wouldn't hurt. She held the icy bottle to her forehead, closed her eyes. She should get some sleep while she had the opportunity, but with so many questions flitting around her mind, rest would be impossible. She went into the living room, stood at the window watching the murky Thames wander by. She knew she could have asked Ewan to stay the night, discussed her ideas with him. But he had clearly been exhausted, and it would have been unfair. She moved over to the nearest sofa, threw herself down. She rubbed the back of her neck, felt the tension there. A third of the beer disappeared in one gulp.

Beckett. She was expecting Caelan to call, to update her. Maybe not at five thirty in the morning, but Caelan retrieved the phone Beckett had given her from her pile of dirty clothes anyway. If Beckett wanted an update, she could have one.

Two rings.

'Good morning.' Beckett sounded bright, alert. Caelan scowled.

'Ma'am.' Even her voice was lethargic. 'I hope I didn't wake you.'

'Not at all. I was heading out the door for my run.'

An image of Beckett in Lycra and fluorescent trainers appeared in Caelan's mind. She hadn't been for a run herself since before she went to Egypt, and needed to make the time. Fitness disappeared much more easily than it was gained. 'You run before six in the morning?'

'On alternate days, I swim.' Beckett's tone changed, became businesslike. 'What happened last night?'

Caelan told her about the conversations she'd had with Adamson and Nasenby. 'Adamson knew nothing about Sam's death, I'm certain. Nasenby... I don't think he knew either. He looked stunned, horrified.'

'But?'

'I don't know. He did nothing out of character, but he didn't like me turning up at his house.'

Beckett chuckled. 'I think I can shed some light on why he might have been uncomfortable.'

'Really?'

'As you know, we've someone watching him and his house. Michael Nasenby had a guest tonight.'

Caelan leaned forward to stand her empty beer bottle on the floor. 'A guest? What do you mean?'

'A woman. A woman who's not his wife.'

It took a second for Beckett's words to make sense. Caelan heard the disbelief in her own voice. 'You mean he's having an affair?'

'You're surprised.'

'I'm amazed. I thought he and his wife were happy.'

'They might be. More likely, she believes they are.'

'Meanwhile, Michael's brought someone else into their home, their bed. Do you know who she is?' Caelan remembered the voice in the background when she had called Nasenby, the one she assumed belonged to his wife. It hadn't sounded familiar, but it had been little more than a whisper.

Beckett sighed. 'I do.'

'And? Are you going to tell me?'

A pause. Then: 'Detective Chief Superintendent Adele Brady.'

Caelan blinked, glad she'd already set the beer bottle on the ground. 'You're joking.'

'I wish I was.'

'But she knows Nasenby's being watched.'

'No she doesn't.' Beckett's voice was quiet. Caelan considered it. Brady had left the room with Achebe before Beckett had told Caelan and Ewan about the surveillance, and it clearly hadn't been discussed beforehand.

'But you said you and Brady were looking at Nasenby's finances, his phone records.'

'We did. No doubt he knows all about that, if not the surveillance.'

Caelan shook her head, struggling to take in what Beckett was saying.

'But Michael was with Ewan and me when we were shot at outside the Wheatsheaf.'

'Means nothing,' Beckett said. 'None of you were hit. We've established that whoever's doing all this, can't be working alone. The shooting could be an attempt to make it look as though Nasenby was under threat, with his accomplice doing the shooting and making sure they missed.'

Caelan knew it was possible. 'I was on the phone to Nasenby when Ronnie received the call at Northolt station. I called Nasenby's mobile. I don't know where he was or what he was doing.'

'Then we need to find out. Do you know where Nasenby was on the day you found Charlie Flynn?'

'Not exactly. He was in the area, everyone was. This is...' Caelan allowed her voice to disappear. What? Unbelievable? Impossible to consider? 'What are you going to do about Nasenby and Brady's relationship?'

'Do? Nothing.'

'Nothing?'

'If Nasenby's innocent – and remember, we've found no evidence of any wrongdoing – then it's none of my business.'

'And if he's not?' As she said the words, Caelan's stomach tightened in protest. Nasenby was her mentor, her father figure. She couldn't believe, wouldn't believe, that he was involved.

'If he's guilty, we're giving him enough rope to hang himself.' Beckett stopped, cleared her throat. 'Sorry. That was insensitive.'

The stench in Sam's bedroom. His hideous swollen tongue. His eyes, wide and bulging. Caelan knew the memory of it would never leave her. In her job, she had seen horror upon horror, heard scream after scream, relived them all until they became an indelible part of her, then carried them around with her. The victims she met were her burden. Their hopes, loves, ideas, all hers to bear. Even some of those who were still alive, those whose tormentors she had helped put behind bars. Their voices were in her head, their touch on her shoulder. Hundreds of them. Nicky. Sam. Ronnie. Charlie.

Nicky.

Her touch, the press of her lips. The scent of her skin, especially in the place beneath her ear where she loved to be kissed. Caelan's past and future, wrapped up in one person. Destroyed by the thrust and tear of a knife.

Beckett was speaking again. '… continue to watch Nasenby. It goes without saying that you're not to share the details of this conversation with Brady, or even Achebe. Stay away from South Harrow. What about Penrith?'

Caelan blinked away Nicky's smile. Coughed to give herself a second to find her voice. 'Penrith? He's on to us.'

'What do you mean?' Another change in tone.

'Says he accused me of being corrupt and killing Charlie Flynn myself to create a smokescreen. He's been doing some digging; he knows I'm innocent. Wants me to trust him.'

'He… what?'

'Pretty much my own reaction.' Caelan stood slowly, stretched her neck. Beckett was silent for a while, and Caelan returned to the fridge, took out a carton of orange juice. Poured a generous measure, took a mouthful.

'That's… unexpected,' Beckett said eventually.

'Yep. Don't suppose Ian's having an affair too? With Achebe maybe? With you?'

A snort. 'What does he want from you?'

'He wants me to believe he's not my enemy. Told me to look at the Charlie Flynn file again.'

'I see.' Another silence. 'Anything else?'

'He doesn't know who told us Lambourne was back in the country.' Caelan waited. Would Beckett tell her? Did she even know?

A pause so long Caelan removed the phone from her ear to check she hadn't lost the connection. What was Beckett up to? Whispering to someone? Checking her emails? Eventually Beckett spoke.

'I don't know either. No one does.'

'No one? How can that be—'

'You're wondering if we sent you on a wild goose chase. If Lambourne's here at all?'

Exhaustion buffeted Caelan, her brain telling her to lie back, close her eyes. 'I wasn't before, but now…'

'It was an anonymous tip. A phone call.'

'Seriously? Another one?'

'Another?'

'Penrith said we found Charlie because of a tip-off. Was the call made from Ealing, by any chance?'

'Ealing? No. Northolt.'

'Northolt.' Caelan smeared her hand across her eyes, the room blurring then coming back into focus.

'The area around the station and the underpass.'

'Shit.'

280

'We don't know who made the call. The CCTV in the station is worse than useless.'

'It's a set-up, it has been from the start.'

'We know that. Why do you think I brought you back here? The only person I could trust to help me was you.' There was a new note in Beckett's voice now, one Caelan had never heard before. She was unsure, pleading. The realisation was unsettling.

'How did you know you could trust me? After all Ian was saying…'

'Because of—'

The truth hit Caelan like a baseball bat. 'Because of Nicky. You knew about Nicky and me, knew I would never be involved in a scheme where she ended up dead.'

Silence. 'It's my job to know. I may seem remote, sitting in my office, a million miles away from my officers on the ground, but I can't be. Your every decision affects me and my ability to do my job. To keep people safe.'

'Safe? Was Nicky safe? Was Sam?'

'Caelan, our work can be risky, you know that. Sam and Nicky knew it too.'

'Risky, yes. Riddled with suicide missions, no.'

Beckett was brisk. 'I want you to get some rest, Caelan. We'll meet later. I want to see where Nasenby's car was when Ronnie Morgan was killed. I want to know where he was last night, before he got into bed with Brady.'

'I thought you didn't want to start alarm bells ringing? We don't know Nasenby's involved.'

'Sam Clifton is dead. This is escalating, Caelan. It needs to stop.'

'How long have you known?'

A pause. 'Known?'

'You said you've known it's been a set-up from the start. When did it begin?'

'Listen, Caelan, I don't want to discuss this on the phone. We'll talk later.'

Caelan swallowed some orange juice. 'What do you want me to do?'

'Like I said, sleep. Call me in a few hours. Hopefully I'll have more information then.'

'About what?'

'Who we need to focus on. We still have five suspects. I want Walker found, questions answered. I want this cleared up.'

'What about Brady? If you think she's feeding information back to Nasenby…'

'She knows what's necessary. I want her to continue to do her job.'

'Nasenby warned me against her, said she's career-minded. Hinted she'd trample over anyone to further her own interests.'

'Well he should know. I've told her you're out of the way for now.'

'She thinks I've been arrested?'

Beckett laughed. 'You're about to be.'

'What?' Caelan left the kitchen, moved to stand at her front door.

'Officers are on their way to your home.'

'But you said—'

'Another change of plan,' Beckett interrupted, her voice cold. 'I've been informed of a new development. Did you see the rope used to hang Sam Clifton?'

'The rope? No, I—'

'A length of clothes line. Your fingerprints were found on it.'

282

Caelan's mouth was dry, a loud buzzing sound filling her head. 'Mine?'

'Yours, Caelan. No one else's, not even Sam's. How did they get there?'

'I've no idea.' Caelan was stunned. Wheels were turning, unseen, out of sight, and she was being dragged along by their momentum.

'The post-mortem on Sam Clifton is scheduled to take place this morning. Brady will be attending, and I'm going myself. We'll speak later.'

'Wait – am I being arrested for real? Do you think I killed Sam?' No reply. Caelan gripped the phone, her legs trembling. 'Ma'am?' Beckett had gone. Caelan's mouth filled with bile, and she swallowed it down.

A knock on the front door – three polite taps. Caelan froze. Was Beckett serious? She crept forward, peered through the peephole. Two uniformed officers stood there, one male, one female. The male officer stifled a yawn; his partner tucked her hands into her armpits, either side of her stab vest. A giggle tried to force its way out of Caelan's mouth, and she pressed her lips together, suppressing it. The situation was ridiculous. The whole case was a twisted mess, a web of nonsense. She no idea who she could trust, if anyone. Beckett, Brady, Adamson, Nasenby... All were changing shape before her eyes. Ronnie Morgan was dead; so was Sam. Glen Walker was drifting around London like a wraith. Lambourne was nowhere to be seen, and Caelan was about to disappear. Beckett was suggesting Caelan couldn't trust the men she had worked with, while Ian Penrith wanted her to have faith in him. The gun used to kill Charlie Flynn had also been used to kill Ronnie Morgan. Who had fired it? Who had the opportunity, the stomach, to murder two innocent young people? The idea that it was one of her three colleagues sickened Caelan, yet she had to admit, it made a twisted sense. Now she was being removed from the firing line. She blinked through her exhaustion, knowing she had to stay alert, now more than ever.

Four more taps on the door. She marched forward, flung it open.

'Good morning, officers.'

The woman mustered a smile. 'You're expecting us?'

Caelan held out her wrists, nodding at the handcuffs. 'Let's go.'

'We're not going to—' The officer blinked, glanced at her colleague. He raised his eyebrows a fraction, but didn't speak.

Caelan gestured towards herself, the pyjamas. 'Can I get dressed before we leave?'

The pair exchanged a glance. 'Of course,' the male officer said.

Caelan closed the door in their faces. It wasn't their fault, they were here because they'd been told to be, but she was furious. Jitesh or Peter would have had no choice but to allow them access to the building. She could trust the concierges' discretion, but another resident might have seen the two officers arrive and make their way up to her apartment; was probably already talking about it on Twitter or Facebook. How would she be able to work undercover after this?

Another thought occurred to her as she pulled off Nicky's pyjamas, found clean underwear. Perhaps that was the point. Perhaps preventing her from working again was the whole idea. Fear gripped her stomach, making her swallow hard.

The net was tightening.

She dressed quickly, throwing on jeans, a T-shirt, trainers. She had locked the gun away when she'd arrived home. It could stay where it was. Would they search her flat? It was possible.

Let them. Let them imprison her, blame her, forget about her. What did it matter?

The two officers were standing where she'd left them. She should have been supervised while she dressed, if they were arresting her for real. She could have destroyed evidence, armed herself. A hint that this was a ploy?

She slammed the door, locked it, pushed the keys into her jeans pocket. She hadn't brought her bag or her phone. Even the handset Beckett had given her she'd left on the worktop in the kitchen. There were a few coins in her pockets, but otherwise they were empty.

The male officer cleared his throat. 'Are you ready?'

'Do you have an arrest warrant?'

His colleague shook her head, bemused. 'We were only told to come and collect you.'

They didn't know whether she was a suspect or a witness. Caelan considered what that meant as she followed the male officer to the lift. The female officer walked behind her, not too close, but near enough to make the point that Caelan had no choice but to accompany them. They were being careful, polite and professional. Caelan stared at the back of the male officer's neck as he pressed the button to summon the lift. She could escape them, even if they were armed to the teeth with pepper spray and batons, but what would be the point? It would be as good as an admission of guilt on her part. She wouldn't give them the satisfaction.

The lift arrived. The journey down to the lobby seemed to take an age, the two officers staring down at their feet and Caelan holding a hand to her churning stomach, wishing she was in bed. Wishing she had stayed in Egypt.

Wishing Nicky was by her side.

Jitesh was behind the reception desk, head bowed, eyes on a textbook open on his lap. He glanced up, flushing as Caelan caught his eye. She grinned.

'Studying hard?'

'I… Yes. Exams next week.'

'Good luck.'

Jitesh nodded his thanks, his face anxious. Caelan wanted to reassure him, to tell him she knew he'd had no choice but to let them in. He had no idea she was a police officer too. Even Peter, with whom Caelan often chatted, didn't know what she did for a living. Most operations had required her to live away from home, so coming and going wearing different wigs and clothes hadn't been an issue. Nicky had been mentioned, especially by Peter, but he had assumed Caelan had bought the apartment in the usual way. She had stayed there with Nicky, but only a couple of times. Moving into the apartment without her had been difficult. Nicky hadn't been close to her family, who had accepted without complaint her wishes about Caelan taking ownership of the flat, especially since her life insurance policies had been paid out to them. At the funeral, Caelan had avoided them, leaving after the service at the crematorium and not attending the wake. Raising a glass in Nicky's memory had not been high on her list of priorities.

The squad car was parked outside the building's main door, and Caelan headed for the passenger seat, before remembering and moving to the back. The male officer opened the door for her while his partner started the engine. Caelan slid inside without speaking, her mind on what Beckett had told her. Nasenby and Brady. Brady had talked about Nicky, introduced doubts about her death Caelan had never considered. Why? She must have known it was nonsense, even before Caelan had told her about inheriting the apartment. But then Caelan had no idea who she could trust. She had only Beckett's word that Nasenby and Brady were having an affair. If she had had more time, she could have asked Ewan to go to Nasenby's house, see who emerged. But Beckett had her own eyes on Nasenby. If Ewan was seen, Caelan's betrayal would have been obvious.

Too late now. They were speeding away from Caelan's apartment building. She wondered where they were taking her.

—

Her question was answered quickly. Within twenty minutes, they had arrived at Limehouse police station. The custody sergeant was a cheery man who showed her into a cell as though it was a luxurious hotel room. As the door closed behind her and the locks engaged, panic hurtled through Caelan's body. If this wasn't a real arrest, Beckett was doing an excellent job of making it feel like one. Caelan had been searched, and had surrendered her house keys and few pounds in change, the only personal possessions she carried. Her shoelaces had been removed, and she'd been asked if she wanted legal representation. Since she had no idea what else to say, she had refused. Now she sat on a thin blue mattress on a bed built into the wall of the cell, and waited. For what, she had no idea.

The walls were white tiles, cold to the touch. The air was stale, but there was a tang of disinfectant, making Caelan wonder what the cell's previous occupant had been up to. She remembered Saturday nights early in her career, bringing people into custody, vomit on the floor, the stench of regurgitated alcohol hanging around the custody area. She retched at the memory, drawing her feet onto the mattress and wrapping her arms around her knees. There was a toilet in the corner should she need to throw up, but she fervently hoped she wouldn't have to use it. High in the corner, a CCTV camera kept its eye on her. Caelan glanced up at it, lowered her face onto her arms. She should use this time to concentrate on the case, on the conflicting statements, ideas and information she had heard. It wouldn't be easy to sort through the rubbish, to pick the gold from the grit.

Her fingerprints had been found on the rope Sam had hanged from. Caelan shuddered. She hadn't touched the rope, hadn't touched Sam's body. She had visited Sam's flat a few times, but had never seen a washing line – Sam hadn't had a garden. She needed more details about the fingerprints. Were they even there at all, or was this another part of the elaborate scheme seemingly designed to trap her? Was Penrith behind it? He had been at Sam's flat after Sam had killed Brendan Milne. Why? Caelan didn't own a washing line either, dried her clothes in the laundry room in the basement of her apartment building, or on hangers in her bedroom. Beckett would know that Caelan wouldn't have been able to hoist Sam into the air herself – no one could do that alone. Were the fingerprints positioned in a way to suggest she had knotted the noose, or that she had handled the rope? Were there other prints on it?

Caelan raised her head, blinking back tears. She didn't know. Nothing made sense, none of it. She needed to speak to… who? Maybe legal representation would have been a good idea. The custody sergeant hadn't mentioned Caelan being a police officer. Did he know? Did any of them know? No crime had been mentioned, no reason for her being brought here. A good sign?

She heard people in the corridor outside, the deep tones of the custody sergeant and a female voice raised in complaint. A door clanked open, then Caelan heard the heavy locks move into place as it was closed.

Then the screaming started, continuously, as though the woman in the next cell didn't have to breathe between screeches. Thumping as she hammered her fists against the blue mattress, her feet stamping the floor, the sounds merging to produce an unholy din, like some dreadful percussion section. Caelan clamped her hands over her ears, willing the woman to stop. More screaming, shouts of abuse. She was pounding her hands against the door now, punctuating each thud with a scream. Footsteps outside, the voice of the custody sergeant again, politely asking her to keep the noise down. Receiving a volley of vitriol in return.

Caelan lay back, curled onto her side, staring at the wall. The woman would tire and shut up eventually – they all did in the end. More screaming, then a loud and prolonged bout of vomiting. The smell drifted into Caelan's cell despite the thick walls, locked door and closed hatch. Someone asking the woman if she wanted water. More screamed abuse. Caelan closed her eyes, exhaustion finally claiming her.

–

She woke to silence, her face turned to the wall. Someone else was in the room, she knew before she turned around. Their presence had woken her.

'Good to see they're looking after you,' Elizabeth Beckett said. She was standing by the door, her hands behind her back. Caelan swung her feet to the ground. The floor lurched as she sat up, though the pounding in her head had receded. 'Yeah, it's five-star accommodation. I'll be leaving a decent review on TripAdvisor.'

Beckett smiled, held out her balled fist. Frowning, Caelan stepped closer, and Beckett deposited her shoelaces, coins and keys into her hands. 'Come on, let's get you out of here.'

As they passed the front desk, the custody sergeant was studying his monitors. 'Mind how you go,' he called without looking up.

Caelan flashed a grin. 'Don't think me rude if I tell you I never want to see you again.'

He raised a hand in farewell. 'That's what they all say.'

Caelan expected Beckett's chauffeur to be waiting, but when they emerged from the station into the grey and misty mid-morning, Beckett kept walking.

'We're getting the train,' she called over her shoulder. Caelan hurried to catch her up.

'To?'

'Cannon Street, then the Underground to Westminster.'

'What's at Westminster?'

'A room I use occasionally as an office.'

'What about your driver?'

'I didn't want anyone to know I was coming to you. I trust my driver, but as far as anyone knows, you're locked away somewhere safe for the foreseeable future.'

'Except the custody sergeant.'

Beckett glanced up at the sky as she strode along, opened her handbag and took out an umbrella. 'He won't say anything.'

'How can you be sure?'

'He's my husband.'

Caelan opened her mouth, unsure how to respond. Eventually she said, 'Oh.'

'Surprised?' Beckett unfurled the umbrella as the first spots of rain began to fall, held it between them. Caelan ducked beneath it.

'Thank you. Why should I be surprised?'

Beckett laughed. 'Most people are when I tell them my husband's a sergeant. He's retiring next year, and he can't wait. I can't imagine him sitting around at home, doing the gardening, but…'

'I thought I'd love not getting up and going to work. I didn't.'

'The circumstances are a little different. I have to admit, though, I expected more of a battle to get you back on board.'

'A battle?'

'Michael Nasenby said you wouldn't even consider it. Richard Adamson wasn't confident either.'

'But you were?'

'They didn't know about you and Nicky.'

'How did you?'

Beckett waited until they had reached and rounded a woman walking five dogs of varying breeds and sizes before she replied. 'Nicky told me herself.'

Caelan had expected to be told to mind her own business. Why had Nicky been confiding in Beckett about their relationship? Caelan hadn't realised the two women had ever spoken. Nicky hadn't mentioned talking to Beckett, much less divulging details of her personal life.

'I didn't know,' she said.

'You wouldn't.' Beckett lifted her arm, allowed her sleeve to fall back so she could check her watch. She increased her pace, meaning Caelan had to hurry too. 'Nicky was reporting back to me, without the knowledge of Michael Nasenby, Ian Penrith or anyone else.'

Caelan stopped, raised a hand to grab Beckett's arm but thought better of it. 'What does that mean? Nicky was spying on us?'

Beckett halted too, met Caelan's eyes. 'Not exactly. When there was something I needed to be aware of, she informed me.'

'Spying, like I said.' All at once, Caelan was furious with Nicky. Their relationship had been none of Beckett's business. It hadn't impacted on their work, had no bearing on their assignments. Why would Nicky tell Beckett about it?

'She wasn't spying, not at all. I told you before, I need to know what's happening. Not the official lines, not the reports and briefing notes. I wanted to hear about the gossip, the arguments, the grudges. Nicky was able to provide the information I required.'

Beckett began to walk again, giving Caelan no choice but to follow, especially if she wanted to stay dry. The rain was heavy, the passing traffic switching on headlights, pedestrians scurrying into shops or doorways. Beckett put her head down, lengthened her stride. Caelan kept quiet, trying to equate the Nicky she had known with the person who had run to Beckett with insider information about her colleagues. It wasn't easy.

Neither woman spoke again until they were on the Underground train between Embankment and Westminster. It was busy, and they were forced to stand closer together than Caelan would have liked. She could smell Beckett's perfume, see the fine lines around her eyes and mouth. Beckett turned her face away, and Caelan wondered what she was thinking. Did she hate being down here in the warm, close air? Resent the crowds, the press of the bodies of tourists and ordinary Londoners? For someone used to being driven in a large, luxurious car, it was something of a comedown. Caelan knew little about Beckett's career. Perhaps she was adept at working undercover, blending in, but Caelan couldn't see it. Beckett wore her intelligence, her capability, like badges of honour. Posing as a drug addict or on a street corner wouldn't come easily to her. In the past, Caelan had loved taking on different personas, the chance to live a life far removed from her own for a time. She didn't think Beckett would understand.

'The office is a couple of minutes' walk from the station,' Beckett said as the train began to slow. As they pushed their way through the crowded carriage, Caelan looked behind them. No familiar faces, no one taking an interest in them. Why then were her senses suddenly charged, her skin prickling? She saw no threat, but her instincts were screaming that danger was close. As they stepped off the train, she pushed near to Beckett, her eyes sweeping over the people around them. On the platform, she grabbed Beckett's arm, heedless of the other woman's glare, and pulled her close to the wall.

'What the hell are you doing?'

Caelan pressed her back against the tiles, eyes constantly scanning the bustling mass of people.

Beckett looked perplexed. 'What is it?'

'I don't know. Have you asked someone to follow us?'

'No, of course not.'

Caelan stared at her, unsure whether Beckett was telling the truth. 'You're sure?'

Beckett pushed past her, clearly exasperated. Caelan turned, her eyes drawn back to the train as it began to move away.

That was when she saw him.

Walker. Glen Walker was on the train. His face was close to the window, teeth bared in a mocking grin. As he saw Caelan watching, he raised a hand, waving as the train picked up speed. Caelan turned, began to run. Beckett stared open-mouthed as Caelan shot past her.

'What is it?'

Caelan wanted to scream at her. Beckett was corrupt, she had to be. How else would Walker have known which train to board?

'Walker's on the train,' was all she said.

Beckett was instantly by her side, both powering along the platform. 'Then we've got a minute before he arrives at St James's Park station.'

People were ducking out of their way, some glaring and muttering. Caelan held up a hand in apology as she barged through a group of young women, her mind spinning through her options. Was Walker a threat? Beckett looked flustered, panicked. But if she hadn't known Walker was going to be there, who had sent him? Should they try to capture him? Caelan kept running. Whether Beckett had been compromised or not, Caelan knew she had to get away from Walker, out of the station to a place where she could safely reassess her situation. She could identify herself as a police officer, order people out of her path, but doing so would cause the kind of panic she wanted to avoid. The possibility of terrorist attacks had made people vigilant, and with the shots fired at herself, Nasenby and Ewan in Whitechapel still in the news, she couldn't afford to take the risk. Mass hysteria would help no one.

'This is hopeless,' Beckett muttered. When they reached the ticket hall, she dragged her phone from her bag. 'I'm going to make some calls. I'll try to halt the train, see if we can grab Walker at the station.'

'You're sending officers into the station, onto the train? People will be terrified. You'll have a stampede on your hands.'

Beckett was already stabbing at the screen. 'A risk I'll have to take. We need to bring Walker in.'

'Can't we do it discreetly? Do you want to tell me what's going on, why I should believe a word you say? This is a set-up, isn't it?'

Beckett held up a hand. 'There's no time.' She strode away. Caelan stared after her, totally confused.

'Where are you—'

'Just follow me. Please, Caelan.' Beckett broke into a jog, moving as quickly as possible in her low-heeled shoes. Caelan glared at her.

'Where are we going?'

'St James's Park station. On foot, we can make it in five minutes if we hurry.'

Caelan shook her head. 'He'll have long gone.'

'Do you have any better ideas?'

Caelan shook her head, her mind still running through the possibilities. Why had Walker been there? How had he known she and Beckett were on the train? His presence couldn't be a coincidence.

Beckett was beside her, the older woman breathing raggedly but easily matching Caelan's stride. Beckett had organised the tube journey, Beckett had sent her driver away. Beckett's husband knew that Caelan had been released, but no one else did. As far as any of her former colleagues knew, she was in a prison cell.

The rain had stopped, though dark clouds loomed above them, the sky as dark as dusk. The pavement in front of them was busy, thronged with crowds heading towards Westminster Abbey. Caelan stopped, moved to the side. Beckett saw the movement and turned her head. 'Caelan? Come on!' She halted, throwing her arms wide, frustration clear on her face. 'There's no time.'

'Why should I trust you?' Caelan heard herself demand. Beckett scowled, shook her head.

'This isn't the time to play the prima donna.' She turned away, but Caelan stood her ground.

'What about my fingerprints?'

'What?' Beckett's voice was icy. She glanced around. 'Caelan, we need to move.' People were staring at them now, and Beckett clicked her tongue. 'We're going to lose Walker.'

Caelan could hear sirens in the distance. 'My fingerprints were on the rope Sam was hanged with. What about the post-mortem?'

Beckett's hands were on her hips. 'What about it?'

'What did the pathologist say? What was the cause of death?'

'The noose wasn't enough of a giveaway?' Beckett's lips were pressed into an angry line. 'You know how he died. All the evidence says you helped him along. Caelan, I'm not going to discuss this here.'

'But you are, because I'm not going any further with you until you do.'

Beckett sighed, moved closer and took Caelan's elbow. 'You see the black van over there?' She nodded towards a vehicle idling at the side of the road. Caelan had already spotted it, but hadn't let Beckett see she had noticed its approach.

'What about it?'

'There are four officers inside watching us. On my signal, they'll come and arrest you again, and this time you won't be home for lunch.'

Caelan smirked. 'You're threatening me. Strange how your true colours emerge eventually.'

'My true colours? What about yours? I'm on your side, Caelan, but we need to get out of here. Finding Glen Walker is our priority, not arguing on the pavement like a couple of fishwives.'

'But you have officers mobilised. Several of them watching your back, for starters. Your job isn't on the ground, it's behind a desk. Why do you need to be out here? I thought you said no one was following us?'

'They weren't, but they are now.' Beckett glanced at the black van. 'Come on.' She grabbed Caelan's arm, tried to haul her towards it. Caelan stood her ground.

'Let go of me.'

'I suggest you moderate your tone.' Beckett's voice was cold. 'For once, Caelan, do as you're told.'

The van swerved into the road, stopped beside them. Beckett clambered inside, two men reaching out and dragging Caelan in after her before she could react. The whole manoeuvre had taken less than ten seconds, and no one on the pavement seemed to have even noticed. Caelan caught her breath, furious. She had been dumped on a seat, a burly armed officer sitting either side of her. Beckett was having a hurried conversation with the driver. The van began to move, rapidly picking up speed.

Caelan turned in her chair. 'What the fuck—'

'Shut up, Caelan, please,' Beckett ordered as she turned back. There were no windows, and Caelan twisted her head from left to right, trying to work out where they were going. The two men she was sitting between exchanged an amused glance, as though she was an unruly child, and she held in a mouthful of abuse. Beckett had fooled her, and now had her trapped. Why had Walker made his presence so obvious? If he had kept his head down as the train pulled away, she wouldn't have seen him. If Beckett had told him to be there, why had he allowed Caelan to see him, drawn her attention to his presence? Her head was thumping again.

'Where are you taking me?' she demanded.

Beckett looked furious. 'I've told you. We're going to the next station.'

'Let me out, and I'll disappear,' Caelan told her. 'I'll go away again, no one needs to—'

Beckett's phone began to ring, and she wrenched it from her jacket pocket, hurriedly fumbling with the screen. Caelan studied her face as she listened. Saw the frown crease her brow, watched her shoulders slump. Slowly she replaced the phone.

'Let us out,' she ordered the driver. He stopped abruptly, and Beckett jumped out, pulling Caelan with her. There was a cacophony of car horns and shouting as the van sped away.

On the pavement, Beckett smoothed her hair, throwing a glare in the direction of the black van as it disappeared.

'Baby-minders gone then? Are you going to tell me what's going on?' Caelan was deliberately chirpy. Beckett's lip curled.

'Walker wasn't on the train. Officers boarded it before anyone disembarked. He's not there, Caelan.'

A rush in her ears, a lurch in her stomach. 'But...'

Beckett folded her arms, tight-lipped. 'He never was, was he?'

'He was, I saw him clearly. He waved at me, for fuck's sake!'

'In your imagination, maybe. In your own head. Come on.'

Caelan stared. 'This is insane. I'm going nowhere with you. You're saying Walker isn't there, was never there? What, you think I'm crazy?'

'Not crazy, no. Under pressure, grieving. Maybe you should reconsider your retirement, Caelan. I'm sure there are grounds for medical discharge.' Beckett managed to sound sympathetic, understanding. Caelan laughed.

'Ten minutes ago you were desperate for my help, and now I'm being retired?'

'Desperate?' Beckett smiled. 'I hardly think so.'

'Walker was there, he—'

'Follow me, Caelan.'

'Where are we going?'

'You'll see.'

28

The building was on Great George Street, a huge Edwardian structure that Caelan had passed many times but never taken much notice of. Beckett marched inside, her head high, her steps unhurried. Caelan followed, unwilling to trust Beckett but not knowing what else to do.

The building's interior was impressive, with crystal chandeliers, marble floors and walls decorated with gold leaf and ornate plasterwork. Beckett kept walking until she reached a plain wooden door set close to the foot of a wide marble staircase. She took a bunch of keys out of her bag, and worked through them. Holding up a silver key, she nodded at Caelan.

'Forget you were ever here.'

'Seriously? Who's waiting through there? Churchill? James Bond?'

Beckett unlocked the door and pushed it open. She waved Caelan through.

The door opened into a stone passageway, cold and lit only by a single, unshaded bulb. Despite herself, Caelan shivered.

'What's going on?' she asked.

Beckett ignored her question. 'Keep moving,' was all she said. Caelan's shoulders tensed, and she walked on the balls of her feet, readying herself to make a dash for freedom if necessary. She began to wish she'd brought the gun.

The passage ran for thirty metres or so, sloping downwards, ending at another plain door. Beckett selected another key and held the door open again, light spilling through it.

'In you go,' she said.

Caelan swallowed. She could see a bland conference room beyond, empty apart from a few tables and chairs.

'This is ridiculous,' she muttered. Beckett smiled, allowing the door to close behind them. The room was hot, stuffy and windowless. The grey walls and carpet didn't feel particularly welcoming. 'Where are we?' Caelan asked.

'You already know. These rooms are under the building. Private and secure.'

'And all this cloak-and-dagger stuff is necessary? I'm expecting to stumble over the Crown Jewels any moment.'

'Do you think this caution is for my own amusement? That I enjoy it?' Beckett shook her head. 'Some of your colleagues may see our work as a game, but I certainly don't. Lives have been lost, Caelan.'

'You mean lives have been taken. People have been murdered.'

Beckett waved a hand. 'As you say. I'm going to explain to you what security measures we have in place here, and then perhaps you'll see you can trust me.'

Caelan narrowed her eyes. 'Why should extra security mean I can trust you?'

Beckett didn't reply; merely pulled a couple of chairs out from beneath a table and poured three glasses of water. Caelan watched with trepidation. Three glasses? Who was Beckett expecting? 'Why should I trust you?' she repeated.

'Because here I can be completely honest. I can tell you everything I know, I can let you into a few secrets. Have a seat, Caelan.'

Caelan remained standing. 'I'm not sure I want to.'

Beckett shrugged as she sat down. 'Up to you, but we're going to be here for a while.'

'What if I don't want to be? What if I want to walk out of here?'

'You're free to leave at any time. I'd remind you, though, you're supposed to be in prison. Any police officer who saw you on the street would have no choice but to arrest you. And if you were in possession of a firearm at the time... Well, you can imagine the years that would add to your sentence.'

'Blackmail. I'm impressed, but you know I don't have the gun with me.' Caelan flung herself into a chair. 'I suppose there are armed officers in the corridor now too?'

Beckett smiled, stood and opened the door. A man stuck his head into the room, grinning, a semi-automatic weapon in his hands. Beckett thanked him and closed the door.

'As I said, when it's deemed necessary, security is taken extremely seriously here.'

'Am I supposed to be frightened?'

Beckett sat back down. She removed her glasses, set them on the table and rubbed her eyes. 'Frightened? No. I was hoping to reassure you.'

'Then tell me the truth. Stop feeding me bullshit and be honest. What happened at Westminster station? I saw Walker, you know I did. You were as shocked and surprised as I was. You spoke to someone on the phone, and then pretended I'd been imagining it. Why?'

Putting her glasses back on, Beckett held Caelan's gaze. 'Of course Walker was on the train. We were in a public place, a busy one at that. Did you really expect me to discuss someone like Glen Walker on the street?'

'Why not? Everyone else is talking about him.'

'No, they're discussing the death of Sam Clifton. I don't have to tell you how many people are overjoyed to hear he's gone. Have you seen the news today?'

Caelan snorted. 'Strangely enough, no. Between discovering my friend's dead body and being arrested, I've not had a spare moment.'

Beckett glanced at her watch, then rested her hands on the table, lacing her fingers. 'The headlines say that one of Sam's former colleagues has been arrested on suspicion of his murder. Who could they mean, do you think?'

Fury erupted in Caelan's chest again. 'You've given them my name? You really are determined to end my career, aren't you?'

'End your career?'

'Sending uniformed officers to my flat to bring me in? How would that have looked to the neighbours? Some chance of me ever being able to work undercover again.' Caelan tipped back her head, blinking tears away. She had no idea why she should be crying – anger, perhaps. Exhaustion.

'You haven't been named, Caelan. The press have no idea who you are. We've fed them the information we want them to have, as usual.'

'Except where Sam Clifton was concerned. You made sure they had his name, you hung him out to dry.'

'We had no choice.' Beckett's expression made it clear there would be no further discussion of the subject.

'It's convenient for you that he's dead, though,' Caelan couldn't help pointing out.

Beckett continued as if Caelan hadn't spoken. 'There's no possibility of your identity being revealed to anyone.'

'The people who live in my building could easily put two and two together.'

'We had to make the arrest look real.' Beckett didn't sound in the least apologetic. 'If necessary, say you witnessed a mugging or saw a shoplifter, and you were coming in to make a statement. I doubt anyone will link you to Sam's death, much less ask you about it. Why should they?'

'You could have had me arrested in the street, in a shop, rather than at my home.'

Beckett eyed her. 'You feel safe there.'

It wasn't a question, and Caelan stared back at Beckett, trying to read her expression. There wasn't one. Her face was as impassive as ever.

'Yes. Doesn't everyone?' Caelan knew it was a stupid thing to say, even as the words left her mouth. No. Millions of people didn't feel safe in their homes; felt threatened and unsafe even in the country they lived in.

'You must miss Nicky.'

Caelan narrowed her eyes. Beckett's statement was even more stupid than her own had been. 'We're not here to talk about me.'

'Fine.' Beckett was brisk. 'The pathologist who performed the post-mortem on Sam Clifton's body confirmed he was strangled.'

Caelan swallowed. 'He was already dead when he was strung up there?'

'Does it matter?'

'You know it does.'

Beckett blinked a few times. 'Then yes, he was.'

'It wasn't me.'

'How do you explain your fingerprints being on the rope?'

'I can't. I wanted to ask you about them – was it made to look as though I'd tied the knot?'

'Numerous prints were found on the surface of the clothes line. Not around the knot specifically, no, or at least no more than on the rest of the rope. You know as well as I do that it makes little difference. Your fingerprints are on the rope that killed your friend and former colleague; your DNA was found in his flat. That's all most juries would need to hear.'

Caelan forced a laugh. 'What about on his skin, around his throat?'

Beckett shrugged. 'No, but it wouldn't matter. A case convincing enough to convict you would be easy to build.'

'You've made your point. I'm in the shit.'

'Which is why we need to find the people behind all this as soon as possible. Today would be preferable. I wasn't going to tell you this, but...' Beckett looked momentarily uncomfortable, 'I'm coming under increasing pressure to have you charged. The arrest we staged should shut them up for a while, but it's a temporary fix.'

'Pressure from whom? You're the big boss, aren't you?'

Beckett shook her head. 'I'm accountable to more people now than when I was a probationary constable.'

'But with a sight more clout.'

'You lived in Camden before moving to your current address, am I right?'

'You don't need me to confirm it. No doubt you know everything about me.'

Beckett acknowledged the point with a quirk of her lips. 'I sent someone there. You had a washing line in the back yard?'

Caelan frowned. 'You mean...?'

Nodding, Beckett spread her hands. 'The line has been removed. No one's bothered to replace it yet.'

'But that could have been anyone, at any time since I moved out – the landlord, a new tenant...'

'It could have been, yes. Or it could have been a person who was planning to frame you for murder at some point, even back then.'

'You don't know—'

'We checked with the landlord. He remembered you, complained that you'd taken the clothes line with you when you left.'

'You're not serious? He checked?'

'It was on the list of items that came with the property, and that should have been left behind by the vacating tenant. I'm surprised he didn't chase you for reimbursement.'

'Christ.'

'It was taken by you.' Beckett lifted her shoulders, let them fall. 'At least that's what someone wants us to think.'

Caelan leaned back in her chair, pinching her lower lip, frowning. None of this made sense. 'It's too amateurish,' she said. 'If Adamson, Penrith or Nasenby were involved, they would have made a better job of covering their tracks.'

'You think?'

'I know. Unless…' Caelan chewed her lip, thinking about it. 'Unless it's deliberate.' Suddenly she slammed the palms of her hands on the table, causing Beckett to jump. Half expecting the armed officer outside to kick the door down and aim his gun at her, Caelan quickly apologised. 'The whole case is frustrating. I thought it was over.'

'With Lambourne still out there, it could never truly be closed,' said Beckett.

'Can I ask some questions?'

'Go ahead. I may not answer them.'

'Why am I here?'

'An easy one to start. Because I need you to find out who killed Charlie Flynn, Ronnie Morgan and Sam Clifton, as you're already aware.'

'Why this building? If it's so secret, why bring me here?'

'You've answered your own question. I don't want anyone to know where you are. The people who work here can be trusted to keep our secrets.'

'Why wasn't Glen Walker arrested earlier?'

'Because we didn't find him. We know he was on the train, and we didn't think anyone got off before our officers arrived. Evidently Walker did. We're still trying to find out how.'

'It's as though he's taunting us.'

'Or being used to taunt us, yes, I agree.'

'What about the surveillance on Nasenby, Penrith and Adamson?'

Beckett blew out her cheeks. 'Nothing suspicious. They're going about their business.'

'I told Adamson you suspected that one of the three of them was involved.' Caelan waited for the onslaught, for Beckett's anger. It had been foolish, stupid in the extreme. She had no evidence Adamson was innocent, except her own gut feeling.

The expected outburst didn't come. Beckett smiled. 'You trust him.'

'He's never given me a reason not to.'

Beckett tapped a finger on the table. 'Shall I tell you something interesting about Richard Adamson?'

Caelan eyed her. 'Is it relevant?'

'It's not gossip, if that's what you mean. You remember the operation where you lived with him? Shared a bed?'

'Six months of hardly sleeping in case I rolled over and ended up on top of him?' She screwed up her face. 'Yes, I remember.'

'And you recall how the assignment ended?'

306

Frowning as she thought about it, Caelan said, 'Abruptly. We were pulled out with immediate effect, the operation abandoned.'

'Were you told why?'

'No. I never asked.'

Beckett nodded. 'And you would no doubt have been told a lie if you had. The truth is, Adamson fucked up.'

Caelan stared at her, almost more shocked by her language than by what she was revealing. 'What do you mean?'

'He managed to jeopardise the whole operation. We had to get you both out quickly, in case your cover was blown.'

'What happened?'

'You remember what you were doing?'

'Spending a lot of time in dodgy pubs and illicit casinos. Richard gambled, played poker – badly. I'm surprised we weren't rumbled straight away. I mingled and flirted, tried to make some friends.'

'All with the goal of gaining the trust of a man suspected of all sorts of criminal activity.'

Caelan scowled, remembering. 'He was a pimp and a people smuggler. That's before you mention the property business renting out some of the worst dives in London to people he'd smuggled into the country, as if he was doing them a favour.'

'The same people he employed in his businesses and brothels, working sixteen-hour days for negligible wages.' Beckett waved a hand. 'Do you recall his name?'

'Seddon,' Caelan said immediately. 'Duncan Seddon.'

'Correct.' Beckett nodded. 'Seddon might remember you too.'

'What?'

'Like I said, Adamson fucked up. Drank too much one night, said the wrong thing, raised suspicion.'

'He told Seddon my name?'

'No, he kept his head, but the damage was done. Seddon was eventually convicted of murder, despite our aborted attempt to gather evidence. Luckily for us, it wasn't long before he knifed a bloke in a pub in front of tens of witnesses.'

'Not so lucky for the person he killed.'

'No, but it got Seddon off the street. He's serving life.'

Caelan shuddered. 'And Richard still has a job.'

Beckett pursed her lips. 'Not my decision. Anyway, Seddon never found out who you really were. The interesting thing is who Seddon is related to.'

'Related to?'

'It's come to light thanks to some bright spark on DCI Achebe's team.'

'And?'

'Duncan Seddon is the cousin of Charlie Flynn's mother.'

'Are you serious?'

'Entirely.' Beckett lifted her eyebrows. 'It may mean nothing, but…'

'But it's a link. Fuck.'

'We're interviewing Seddon later today.'

'In prison?'

'That's where he lives.' Beckett gave Caelan a hard stare. 'And before you ask, no, you can't be the one to talk to him.'

'I wouldn't expect to. Anyway, I wanted to read the Charlie Flynn files again.'

'Because Ian Penrith told you to?'

'He suggested it. And I haven't visited Brendan Milne's flat yet.'

'Why? Walker had never been there, forensics proved that.'

'He doesn't want to be found. He was a few metres from us earlier today and we didn't get him. Have you thought about how he knew we were going to be on the train?'

Beckett grimaced. 'Maybe he was watching your flat. Maybe he followed us when we left Limehouse. I've no idea.'

'You didn't tell anyone where you were going?'

'No one, not even my husband.'

'Really?'

'He knew I was coming to collect you. He didn't know where we were going. He doesn't know I use this office either.'

'Can't be easy to have secrets from him.'

'Don't be naïve, Caelan. Secrets are part of the job.' Beckett heaved a sigh. 'Study the Charlie Flynn files. Maybe you'll spot something everyone else has missed. I include myself in that.'

'You've read them?'

'Of course I have.'

'You've known that the truth about his death was covered up for longer than you said.'

Beckett spread her hands on the table. 'All right, I'll be honest. I've been looking at this case since the day Charlie died. It's never added up, none of it. I knew I had to be careful, discreet – I didn't want to put any more of my officers at risk. You resigned, Sam and Nicky were out of the picture, and I was left with Nasenby, Penrith and Adamson – the three I had an inkling I needed to focus on.'

'Nicky was out of the picture? She was murdered.' Caelan rubbed her eyes, exhaustion dulling her vision. Beckett nodded, acknowledging the point.

'I've believed for a long time that someone in our department was dirty, but I could never pin down who it was.'

'Dirty? How do you mean?'

'Come on, Caelan. We tried for years to collate enough intelligence on Seb Lambourne to bring him in. The National Crime Agency has been digging around him too, and found out about as much we have. Nothing. Why?'

'Lambourne's clever, he—'

'My guess is he had inside information. Someone was warning him we were sniffing about, every step of the way, allowing him to move assets around, cover his tracks. Allowing him and Walker to disappear after Charlie died.'

'You think Lambourne was paying someone to keep him informed? Who?'

'If I knew, we wouldn't be having this conversation.'

'You said you'd looked at the financial records of everyone on the team. No clues there?'

'We have, but this is someone who knows how to leave no trace. You said it yourself – we're not dealing with amateurs here. Cash must have changed hands. Seb Lambourne would have no shortage of notes he needed to be rid of from his various schemes.'

'It must have been huge amounts of cash, though. Why would you take the risk otherwise?'

Beckett sat back, rubbing her chin. 'A fortune, yes. But something went wrong – the kidnapping of Charlie Flynn. Suddenly our bent cop is worried. I think Charlie saw him, could have identified him. That meant the boy had to die.'

Caelan shivered. 'But why was he kidnapped in the first place?'

'Maybe he saw something he shouldn't have done and was removed to keep him quiet. I don't know. Maybe Seddon will be able to help us, though I'm not hopeful.' Beckett tapped her fingernails on the arm of her chair. 'Thinking about it, perhaps you should visit Seddon, Caelan. I've no concerns he'll remember you from your operation with Adamson. It was a considerable amount of time ago, and no doubt you played your role to perfection. I don't want to tell anyone else about these ideas of ours.'

Caelan raised an eyebrow, uncomfortable with Beckett's flattery. She was crawling, and it didn't suit her. What was she up to? Caelan focused on the other woman's face, unease creeping through her again. 'Our ideas?'

Beckett laughed. 'Okay, mine. But someone is pulling the strings, someone dangerous and with no conscience. Someone who would kill a ten-year-old child to protect themselves.'

'We don't know that. How would Ronnie's death fit in with your theory?'

'A brutal and no doubt effective way of telling Seb Lambourne to stay away and keep his mouth shut? I don't know.'

'Did you ever expect me to be able to find Lambourne?'

'I hoped you could.' Beckett glanced away, and Caelan pounced.

'I thought you were being honest with me?'

Beckett held up her hands. 'All right. I doubted you'd be able to. I had an inkling that Lambourne's supposed reappearance was smoke and mirrors. Something else is going on here, Caelan. Something we don't yet fully understand.'

'What about Walker? He's back for sure.'

'I'm not disputing that.' Beckett's mobile began to ring, and she took it from her bag. 'Excuse me. It's Adele Brady. I should answer.' She raised the handset to her ear. 'Adele. I assume you're ringing to update me on the situation with Glen Walker?' Caelan watched Beckett's expression change as she listened. 'You're certain?' A pause, colour rising in her cheeks. Then: 'It's disappointing. Keep me informed, Adele.'

She placed the phone on the table and closed her eyes. Caelan watched, concerned, until they opened and Beckett said, 'Walker bribed a Transport for London employee to let him off the train when the announcement was made that people needed to stay where they were. He evidently then managed to disappear in the crowd. We've found footage of him leaving St James's Park station, but then we lose him. As usual, he's one step ahead.'

'Doesn't explain how he knew we'd be on the train.'

'All I can think is that he must have followed us.'

'I would have seen him.'

'Perhaps not. We were hurrying, we had the umbrella. You may not have noticed one man behind us in the crowds.'

She would have. Constantly surveying her surroundings was second nature. Whatever Beckett said, Caelan knew Walker had not been following them. She decided to let it go, for now. Beckett would never agree, never admit there could be another explanation, one Caelan didn't like to consider. 'How much did he give the TfL employee?' she asked.

'Fifteen hundred pounds in cash.'

Caelan whistled. 'Tempting.'

'He said he had an important meeting to get to and couldn't wait around. The staff and passengers weren't told why they were having to remain on the train; only that it was being delayed.'

'Bit of a giveaway when twenty police officers boarded, though.'

'They were plain-clothes.' Beckett managed a tired smile. 'We did try for discretion.'

'Walker must have suspected that we'd stop the train from leaving. Why else would he be carrying such a large amount of cash?'

'It was in a brown envelope, ready to be handed over. The guy he bribed is young, in debt, he has children. He saw the cash, forgot his principles and his training.'

'Good thing Walker didn't have explosives strapped to his body. Are they going to sack him?'

'I don't know. It's not our issue.' Beckett blinked, and Caelan knew she would make sure the employee kept his job. Caelan would have done the same. He would appreciate the seriousness of his actions, how catastrophic the outcome could have been had Walker been a terrorist. He wouldn't make the same mistake again.

'We're continuing to look for Walker,' Beckett said.

'I don't think we'll find him until he wants us to.'

Beckett checked her watch. 'He? Who do you mean? Walker himself, or someone else?'

'Whoever Walker's boss is.'

'He could still be working alone. I want you to go and speak to Seddon. Take Ewan Davies with you.'

'Will he be free?'

'He's on his way here now. Keep him close, Caelan. Leave the gun at home for now, but I want you carrying it when you return from the prison. Call me when you've spoken to Seddon.'

'What do you want me to ask him? He could have friends on the outside, people who know Lambourne and Walker. We might be making a mistake by even going there.'

'I'm not concerned. Walker knows we're looking for him. There's no need to be cautious. Seddon's in the first year of a lengthy stretch. He'll be lucky if he doesn't die in prison.'

-

The room Caelan and Ewan were led to was square and stuffy, empty except for three chairs and a table. Caelan sat in the chair nearest the wall. At some point in the distant past, it had been painted white, now faded to a dismal grey. She heard faint shouting, another voice bellowing a response. On the floor above them, feet were pounding, faint cooking smells conjuring images of hundreds of prisoners queuing for their dinner. She wished she had a bottle of water to hand, knowing her suddenly dry mouth was a result of the trepidation and anxiety being in this place provoked. They had surrendered all their possessions before being allowed into the main buildings, been searched, then ignored by a bored-looking drug detection dog. Beckett had given them police identification bearing fake names to use at the prison. As far as anyone else knew, Caelan Small was languishing in a cell somewhere.

Caelan had been in many terrifying situations, had felt fear grab her throat more times than she could remember. She had known that her best chances of survival hinged on trusting her instincts, her training and her ability. So far, she had managed to emerge physically unscathed. Here, though, she felt vulnerable. She assumed they were being kept well away from the cells, but there was no escaping the sounds and smells of over a thousand incarcerated men. The air seemed charged, tension simmering, tempers constantly close to fraying. It wasn't the first time she had visited a prison, but she hoped it would be the last.

Ewan sat down beside her. He folded his arms, looking around the room as uncomfortably as if the door had been locked behind them.

'First time in a prison?' Caelan asked.

He nodded. 'It's about as much fun as I expected. I want to run.'

'I know the feeling.'

'How do people survive in here for years? I couldn't get through an hour.'

'They've no option, I suppose. They might ask how you survived the army for so long.'

He grinned, but Caelan could see it was an effort. 'At least I was there by choice.'

'You made the decision to join up. After that, you were told what to do, same as all the blokes locked up in here.'

'True. Prison food's probably better too.'

The door was pushed open and a man appeared, followed by a prison officer.

'I wouldn't bet on it,' the officer said with a grin. 'Here he is. He's promised to behave. No doubt he'll tell you nothing, but it gets him out of my hair for a while.'

Seddon looked much as Caelan remembered him. He was in his early fifties, but appeared younger. He wore jogging bottoms and a matching sweatshirt, his dark hair neatly combed into a side parting, turning white above his ears and receding at the temples. The clothes, though clean, were well worn, old stains visible on the thin grey fabric. He was six feet tall and stocky, his eyes deep-set and shadowed. An intimidating presence, especially in the close confines of a prison. Caelan didn't move, didn't allow her expression to change as his eyes ran quickly over her face and body.

Seddon moved to stand in the centre of the room, staring at Ewan, then at Caelan. His gaze was neither challenging nor lascivious; he viewed them both with the same calculated intensity.

'Why would two coppers want a chat with me?'

The prison officer nodded to the chair and said, 'Sit down.'

'What if I don't want to speak to them?'

'You said you would. Now sit.'

Seddon smirked. 'They talk to us as though we're dogs, you see.' He moved to the chair and sat down, leaning back, his legs spread wide. 'Isn't that right, Mr Grandby, sir?'

The prison officer laughed. 'Part of the training, Mr Seddon. Humiliate and degrade the prisoners at every opportunity.' He winked at Caelan and Ewan. 'I'll be outside.'

As the door closed behind him, Seddon leaned forward. Caelan remained still, though she felt Ewan tense beside her. Seddon saw it too, and one corner of his mouth lifted. 'It's all right, son. I don't bite.' He lifted his hands, cuffed together. 'No threat at all, you see?'

Ewan blinked, but said nothing. Seddon turned his attention to Caelan.

'How about you, darling?'

Caelan stared back at him. 'Me?'

'How does it feel to be locked up with twelve hundred men? Some of the blokes in here have barely seen a woman in more than twenty years. I'd imagine they'd love to be sitting where I am right now.' He smirked, using his fingertips to adjust his trousers around his crotch, moving his knees even further apart. Caelan watched the performance, unimpressed. If Seddon thought he was going to rattle her with one of the most pathetic attempts at intimidation she'd ever seen, he was mistaken. She lifted an eyebrow.

'Finished?' she said. The effect on Seddon was immediate; he sat up straight, his features contorting.

'Hard-nosed bitch act, is it? Fine by me.'

'More convincing than your perving,' Caelan shot back at him.

'Telling you, when my mates on the wing hear I've been talking to a young woman, they'll want to hear every detail. Your face, your figure, the smell of your skin...' He leaned forward again, sniffing, treating them to a passable impression of Anthony Hopkins playing Hannibal Lecter. He groaned. 'Beautiful.'

'Oh piss off,' said Caelan. 'If you don't want to listen, go back to your cell, and we'll go home. Some of us can do that, Duncan.'

'And I won't be able to for another twenty years?' Seddon nodded, grinning widely. 'Good point. You've hurt me deeply by mentioning it – well done. All right. Tell me why you're here and I'll decide if I want to hear you out or not.' He widened his eyes, tipping his head to the side as if to prove he was listening.

'We were told you'd agreed to help us,' Ewan said. Caelan wished she had told him to keep his mouth closed, and let her do the talking.

Seddon chortled, displaying beige teeth and several gold fillings. 'New boy, is he?' Ewan blushed, and Seddon laughed harder. 'Leave him at home next time you come to see me, darling.'

Caelan was losing patience. 'We're here to talk about your cousin.'

'My cousin?' Seddon raised his cuffed hands to scratch at his jaw. 'Have to be more specific, treacle. I've thirty or more cousins, not to mention a shitload of half-siblings – my mum was an old slag, what can I say?'

'This cousin's young son was murdered,' said Caelan quietly. Seddon stared.

'Son? You mean Charlie?'

'You do know then.'

'Know? Of course I fucking know.' Seddon's lips were drawn back in a snarl. 'Shot in the head by some fucking paedo who'd been doing God knows what to him while the police sat around scratching their arses like the useless bastards they are.'

He showed his teeth in a parody of a smile. 'Present company excepted.'

'There was no suggestion Charlie was sexually assaulted.'

'So you say. I know how these fuckers work. Why else would you grab a kid and keep him locked up?'

'I can think of several reasons. We were hoping you might be able to help us decide which version is the right one.'

'I doubt it. Why are you asking?'

'Were you close to your cousin?'

He snorted. 'Close? No. Like I said, my family's huge. If I was close to everyone, I'd never get any business done.'

'Business?' Caelan remembered the briefings about Seddon's entrepreneurial activities, and suppressed a shudder.

'It's hard to believe, I know, but I have a successful plumbing and building company on the outside.'

'Plumbing? Right.'

'What does that mean?'

'Nothing, Duncan. Nothing at all.'

'My sons are running it while I'm otherwise engaged.' Seddon wiped his nose on the back of his wrist, the handcuffs clinking. 'Lucky I started paying into a pension early, isn't it?' Caelan couldn't help smiling. Seddon saw it, and winked. 'Think you and I are going to be mates. Not sure about him.'

'You knew your cousin's son was murdered, though?'

'Hard to miss it. All over the news, front page of the papers when he went missing. Then when he was found dead...' Seddon swallowed. 'I couldn't believe it. I went to the house, told them they should have paid the ransom.'

Caelan was careful not to alert Seddon to the fact that he'd given them information of interest. The Flynns had always denied receiving a ransom demand.

'And what did they say?'

He looked at her as if gauging whether to tell the truth. 'Listen, Miss Police Officer, what am I getting out of this?'

'Half an hour off work?'

'Meaning I'll lose some of my wages. A few pence less in the pittance I'm allowed.'

'I'll make sure you're not docked any money.'

'Good of you. What else?'

'You're starting a life sentence. I don't think you're in a position to make demands.'

'Don't you? Seems to me like the ideal time to try.'

Caelan sighed. 'What do you want?' It was a stupid thing to say, and the look he flashed her was pitying.

'Apart from you naked, bent over this table?' He licked his lips. 'I want out of this shithole. I've been in here before, but it's changed. It's all kids and blokes who can't speak English now. Most of them are mental, or pretending to be. I want my category to be reconsidered.'

'I bet you do.'

'Only fair. You scratch my back, and all that.'

'You know that won't happen, not yet. You killed a man.'

'Not intentionally. I never meant for him to die.'

'You stuck a knife in him, Duncan. What did you think was going to happen? It's not as though you tickled him.'

Seddon stuck out his lower lip. 'I'm not going to argue over the details. Tell me what you can do for me, or I'm off.'

'You won't even discuss it? This is about your own flesh and blood,' Caelan said. She doubted Seddon had a conscience, but it was worth a try. He lifted his shackled hands again, rubbed his top lip, scratched the stubble on his chin. Eventually his index finger disappeared inside his nostril. Caelan watched, not giving him a reaction. Eventually her patience was rewarded.

'They wouldn't even see me,' Seddon burst out. 'There were journalists, TV cameras, nosy neighbours. People laying bunches of fucking flowers everywhere, like it was going to help. Pricks.'

'How did you know a ransom demand had been made?'

Seddon stared at her. 'I guessed. "Pay up or we'll start chopping bits off your son and posting them to you." You know how it goes.'

'If you say so. Did your cousin ever confirm the kidnappers had contacted them?'

'I've told you, I never spoke to her.'

Caelan held in a scream. 'You were winding me up before? You're telling me you don't know if your assumption about the ransom was right?'

'I've no idea.' Seddon's grin was smug. 'Irritating bastard, aren't I?'

'What about other members of the family? Did anyone else talk about Charlie's murder?'

'What do you think? It was all anyone spoke about.'

'How did the family feel when the man who killed him escaped?'

Seddon sneered. 'When you lot let him get away, you mean? Shame you couldn't look the other way when I used my knife on a mouthy bastard who was taking the piss, wasn't it?'

'Taking the piss? What do you mean?'

'The whole pub was talking about Charlie's death. The bloke I killed? He made a smart remark, something about thinking the parents had done it and shifted the blame. I lost it. Next thing I know, he's on the floor, blood pumping over my best shoes.'

'How inconsiderate of him. You were defending your family's honour then, is that it?' She tried to keep the sneer out of her voice, but it wasn't easy.

'Didn't wash with the judge either.' Seddon sounded regretful.

There was a silence, Caelan wondering how best to play this. Seddon was wily, and clever. He might be able to help, but was equally likely to be stringing them along for his own amusement. Anything to break up the tedium of the day. 'Your victim wasn't the only one to think that maybe Seb Lambourne didn't kill Charlie,' she said, choosing her words with care.

Seddon let out a bark of laughter.

'Yeah, and maybe the *Titanic* sprang a leak. Maybe this whole world is a reality TV show, watched by little green men.'

'You believe Lambourne did it.'

'Wasn't I clear enough? Yes, I do. He didn't get his money, so he murdered the boy. Killed some copper too, I heard.'

Some copper. The image of Nicky slumping to the ground flashed through Caelan's mind again. She ran a hand over her mouth. Seddon watched with interest.

'Colleague of yours, was it? A friend?'

'No.'

'Still, it was only a copper,' Seddon taunted. 'Not as though you lot count, is it?'

Caelan met his eyes. 'Not as much as a ten-year-old child does, you mean?'

Seddon sat back, pouting. 'Why are you asking about this, anyway? It's ancient history.'

How much should she reveal? Fuck it. Beckett had said there was no need to be cautious.

'We've heard Lambourne's back in the country,' she said.

Seddon looked unimpressed. 'And?'

321

'And his son was murdered recently.'

'Lambourne's son was? Fuck me. Well, what a shame. Am I supposed to be upset?'

'Can you think of anyone who might have wanted to teach Lambourne a lesson?'

'Apart from the whole country? Got the "bring back capital punishment" brigade hot under the collar when he killed Charlie, didn't he? They all wanted him stringing up. Sounds a good idea to me too, now you can do your magic with DNA.'

'Except you'd be dead too by now. Hanged by the neck…' The memory of Sam's prone body flashed through Caelan's mind again. At least he had been dead before he was strung up there. It gave her little comfort.

Seddon smiled, unconcerned. 'Hardly the same. I'd never touch a kid.'

'Noble of you.'

'I try.'

'You've narrowed the list of suspects down to the entire population of the British Isles for us. Excellent work, Mr Seddon.'

'All right, sarky. Doesn't suit you, you know.' He shuffled in his chair, his brow wrinkling. 'My cousin and her husband might have had a go, but they're dead.'

'Seriously? You're suggesting your own cousin as a suspect?'

'Nah, not unless she's doing it from beyond the grave. Her husband's lot were well dodgy, though. Have a poke around his family tree – who knows what might fall out.' He struggled to point a finger at her. 'I'll give you that for free. Nasty bastards, all of them.'

'Says the convicted murderer,' Caelan couldn't help reminding him.

'Now don't be like that.'

'Anyone else? Preferably people who are still breathing.'

'What about the other geezer, the one who worked with Lambourne?'

'Glen Walker. We can't find him.'

'There's a fucking surprise.' Seddon clicked his tongue, considering it. 'No idea then.'

Caelan pushed back her chair. 'This is a waste of time. Goodbye, Duncan.'

He held up his hands. 'No, wait. You're serious about it not being Lambourne, aren't you?' His expression changed, his eyes narrowing, a smirk crawling around his lips. 'I'll ask you again. What are you going to give me?'

'What do you know?'

'Not how this works, darling.'

'I'm not your fucking darling.'

'Temper, temper. The copper who died... There was someone else there, wasn't there? It was supposed to be a rescue mission, turned into a total fuck-up. The bloke in charge was sacked.'

'And?'

'I don't know. In here, I'm shut off, but out there... Out there, I heard things.'

'What? What did you hear?' Caelan knew she sounded too eager. He would pick up as much information inside as he had when he was free. Men like Duncan Seddon didn't stop their activities because they were in prison. Seddon had nothing concrete to tell her, she was certain. And yet... she couldn't take the chance.

'I want to be moved,' he repeated.

'No chance. Tell me what you know.'

'Or else what? My life's fucked already. I'm going to die in here while my sons piss everything I've worked for up the

323

wall.' Seddon twisted in his seat, calling towards the door. 'Mr Grandby? I'll go back to my cell now.'

Caelan thought quickly. Beckett had the power to make things happen. What harm could it do to promise to try to help Seddon? He was right, his life was a write-off. He could wheel and deal all he liked, but he would still be inside. His power had been diminished. Did it matter where he spent the rest of his days?

'Listen, I'll speak to my boss,' she said quickly, urgency bleeding into her voice.

Seddon heard it, cocked his head. 'I'm listening.'

'You're a Category A prisoner, and I can't change that. What I can do is try to make your time here more palatable.'

'Still listening.'

'What can I say? Your own clothes, full privileges? Money, cigarettes.'

He sketched a yawn. 'Not good enough.'

'Then we're finished.' This time Caelan got to her feet.

Seddon managed to click his fingers. 'Not until I say so.'

She looked down at him, not hiding the sneer now. 'You're in charge, are you?'

'I did some business with Seb Lambourne once. I regret it, of course, now I know what he is. It was years ago, but you never know, I might be able to tell you something, if…' He sat back, waited.

'What do you want? Tell me, and I'll see what I can do – within reason.'

He smiled. 'Good girl. Like I told you, I want a transfer. Somewhere with fresh air, scenery. I want to do some gardening, grow some vegetables, maybe flowers. I'm sick of London.'

Caelan stared at him. What was his game? People like Seddon didn't do anything without a reason, and she couldn't see him digging or weeding. 'What about your family, your business?'

'My missus has been shagging my brother for years. They think I don't know, but it suited me to let them get on with it. Allowed me time to have plenty of fun of my own. He moved into my house the day I was arrested. The business is fucked. Let the boys wreck it. My time's over. Think of it as me wanting a retirement home.'

'Scenery? Gardening? Not the top of most prisons' list of priorities, I don't think.'

'Which is where they get it wrong. Some trees and fields to look at, even through the bars on the windows, would do most cons the world of good.' Seddon's voice was dreamy.

Caelan shook her head. 'Now I know you're taking the piss.'

'Not at all.'

'What about HMP Wakefield?'

'Monster Mansion? Funny. Anyway, it's surrounded by houses.'

'Frankland?'

Seddon rubbed his chin. 'Better. Still full of perverts, though.'

'You're Cat A, Duncan. Your fellow prisoners aren't going to be angels.' Caelan was losing patience. 'I need to leave here in the next ten minutes. I'll see what I can do about a transfer, but I don't have much authority. I'm making no promises. Take it or leave it.'

Seddon scowled. 'If you have no authority, why are you here?'

'Because we thought you might want to see the person who murdered a ten-year-old relative of yours behind bars for the rest of their life. Seems we were wrong.'

'Reverse psychology now? You know how it is. No such thing as something for nothing. Now,' he leaned forward, 'let's talk.'

'You said you did some business with Seb Lambourne. What did you mean?'

He laughed. 'I'm not giving you details. I had some merchandise to sell, he heard, wanted to buy. We agreed a price, did the deal.'

'Did you meet face to face?'

'Once, in a pub. Horrible place.'

'Where was it?'

'Whitechapel.' Seddon made guns from his index fingers and thumbs, pointed them at Caelan. 'Not the Blind Beggar, it was some other shithole.'

What the hell? 'The Wheatsheaf?'

'Bingo! Do you know it?' The look Seddon gave her was impossible to read. Deafening alarm bells shrieked in Caelan's head. She was being played, manipulated. Seddon was leading her in a dance, and she had been forced to fall into step. She folded her arms. Something was wrong, and she had no idea what. Was this Beckett's doing? She had arranged the meeting. Seddon was a pawn, she was sure, dragged along for the ride. He'd probably been promised his transfer long before Caelan and Ewan arrived, having agreed to play his part.

'I've heard of it,' she said slowly.

'Plenty of meetings go on there. Lots of deals struck, agreements made. Tempers lost, sometimes.' He smiled at her. Caelan felt colour rise in her cheeks. Did he know what she had done in the Wheatsheaf? How could he? It was impossible, and

326

she told herself to stop being paranoid. Seddon was a gangster, vicious and violent, nothing more.

'Tell me more about your meeting with Lambourne. Was he alone?'

'No. Someone like him rarely is. Have to have their muscle, their heavies, showing how important they are.' He cleared his throat. 'Pathetic.'

'Who was with him?'

'The geezer you mentioned before. Walker.'

'You're sure?'

Seddon lifted his shoulders. 'He called him Glen.'

Caelan shook her head. 'Not good enough. We already know Walker used to drink at the Wheatsheaf.'

Seddon gave a slow, smug smile. 'Did you know he lived in the flat above it?'

Caelan's stomach dropped. She stared at Seddon, more certain than ever that he was telling her what he'd been instructed to.

'Are you serious?'

'Absolutely.' He grinned. 'Didn't know that, did you?'

'No.'

'Best get over there.'

29

Outside the main entrance to the prison, Caelan turned to look at the buildings. Ewan stood beside her, keys already in his hand. Caelan saw them, smiled.

'Ready to go?'

'Have been since we arrived.'

In the car, Caelan remembered she didn't have the phone Beckett had given her.

'Shit. We'll have to go to my place,' she told Ewan.

'No problem.' He accelerated away from the prison, clearly happy to be leaving it behind.

'But it is a problem. I'm supposed to be locked up.'

'What?'

Caelan explained about the arrest, the subterfuge, Glen Walker's appearance and the failure to capture him. 'I need the phone Beckett gave me. She wanted me to report back.'

'And the gun?'

'Yes,' she said, reluctant. 'I suppose I should have it. I'm not a fan of carrying firearms.'

'It could save your life, especially if you're going back to the Wheatsheaf.' He hesitated. 'Are you?'

'Not without a search warrant and some backup. I'll report back to Beckett, let her decide. It would be stupid to barge in there again. What did you think about Seddon?'

Ewan drummed his fingertips on the steering wheel. 'I don't trust him.'

'You didn't think he sounded as though he'd rehearsed what he was going to say?'

'Now you mention it…'

'I don't even know whether I can trust Beckett. How did Glen Walker know we were on that train? Why did Duncan Seddon sound as though he was playing a role?'

'Because he's beginning a life sentence and was out for what he could get?'

Caelan gazed out of the window, unconvinced. 'Beckett's told me things I have no way of verifying. She's been clever, making sure I can't trust Nasenby, Penrith or Adamson. Even Brady and Achebe are out of bounds now. She's separated me from everyone I had faith in.' She glanced at Ewan. 'Except you. Which makes me think.'

He gave her a sideways glance. 'What do you mean?'

'Why? Why does she insist you come with me everywhere I go?'

'I don't know.'

'To protect me? Or to keep an eye on me?'

'Wait a minute.' Ewan glared at her, his tone sharper than she had heard before. '*You* wanted me to be with you. From the first time we met, you asked me to tag along.'

'I know. Now I'm wondering whether I was supposed to.' She studied his profile. His jaw clenched, his frown fierce.

'This is ridiculous. I'm here because you wanted me to be.'

'No, I sent you away. Beckett told you to come back.'

'You sent me away? I'm not your bloody servant, Caelan.'

'No, but you're Beckett's.'

He exhaled. 'I'm not. I'd never heard of her until you spoke about her.'

Caelan closed her eyes. 'Bullshit. She's an Assistant Commissioner. Stop the car, Ewan.'

'No. I'm supposed to be—'

'What, watching me?'

'Protecting you.' He mumbled it, and she laughed.

'Are you joking? Do you think I need your help? Stop the car.'

'Fine. Have it your way, but when you're the next person found dead, it won't be my fault.'

'I'll take the risk.'

Muttering, Ewan yanked the steering wheel, stamped on the brake. To a cacophony of car horns and yelled abuse, he stopped at the side of the road. Caelan climbed out and strode away without looking back.

—

She ducked into a café, her heart thumping. Had she made a mistake? What would Ewan do? He knew too much, would be able to guess her next move. She knew there was a possibility she was being unreasonable. She had no evidence, no real reason to believe he was working for Beckett. But people around her were dying, and she had no idea who to trust. Seddon had given her a new lead, but without a search warrant, without Beckett's backing, she was stuck.

Approaching the counter, she asked for a latte, handing over most of the money she had and taking her drink to a table near the back of the room. She needed to get into her apartment to retrieve her phones and the gun. She had no way of getting in touch with Elizabeth Beckett otherwise, but anyone who wanted to find her would be aware that she would head home eventually. If she didn't make contact soon, Beckett would no doubt send people to bring her in. And then what? She could be charged with Sam's murder, be blamed for everything else. She took a mouthful of her drink, her thoughts rampaging.

Where to go, who to call? She had no money, no transport. She was stuck in the middle of Woolwich, more than eight miles from home, carrying only her keys, a few coins and a warrant card bearing someone else's name.

In other words, she was fucked.

The café was quiet, the only other customers an elderly couple who sat ignoring each other over cups of tea. The barista was a young woman with tired eyes. As Caelan watched, she removed a bottle of water from under the counter, unscrewed the cap and drank. Caelan knew she had no choice. She finished her coffee and picked up the cup.

'Hi there.'

The barista took the empty mug, flashed her a wary glance. 'Hi.'

Caelan held out the ID Beckett had given her. 'Do you have a phone I can use, please?'

Her eyes widened. 'Of course.' She moved to the end of the counter, gestured to Caelan. 'There's an office in the back, you're welcome to—'

Caelan was already by her side. 'Thank you. Is there another way out of here?'

A frown. 'Well, there's a rear door, but it's only supposed to be used for deliveries.'

'I'll need to use it. Thanks.'

'But...'

Ignoring her, Caelan pushed into the office the girl had mentioned. It was tiny, little more than a cupboard, but there was a phone on the desk as promised. She grabbed the receiver, stabbed at the numbers. Crossed her fingers, hoping she wasn't making a mistake.

'Another mistake,' she muttered to herself as the tone changed and the phone began to ring.

'Hello?'

She took a breath. 'Listen. I need your help...'

—

The journey would take him at least forty minutes. Caelan left the café through the delivery entrance, glanced around. She didn't think she and Ewan had been followed from the prison, but how could she be sure? Anyone watching would go into the café when she didn't emerge after a reasonable amount of time. It wouldn't take much detective work to question the barista and follow Caelan's route. She had to move, but not too far. Where? She had no way of disguising herself, nowhere to hide. She was in a narrow alley that ran behind the row of shops the café was part of. There were industrial bins, piles of rubbish, but nowhere to duck out of sight. Not unless you wanted to stink for weeks.

She walked to the end of the alley and waited. The road beyond was busy, and Caelan emerged onto a cobbled pavement. She looked around. A car with its engine idling had parked in a bay across the road, and she turned away, her heart rate rocketing. Her enemy was faceless, at least for now, but Beckett had the whole of the Metropolitan Police at her disposal. If she wanted Caelan found, evading capture would be next to impossible. Walker had managed it, though. How?

Caelan had to keep walking. There were no shop windows to pretend to admire here, no reason for her to be standing still. She kept her face averted from the car. Risking a glance behind her after she'd counted thirty steps, she realised it had pulled away. To follow her? It had vanished. Was she imagining threats where none existed? She rubbed her eyes, wishing herself miles away. She should have known, refused to do their bidding. This world was dark and murky, with a thin, vague line between right and wrong. During the Charlie Flynn case, the line had been rubbed away, and was now obliterated. She was alone.

How long had passed since she'd phoned him? She had no idea. She couldn't stray too far from their agreed meeting place. She rounded a corner, hoping to double back to the alley. The car she had been suspicious of was coming towards her. She kept walking, her eyes on the pavement. As it shot past, she glanced up, trying to confirm how many people were in the vehicle. She thought two, the driver and a passenger, but it was impossible to be sure.

Another car, slowing, stopping beside her. She froze.

'Excuse me, love. Any idea where Parry Place is?' An older man, chubby, his Yorkshire accent reminding Caelan of her grandfather. He stared at her expectantly, and Caelan shook her head.

'Don't live here, sorry.'

'Don't live here? No bugger seems to! Never mind.' He sped away and Caelan told herself to calm down. She was forgetting all she'd been taught – her training, and what she had learnt on the job. Staying calm and in control was a priority. If you didn't, you risked putting yourself and others in danger. She hadn't felt so panicked in years.

Outside the railway station, she huddled close to the wall and kept her head down, hunching her shoulders, attempting to disguise her face. Where the hell was he?

Eventually, when she was close to giving up hope, a battered car approached and stopped. Caelan hurried over when the driver wound down his window and she saw his face.

'Thank you, Jitesh. You're a lifesaver. I'm sorry I had to ask you to do this.'

The young concierge grinned. 'It's okay. It's my job to help, I'm happy to do it.'

'This is above and beyond the call of duty, though.' Caelan shoved the two phones he'd brought into her jeans pockets. He handed over a jacket, bundled with a scarf.

'The other stuff's inside,' he told her.

'Thank you. I promise I'll explain when I can.'

'No worries.'

'Thanks again. You'd better get back to work.'

'My brother's covering for me, there's no hurry.' He looked at her, worry creasing his face. 'Take care, okay?'

'I will.'

He pulled away, and she watched him go, then took out one of the phones again.

'Caelan, where the hell are you?' Beckett demanded.

'No doubt you know. I'm sure that tracking me via this phone is only too easy.'

'What? What did Seddon say? Could he help us?'

'Yes. He told me that Walker lived above the Wheatsheaf.'

'The Wheatsheaf?' Beckett paused. 'I'll send someone over there.'

'You need to work on your surprised voice. Duncan Seddon could use some acting lessons too.'

'What are you talking about?'

'You knew what Seddon was going to say, probably wrote the script for him. I'm not sure what game you're playing, but I've had enough. I'm going to drop this phone down a drain and get out of here.'

Beckett laughed. 'Now you're being melodramatic. I'm not playing games, Caelan. I want the truth and you're the best person to help me find it.'

'Yeah, bullshit. I'm ending the call.'

'Caelan, listen. You're right – I've not been honest with you, but you need to trust me. I'm sending a car for you.'

'Someone else I have to trust?'

'Listen carefully. Ian's coming for you.'

Caelan clutched at the phone, shrinking back against the wall. 'He's coming for me? What do you mean?'

'Ian Penrith. He's on his way.'

'Penrith? But I thought—'

'You can trust him. You must. He'll bring you back here and we'll discuss our next move. The end is in sight, Caelan.'

'It certainly is. I quit. Goodbye.'

'Caelan, wait—'

She ended the call, turned off the phone. Her hands shook as she pushed it into her pocket. What was Beckett talking about? Penrith had told her to trust him, and Beckett kept echoing his words. But Caelan didn't, she couldn't.

She scanned the area around her. Beckett hadn't said where Penrith was, but they had known she had been at the prison, knew she was no longer with Ewan. No doubt he had reported straight back to Beckett. For a second, the world blurred around her. Blindly, she reached for the wall, leant against it. What should she do? If she stayed here, she was a sitting duck. Penrith would find her. There was nowhere to run. She should have asked Jitesh to bring cash, her own ID. He couldn't have retrieved the gun because it was locked in her safe, and she would never have asked him to anyway. All she had to disguise herself with now was a jacket, a blonde wig and a hat. Penrith wouldn't be fooled for a moment.

The car she had seen before was back. Abruptly, it halted. Caelan watched as the driver's window was wound down. She couldn't make out a face, only the top of a dark baseball cap. Then... She heard nothing but felt the heat, the rush of air, saw the orange spray of brick dust. Instinct drove her, her body hurrying to catch up with her brain. She flung herself to the side as a second shot embedded itself in the brickwork an inch from her skull.

She hit the pavement hard, rolled away. The car engine revved as she sprang to her feet. Time stopped as she straightened, frozen by horror.

He was going to drive straight at her.

'Caelan!' It was a bellow, off to her left. She turned her head towards the voice as the gunman flung his car into reverse, tyres screeching.

Ian Penrith was racing towards her, his face red, a gun in his hand. He tackled her, the force of the impact flooring them both. He covered her body with his own, lifted his head, breathing hard. Caelan's ribs screamed, her palms and knees burning where she'd hit the cobbles for a second time.

'Ian, what the fuck—'

'Shut up and keep your head down,' Penrith ordered. Caelan closed her eyes, took a breath.

He heaved himself away and onto his hands and knees. 'He's gone. Caelan, he's gone.'

Sirens hurrying closer, people spilling in all directions. Penrith reached out a hand, hauled Caelan to her feet. 'We need to get out of here.'

'But—'

'I'll explain in the car.'

He hauled her along by the arm, his eyes constantly searching the area; bundled her into the passenger seat.

'Who was it?' Caelan managed to ask.

'Didn't you see?'

'No. He was wearing a hat, pulled down low, a scarf over his face.'

Penrith gritted his teeth. 'I'm taking you back to Westminster, to Beckett's underground lair. The shit's hit the fan, Caelan.'

She allowed her head to fall back, closed her eyes. 'Didn't that happen when Ronnie Morgan died?'

'Not like this.'

He pulled out into the traffic. Marked cars were arriving at the scene, officers tumbling out of the vehicles.

'Shouldn't we have waited?'

'For him to have another pop at you? I thought maybe not.'

'Who was it?' she asked again.

'Wait until we get back to the office. You can work it out for yourself.'

Penrith drove as quickly as the heavy traffic would allow. Caelan glanced at him, his hands tight around the steering wheel. He felt her gaze, turned his head.

'Are you okay? You're making a habit of being shot at.'

'What's going on, Ian?'

He sighed as the car in front of them began to move, released the handbrake. 'I told you I've been doing some investigation.'

'While making a song and dance about me being corrupt? Yes, I remember.'

He nodded. 'Which has borne fruit.'

'Meaning?'

'Meaning I can guess who killed Charlie Flynn, Ronnie Morgan and Sam Clifton.'

'And Charlie Flynn's parents?'

Penrith raised a hand, rubbed his chin. 'Them too.'

'You're *guessing*? Christ, Ian. It's not like you to be cautious.'

'We have to be, you know that. I don't have any evidence. If we can't prove it yet, we have to keep quiet until we can.'

'This is stupid. If you know who did it—'

Penrith thumped the steering wheel. 'What? What do you want me to do? Go and bring him in like any other criminal? It won't work, not this time.'

'Beckett had no problem doing it to me.'

He sighed. 'Hardly the same. We knew you weren't guilty.'

The sound of a phone ringing filled the car, Beckett's name appearing on the screen on the dashboard between them.

'Ian? Is Caelan with you? Is she safe?'

'Yes, she's here. She's fine.'

'I'm glad to hear it.' Beckett didn't sound glad. She was clearly pissed off, her tone sharp, the words clipped. 'Why did you send Ewan Davies away, Caelan?'

She saw no reason to lie. 'Because I didn't know if I could trust him.'

Beckett made a sound of exasperation. 'He's one of the few people... Look, never mind. Get back here, quick as you can.' They heard another voice mumbling and Beckett said, 'Excuse me a moment.' There was the murmur of conversation, and Penrith cocked his head, squinting, trying to make out the words. *What are they saying?* he mouthed at Caelan. She shook her head, as clueless as he was.

Beckett came back on the line. 'Okay, change of plan. We think we've found him.'

Penrith was frowning, and Caelan said, 'Who?'

'The man who shot at you a few minutes ago.' Beckett was impatient. 'I want you to go and verify it's the same car. Shouldn't take a second, then straight back here. Okay?'

'I thought we'd agreed that getting Caelan safely back to base was my priority?' Penrith said.

'We had, until I heard we'd found the vehicle.' She gave the location. 'I'll be waiting.' There was a click as she ended the call.

Penrith accelerated. 'She's efficient, I'll give her that.'

'She didn't say if they've found the shooter, and she's telling us to go to the car?'

'They must have him in custody.' Penrith's voice was tight. He flicked on the indicator, waited for a gap in the oncoming traffic. 'She was worried about you. Beckett, I mean.'

'She's a strange way of showing it.'

'You shouldn't have sent your babysitter away.'

'Ewan? He wasn't armed. What was he supposed to do against a gunman?'

'Well, what did you do?'

'You saw. Got out of the way.'

'A wise move.' Penrith made the turn. 'It's not far.'

Caelan said nothing, uneasy and rattled. Where was Ewan? Was he safe? And who had shot at her? Penrith had said he knew who was behind the murders. Was he telling the truth, or was it another bluff?

'There.' Penrith pointed a meaty finger in front of them. Caelan craned her neck. A squad car, its blue lights strobing, was parked across the road, blocking access or escape. A few uniformed officers milled around. Penrith brought the car to a halt fifty metres away from them, and climbed out. Caelan followed, her legs shaking. Penrith looked at her, clearly concerned.

'All right?'

'I'm fine. Let's get this over with.'

He nodded. For a second, she thought he was going to offer her his arm to lean on, but he turned and strode away. He had his warrant card out, approached the nearest uniform. The officer, a middle-aged woman, pointed over her shoulder.

339

'Vehicle's back there. We got the call to look out for it, saw it abandoned a few minutes later. We're waiting for forensics and God knows who else. I warn you, it's a mess.'

Penrith frowned. 'What do you mean? Did he crash, smash himself up?'

She grimaced. 'Not exactly. Looks to me as though he's blown his own brains out.'

30

Beckett had organised coffee, was standing at a table pouring it into dainty china cups as Caelan and Penrith hurried into the room. She turned to look at them, cradling her cup and saucer to her chest.

'It was Glen Walker, wasn't it?' She was looking at Penrith as she spoke, but he was staring at the carpet.

Caelan nodded, the image of Walker's ruined head slumped over the steering wheel fresh and immediate. She could still smell the blood, though she hadn't been allowed to get too close. Near enough to confirm that what was left of the face had belonged to Glen Walker.

'This is… unexpected.' Beckett drank. Her hands were steady, though she looked pale and exhausted. She lowered herself into the nearest chair and crossed her legs.

'I don't know, it seems being shot at is a daily occurrence for Caelan,' Penrith said. Beckett ignored the comment, nodding towards the coffee.

'Have a drink, Caelan. Sit down.' She indicated one of the chairs near her own. Caelan obeyed. The coffee was strong, and scalding hot. She sat and drank half before speaking again. The kick of caffeine would be welcome.

'Will someone tell me what's going on? Did Walker fire the shots, or was it someone else?'

Beckett and Penrith exchanged a glance. 'The pathologist is on his way to examine the body now,' said Beckett. 'We believe we're looking at another staged suicide.'

'Do you think Walker killed Ronnie and the others?'

Setting her empty cup down, Beckett shook her head. 'We know he didn't.'

'How can you be sure?'

It was Penrith, leaning against the wall with his hands in his pockets, who replied. 'Because Glen Walker was working for us.'

Caelan turned in her chair to stare at him. 'What?'

Penrith poured himself some coffee, not bothering with a saucer. The cup looked tiny in his hand, as though it came from a child's tea set. He grabbed a chair, dropped into it. 'Walker was working for us, reporting back when he could.'

'I had asked him to come here to speak to you. He was supposed to meet us here, though I didn't expect him to be on the same train.'

Her mind reeling as she absorbed what this new piece of information meant, Caelan said, 'Then why did he wave at me?'

Beckett's expression was thunderous. 'Because he's an idiot, an amateur. Was, I should say. He was playing a dangerous game, obviously decided that going to meet his employer was more important than coming here to speak to us.'

'What was he supposed to be reporting back on?'

'Anything we would find useful. Most importantly, who he was working for.'

'But he didn't?'

Penrith shook his head.

'He wouldn't tell us, because he wanted to protect himself. He did feed us some useful information, reasoning that if we worked it out for ourselves, he wouldn't be a grass.' Beckett's mouth twisted. 'Because it matters, of course.'

'But now he's dead. He obviously didn't see that one coming.' Caelan felt a hysterical giggle trying to push its way out of her mouth. 'We allowed Sam to be killed, now Glen Walker. Why are we doing nothing?'

'We're not, however it might appear,' Beckett told her.

'While you've been haring around London dodging hails of bullets, I've been doing some old-fashioned detective work.' Penrith crossed his arms over his belly. 'Want to hear about it?'

Caelan finished her coffee, put the cup and saucer on the nearest table with a clatter. 'As long as it's not more bullshit.'

'It won't be. Scout's honour.' Penrith unfolded his arms, planting his feet squarely on the floor, knees wide apart. 'We tracked Glen Walker down a couple of days ago. You don't need to know how, or when. He confirmed that he hadn't seen or heard from Lambourne since Charlie Flynn's death. Walker had been lying low; he never left London. We set up surveillance to be sure he was telling the truth, and when we were satisfied, we offered him a deal.'

'Information in exchange for his freedom?'

'Sort of. We made no promises, but why wouldn't you be keen to help when the alternative is to spend the rest of your life behind bars?'

'I bet that'll be a real comfort now he's had his head blown off.' Penrith's expression didn't change, and Caelan continued. 'You knew from the start, didn't you? You knew Lambourne and Walker hadn't killed Charlie. You wanted to use Walker to find out who had.'

Another quick glance at Beckett, as if Penrith was asking for permission to speak. 'Correct. We had no illusions about

343

Lambourne – we knew the chances of finding him were close to non-existent.'

'Why?'

Beckett cut in, holding up a hand. 'The point is, we hoped Walker could help us, and in return, we promised to help him. He'd be looking at a much shorter prison sentence, if he went to jail at all. He had no real choice.'

'Who is it? Adamson, or Nasenby?'

Beckett said nothing, watching Caelan's face. Caelan shifted in her chair, wondering if she'd missed something. 'Ian?' Penrith was silent too, his eyes on the floor. Panicking now, Caelan turned back to Beckett. 'What aren't you telling me?'

Beckett's sigh was long and heartfelt. 'We still don't know.'

Caelan threw back her head, her skull thudding into the chair. 'Are you fucking kidding? How can you not know? Ian said—'

'I said I could guess, but had no evidence,' Penrith reminded her.

'What about the surveillance on them? Someone shot Glen Walker today – if you're watching Nasenby and Adamson, you must have seen who did it.'

Beckett was shaking her head. 'But we didn't.'

'What are you talking about?'

'When the shots were fired at you earlier, was Walker in the car alone?'

'No, I think there was a passenger. I couldn't see, not for sure.'

Beckett nodded. 'Walker shot at you, missing deliberately because he knew that killing you wouldn't be a great idea, then once he had driven them away from the scene, the passenger killed him.'

'We're supposed to think Walker was behind all the deaths,' Penrith said. 'Needless to say, we're not buying it.'

'Did the surveillance team fuck up then? Lose them?'

'Not exactly,' said Beckett. 'I told them to stand down this morning.'

'You... you did what?'

Beckett was unruffled. 'You think I made a mistake?'

Caelan stared at her. 'In the event, don't you?'

'Not at all.'

'I'm two seconds from walking out of here,' Caelan snapped. 'What the fuck is going on?'

'We knew Glen Walker had been asked to meet his mysterious boss in central London earlier today. He was supposed to report back to us, as you know. Instead, he met his boss and they went to find you. We had an idea something was going to happen, so I took the surveillance teams out of the equation.'

'You're not serious?'

'I'll admit, I didn't expect Walker to be killed, or you to be shot at, but I didn't want Nasenby and Adamson to realise anyone was following them. They're both highly trained officers with excellent records. I knew that every day they were under surveillance was a risk. The longer it went on, the higher the chance of them spotting the surveillance.'

Caelan gave a slow handclap. 'But instead of risking being rumbled, we've got another dead body and are no nearer discovering who pulled the trigger? I'm sorry, but you fucked up.'

Beckett continued as though Caelan hadn't spoken. 'We're going to let Walker's death be reported as suicide. Allow people to think he was behind everything, then, filled with remorse, decided to end his own life.'

'You've got to be kidding. As if he would.'

'It's perfectly feasible.'

'And covers your fuck-up. No doubt you're glad he's dead.' Beckett said nothing, and Caelan baulked as she realised. 'You knew, didn't you? You guessed this would happen. You allowed Walker to meet this person knowing they would kill him.'

'Nonsense.' Beckett was perfectly calm.

'That's why you stood down the surveillance. You knew Walker would be killed, and you didn't want anyone to know you could have prevented it. It's a neat ending for you, saves you having to deal with Walker, and means you can quietly deal with who's *really* behind all this, whether it's Nasenby or Adamson, with no fuss or bad publicity. Jesus, you're cold.' Caelan swallowed, bile filling her mouth.

'Enough,' Beckett said. 'I've told you what happened. You'd be advised to accept it.'

Caelan looked at Penrith, who kept his face turned away. Fear pulsed through her. She was at their mercy down here, and they knew it. She had to play their game, for now at least.

'Fine. If we go with your version of events, why would Walker kill himself?'

'Because he knew Seb Lambourne was coming for him.' Beckett paused, allowing her words to sink in. '*We* know Walker didn't kill Ronnie, but no one else does.'

'What about Ronnie's mother?' said Caelan. 'Doesn't she deserve to know the truth?'

'Of course, and when we know it ourselves, we'll tell her.'

'And in the meantime, she'll watch the news and be told that Walker murdered her son?'

'We'll speak to her. It's not your concern, Caelan.'

'I've met her, talked to her. Yes, it is.'

'All right. I said we'd speak to her.' Beckett saw Caelan's glare, shot back one of her own. 'I need *you* to focus on finding our killer.'

'And how do you expect me to do that? If you hadn't cancelled the surveillance, we'd already know who it was.' Caelan knew her tone was close to insubordination, but was beyond caring. Did it matter anymore?

Beckett inclined her head. 'Could you show Caelan the footage, please, Ian?'

'The footage?' Caelan narrowed her eyes. *Now what?*

Penrith lifted a tablet computer from one of the tables.

'I'll warn you, Caelan, this recording was made by the camera Nicky was wearing on the day Charlie Flynn died.' Caelan began to protest, not wanting to see it, but Penrith shook his head. 'It's from after Nicky was attacked. When...'

'When she was lying on the ground, bleeding to death?' Caelan forced him to meet her eyes. Penrith nodded, his expression impossible to read. Her hand trembling, Caelan took the device.

Darkness. Silence. Caelan watched for thirty seconds, but nothing happened. 'What am I supposed to be seeing?' she demanded. Her skin was prickling, her mind begging her to throw the tablet down and run from the room. She didn't want to watch these images, taken from a camera worn on Nicky's dead body. How could she continue to view them knowing that the picture was blurred because Nicky's blood was obscuring the lens?

'Keep watching.' Penrith's voice was uncharacteristically soft.

'And listen carefully,' said Beckett. Caelan hunched her shoulders. This was horrible.

She concentrated on the dim screen, keeping clichés about watching paint dry to herself.

Then she saw it.

A shadow, a shade darker than the murk of the rest of the screen, moved quickly across the camera's line of vision. It paused for a fraction of a second, presumably looking down at Nicky's body, then disappeared. Caelan was transfixed, wanting nothing more than to turn away, yet at the same time unable to do so. The screen was blank again. She made certain the volume was as high as possible, knowing what she was waiting for, and dreading it.

A gunshot. Muffled, but unmistakable. She started, flinching as if the gun had been pointed at her.

She had just witnessed the murder of a ten-year-old child.

'The figure you saw,' said Beckett, hammering home the point. 'That's the person we need to find.'

Caelan scrolled back, watched again. It was a vague outline, a shape; there was nothing recognisable. No face, not even enough detail to say whether the person was male or female. Caelan took a moment, focused on what she was seeing rather than imagining Nicky lying there, the camera still recording. Rather than thinking about Charlie now lying dead on the ground.

'Is there no way of making this clearer?' she asked. Penrith shook his head.

'You're watching the enhanced version. Took one of our tech geeks a while to get anything more than a completely black screen and the gunshot.'

'But it's useless.'

'No,' said Beckett. 'It was our first clue, and proof that Charlie Flynn wasn't killed when we originally thought, but ten minutes later.'

'Ten minutes?'

'Per the recording, yes.'

'And who had the opportunity to go back in and kill him?' Caelan felt sick, her mind refusing to accept what she had seen and heard. She knew she had to push the horror and fury away, to concentrate on the only thing she could do to help Charlie now – finding the person who had killed him.

Finding the shadow.

The knowledge that she and Sam had left Charlie, drugged and alone, to die in that place haunted her, and she knew it would for the rest of her life. But she had trusted Sam's judgement, followed his lead as she had been trained to.

'Sam knew, didn't he?' Her own voice sounded strange to her, the words hesitant as she struggled to even acknowledge the thought.

Beckett squinted at her. 'Knew? What do you mean?'

'He knew Charlie was alive. He must have done.'

'We've no evidence to suggest—'

'I don't need evidence. That's why he hid away, drank himself stupid every minute of the day. He fucking knew. He was part of it.' Caelan ground her teeth, white-hot fury tearing through her again. Sam was dead, removed and disposed of. He was a victim too, but Caelan could no longer feel any sympathy for him.

'We don't know for sure,' said Penrith. 'Not until we find our killer, anyway.' He nodded at the tablet. 'Check the emails. There's CCTV footage from today, some from the street Walker was found in. I've not been through all of it yet.'

Caelan looked at the screen again. 'Today was reckless. Before this, he'd planned carefully, left nothing to chance.'

'He's desperate now,' said Beckett. 'He must have guessed we'd turned Walker, probably after he missed when he shot at

349

you today. He wanted Walker out of the picture, unable to talk. He's backed himself into a corner.'

'You told me the Charlie Flynn files were interesting.' Caelan turned to Penrith. 'Was this what you meant?'

He nodded. 'Unanswered questions.'

Beckett's phone rang. 'Our crime-scene manager.' She lifted the handset to her ear as she stood and moved away. Caelan looked at Penrith.

'Why didn't you tell me what you were up to, instead of making me hate you?'

'You know why. Having all eyes on you was the best way of keeping you safe.'

'It's hard to believe Michael or Richard could be behind this.'

'Nevertheless, it's true. Walker must have been acting under instruction.'

'Who is it, Ian?'

Penrith looked at the carpet. 'I've told you, I don't know. My guesses are useless. We need evidence. Watch the CCTV footage, read the reports.'

'Surely they'd both know how to avoid the cameras? Half of them don't work anyway.'

'But half of them do.' He stood, stretched his back. 'See what you think.'

Caelan watched him move to the table where the flask of coffee stood and pour himself another cup. Beckett hurried towards them.

'The pathologist has confirmed that Walker *could* have shot himself. The weapon was found in the footwell of the car. Walker's fingerprints are on it – he's definitely fired the gun recently.'

'A few minutes earlier, at Caelan,' said Penrith. Beckett nodded.

'The bullet entered his left temple, and we know he was left-handed. It could be suicide, but...'

'But it's murder,' Caelan said.

'They're going to take the car into the lab, investigate it fully. I've told them I want results as quickly as possible, and screw the cost.' She ran a hand through her hair. 'I'm not hopeful, but we have to check.'

She was interrupted by a knock. She checked her watch. Penrith muttered, 'And behind door number one...'

'Come in,' called Beckett. Adele Brady appeared in the doorway, followed by Tim Achebe. As Caelan got to her feet, Brady saw her expression.

'Surprised to see us?'

Caelan lifted her chin. 'How's Michael?'

'Fine when I saw him last.' Brady grinned at her, and realisation dawned.

'You were the surveillance.'

Brady gave a gleeful nod. 'I was part of it.'

'You slept with him? That's commitment.' Caelan raised her eyebrows, and Brady laughed.

'We didn't have sex.'

'A comfort to his wife, I'm sure.'

'Not my problem. Come on, Caelan, you've done it too. It was work. He's not my type.'

Beckett clapped her hands. 'Enough. Caelan, I'd like you to go through the CCTV footage, as you discussed with Ian.'

Caelan nodded, picked up the tablet again. Closed her mind to everything except the images rushing by on the screen.

It was fifty minutes later when she stiffened, scrolled back, and watched again. She tapped her finger against the screen, tears in her eyes.

'Bastard. You utter shit.' She stood, raised her voice. 'We've got him.'

31

When Caelan emerged onto the street, rain was falling. She lifted her face to the sky, relishing the coolness for a second, before running for the car parked across the road.

'Evening,' Ewan said. His tone was courteous, but without warmth.

'I'm sorry. I was… Well, I was out of order.'

He nodded, his face grave. 'Forgotten. You're armed?'

She patted her hip. 'Let's go.'

Caelan was surprised how matter-of-fact she sounded. The discovery she had made a few hours before had rocked her, shaking the foundations of what she had believed. She had been wrong, and the realisation had hurt. Now, though, she was focused, fully engaged with the role she had been offered.

The sky was dark; the early evening air felt charged. Caelan knew that the sensation was caused by the usual pre-operation fear sending adrenalin skittering through her veins, giving the illusion of heightened senses and invincibility.

That illusion was dangerous. Fear was a friend, as she had been told early in her career. It kept you sharp, alert. Ewan had said the same when talking about his time in the army.

She smoothed a hand over her forehead, a few strands escaping the ponytail she had coaxed her hair into before leaving Beckett's underground bunker. Ewan tapped his fingers against the gearstick.

'You're sure about this?'

'Yep.'

'He's killed… what? Four people?'

'At least.' Caelan swallowed. 'It's okay, he won't hurt me.'

'Know for sure, do you?' Ewan shook his head. 'At least you have the gun.'

But would she be able to use it on him? If her own life was threatened, perhaps. Otherwise…

She leaned back, not wanting to think about it. It wouldn't be necessary anyway. She would have backup – Ewan, and others. Her safety wasn't the issue here. Justice for Nicky, Charlie and the other victims was.

The journey seemed to take no time at all. Ewan looked at the building, raised his eyebrows.

'Wonder if he'll be more welcoming tonight?'

Caelan grinned at him. 'Why shouldn't he be? Brady's not here.'

As she got out of the car, she touched the gun at her hip and glanced up again at the sky. She didn't believe in heaven or hell, but who knew what else was out there? Logically, scientifically, she knew Nicky couldn't see her, wouldn't be looking out for her. The instant her heart and brain had ceased to function had been the end of Nicky's love. Yet Caelan looked at the stars and remembered her. She hoped she was right; she wanted to draw a line under this.

Time to move on.

She stepped up to the door and knocked without giving herself time to think about it. Immediately, he was there, opening the door and peering around it, his face quizzical.

'Caelan? Another visit?'

'Michael.' Caelan looked into his eyes and smiled. 'We need to talk about Richard.'

'When did you first suspect him?' Nasenby crossed the kitchen, set a bottle of water on the marble table in front of Caelan and handed Ewan a glass of orange juice.

'Honestly? A few hours ago. You know Beckett has had people checking everyone's finances, poking around to see what we've been up to?'

Nasenby pulled a face. 'I'd guessed.'

You mean Brady told you. Whispering the secrets Beckett wanted you to know. 'Well, one of her people found out that Richard had bought a house up north somewhere, near his parents. No recent credit checks, no mortgage. No lump sum taken out of a savings account either. He lives in a shitty little place in Kentish Town, but this was a modern house he'd bought off plan. How?'

Nasenby rubbed his chin. 'Inheritance? Gift from his parents?'

'They're retired, barely managing. In fact, Richard sends them money each month.'

'A loving son.'

'Like Charlie Flynn, Ronnie Morgan.' Caelan paused, gave the names space to breathe, to settle. Nasenby was nodding.

'I've noticed Richard wearing expensive suits, a different watch…'

'Exactly. Nothing too flashy, but they're new. Could be as innocent as a bank loan or an increased credit card limit, but we've checked. Nothing.'

'Cash transactions then.'

Caelan nodded. 'We've even got some footage of him buying shoes in Harvey Nicks. He paid in notes.'

Nasenby leaned back in his chair. 'Didn't know you could. Thought it was invitation-only credit cards all the way in there.'

Caelan laughed. 'I began to wonder where the money had come from. Then there's the camera footage.'

'What footage?'

'When Lambourne attacked Nicky, the camera kept recording, even as she lay there dying.' Caelan's throat caught as she said the words, but she forced herself to continue. Now was not the time to let emotion derail her. She needed Nasenby to listen, to understand. 'It's obvious when you think about it, but for a while, no one did. Unacceptable, but mistakes happen, as we all know. When they played it back, they thought it was useless at first. Grainy, dark – looked like the bottom of the sea. There was sound, but the visuals were shit.'

'Then you got one of the tech geniuses on board.' Nasenby was nodding, already one step ahead.

'And he managed to clean it up. Not much, admittedly, but enough to be able to make out a figure.'

'Richard Adamson.' Nasenby blinked at Caelan. 'I can't believe it.'

'Neither could I. A man I'd worked closely with, had trusted with my life. But, as they say, the camera doesn't lie. Did you hear about the shooting?'

'Glen Walker? Yes. The same gun, I was told. The one that killed Charlie and Ronnie Morgan.'

'The one used to shoot at us the other day. The one used to shoot at me earlier.'

Nasenby stared at her. 'You've been attacked again? Christ, Caelan—'

She waved his concern away. 'Glen Walker apparently killed himself, filled with remorse because of his role in the death of Charlie Flynn and everyone else. Case closed with no loose ends.' She picked up her bottle of water, cracked the seal and drank. 'But we know it's not the truth. We know Walker and

Lambourne didn't kill Charlie Flynn. In fact, Walker didn't kill anyone.'

'Lambourne did. You saw him.'

Caelan nodded, acknowledging the point. 'We found Walker's body in his car. We've had preliminary forensics back.'

'Already?' Nasenby whistled. 'Must be a record.'

'Brady's shitting a brick about the cost, but it was necessary. We need answers, and we have to be sure before we arrest anyone.'

'What did forensics say?'

'There were no fingerprints, at least none we weren't expecting. Walker's own, mainly. But they found a hair.' Caelan shrugged. 'Doesn't mean much on its own, of course.'

'A decent defence would explain it away. Easy to obtain a hair and plant it.' Nasenby nodded.

'So we looked around for any cameras in and around the area where Walker's car was found. Also the place where I was shot at today.'

'And?'

'Inconclusive on their own. But if you add a couple of the stills to the evidence of increased cash flow, the hair and the images from the camera Nicky was wearing, a clearer picture begins to emerge.' Caelan took the tablet computer from her bag, laid it on the table. She drank some more water, her throat tight. Once she had shown Nasenby the proof, there would be no going back. These weren't accusations anyone would forget. Beside her, Ewan shuffled in his seat, no doubt sensing her tension.

Nasenby smiled. 'Show me.'

Caelan picked up the tablet. 'This is the footage from Nicky's camera. I'll scroll through until the time we're interested in. The first part is… distressing.'

Nasenby gulped, moving to stand beside Caelan. 'I'm sure.'

Caelan touched the screen. They watched the shadow flit across the screen, all three wincing at the sound of the gunshot. Nasenby had paled.

'Was that…?'

'The shot that killed Charlie Flynn, ten minutes after we first thought he'd died? Yes.'

Nasenby's Adam's apple jerked in his throat. 'God, Caelan. I can't believe it.'

'I know. I couldn't either at first. So I watched again. Then I blinked a few times, had a walk around the room and a cup of coffee, and watched it through again. On the third viewing, I noticed something else.'

Squinting at the screen, Nasenby frowned. 'What do you mean?'

'Let's have a look.'

Nasenby shuffled closer as the footage played again. 'I'm none the wiser, Caelan.'

'Okay. Watch carefully.'

'Can't you tell me? We could be here all night.'

'One more time. I'll point it out.'

'Fine.'

This time, as the shadowy figure flitted into view, Caelan tapped at the screen, freezing the picture. 'There. Do you see?'

Nasenby was clearly growing frustrated. 'What? I've no idea what you're talking about.'

She pointed. 'There. It's faint, very faint, but there's a tiny glint. I spotted it, asked the technician to work on it a little more.' She brought up another image, a still. 'There. Now do you see?' As Nasenby shook his head, Caelan looked up at him, smiling. 'I know it's difficult to make out, but we're fairly certain. It's a wedding ring.'

'But Richard's not married. He doesn't wear one.'
'No. But you do.'

32

Caelan set the tablet on the table, her other hand resting on her gun. 'It was you, Michael. You shot Charlie Flynn and Ronnie Morgan. You killed Glen Walker and,' she swallowed, 'you murdered Sam.'

Nasenby stared at her, then burst out laughing. 'You're delusional. Why would I do that? How could I have killed Ronnie Morgan? I was talking to you when it happened.'

'No you weren't. You called Ronnie's mobile when you were still talking to me, using a different phone. We were still at the station. You lured him to the underpass, and shot him. You knew I'd be following, but also that I'd be keeping my distance. If you waited inside, you could step out in front of Ronnie, shoot him and get away. I don't know the details, but that's how it happened. You've been clever, Michael, but not clever enough.'

Nasenby's hand whipped out, grabbing Caelan's throat. Immediately, white light exploded before her eyes, a humming filling her head. This was not how it was supposed to go. Ewan leapt to his feet, his chair clattering to the floor behind him. 'Don't bother, or I'll kill her now,' Nasenby told him. 'Are you armed?' Caelan managed a nod. 'Hand me the weapon.' She did so, not daring to risk anything clever. Best to try and talk him down. Nasenby took the gun in his free hand, glanced at it. He turned, smiled at Ewan, and shot him in the chest. A cry escaped Caelan's lips as Ewan fell, cracking his head on the marble table as he disappeared beneath it.

'Now look what I've done. Shame, he was a nice chap.' Nasenby grinned. 'Now, tell me what you know.' He removed his hand from Caelan's throat but jammed the gun against her temple. Caelan's knees had liquidised, her mind screaming. Ewan. He'd shot Ewan, and she was to blame. She had suggested this approach, attempting to catch Nasenby out, make him think they believed Richard Adamson was guilty. Now she realised that it had been naïve, foolhardy.

And Ewan had paid the price.

Nasenby cracked the gun against her temple, his other hand seizing her throat again. He squeezed. 'Well?'

Caelan forced herself to choke out the words. 'You were the one instructing Walker. He followed Ewan and me, shot at us outside the Wheatsheaf, all under your orders. Your hair was found in Walker's vehicle. We've got CCTV from one of the houses on the road where you shot him. It shows you getting out of the car.'

Nasenby laughed. 'Come on, Caelan, that's pitiful.'

'The wedding ring.'

'Because I'm the only person in London who wears one.' He laughed. 'Christ, I knew you were slipping – I didn't realise how far.'

'You were in Sam's flat. You left fingerprints, Michael. Amateurish. But then if you'd gone in there wearing leather gloves, Sam would have smelt a rat. You don't like people who fight back, do you?'

Nasenby released his grip on her throat to slap her face with such force the room darkened for a second. He grabbed the front of her shirt, almost lifting her off her feet. 'A bulletproof vest? Won't save you when I blow your head off.' He shoved the gun under her chin, then lowered it, tracing a line between her breasts. 'Maybe I should do it now?'

Choking on the blood gathering in her throat, Caelan kept talking. 'Seb Lambourne had been paying you for years for information. We never caught up with him, because you made sure we couldn't. Then you decided to be rid of him for good. Maybe he threatened you with exposure, we don't know yet.' Nasenby stared at her, shaking his head, his eyes wild. 'You suggested a kidnapping plot. Did you tell him it would be an easy way of making some cash? Make him a major-league criminal? Either way, it backfired. Lambourne panicked when he saw us, armed police. He wasn't expecting us. He killed Nicky so he and Walker could escape. You were sitting outside, waiting for the rescue operation to take place. How did Lambourne and Walker get away?'

Nasenby smirked. 'Wouldn't you like to know?'

'You helped them.'

'I left a van with the keys in it nearby. They hid in the back and waited. I drove them away later.'

Caelan blinked. 'It couldn't have happened like that. We were watching every vehicle; every house was under observation. We searched every property on the street.'

Nasenby's laugh was scornful. 'We did, but I might have missed something in the adjoining property. Those druggies living in the squat next door wouldn't have realised if Father Christmas had turned up in their living room. A quick change of clothes, and the guts to try it. There was a hole in the wall between the two properties, up in the attic. It's bricked up now, of course. Loose ends need tidying up, after all. Isn't that why you're here?'

'I don't believe you.' Caelan was swaying, her ears ringing, her nose leaking blood. He hadn't said enough, not yet. 'Half the Met was out there – the helicopter, dogs…'

'It's the truth. You think the cordon was watertight?'

'It should have been.'

'An army of people could have got away from there without being seen. It was chaos, especially once they knew the boy was dead.'

'You mean, when you killed him.'

Nasenby shrugged. 'Like I said, the house was empty until forensics arrived. Sam was a big help, though.' He grinned at Caelan. 'He knew how to keep his mouth shut, drunk or not.'

Hating him, Caelan resumed her summary. 'When you found out Nicky was dead, you had to act quickly. You knew Charlie was alive, but drugged. In the confusion, you rushed in and killed him. Why, Michael? Why did you do it?'

Pain exploded in her skull as Nasenby smashed the gun against it, releasing his grip so she fell to the tiled floor. Blood running down her cheek, she pushed herself to her knees, knowing she had to stand if she could. She was too vulnerable on the ground. Nasenby saw her struggling and drew back his foot. The kick to her kidney sent new shockwaves of pain hurtling through her chest, radiating across her back. Nasenby chuckled, her agony amusing him. Caelan twisted her body, turning onto her side, panting, spitting blood onto the floor. She caught sight of Ewan lying on his back under the table, and, gripped by fury, she forced herself to her feet. Nasenby watched, a mocking grin on his face.

'Have you finished your fairy story yet, Caelan?'

She staggered, holding onto a chair for support. 'I assume Charlie had seen you, could have identified you. Lambourne and Walker fled, knowing you'd set them up. With their

363

records, who'd believe that a high-ranking police officer had told them what to do? Then you heard a whisper that Lambourne was back. You couldn't take the chance. You killed his son as a warning.'

Nasenby sighed as if she was boring him. He stepped forward, slapping her face again. 'Rubbish.'

Caelan gasped, her ear ringing. He was going to kill her. She had to keep going.

'You'd already got rid of Charlie Flynn's parents. Then Sam, Glen Walker… You couldn't stop until everyone was dead, because any one of them could have exposed you.' She wiped blood from her nose with her hand. 'All those deaths, and for what? To save your reputation? A reputation you didn't deserve.'

Nasenby let out a roar, an animalistic bellow of fury. He threw himself towards her, wrenching her arm behind her back, ramming the gun against her temple. Caelan froze, breathing hard, knowing he would kill her without a second thought.

'I admired you, Michael,' she managed to gasp. 'I respected you.'

'Why wouldn't you? I'm the best there is. I get results. When I tell everyone how you and your sidekick barged in here and attacked me, I'll be believed. What are you doing here, anyway? You're supposed to be locked up.'

He twisted her arm, wrenching it in its socket until Caelan thought she would pass out with the pain. She had to keep him talking. 'Because I murdered Sam, killed Charlie, Ronnie and everyone else? Maybe you're not as convincing as you thought.'

It was a risk, and she knew it. He pressed his mouth against her ear, his breath wet and hot. 'I think I am, Caelan. I convinced Lambourne to kill Nicky, didn't I?'

Caelan's mouth opened, but for a second she couldn't speak. 'What did you say?'

'You heard me. The way she looked at me sometimes – she knew, I was sure of it. She had to disappear, and Lambourne was only too happy to oblige.' He grabbed Caelan's ponytail, gave it a savage twist. 'Never mind, I'm sure the apartment she left you was a comfort.'

He released his grip, shoved her away. As she sprawled across the floor, he smiled down at her, raising the gun.

'It's regrettable, Caelan. You were keen, clever. Promising. I was pleased when you retired. Too smart for your own good. Pity you came back.'

He laughed, pointing the gun at her head. Caelan closed her eyes, wondering where the hell her backup was. A gunshot shattered the air, the window behind her exploded.

The world disappeared.

33

Elizabeth Beckett was standing over her when Caelan opened her eyes. She looked around – white walls, gaudy curtains. Unsettling smells in the air. Hospital. She focused on Beckett.

'I'm not dead then.' The amount of pain she was in confirmed it.

Beckett laughed. 'Not quite. Neither is Ewan.'

Caelan's heart thumped. Ewan. She'd forgotten about him. 'Is he okay?'

'He'll live; the vest protected him, but he's still in a mess. He's not happy he was forced to stay on the ground while Nasenby was beating the shit out of you.'

Caelan managed a laugh. 'Seemed a sensible move to me.'

Beckett shrugged. 'It saved his life. Nasenby obviously wasn't expecting bulletproof vests until he realised you were wearing one.'

'He should have been, though he wasn't expecting us to be on to him either. Even when I showed him that the figure was wearing a wedding ring, he still frowned, shook his head and said he couldn't see it.'

Beckett shrugged. 'His arrogance blinded him to the fact that we were getting closer and closer to the truth.' She paused, blinked. 'You did well.'

'Anyone might have noticed the ring.'

'But they didn't. I'd watched the footage, so had Ian, as well as the technicians. We all missed it.'

Caelan turned her head. She didn't want praise, didn't deserve it. 'Is he dead?'

'Nasenby? No. The shot took him down, but he was in no danger of serious injury. He's still maintaining his innocence.'

'Even though you heard every word he said?' Caelan reached up to her ponytail, felt for the bobble that held it in place. 'Clever trick, this.'

Beckett held out her hand, examined the tiny length of elastic and the silvery bead attached to it. 'I can't see the transmitter, and I know it's there. Your plan worked a treat.'

'Not really. He didn't confess.'

'As good as – what he said was pretty damning. Wait until we get him in an interview room. He won't be so smug on the other side of the table.' Beckett bared her teeth. 'I'm sorry I had to keep you in the dark for so long. I hope you understand why it was necessary.'

'You lied to me.'

Beckett bit her lip. 'Occasionally. I didn't want you storming off to confront Nasenby, or Richard Adamson if he turned out to be our man. I know you're close to both of them.'

'Not close enough.'

Beckett checked her watch. 'I think you'll be allowed to leave soon; they're happy there's no concussion. Take some leave. I'll stay in touch, but I don't want to see you for a couple of weeks.' She smiled. 'Maybe go on holiday, or spend some time at home.'

Tears blurred Caelan's vision for a second, and she blinked them away. 'I want to see Nasenby interviewed.'

'You can watch the recordings.'

Caelan didn't have the energy to argue. 'Do you think he killed Lambourne?'

Beckett sighed. 'I think we can both guess the answer. We'll ask him. Now, I need to get back to the office.' She began to walk towards the door. 'I'll call you later, update you on Ewan's progress. I want you to go home.'

'But—'

At once, Beckett was stern. 'I'm ordering you, Caelan. You need to stay away while we clear up this mess.'

Caelan collapsed back onto the pillows, knowing when she was beaten. 'Fine.'

Beckett nodded, all smiles again. 'Well done today.'

'Can I ask one more question?'

A sigh. 'Make it quick.'

'The anonymous phone call, the one saying Lambourne was back in the country. Did you make it, or did Ian?'

Beckett tutted, thinned her lips. 'I couldn't possibly comment. Don't mention that again, Caelan, not if you know what's good for you.'

Epilogue

Three hours later, Caelan climbed slowly out of the taxi and staggered towards her building. Jitesh was behind the desk and he looked up, concern clear on his face when he saw her bandaged head, her battered face and pained movements.

'Are you okay?'

She tried a smile. Winced. 'I'm fine. A little sore.'

He glanced over his shoulder, lowered his voice. 'Did the police do that?'

Caelan laughed, her throat aching. 'Shall I tell you a secret, Jitesh? I *am* the police. Keep it to yourself, though.' She limped over to the desk. 'Thanks again for what you did.'

'No problem. No bother at all.'

She dropped an envelope in front of him. 'A thank-you present.'

Frowning now, he picked it up, looked inside. 'No. Thank you, but I can't.'

Caelan waved his protestations away. 'You saw the police take me away, but you were a good enough friend to still do me a huge favour, one that could have lost you your job. Take the money, Jitesh. Please.'

'I don't like to.'

'Well, I'm not taking it back.' She stepped away, bruises aching, the stitches in her head beginning to itch under the dressing.

'Do you need a hand to get upstairs?'

'I'll be okay, thanks.'

She wished him goodnight, shuffled towards the lift. As the doors closed, she leant against the wall, suddenly exhausted.

The flat was cold, and as she moved slowly through the rooms, she switched on every light. She ordered a pizza, called down to tell Jitesh she was expecting a delivery, then got into the shower, being careful to keep her bandages dry. She longed to have a bath, but knew she would struggle to climb out with her bruised, aching limbs and pounding head.

As she pulled on Nicky's old pyjamas and a thick pair of socks, the doorbell rang. She staggered over, pulled the door open without bothering to check the peephole, knowing Jitesh would have let the delivery driver in.

Nicky stood there holding a pizza box, her expression guarded. Caelan yelped, staggered, clutching at the door frame as Nicky hurried forward and grabbed her.

'All right, you're okay. I've got you,' Nicky was saying. The pizza was on the floor, and through her confusion Caelan wondered whether the bang on the head she'd received had been more serious than the doctors had realised. Nicky was still holding her, staring into her eyes. Caelan gazed back. She looked real; the arms around her felt real. There was concern in Nicky's eyes as she saw the dressing, the bruising on her face.

'It's me, Caelan. I'm here,' she whispered. 'I know it's a shock...'

'Nicky, I don't...'

Caelan's stomach heaved, the floor rushing towards her as her knees gave way. Nicky hauled her into the flat, slamming the door behind them. 'It's me, Caelan, it's okay.'

'You're dead,' Caelan said, her voice tiny. 'I saw you die.'

Nicky shook her head, tears in her eyes, her lips trembling. 'I'm fine, but I had to go away for a while. It was a set-up, Caelan. I'm so sorry.'

'I don't understand. You pretended? How could you... how could you do that? I thought you were dead. I held you, knelt in your blood, tried to help you. Sam had to drag me away; I didn't want to leave you.'

Nicky was sobbing now. 'I know, I remember.'

'How could you? How could you let me think you were dead?' Dazed, Caelan looked around her, remembering. 'But this is your flat, not mine. If you're alive... Jesus, Nicky. I went to your funeral. Your family were devastated too.'

'They know.' She swallowed hard. 'They didn't, but they do now.'

'And they've accepted it? You let them think you were dead and they've forgiven you?'

Nicky bowed her head. 'Not exactly. Listen to me, Caelan, I had no choice.'

'Fuck off, Nicky, of course you did.'

'No. I had to go. I suspected something wasn't right. People were already dead; I knew I'd be next. I did some preliminary work, went to Beckett. She offered me a safe place to stay, and took over.'

'Did Ian know?'

'Penrith? You'd have to ask him.'

Caelan gaped at her. This was too much. He did, she knew it. 'You're telling me Beckett knew about Nasenby from the beginning? She lied to me all along?'

Nicky shook her head, her eyes pleading, willing Caelan to understand. 'We didn't know who it was. She wanted time, a chance to begin some discreet investigations. She didn't think

I would be safe, so we… we arranged for me to disappear for a while.'

'Disappear? You died, you fucking died. All the blood…' Caelan shook her head, speechless.

'Pig's blood, I think. I had it ready, a pump and tube…'

'Ready?' Caelan stared at her. 'How did you know Lambourne would attack you?'

'I didn't, but if there was a chance to make it look as though he'd killed me, I had to be ready. Lambourne barely touched me; he just wanted me out of the way. He didn't hurt me.' Nicky shook her head, helpless.

'He didn't hurt you? You lay there gasping and choking, letting me believe you were dying, and he hardly touched you? I blamed myself for not saving you, have done ever since, and you were in a safe house somewhere?'

'I—'

'I went to your funeral, grieved for you, dragged myself back here to find Lambourne, to make him pay.' Caelan wiped a hand across her eyes, barely able to force the words out. 'And then you turn up here like nothing's happened? Did you think I was going to be pleased to see you?' She turned away, shoulders heaving. Nicky was sobbing silently, her body shaking.

'It wasn't meant to be like this. I don't know what to say. I'm sorry, Caelan.'

'*You're* sorry.' Caelan strode through to the bedroom, stripped off the pyjamas, pulled on a pair of jeans and a sweatshirt. Nicky watched, her hand over her mouth, silently weeping. Caelan grabbed her bag, her keys.

'Caelan, please. Where are you going?' Nicky hurried after her as Caelan strode towards the door.

Caelan turned back to face her, tears soaking her cheeks. 'I don't know, but I can't stay here.'

She slammed the door behind her, limped down the stairs, and went out into the night.

Acknowledgments

This is the first Detective Caelan Small novel I have written, and I'd like to offer my heartfelt thanks to the people who have helped me along the way.

Firstly, a huge thank you to the wonderful team at Canelo, who are an absolute pleasure to work with. They have done an incredible job of publishing my work and it's a dream come true for me to be part of such a brilliant team. Special thanks to Michael Bhaskar for his advice, encouragement, patience and understanding.

Thank you to all the friends whose support means so much. I won't name you all here for fear of accidentally missing someone out, but I hope you know who you are and that I'm hugely grateful.

Huge thanks to the bloggers who have taken the time to review the book and to the readers, especially those who have written reviews or have contacted me to say they have enjoyed my work. It means a huge amount to me, and I thank you all.

Thank you to Tracy, who believes in me and my work even when I'm struggling to. I will be forever grateful for her faith in me. Thank you to Mum and Grandma for everything you've done for me, especially your constant encouragement and support, and to my son and the rest of my family. A mention too for my furry writing companions, Evie, Poppy and Alexa. I am lucky to have you all in my lives.

Detective Caelan Small Novels

Ask No Questions
Tell No Lies
Time to Go